THE TALES OF AMCRONOS

BOOK 4

THE QUEST FOR THE TITAN'S HEART

D1512315

COLSON ROSA

THE QUEST FOR THE TITAN'S HEART

ILLUSTRATIONS BY JODY BALL

Mom and Dad,

I can scarcely find the words to thank you enough. You have been emotional supports, constant encouragers and incredible editors of this and all my stories. I hope that all the amazing life lessons you have taught me never slip from my mind. I will cherish them always, but never as much as I cherish you.

To My King whom I love,

Thank you for guiding my heart,

Thank you for judging my steps,

Help me cling to Your side,

Help me to never falter off your path,

Though I may lose sight of You,

You never lose sight of me.

Thank you.

CONTENTS

Highternmore
Vanswick
Pelios
Molten Wasteland
Mountain Pass
Saberlin
Kala Lake
Dreyron
Srayo
The Towns of Fairfick
Forest of Torin
Forest of Bane
The Plains of Naldor
Mazaron Mountains
Sevrathan Fortress
Aphenter
Hessinejon
Sadron
Helix
Hills of the Gorills
Bactran Desert
Toga
The Bay of Cinon
Forest of the Unknow

6

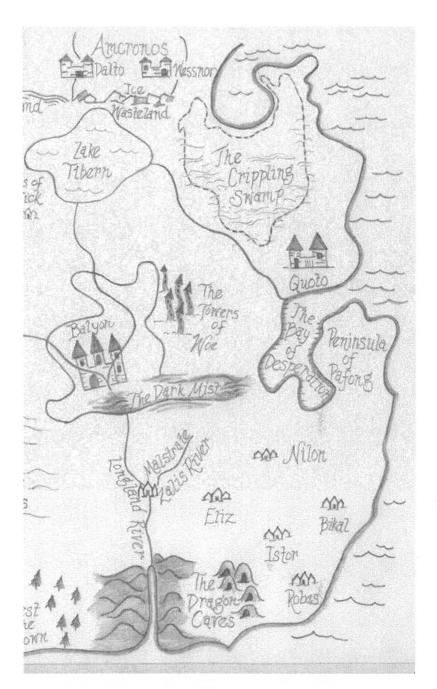

CHAPTER 1

THE WAR FRONT

This was not just chaos; this was frenzied madness. Warren's head was spinning as the world seemed to crash around him. How could this be? How could an army of Natas be gathering on their doorsteps right when Srayo was weak? They would not be weak and unprepared for long. Warren would make sure of that.

He declared to those around him, "Remain calm. Soldiers and civilians, remain calm! We need to prepare defenses. This castle is strong, and can easily be defended. Now that we know a siege is coming on Srayo, we have the upper hand. Someone please find Auden and Denethor and bring them to me. We will figure out the best way to proceed. In the meantime, store all the resources in the storehouses then return to your homes."

Soon enough, Warren, Auden and Denethor were united beside the gateway. Collectively, they took a deep breath. Denethor had already calculated some defensive strategies, Warren could tell. Auden turned toward him. "The unfortunate scout is being buried as we speak. It is sad he had to die in such a tragic way. But we need to focus on the present, and most of all, the future. You know this fortress better than anyone. How should we move forward?"

"Luckily, the defenses of this city are already built up for the most part," Warren said. "I have a feeling, though, thick walls and archer towers will not be enough to hold this attack off. We have mighty creatures at our disposal; we should make as much use of them as possible. Have the stone golems dig a moat around Srayo, and have spikes made to form a defensive ring around the moat."

"I will assign archers to mount the towers, and double the guards to patrol the eastern wall," Denethor said.

Warren agreed. "That's very good. Auden, can you get started on the moat and the spikes? I will make sure weapons are distributed, supplies are put away, and barricades are built. I have already asked my general to make sure the soldiers remain ready at all times. We can successfully hold off this attack if we are vigilant." The three lords said nothing more as they thought through the current events. Then, with passionate focus, the trio split paths to ready Srayo for an assault.

Auden rounded up the stone golems and the lumberjacks from the mountain pass. They began their tasks promptly, knowing the faster they could finish their work, the safer Srayo would be. Dirt flew and rocks soared away from the stone golems, who shoveled the trenches with their bare hands. Auden stood in awe of their power as the beginnings of a moat were already forming.

The loud crackling of falling trees sounded as the skilled lumberjacks worked with excellence. The mountaineers could be stubborn and stiff-necked at times, but they had harvested more trees than anyone else in the land. The first few spikes were piled by an assembly of workers willing to help.

Auden allowed himself to grin briefly. He then began tapping his fingers methodically. "May the King reign and His followers prosper," he said to rally the morale of his taskforce.

They stopped their work. "May the King reign and His followers prosper," they replied.

Auden walked toward a fallen tree and picked up a saw. The workers fell silent as they witnessed the revered Lord Auden of Hightenmore joining them in the assignment. They lifted a cheer and continued their work with a renewed effort. No force could stop the true courage and zeal of the Light.

*****

Warren looked across the expanse of the castle he had helped rebuild. A tear descended down the slope of his cheek. He had fought too hard to prepare this stronghold as a launching point for the crusade of the Light. He would not let it go to waste. He would not lose Srayo, not when he had poured his life into rebuilding it. The grays and browns seemed increasingly prominent throughout Srayo. What would become of his new home? Warren fought back his emotions and headed toward the storehouses.

He witnessed numerous workers carrying bags full of food and pilling them into the spacious storehouses. A woman walked up to him, her face was completely flushed. "Sir, we are almost out of room. Should I have the rest of the helpers carry the medical supplies and extra food stuffs into your mansion? That is the only place I can think of besides the stables."

"That's fine. Load it to the brim if need be. We can use it as our infirmary. We need to do whatever is necessary. You're doing good work. The soldiers are being kept fed, I presume."

"Yes, sir. They are fed, armed and practicing in the training grounds. The army is in top fighting form, so I hear. Srayo's smiths continue to make extra weapons and armor, just in case."

Warren looked her in the eyes. "You don't need to address me as sir. I am like you, a person. In fact, you may know as much as I do. It has been less than a year since I accepted the task of governing Srayo. Great things

12

have happened in this city so far. I only hope I do not falter because of my inexperience."

"May I return to my duties, sir?"

"Please call me Warren, and yes, you may."

Warren followed her into the heart of the city, then veered off toward the training grounds. Unbeknownst to them, Warren admired his troops as much as they honored him. His thoughts wandered until his eyes fell on the eastern wall, where guards stood, focused on the open horizon. What were they seeing out there? How long until they saw enemy ranks advancing upon Srayo?

These were questions that lead to worry, and Warren had no time to be anxious. He doubled his speed toward the training grounds. Before reaching his men, Warren came across Hannah, who grinned when she noticed him. She brushed a stray hair out of her face and said, "Glad I get to say goodbye to you, Warren."

He frowned. "What do you mean?"

"Our family is returning to Vanswick. With Srayo under threat of attack, my father told us to return home. We will be protected there. Far away from danger. I wish I could stay and help ready the army of the Light, but that is not my place."

"Denethor has made a wise decision," Warren answered. "Keeping you and your family safe is not negotiable. Though I hate to say it, I probably could not protect you if you stayed. You belong with your mother and sisters. To ease them and be a comforting shoulder for them. Tell your mother that she is a wonderful woman, and your sisters, they are bright stars in the sky. I will truly miss you, Hannah. When, if, I return, I hope to see you again. Maybe you can teach me to shoot the bow someday."

"Goodbye, Warren."

He hated how that sounded. He could not let it go with that. Hannah turned to leave, but Warren said, "Hannah, do you know that your father and I have something in common?"

"Of course," she answered. "You have many things in common."

Warren continued. "One thing in particular."

Now she was curious. "What might that be?"

"We're both fighting for people like you."

She blushed.

They locked gazes, took a deep breath, nodded, and continued on their ways. They hated that the war had strained their friendship. He tried to get his mind off Hannah's departure. He looked for anything that would take his mind off the war. War split friends. War broke hearts and families. As a leader, he owed it to his people to think positive. At least, that is what Warren told himself.

The cobblestone path pressed hard against his boots, and horses trotted alongside him. There was no breeze that day, something unusual in the city. Warren tried to clear his head, something he found impossible to do. Eventually, he gazed upon the arching swords and thrusting spears of Srayo's warriors.

Whether driven by fear or by courage, the warriors at the training grounds pushed themselves to their limits. They fought harder, struck faster, and locked themselves deep into their exercises. Maybe that was what Warren needed: the distraction of clashing steel to guide his wandering thoughts. Warren's general advanced toward him and said, "I am afraid I'm fresh out of new drills for these men to complete. They have plenty of skill to go into battle."

Warren raised his eyebrows and turned his head. "You aren't telling me everything, general."

"Their bodies and minds may be ready, but their hearts are uneasy. Uneasy at best. I have heard whispers traveling through the ranks, and doubt is growing. You know I'm not very good with speeches. Could you encourage them?"

Warren walked alongside his general toward the troops. "I would be glad to. In fact, it is one of my favorite parts of being a lord. I will teach them a few new exercises, as well. In the meantime, could you gather some soldiers and begin building barricades? When the time comes, we can place them strategically throughout the town."

"Why would we possibly need barricades?"

Warren bit his lip. "I fear the walls won't hold out the enemy. They might, but we should take the side of caution."

Before Warren began talking to the soldiers, his general gathered fifty capable men and led them toward the eastern side of the city. Warren cleared his throat several times. He grabbed a rope hanging on a fence and held it in front of him. "Soldiers, army of the King. You have worked hard for this moment. This rope represents our forces. Who among you is the strongest? Bring the strongest men forward." Two sturdy men came toward him from the crowd. Warren handed each of them a side of the rope.

"Pull the rope apart. Break it with your strength." Warren stared intently at them, and they used all their might to rip apart the rope. After several tries, they laid down the rope, defeated.

Warren was not surprised. "You see, valiant troops, we are the rope. We seem small, insignificant and limited. But when the forces of Natas try to pull us apart, we remain undeterred. The rope was not broken, and we will not be either. Though the threat of Natas seems like it may overpower us, it will not. It cannot. For we are bound together, and nothing... nothing can tear us apart."

The soldiers lifted a heroic call, and raised their swords in the air. Warren drew his blade and lifted it in the air with theirs. He watched their spirits lift and it encouraged him. In truth, Warren's speech was to himself more than to anyone else.

When he sheathed his sword, he said, "Soldiers, I have a new challenge for you. You have done enough drills for the day; now it is time to show what you have learned. When it comes down to the heat of battle, your resolve and your intuition are what save you. I will split you into two armies, and have you fight large scale. Once the armies are formed, each side must select a leader, and strategize for the battle. This will be just like a real battle, so use your heads in this fight. If you are hit, fall to the ground."

The troops were divided, and each side chose their wisest, most honorable men as their leaders. The leaders gathered their armies together and planned the battle. The two squads stared at each other with eyes of steel. They viewed it as more than a simple competition, but as a true test of their training and determination.

Swords were drawn and spears were brandished. Then at the sound of Warren's voice, the two groups charged at each other. As Warren, had hoped, it was not a mad frenzy. Rather, the soldiers were organized, fighting in formations and using specific tactics. Warren kept himself completely engaged in the battle, critiquing every move and countermove. He knew these men were ready for war.

The duel raged on for half an hour, and most of the sides had cleared the area because they had been defeated. Both armies focused more and more on protecting their leader as the battle began to slow. The men were breathing so hard it was distinctly noticeable to Warren. "Soldiers, you have fought hard. The fight is almost complete. Now make sure to act wisely in the next few minutes, for it will decide the fate of the battle. This is a turning point. Show me what you have learned, and attack."

The men took heart, and their leaders shouted out commands. The final moments of the exercise showed Warren the hearts of his warriors. They were valiant, brave, and smart. He smirked as the second team's leader was tagged and the fight ended. The men complimented each other and laughed at the accounts of the skirmish. It was good that they were joyful. Warren would not have it any other way.

He left the men to rest and heal any minor wounds from the exercise. He looked around Srayo; buildings were being prepared and repurposed for defense, guards were standing alert on the eastern wall and archer towers were being loaded full of arrows and bolts. They could pull it off. Srayo was a mighty fortress which had cost them many brave men to take, and they had had the element of surprise. There would be no surprise attack this time, thanks to the sacrifice of the loyal scout. His message had given them the most important thing - time.

For a moment, the town was calm and still. Although war was on their doorstep, everything seemed at peace in the city. It seemed as though life would go on past this coming battle. Sadly, this tranquility did not last long. The brief scent of serenity passed by, and the city leapt back into the flurry of preparation. Warren wished war could save everyone the trouble and leave them. There was nothing they could do to stop it now. Not when Natas was forcing their hand. They had made a choice, a risky choice. Now they had to stick with it to the end.

*****

"We should keep our creatures centralized on the eastern side of the citadel. There they can do the most damage to the enemy," Auden told the other lords.

"I think the warriors of Pelios and the forces from Xala Lake should guard opposite sides of Srayo. There seems to be something beneath the surface with them. I do not know the history they share, but they stay far away from each other whenever possible. I would trust either of them with my life, but I believe their past may affect our future. They simply need more time to trust one another," Warren said.

Auden slumped back in his chair. "That's true. The same goes for the stone golems and Seviathans. Though they are now on much better terms, we do not want to risk any hostility among our ranks. I hope one day we can leave the wars of the past where they belong, but for now we should take every precaution. I propose we divide our creatures to the southeast and the northeast. That way, we can position our men between them."

Denethor nodded. "That sounds like a good plan. I think we should place as many men from Dalto on the walls as possible. They are masters of ranged warfare, and our archers are still new at the trade. What should we do with our secret weapon?"

"You mean our dragon?" Warren looked at Denethor with curiosity.

"Yes, our dragon."

Warren brushed some dust off the map of Srayo. "I think we should save him for the heat of the battle. If we can hide him for long enough, then the enemy will be utterly caught off guard."

Auden joined in the conversation. "How will we signal him when we need him?"

"We could always use a simple horn blast."

"Fine by me, but we should make sure multiple warriors know the call, so that if one is unable, another can signal our mighty dragon. Having that kind of firepower on our side will always lift my spirits." Auden let out a miniscule grin.

As the lords planned for the oncoming storm, no citizen of the city sat idle. Throughout the fortress of Srayo, weapons were readied, barricades were built and soldiers were training. Everyone looked to the east, wondering how much time they had before the attack.

Wondering how much time until all-out war began.
Wondering if they were strong enough to face their enemy.

*****

"We've spotted enemy forces gathering in the trees. The attack will probably come within the hour." The archer bowed and left the room.

Auden ran his hands through his hair. It was an intense and critical moment in the history of Amcronos. This weight fell mostly on his shoulders. The army was counting on him now more than ever. Deciding to rally the men for a final speech, Auden ventured to the center courtyard and called the soldiers together. They all looked up to him, expecting something to calm their tensed nerves.

Auden made sure his voice was loud and determined. "Men of the Light, raise your heads. May the King reign and His followers prosper. We are more than a group of men fighting for our homes and our lives. We are more than soldiers trained and hardened in war ready to face any foe. We are followers of the King! This makes us more than men; this makes us men fighting for a cause that is greater than our lives and even all of Amcronos. Take hope, soldiers, that we have the greatest power on our side, and no force of darkness can blot us out."

Before Auden could continue, a little boy stood on a crate and held his wooden sword in the air. "I will fight for the King, though my sword is a little small."

With a new perspective, Auden continued his speech. "Young knight, your strength is not in your arm but in your heart. Come here, child." The young boy went up next to Auden. The Lord of Hightenmore then turned to the crowds. "When I look into the eyes of this little boy, I find so much valor and passion that I am in awe. I would gladly lay down my life beside someone with such zeal. Now, if a child is willing to stand for all he holds dear to give Amcronos a brighter future, what say you, men?

"Are you willing? Willing to lay down your life and stand against the wickedness of Natas until you have nothing left? Are you willing to hold nothing back, never look back? Do you remember why we are here? Raise your swords and shields and fire your arrows with righteous fury, for this day we stand up to the threats against our King!"

A cheer like never before sounded through Srayo that would make the mighty waves of the ocean jealous. No enemy could match this power of heart and mind. Auden knew this war would be the greatest of all time. The forces of the Light were up against a wall. If they lost this battle, everything would be for nothing. But if they were victorious, they could advance straight into the enemy lines. If they won, it would mean everything.

CHAPTER 2

THE GREAT BATTLE

There were five of them. They were running toward Srayo with all their might. The three lords knew as they watched from the wall that the five scouts would not make it. Trapped by a helpless fate, the fleeing scouts used all their energy dashing through the open fields toward the castle.

Behind them, waves of wicked men swarmed past the dark trees and into the light. Like an impending cloud blotting out the sun, the enemy legions covered the fields. They lifted up a mighty shout. It was not a shout of hope or of courage; it was a roar of violence. These enemies were bent toward chaos and destruction.

All Srayo mounted the defenses and readied themselves for battle. This would be a straight-up fight, no secrecy, surprises or sabotages. Or at least that was how it seemed. Archer towers were filled with bowmen from Dalto. Seviathans brandished their scimitars. Xalaians twirled their spears. Warriors from Pelios heated the fires inside of them. Humans mounted their bravery.

Four of the five scouts had already been taken down by the onslaught. One quick man was still alive. He was close to the gate, but the enemy was closing in around him. With a clash, he hit the gate and pounded on it. Yet they could not risk opening it. Auden lowered his head, unable to watch another scout devoured by this menacing monster. All of a sudden, Boranor leapt over the wall and threw the scout over his shoulder. The powerful leap of the stone golem landed him and the scout atop the wall. Boranor's honest heart would save any life, however small.

He laid the man on a bed of hay. He was then taken away to the medics. Meanwhile, Boranor returned to the gate, where the stone golems were bracing it for impact. As the forces of evil neared Srayo's walls, Warren called out, "Archers, fire at will." A barrage of shining arrows bolted down onto the warriors of Natas. Many of them defended themselves from the strike, but others fell from the blows. The shots of Dalto's experienced archers proved the deadliest. Although the evil soldiers were ready for the arrows, many fell because of the incredible accuracy the archers displayed.

While the arrows flew back and forth, Natas' men carrying cauldrons of acid moved toward one of the gates. They poured the acid onto the gateway, and it began to dissolve. This was a trick no one had expected. Above the

24

gate, soldiers threw down spears and boiling oil to hold the evil warriors back. Warren was the first to see how desperate things were becoming. How could they defend a gate that no longer stood? Luckily, his fears were relieved when the acid did not completely destroy the massive gate.

Some of Natas' other soldiers tried to get to the wall by the moat, only to be stabbed by the sharp poles blocking their way. The defenses of Srayo seemed to be holding, for the moment. Casualties fell from both sides, but the majority fell from the dark armies.

Warren called out to the men on the wall, "Move back to the towers. Remain protected." They could not see what their lord saw. An enemy barrage landed upon the troops before they could reach the safety of the towers.

Almost instantaneously, Warren's mind flung into action. "Bring every single man who can wield a bow, and file them into the towers. Have no men on the wall except in the towers. Don't spare a single arrow!"

This adjustment filled each turret with twenty men apiece. While ten loaded their arrows, the other ten aimed and fired. They then quickly switched positions and continued the barrage. The once bountiful supply of arrows and shafts thinned at a rapid pace. That, however, was a very good sign. Those arrows were finding their marks.

Then, as the tide of the battle seemed in the favor of Srayo, the enemy brought out a single, giant catapult. They loaded it with a dark boulder, and let it loose on the city. A hail of rocks plummeted into the castle like a meteor shower. Soldiers were sent flying by the impact. The destruction of the avalanche was indescribable. Roofs crashed to the ashen streets, torn from their buildings like loose teeth. Craters dug into a once peaceful town and left their wreckage. Enemies of granite and sulfur had been launched over the walls, with wills of their own to seek and destroy.

Of course, the forces of evil had also planned for this encounter. They were prepared, too prepared. What dark architect had designed this beast, and what worker had fastened its horrifying will to kill? No one could say. Their ears were still ringing from the shockwave.

Auden in distress witnessed the familiar face of Denethor nearby. "What kind of weapon is that? No machine can cause this much damage on its own."

Denethor dove under some debris. "It must be some sort of new creation of Natas. Its power is amazing. We will not be able to last long if it continues to barrage us. There is still hope, though. Call out the dragon."

Auden let out a clear blast from his horn, and the Xala dragon burst into the sky. Its glorious wings thrust it from its hiding place and shot it above the castle. Auden shouted, "Take out the catapult!" It knew its target even before it heard the command.

All ranks were broken in the city as men hid under any cover they could find. Most of the city held fast during the strikes, but the hailstorm was relentless. Denethor grimaced in pain as he felt his leg trapped under a flipped cart. He tried to free himself from it, but it was no use. He was not the only one ensnared. Many others also struggled to free themselves from the rubble.

Denethor looked up into the sky for a fourth bombardment, but it did not appear. He powered his way out of his trap and ventured to the wall. He only dared go high enough to peer out toward the dragon.

The catapult had targeted it instead. Denethor shuddered as he witnessed the catapult tear away some of the dragon's scales. It was a dual of beast against machine, and the beast was losing. Soon enough, the dragon realized a direct attack was futile, and soared high in the air where it could dodge the projectiles. It maneuvered around the oncoming attacks masterfully. Enemy archers and the catapult could not hit it at such a high altitude. Diving at headlong speed, the dragon plummeted into the catapult and began ripping it to shreds. The impact alone had splintered the immense contraption, but the glistening claws of the mighty dragon did much more damage. The immense catapult was reduced to mere shattered boards.

Denethor overheard Warren saying, "Get out of there. Get out of there." But it was to no use. The mighty creature hurled enemies left and right, clawing and biting them with fury, but to no avail. It was struggling against the onslaught of strikes. Still, it continued to end enemy lives with every breath. Hundreds fell by its wrath. The dragon was crippling the enemy, and giving Srayo a fighting chance to reassemble its troops. This chance could not have been too soon.

While half of the enemy retreated from the gate to help slay the dragon, the rest pounded into Srayo. The corroded gate could not hold. The forces of Light flocked to the south to meet the enemy. They would not let the enemy gain any more ground. Not a single step.

The first foes the assailants encountered were the massive fists of the stone golems. A horrible foe to attack. Nonetheless, swords, spears, arrows and axes dug their way into the golems' hard rock as they tried to fight them off. But the stone golems brushed the blows aside like straw and plowed their way into the heart of the enemy forces.

Boranor led his team with such determination that they plowed a path through the lines, and rushed to the east to try and save their ally. If anyone could save their dragon from its desperate state, the stone golems could. Even with all this damage done to their army, the forces of the darkness kept coming.

Auden took charge of the army of the Light. "Men, form ranks near the gate. Shields in front, then spears, then archers. Shield bearers, draw your swords for melee combat. Seviathans, cover the left flank. Men of Pelios, cover the right.

"Xalaians, take heart, your ruler may yet live. Spread yourself through the castle, forming a line between the buildings to the south. Make sure any forces who try to sneak around our troops are dealt with. Use secrecy to your advantage."

In full obedience, the unorganized army shifted to a well-prepared front. The enemy, on the other hand, was full of wild men, savages and cutthroats. Thus, their attack was completely offensive, without structure but with vengeance. Many of them were determined with all their beings to turn Srayo back to a fortress of Natas. This zeal made them dangerous, a cornered viper.

As expected, most of the dark soldiers charged straight at the large rank of men. Spears and arrows were launched at the attacking flood of enemies, and many of them fell lifeless. Thinking the row of shields was for defense, the dark warriors went straight at it. But as they started fighting against the iron shields, the shield bearers drew their weapons and started slicing down the attackers. They shifted from a wall of shields to a wedge, driving into the heart of the enemy flank.

The Seviathans and swordsmen of Pelios joined in the assault with fury. With zeal, the Seviathans leapt onto their enemies and brought them down with swift strokes of the sword. They used their acrobatics and battle skill to outmatch their opponents. No one could counter their talented moves, and their spiked tails gave them a major one-on-one advantage. These foes had never fought Seviathans, and were devastated by their skill.

Like the fires in their hearts, the swordsmen of Pelios were lit ablaze with power against Natas' minions. Instead of using cleverness, speed or agility, they powered through their foes. With swords unleashing fiery wrath, they disarmed their opponents leaving them helpless, and thwarted any strategy used against them. They used the rage of Natas' warriors against them, proving that their fury was far more deadly.

As impressive as the counterattack of the light was, the mercenaries of Natas gathered themselves. They had not been expecting this enemy, but for savages they adapted swiftly. Maybe they were not savages at all.

The men of the Light were soon pushed back. But as they retreated to safer ground, the squid men dragged away many unsuspecting enemies and they were no more. The forces of the darkness were weakening.

It comforted the lords that the civilians had already been evacuated. This gave them extra room to maneuver and fight. Their undivided attention was on the battle at hand. Auden and Denethor stood side by side as the ranks reformed near the citadel. All of a sudden, a heavy downpour of rain drenched both sides. It blanketed the entire city in a matter of seconds. Most of the soldiers kept fighting like nothing had changed, but the swordsmen of Pelios struggled to find cover. They gasped in pain as if drowning, as if Natas himself had a hand to their throats.

In disarray, Auden and many others hurried to drag them under overhangs and into buildings. They could not lose their allies from Pelios; they were vital. Suddenly, Auden remembered the potions Warren had given to him in case of an emergency. At first Auden was doubtful of their usefulness, but now they mean everything. One in particular caught his eye, one that could supercharge the immune system.

Auden thanked the King for the mage's potion and hoped it would work on the fire beings. Did these potions only heal humans? Auden had no choice.

Giving several of them a few drops of the concoction, they got up as if nothing had happened. Auden had to back away from them, because their flames were immensely hotter than ever before. No drop of the vial was spared, but there had only been enough to aid half of the warriors. Nonetheless, the troops rallied as the blazing swords of Pelios returned to the fight. The rain evaporated around them, covering the area in mist. No power could stop their fire. Not this time.

While the men of the Light fought through both mist and rain, the men of Natas could not function within it. They had once seemed unwavering, but they were all too human. They grew tired. The combined forces of the creatures and men of Srayo overwhelmed their foes with zealous brilliance and unyielding loyalty. Cries of defeat echoed from the fleeing minions of darkness as many fell by the sword.

One cry stood out louder than them all. It was not coming from within the castle, but outside of it. The powerful Xala dragon had uttered his last roar.

After Srayo had been cleared of all enemies, the army met together to survey the victory and count their losses. They did not chase Natas' army past their walls.

There was no need. Those that survived would spread the message of the great victory at Srayo. The darkness would think twice about attacking Srayo again.

Boranor lifted his voice for all to hear. "Our brave dragon died with honor. His sharp teeth finished many of his oppressors, and his claws shredded the armor of his foes. I'm sure he would want us to press on against Natas and ready our path toward the strongholds of wickedness." Though the Xalaians could not cry, they each bowed their heads and lowered themselves. They made no sound, but everyone could tell they were devastated.

Warren answered, "Surely, we will do that and more for his honor. Though I did not know him well, I considered him and the others who fell close allies and true friends. Their willingness to lay down their lives for the King will never be forgotten. But we do not have time to mourn, for the hour is drawing near. The hour of the Light, where the forces that corrupted Amcronos cower from our blades. We need to bury our dead not in sadness, but in hope for the future. If we are not driven onward by their sacrifice, then our future may not be one of hope."

Denethor addressed the group next. "Men, we won a great victory this day. Srayo was defended as well as could be expected. No... better. We had a minimal number of casualties compared to the army sent against us. Do not worry about repairing the city. The citizens of the city will rally together for that task. Now is the best time to strike at the enemy. Gather your supplies and weapons. Prepare your minds for the journey and ready the caravans of resources. We will bury the dead, for they deserve that courtesy. Mourn for them now, for by the time we leave, our hearts need to be focused on the task ahead."

The army dispersed throughout the city, and the townsfolk were called from the mountain pass back. They were shocked to find so much in ruin. Moans of sorrow fell among the soldiers, but they quickly ceased. It had been a great stand for the King, yet the deaths weighed down on the soldiers. The Xalaians gathered around their lifeless leader and recalled the solemn event. They were deathly silent, which said just as much, if not more.

As the warriors were buried, one of the soldiers came up to Auden. "Sir, are we to bury the bodies of our fallen enemies?"

Auden gazed down at the face of a fallen enemy warrior and removed his helmet. He was neither a disfigured brute nor an enraged maniac. He was simply a man. A man who did not understand who or why he was fighting, only desiring to appease his master. He could have been fighting to spare the lives of his family or earn money for his impoverished friends. No one would ever know now.

Auden's heart was smashed to pieces as he stared at the unfortunate middle-aged soul who had perished in the battle. If only they could know. If only the armies of darkness could see they were fighting for the wrong side. All they had ever known was evil; if only they could see the light for what it truly was. "Yes, we will bury all of the dead, friend or foe, for we will keep our honor no matter the cost. The state of our minds and the cause of our plight are the only two things that set us apart from the minions of Natas. Thus, we must keep our minds humble and honest, and keep our focus on the King."

The soldier saluted, and went away to inform the other men. Auden looked across the aftermath of the battle, and knew they had been lucky to win without major casualties. But Natas always had more men to fight, and for every one dead soldier of the Light, there would need to be five dead enemies. Most importantly, the enemy now knew everything about them. The stone golems would no longer be a surprise, and swords of fire would not terrify their adversaries again.

Denethor stood a few feet from Auden, helping carry a wounded man to the medics. After several minutes, Denethor returned. "Auden, should we leave this work to the civilians? The hour to move is upon us. If we could get a day's journey to the east, we will be much closer to defendable locations."

"No. Burying our soldiers is part of our homage. I know you are eager to get moving, but we must honor our fallen. Our men would feel cheated if they were not allowed to bury their fellow warriors. We will leave soon enough, my friend, and you can push the men onward with all haste once we've left. Surely, you see that a proper burial must be given, for the honor of the living as much as for the dead?"

Before Denethor could respond, Warren rushed up to both of them. "Come with me," he said. "There is something you need to see."

Without a moment's delay, the three lords approached a group of soldiers huddled around a single dying man. Auden was shocked that the man was still alive. "Why is this man not being treated? You are standing around like he is poisonous to the touch. Someone help him."

The men turned to Lord Auden. "Sir, this is not one of our men. This is Halithor, fifth son of the wicked Natas himself."

Auden and Denethor were speechless, but Warren backed the men away from Halithor's crippled body. Warren gazed over Halithor briefly, and knelt beside him. "You don't have long to live. Your father has abandoned you, used you as a blunt instrument and tossed you aside."

Through clenched teeth Halithor replied, "Never. He would not betray me. I will not betray him. You will never reclaim Amcronos."

"Poor Halithor. You are lost in your ways like a calf without parents. You don't realize we are trying to free Amcronos, not imprison it. Your father is a cruel, devious man who has enslaved and tortured thousands. Is that who you want to follow?"

Halithor tried to sit upright, but could not. "To the very end of my days. I know my father is merciless and heartless, but he has power and strength over Amcronos. Two things your naive King will never be able to know."

Warren gave Halithor one last chance. "What are Natas' plans against us? Where will he concentrate his troops? How many forces is he mustering against us?"

Instead of answering, Halithor used all his remaining energy to draw his dagger and finish himself with it. Everyone cringed in disgust. It was horrible how devoted he was to the ways of evil and bloodlust. Hopefully, not all the followers of Natas had been this blinded and consumed by the darkness.

The soldiers surrounding the area looked toward the lords. Were they going to bury the son of their greatest enemy? Could they honor such a malicious man as Halithor? Auden and Warren locked eyes, unsure themselves.

*****

Denethor had left the scene, finding it necessary to check on the recovery of the fire beings. His mind was not on the dead, but on the living. He knew that the battle was over, but thought instead on the battles to come. Battles that might come down to the strength of Pelios.

They had taken a major impact from the heavy downpour during the fight. Denethor hoped their inner fires had not been snuffed out by the powerful storm. Right before reaching the medical building, Denethor stopped dead in his tracks. What if Natas had sent that sudden

36

onslaught of gushing cold rain? It was possible that his dark arts could grant him that kind of power.

If that was true, then the swordsmen of Pelios were in far greater trouble than he had thought. They could recover from rain; but could they recover from an evil torrent of Natas? No one could know.

Denethor entered the building to see the doctors treating numerous wounds, most of them small. There was only one man checking over the fire beings, but he did not look like a medic. No, it was the mage. The very same mage Warren had found not long ago. What was he doing beside the crippled men of Pelios?

Denethor calmed himself and paced over toward the mage. "Do you know how to help them?"

The mage whispered something to himself then looked up to Denethor. "I've been covering them with hot coals from the smith's fires. This seems to be helping them. Also, I gave them some of the Xala dragon's poison."

"What? You gave them poison? Why in the world would you ever consider doing something as foolish... no worse than foolish, it's murder."

With eyebrows raised, the mage replied, "No, it is not murder. I know what I'm doing. You see, underwater is no place for a dragon. As a cold-blooded creature, it needs temperature regulation. As you can guess, Xala Lake can get very cold at times, especially during the winter. So how does it live? Its poison is so specifically suited to its body that as it circulates, it keeps it warm. Thus, you could almost say that when the dragon would bite something, it was injecting its blood into it. The dragon seems to be helping us long after the battle."

Denethor had nothing to say to that. He glanced over the sleeping warriors of fire, and noticed they seemed to be improving. Content with their status, Denethor began to walk away. He realized he had been wrong about this mage. When Warren had first presented him, Denethor had inwardly scoffed. Now it seemed that the intellect of this strange man had saved everything. Of course, Denethor would never admit this to Warren.

"Alert me when they have awakened."

The mage nodded then returned to his work.

*****

The tombstone read:

Here lies Halithor, fifth son of Natas, defeated in the attack against Srayo. The forces of the Light prevailed against him. He can no longer stand against the Light, and his defeat marks a new era. An era where the darkness will fall and Natas will be cast from his pitiful throne. May the King reign and His followers prosper.

Content that justice had been done, Warren and Auden left the graveyard trying not to show his delight. They now heeded the words of Denethor and turned their minds to the future. They needed to make sure the city recovered to its former glory before setting out eastward.

The caravans had already been loaded with supplies necessary for the journey ahead. This greatly sped up the process. The soldiers were recuperating in the barracks, and could put on their armor in a moment's notice. Everything was ready. Everything except for preparing the city for the months ahead.

The three lords met together with the other leaders. These included the Lord of Hessington, the assembly of Dreylon, Quinn of Dalto and the generals of the forces. In a small building off the main road, the group discussed how to stabilize the city.

"We have many of the structures being repaired right now, and the civilians have safely returned to the city," one of the generals began. "Statements have been ushered forth to them that they need to begin gathering supplies. They know they must restructure the city and initialize business and trade again."

Warren answered, "That's good. I've gotten to know these people for a while now, and believe they will bounce back soon enough. We don't need to be here while they do. They can manage on their own. We need to gather our men and set off toward Lake Tibern sooner rather than later."

The Lord of Hessington sat up in his chair. "The leaders of Dreylon and I will make sure the lands of the Light remain functioning and prosperous. We will remain to protect the lands of the light. If any further attacks come against our borders, we will rally men and call upon the aid of the remaining stone golems in the Mazaron. Auden, Denethor, Warren, hurry now to make ground against the enemy, so you may face them on favorable terrain. We have the advantage; this is no time to lose it. You have control of the army, and the creatures of our banner are loyal to you. Hurry now and assemble the troops. Nothing more needs to be discussed."

With all haste, the lords rounded up their men from the barracks. They were glad to hear that the creatures and men alike were faring well. The Xalaians had rallied behind the heroic sacrifice of their leader. Their final request had been that dragon's body be ceremonially burned, something Warren never would have expected. Nonetheless, Warren agreed to their wish and assured them the mighty Xala dragon would be honored and remembered.

The fire that blazed over his body leapt into the night sky with fury. Its white-tipped fingers shot both light and sadness into Amcronos. Its embers glowed for all to see, even as far as the mountain pass. It was a historic moment for all, symbolizing not only the loss but the gain. Through the pain, they had achieved something remarkable.

Warren was glad to see the Pelios warriors had overcome their injuries and, though not at full strength, were ready to march out. The stone golems and Seviathans seemed more zealous than ever to make an end of the tyranny over ruling the land. Quinn furthermore rallied his Daltonians, and their bravery was impossible to hide.

Spears were lifted, belts were buckled and packs were shouldered as the army centralized. The goodbyes were brief, but not nonexistent. The slow clank of the cart wheels was followed by the loud noise of the rising gate. Forming loose ranks, the men were positioned in a long line exiting Srayo. They looked back to the mighty fortress one last time, then set their eyes to the dim forests awaiting them.

Warren surveyed the familiar faces moving beside him, and noticed one he did not expect to see. Gevnor was traveling beside him, his sword strapped to his back and his steps unwavering. Warren inched closer as they moved onward. "Gevnor, aren't you staying to await the arrival of Lavrin?"

Gevnor shrugged. "Lavrin is living out his own life, wherever that might be. I've made up my mind that he'll be alright with the King on his side. Doubting and fretting will get me nowhere in the end. It's time for me to leave the struggles of my past. Now I must unleash the potential of the King's cause in my life. Hopefully, it's a future I'll remember for years to come. Hopefully, it's a future Lavrin and I will look back upon with pride."

CHAPTER 3

THE ENCOUNTER

He could not let it happen. He could not let this war wage. Natas' trickery, his devious lies, could not ruin so many more lives. The future of the nomadic races of southwest Amcronos pressed hard on Uminos' mind. His feet could not move any faster. Uminos raced over the sand to the best of his ability. He hurried onward for minutes on end. Then he beheld it. His stomach wrenched into a tight knot.

A long line of horseback riders stretched the horizon on a sloping dune of the desert. Uminos could not tell if the battle was taking place, because the nomads in the distance were blurry in the blazing heat. All he could tell for sure was that a strand of desert warriors was brandishing long halberds at their sides and spears on their backs. If the battle had not already started, they were surely readying for it.

Uminos was less than a mile away from stopping civil war. He was so close. Now he had to reach the forces in time, or else watch the battle unfold in its brutality.

*****

They knew the unfolding moments would decide the fate of the desert. They were two evenly matched sides, both hungry for revenge. They had no idea this revenge was fueled by Natas' hand. They prepared to face off in the greatest battle in southwestern Amcronos' history. The two armies did not consider how the battle could destroy their ways of life, only that victory was crucial.

Lavrin searched the ranks of the other army for Felloni or Kasandra, but could not find them. He knew that this fight would not end well if Kyra's vision at the oasis was going to come true. His heart turned to the King. Would he sit by and let this happen? Lavrin had no answer, only a hope that something would stand in the way. They needed something, anything to block this battle.

Yakwan was at the front of the western army; Lefsont was at the front of the eastern army. The two brave, passionate leaders stared at each other. One hardened by a lifetime of determination and leadership. The other hardened by youthful drive and focus. Lavrin had tried to convince Yakwan to turn to the lands of the Light to settle this dispute, but he would not listen. No one would listen to him except Kyra.

Kyra stood a short distance behind the army. She wanted to turn around and sit in the far corner of the medical tent. At least there, she could wait for the battle to be over, but she could not bring herself to it. Her eyes remained fixated on the riders in front of her. They grasped their weapons tightly, trying to push fear out of their minds. The constant trickle of sweat from their foreheads confirmed this. Kyra knew they had ample reason to be afraid; their entire nomadic race could be wiped out this day. She felt like the pressure would never be released, but would keep building until the fight began. She was right.

Doubt began to show on the faces of the nomads, and the two sides seemed to stir in anxious anticipation. It was as if this was the only moment they had ever lived. It was surely the most important moment.

Kyra decided that instead of trying to master her shaking senses, she would pace behind the tent. It was somewhere she would feel safe. Somewhere she would not have to watch the horrific battle unfold. She let the doctor know where she was going, though he did not answer.

Behind the tent, Kyra stomped her foot on the ground and ran her hands through her hair. Had they really failed? Her dream at the oasis was going to come true. No, but it was not a dream, it was a nightmare. A nightmare she could do nothing to stop. She did not care whose fault it was. She did not care if it had been the Sadron's fault or the fault of Ioga, or if no one was responsible. All Kyra wanted was a way to stop the battle from happening.

Something impactful would be necessary to stop decades of mounting hostility and anger.

Then, off in the distance she saw something and rubbed her eyes. Was that Uminos? How could he be here? He had been left in the camp to interrogate the ambassador. Could he have learned something from this diplomat from the Northeast? This could be exactly what she was hoping for. As Uminos drew near, she heard him yell, "Stop. Stop this war. It's all a mistake. I have proof. Stop. Do not fight each other."

Kyra was overjoyed, but then she turned toward the army, which was letting out a battle cry. Before Uminos could bring the vital information, both sides began to rush toward each other, bent on victory. No one could stop them from destroying each other now.

They drew closer and closer as their steeds galloped intently. When they collided, it would shatter the entire foundation of the nomadic tribes. Uminos would have burst into tears… if he could cry. Nevertheless, he collapsed to the ground with his face in his hands. He was worn out, partly from exhaustion, but more from Natas' successful campaign to ruin these people.

As spears were raised high, and the two sides hurried toward the center of the battlefield, something unexpected happened. The shout was too late to warn the armies in time. It was one word, but it had the impact of thousands. "Sandstorm!"

A blistering hurricane of sand approached, and it lifted riders off their horses and threw them to the ground. With the strength of an earthquake, the sandstorm blasted the entire area. Everyone was engulfed by the thrashes of the storm. It clawed at their skin and bit them like a wild dog. There was nothing to hold onto. Nothing to cover them from the angry tempest. It was one of the greatest sandstorms the nomads had ever seen, and they had not been ready for it.

The tornado of flying sand continued to pile upon them and sent their minds into a frenzy. They tried to gain their bearings, but all they could do was cover their faces to shield their eyes. For what seemed like an eternity, Lavrin lay pummeled by the barrage. He tried to stand up, but could not.

His body was not harmed, but in shock. It refused to budge. No longer calm, the urge to move overwhelmed him. It was then that he found his bearings, and realized he had been buried alive. He was terrified of dying this way, and dueled against the ground above him. The ground seemed to fight back. Sand covered him on all sides and was burning his skin. Eventually, he shot his hand free, and began to shovel sand off him. Trying to relieve himself of the pain, he threw as much off as he could. Soon most of his body was free.

He lay there in the sand, feeling helpless and alone. Though he knew there were many around him, he could only notice a few through clouded eyes. With his faded vision, Lavrin could not make out any of his companions.

He could only hope they were alright. At least the storm was over.

For several moments, Lavrin did nothing but breathe. Each breath singed his lungs.

Although it was difficult, he was able to shake out his legs and raise them above the sand. He was one of the first to rise from the impact. His feet wobbled at first, but then braced to hold him.

He looked to his right and to his left. Slowly, men were rising out of the ground, recovering to the best of their abilities. Lavrin spied the confused and shocked expressions painted clearly on every face. With each passing moment, the hatred between the tribes seemed to fade, and the reality of the unexpected, massive sandstorm sunk in. Turning to the tents behind him, Lavrin could see Kyra being helped by Uminos. Lavrin was shocked to find Uminos had arrived onto the chaotic scene. This shock faded quickly… it seemed in comparison a far less dramatic surprise.

Like crops sprouting after a harsh winter, the two sides began to recover and look like armies again and less like victims. Yakwan returned to the head of his force, as did Lefsont after checking on his men. It seemed like the mood of the battle had been shifted, like no one had the strength left to fight. Only the setting remained the same... but it was not the same. There was one difference, the warriors began to realize.

Between the two armies stood four soldiers. Not nomads. Not men layered in cloth and clutching long halberds. These four fighters were an impressive sight to behold. They wore shimmering armor, more decorative than that of kings. No one could tell what it was made of; it was not iron, gold or even gems. It was some element greater than them all. Each warrior was unique: one had a mighty hammer hoisted above his shoulder, one held a bow loaded with three arrows, the other two carried swords with more sheathed across their backs. Their weapons were greater than any expert craftsman could form.

The large man carrying the hammer had an air of magnificence and power about him. His weapon had a head of diamonds, smelted together. It appeared able to smash a boulder into bits. The engravings down its hilt were so complex that they could never be copied. They read of a language never seen before. Like a statue, he stood tall and ready.

With arrows lit in white flames, the archer had the poise of a leopard. She kept her fingers lose and scanned the ranks with intent. As if in complete control of her surroundings, she looked unfazed by the two armies. Her bow and arrows seemed ready to obey her every command.

The third soldier appeared to be the leader of the group. Dragon scales seemed to cover his entire body. They gave him the presence of someone who truly could hold his own against a dragon's rage. The tip of his sword was piercing, ready to face any obstacle. He had the eyes of a scholar, but the air of a seasoned duelist.

No one could see the eyes of the last man. His face was covered, and no one could get a sense of his characteristics. The part that stood out the most, was the necklace he wore. Its totem was a perfectly carved emblem of the King. As if part of a star, it glowed with a soft light.

Who were they?

No man dared draw near to them. The desire to fight between the armies seemed divided by this wall of four. Though they appeared like humans, everyone took them as unnatural beings. It was like the first time seeing the ocean... breathless awe. The sandstorm and all its destruction was washed away when one of the four spoke.

He took off his dragon scale helmet to reveal his face. It was a pale white, without any imperfections. It was like he was a ghost, but an amazing ghost rather than a horrifying one. Everyone focused on his voice. "This war must end."

Lavrin ran his hands through his hair. There was something eerily familiar about this man. His voice sounded like one he knew well. One he used to know, but had since forgotten. His face, however, seemed unique, like one he had never seen before. How could he have forgotten a man like this? Surely if he had met this man, he would have remembered.

"My name is Chan. I have come with my three companions from the Haven Realm itself."

Lavrin's mouth dropped. His mind blurred and his head spun. It became hard for him to breath. How was this possible? Lavrin looked behind his shoulder to see Kyra faint in disbelief. Lavrin could not hold his body still. It began to shake, as if having a mind of its own. Should he go to them? Should he hug them and hold him tight for a thousand years? If this was Chan, that meant the warrior beside him was... No, it had to be. The one and only Calix Windrider. Holding back his joy was impossible.

Overwhelmed, Lavrin dropped to his knees as his body continued to quiver.

Chan continued with his speech, though Lavrin's heart began skipping beats. "We have come to warn you about the dangers of this battle. We will show you the trickery you have been under since this hostility began. You see, the entirety of your anger toward each other is grounded on a platform of lies... lies that have been forced upon you for years by men you thought were advising you. Men you thought could help you have harmed and wronged you in a cruel way.

"Natas has always desired to have you join his cause. But he has realized that if you would not join him by desire, you could be tricked into following him. It has been his plan to have you cripple each other in war, so that he could come as a savior to you all. When both sides grew desperate for support, he would be there to lean on. But he is no savior. He is a tyrant who has planted the seeds of this war in your hearts. I will not let your noble heritage fall under such a darkness."

Yakwan could not believe it. "How could you know this?" he countered. "There is no way this has all been false. What they did to us must be punished. How can we believe you when we know nothing about you?"

Chan laid down his sword. "We are your friends. The King has made everything here in the desert known to us. I can wager every leader of these tribes has been receiving ambassadors who have been offering advice and resources for you. Each tribe has given these ambassadors a position of the highest honor. The advice they give you has been to benefit Natas. The weapons you have received come from storehouses of evil cities."

A man stepped out of the ranks next to chieftain Lefsont, and proclaimed, "This is not true. The advice I have given to the Iogan tribe has not been for any evil purpose or for cruel gain. You are the liar, and you have no right to trick these men."

Knowing the intentions of the man's heart, Calix lifted the mask of his helmet and turned toward the advisor. He said to him, "You try to deceive men with your talk. But I can see straight to your heart. The King reigns and His followers prosper. You are not one of His followers. You are a snake, just like your master. Natas shall never defeat the King."

With anger spurred in his eyes, the man drew his blade and charged toward Calix. "How dare you insult the powerful Natas!"

Calix drew his sword at lightning speed, and confronted the man. With a few precise strokes, Calix disarmed his opponent and placed the edge of his sword on his neck. Instead of finishing the man, he decided to force him back toward the tribes. Handing him over to the host of nomads, Calix bowed to the chiefs. "Do with him as you see fit. I will not decide how you handle betrayal."

Lefsont drew his crossbow, and cut a small dash into the betrayer's hand. As the man stumbled back gripping the wound, Lefsont pointed south. "Cast him into the desert with no supplies. No man is to grant him water or food. We will see how much Natas really cares for him. I wager he will doubt his loyalties under the desert sun. If anyone ever enters our tribe, check his wrists. We will never allow him in our sight again."

As this scene unfolded, the other followers of Natas mounted their horses, trying to escape. Nadrian caught them in the corner of her eye and yelled, "Do not let them escape."

In a moment, the nomads turned on the advisors they had once respected. Most of them were apprehended by the upset desert dwellers, but one man escaped, riding hard to the North. Nadrian pulled back her bow, aiming toward him. Chan put his hand on her shoulder. "Let him go. We have more important matters to deal with." The other henchmen of Natas were cast south like the other man, never to return to haunt them. They stumbled into the endless tide of golden death with spite, dread and clenched fists. They knew their master would not come for them.

Calix returned to the center of the battlefield with his companions. He knew reuniting these tribes would be difficult, but it was ultimately something they needed to resolve on their own. No matter how much Calix and his friends could persuade them, some wounds would take time to heal. What they could do was give the healing a platform to start.

To begin the process, Calix told the two sides, "Please consider that you tribes have no reason to hate one another. There's no purpose to this war except to fuel hatred and malice. You saw for yourselves the way your ambassadors fled, for they know what they had done. I can only hope that there will no longer be two armies of five tribes. Rather, I believe you can unite together in peace, strength and friendship, heal these scars and become one army for one tribe. You have great respect for your culture, now you need to transfer this honor you cherish to your fellow kinsmen."

Lefsont looked toward Yakwan and asked, "What shall it be? Is peace possible between our tribes?"

Yakwan cast his hammer onto the sand and motioned for his warriors to do so, as well. They unloaded their weapons onto the ground, following their leader's example. Though the sudden shift from war to peace made them doubtful, they raised hope in their hearts. They had witnessed the extraordinary, and it gave them assurance. Yakwan walked forward, past Calix and the others, and stood face to face with Lefsont. "I'm willing to try if you are. Kill me now if you wish, and slay all my men, but we won't raise our arms against you."

Lefsont brought out one of his knives and everyone gasped. Instead, he knelt and stabbed it into the ground. He then set down his crossbow, as well. "I am tired of the talk of bloodshed. We are not murderers; we are nomads trying to survive. If you will accept my offer, would you please join me for a meal in my tent?"

Yakwan replied, "I would be honored, though I may desire to use utensils instead of my hands."

Lefsont smiled and nodded. The armies slowly walked toward each other, and though they did not embrace each other with open arms, their hostility dwindled. At the very least, they were not fighting. It was the war that never began.

Lavrin met up with Kyra and Uminos to venture toward their friends. Friends they hadn't seen in many months, if not years. Friends they thought they would never see again for years to come. A short distance away, Felloni and Kasandra also dared closer and closer. They were only a few steps away from getting to finally reunite with their companions again. Lavrin, Kyra and Felloni were almost besides themselves in excitement, and Uminos and Kasandra were just as anxious. They had heard stories of Calix, Chan, Grax and Nadrian, but never pictured them like this... knights of the Haven Realm.

It felt like an eternity, striding closer and closer. A lot had changed since they had last met. Memories of the wonderful and painful times they endured together brought floods of emotions to Lavrin. So many great times, so many hard-fought battles won, and now they had turned the tide together once more. Stopping a civil war would surely be a highlight of their journeys.

Finally, Lavrin and the rest of the team, weary from the desert, reached the Haven Realm warriors. Nothing could be more fitting for this joyous occasion than a long embrace, and they embraced with a bond deeper than friendship. Kyra and Nadrian held each other close. Felloni had forgotten the strength of Grax as he unleashed a bear hug on him. Chan wrapped one arm around Uminos, and the other around Kasandra. Though they had never met before, it felt like they were all part of a family.

The most emotional and impactful embrace was between Lavrin and Calix. They gripped each other tightly and would not let go. After what felt like ages, they were finally reunited. The pain Lavrin had harbored with him - the pain of Calix's fate at Hightenmore - was washed away in this moment. He had held onto it for so long, and now it was finally released. Calix knew how much Lavrin had gone through without him, which made the bond between the two that much greater.

Speech seemed a foreign concept as the united confidants were lost in the presence of the moment. Even Nadrian was tearing up, though heartfelt moments were against her typical nature.

Like all amazing times, however, this reunion had to end. The nine knew all was right in those few seconds. They had wished to see each other again for months on end. Even for those from the Haven Realm, the draw had been great. Now they finally had reunited. There was so much to say, but no one said a thing. So much to be remembered, and so much to be learned. Still, with thousands of things they wanted to say, they could not find the words.

Kasandra eventually broke the silence. "I've heard so much about you four. I feel like I know you through the stories Lavrin, Felloni and Kyra have told."

Grax chuckled. "I hope it has only been the good things." Everyone smiled.

"Nothing but good things." Kyra laughed as she said it.

"I'm so glad to see all of you," Chan said. "I fear we may need to cut this moment short, at least for a little while. We can catch up on each other's lives later. In the meantime, we need to see if everything is faring well with the desert peoples. That is first and foremost our mission. After that, I want to hear about everything."

"I want to hear everything from you first," Lavrin said.

The group strolled over toward the mass of nomads engaging in varied conversations. They made their way to the chiefs of the tribes. Calix was the first to reach them. "Hello, noble rulers of the desert. My companions and I were wondering if you had made any decisions about the future of your peoples."

The chieftains answered, "We have come to a few key verdicts on this matter, though progress is and will be slow for a while now. Our tribes have become so entangled by the mass of lies, bitterness and anger, that learning to trust each other will take time. Without the ability to rely on each other, we cannot engage in much of anything on a larger scale until resolving these inner matters. Because of this, and the standings of our culture, we cannot join the King's army."

"That's understandable. It's the highest priority that you get your kinsmen up on their feet. However, when you do stabilize as a land, if you do decide to join the war…"

Yakwan interrupted him. "Yes. We'll make sure never to join the side of Natas. You have our word on that. I fear, though, if we do join this struggle, it may be many years in the future. The only thing we can promise you now is that trade is certainly possible between our realms."

"Is there any way we can help your tribes now?" Lavrin asked.

Yakwan shook his head. "I'm terribly sorry for how the Sadron tribe may have wronged you and your friends. I'm sure your time here was less than pleasurable. All along you were trying to steer us clear from this fatal course. I thank you for that effort. You have done your part, now it is time for us to do ours. We will be able to revive our fallen peoples. For now, we can provide you with supplies for your journey, since I expect you do not plan on staying here."

"Thank you for your generosity. I believe we head on planning north, back toward the Mazaron Mountains."

Chan stepped forward. "I'm quite sorry for the confusion, but we will actually be heading east first," he said. "Anything you could supply us with would help us, though we have enough resources to last us a long distance."

The chieftains bowed. "Any assistance we can give, we will. You deserve our gratitude. Yet if it is all the same to you, we would like you to leave quickly, to avoid unnecessary tension. Our men may have trouble with you remaining, as some of them believe you brought the sandstorm upon us. We will try and ease them. I hope you understand."

"Of course, we understand," Grax replied. "You need time to fix your own wounds, both internal and external. I'm only sorry that we could not have arrived sooner, and stopped this rivalry before it ever began. When will we leave, Chan?"

"As soon as we can. We'll gather our equipment and supplies, and leave you to your tasks. I wish you the best of luck. I pray that the King will grant you fortune, favor and freedom under your newfound light. Please, when all of this is over, consider joining the King's cause.

You will not regret it. Now, where can we go to find horses for our travels?"

"We will certainly consider it," Yakwan answered. "The horses and supplies are spread out around the area. Our soldiers are still stirred up by the storm. You can take whatever you need from the battlefield… if you can even call it that. Our men will start restoring our camps and recovering our materials spread about by the sandstorm."

Lavrin and the others bowed, then left the chieftains. They surveyed the tossed about bags of supplies and flipped caravans. Kyra walked up to a horse and noticed it was not afraid when she neared it. In fact, it almost seemed to approach her. Kyra gracefully stroked its mane, and it neighed in reply. A nearby nomad came toward her and said, "Her name is Lyris, after my mother."

Kyra let her hand fall from the horse's side. "I'm terribly sorry. I didn't know that she was yours. She looks like a fine horse."

The man bit his lip, then answered, "You need her more than I do. She is a noble horse, though she is afraid of fire."

"Thank you very much, kind sir. There is nothing wrong with being afraid of fire; fear can save you much pain. I wish I could pay you for her, but a wicked man named Faeth stole my money."

The man motioned to Lyris, nodded, and left to help flip over one of the caravans. He did not say another word.

Kyra took a deep breath; she was glad he had shown her kindness, since she was a stranger. Sometimes it was small acts of generosity that mattered the most. She headed off to find the others.

They were gathered around a minimal stack of provisions. Lavrin was the first to start loading his sack full of food. He made sure only to take what he needed. Everyone strapped a canteen to their side and readied their packs for the long trip. They could not get out of the desert fast enough.

Uminos made sure to find Tagon and thank him for the kindness he had shown. He had freed them from captivity, and saved their lives at least once or twice. He had shown them hope and hospitality, even when the rest of their tribes were cautious and untrusting. Without him, they may never have succeeded. Tagon had become a friend, and Uminos would be glad to help him in the future, if he ever got the chance.

The nine mounted their new horses and bowed to the chieftains. They could only hope the chieftains could bring order and unity, or else civil war might break out again. Everything they fought for would mean nothing if war broke out anyway. Hopefully, the tribes could finally band together.

Everyone thought back to their experiences in the desert, and all the struggles they had endured. Everyone except for Lavrin, who looked ahead toward the future. Why had Chan insisted they head east?

CHAPTER 4

TIMES LONG LOST

It was a perfect day. The sun was partially covered by a silver cloud. Not too much to cover its light, but just enough to be noticeable. The air was neither thin nor heavy. The gentle touch of the wind was delicate, like a rose's petals. The end of the desert was in sight, and they could see the rolling hills that lay just beyond it. The hills were a light green, portraying life and freedom. They gradually carpeted the horizon with their beckoning smiles. How grand it was to see green again. To some, gold is the color of riches… if that is true than these followers of the King would rather be poor.

Lavrin slowed his horse to a trot and the others followed. Kasandra rode up upon Lyris. "I'm so glad to be at the end of our time in the desert. I know we've accomplished many great things and helped save the nomads, but the heat was really getting to me."

"I agree. It was an unusual feeling, and not in a good way."

Chan smirked. "The short time I've been in the desert, I've had no trouble with the heat. I'm watching you all practically die from your sweat. Funny, I hardly notice it. It's probably the dragon scales."

Kyra rode up beside them. "I am jealous, Chan. That reminds me. How did you, Nadrian, Calix and Grax not get blown over by the impact of the sandstorm? Surely that was not your dragon armor as well."

"It carried us."

Kyra was utterly puzzled, and it showed on her face. "Come again? What do you mean, it carried you?"

At this time, everyone had gathered closely together and were riding in a tight pack. They were eager to join in the conversation. Nadrian was the first to answer Kyra's question. "The King is marvelous in His ways. He has used some very unusual means of sending out his messengers in the past. I have read about some of them in a book the King granted to me. He has used both natural and unnatural occurrences for His benefit. The King formed the sandstorm and sent it on its way so that it would arrive at the right time in the right place."

"At the right place, at the right time, bringing the right people, you could say," Lavrin added.

"I suppose you could say so," Calix said. "I mean, we knew the most about the situation."

"What do you mean, Calix? How could you have known anything about it, except that we were there?"

Calix slowed his horse. "Oh, that's right. You didn't even know. We've been watching you from the Haven Realm. There is a pool there which allows you to see into Amcronos. We have been carefully following your progress in the Mazaron with its conversion to the Light. We also watched your efforts here in the desert."

Kyra grinned. "That's amazing. I'm very glad you remembered us and kept us in your hearts in the Haven Realm. If only there was some way you could have told us you were watching over us. That would have helped us when the struggles hit. Some of the trials would have been much easier with your help."

Grax gazed over his shoulder back toward the dunes of sand. "But we did. You must not have realized it in the heat of the moment. The oasis you found was sent by the King to aid you. We asked him to grant you a gift to help you continue on your journey."

"Really? You sent that to us? Oh... I suppose that means you also watched all our bickering. That must have been a horrible sight to see. I wished it could've been any other way. I wished you could have seen us living in

65

perfect harmony. You must have thought rather poorly of us." Kyra twisted a few locks of her hair.

Calix said, "No, quite the opposite. I'm glad we got to see exactly what was happening in the desert, or else the King would have had no reason to send us. Struggles build character. I think all five of you are now better people because of the hardships you have gone through."

Lavrin nudged Calix. "Glad to have you back. I always missed your little words of wisdom."

"Wisdom comes from the King, not from me. I'm only trying to help as best I can. Still, I'm sure my time in the Haven Realm has given me more knowledge than I could gain here in Amcronos. Also, it was not just a guess that you have become better people. The light of your hearts has grown brighter since we came from the Haven Realm."

"The light of our hearts?" Kasandra asked him. "What do you mean?"

Calix paused. "My mistake. I completely forgot we haven't told you about our new gifts and abilities. In the Haven Realm, there was a great ceremony where everyone received a special token from the King. That is how Chan got his dragon scale armor, and Nadrian received her book of Amcronos' beginning. This necklace I wear is more than the King's emblem. It allows me to do two things I could never do before.

"I can tell the purity of one's heart. Followers of the King are white or blue. Followers of Natas are red or black. There are also some like the nomads, with hearts of gray or brown. They have not chosen their side. I'm still trying to get used to this ability, but I'm glad your fires for the King burn brightly. Also, my necklace lets me recognize if someone is lying or telling the truth. In the Haven Realm, there was no real use for this gift."

"That is amazing. That would have been very helpful when we were captured by Faeth. We would never have been in this mess. But as you mentioned, it turned out for the best. The King knew the perfect time to send you to our aid. The gifts you all received sound incredible, but what was Grax's present?" Lavrin looked toward Grax, who was staring into the distance.

"It's hard to say exactly. He has not let anyone see the letter he received. All that I know is he was given a personal note from the King himself that has reassured him and given him hope. It has set his heart aflame with passion. Surely, he would not have wanted anything else."

Lavrin thought it over, and realized Grax did seem different, as though he carried a new responsibility. But it was not that. More of a new honor or deeper loyalty. Either way, Lavrin was glad to see the mighty warrior becoming even more of a righteous man. Truly, no one could find better friends than Calix, Grax and the rest of their group. It was like they were a family... a family that may have its difficulties, but which was knitted together like rope.

Meanwhile, Kasandra asked Nadrian, "I've always wondered what it is like in the Haven Realm. What do you do there? Is it quiet, or loud because of cheers and laughter? Is it always bright there, or more shaded to ease you from the heat?"

Nadrian spun an arrow in her hand as she rode. "Where to begin? The Haven Realm is a place of unity and peace. It's almost like a paradise, but with thousands of other followers of the King there with you. We live in the capital city, and it is massive. To answer your questions, I spend most of my time admiring the capital, meeting others with zeal for the King and watching the events happening in Amcronos. We always have something to do, but are never busy. Training seems easier, food tastes better, meeting others is natural, and life is enjoyable."

"That sounds wonderful. Did you happen to meet a man named Rowan? He would be mid-height, with darker hair. He…"

Nadrian interrupted her. "Yes, Kasandra, I actually did get to meet him. He seemed like a good, honest man. Every now and then he would come with us to the Lake of Revelation where we would watch the situation in Amcronos. He trained with Calix and Chan occasionally, and seemed connected to us, since we knew Lavrin and the others he had met. He told me a lot about you, you two seemed like deep friends. It was a shame that he died the way that he did. Rest assured that he is safe and joyful in the Haven Realm. How are you taking it?"

"Much better." Kasandra smirked. "Knowing he found his way into great company helps a lot. I cherished our times together; he was more than a friend to me. In fact, I've known him for so long that life feels different now that he's gone. At least I will see him again one day in the Haven Realm. You must have mixed emotions about having to come back here. You went from living in perfection to stopping war in a desert. But why did Rowan not come with you? I would have really enjoyed seeing him again."

Nadrian frowned. "It is complicated. Personally, I'm glad we were sent back to Amcronos. Though I definitely miss all the amazing things of the Haven Realm, I know will see them again. Besides, helping defeat the darkness is a worthy goal to return for. About Rowan, his death was permanent. With Chan, Grax and I, we traveled to the Haven Realm across the Western waves. Thus, we technically never died, and are still able to return."

Kasandra turned to Calix. "Nadrian didn't mention you. How did you travel to the Haven Realm? Felloni and Kyra have told me several times about the brave death you suffered at Hightenmore castle."

"I was taken from my body by the King. Little did I know it, but the King took me from Amcronos for this very purpose. He needed those around me to keep fighting, and knew my death would shatter their hearts. Thus, and so I could return now, he could not afford to let me die slowly. It was an extreme case, however; I am the first time in

69

history the King ever took someone to the Haven Realm before it was their time."

Kasandra nodded. "So, you never died either. I think I understand how that works. So, does that mean all of you could still die now that you are back in Amcronos?"

Calix bit his lip. "It is possible. Though in such good company and with the gifts of the King on our side, that is unlikely. But, eventually the King will call us back to the Haven Realm. He will allow us to remain only until our mission is completed."

The soft steps of the horses transitioned from sand to dirt. After traveling through a section of dry clay and dirt for several minutes, they reached grass. The ensuing scene was marvelous. After having left the monotonous desert, the bright greens of the grassy plains left one in wonder. The colorful flowers, circling bees and swaying bushes all seemed in the right place. Most people would have taken it as ordinary, but to some of the adventurers, it was incredible.

To Lavrin, Kyra, Felloni, Uminos and Kasandra, it was terrific. They lay on the peaceful beds of grass and soaked in the moment. It felt like their hard times were finally over, and that they would never have a care again. They took in their momentary freedom like they were never going to have to struggle or battle again. Little did they know what lay in store for them in the coming weeks.

Chan, Calix, Grax and Nadrian remained on their horses and thought back to the splendor of the glorious city of the King. In the Haven Realm, scenes like this paled in comparison to rich splendor of the land.

After several minutes, Lavrin returned to his horse. "Why do you not look excited?" Lavrin asked Chan. "This is amazing. We've finally made our way out of the desert and are ready to continue our journey together. Our group has been reunited... finally reunited. We will remain together to build each other up. With your return, we will be able to accomplish more for the King than ever before. Doesn't the future look bright?"

Chan was slow to reply. "It depends on how you look at it, I suppose. The King has sent us here for a mission... a mission that involves all of us. That is the reason we have been traveling east from the desert, not back north to the Mazaron Mountains."

"What kind of mission? You realize that our time in the mountains and through the desert have taken their toll. Can we have a week or so to rest and recover?"

"I'm afraid not," Chan replied. "Events happening in the North are speeding up our quest, as well. I don't know much about the mission, except that we need to find some sort of weapon or item. The way the King described it, it sounded ancient - a relic of Amcronos' past. We're headed toward a village in the plains. There, one of his messengers will tell us where to begin searching. If you want to know more, you can probably ask Nadrian. She has been learning about Amcronos' history for some time now."

Lavrin lowered his gaze. "I suppose it's for the best. I only hope our group can give their all to this task. The farther east we head, the greater chance there is that we will be attacked. I will do the best I can to rally us for such an encounter."

Chan nodded. "We will do it together."

"How do you know this weapon is so important, anyway?"

"The King himself told us to head into the desert to rescue you from war and end it before it began. Then we were to escort you to the East to find a weapon that would help the lands of the Light fight the darkness. The words of the King are never wrong. I have a feeling he would not have had us return if this item - whatever it is - was easy to obtain."

Lavrin took a deep breath. "I'm very sorry. I did not know the King himself had told you this. It must be quite an honor to be acting on behalf of the King directly. We will keep moving soon."

Chan did his best to smile. "Take heart. You are acting on his behalf just as we are."

After recovering from the joy of leaving the desert, the rest of the group returned to their horses. Lavrin relayed to them Chan's instructions, and the nine set off eastward. Eastward... toward Natas' domain. They were headed closer and closer to the place Lavrin never wanted to enter. If the mission had not come from the King himself, Lavrin might have questioned it. For now, at least, they were far from Natas' looming hand.

The horses traveled faster over the swaying grass, glad to be out of the harsh terrain. Uminos still had not found a horse that could carry his heavy scales, but he was alright with that. He could not fathom how to ride a horse, anyhow. His only hope was to eventually find some creature that he could relate with, or he would be forced to run on foot the rest of their quest.

As he sped through the area, he was amazed it had not been reached by the dark grasp of Natas. It might be one of the few places left in Amcronos that was not tainted by war or by the slavery of Natas. It would be a great place for his people to live. But there would be nowhere left for his people to thrive if Natas won this war. Uminos suddenly realized the weight placed upon those fighting this war. On his shoulders, he carried the entire Seviathan race. Uminos, once an outcast of his people, now represented every one of the them. Somehow, though the burden was heavy, it was also comforting. It was a responsibility he gladly accepted.

Uminos might have dwelt on this thought for hours, but the conversation of Lavrin and Calix distracted him. He knew Lavrin had been waiting months, if not years, for this moment. Now, of all the times, he could only find it within himself to answer Calix's questions.

"So, what happened to the swords Auden gave us?" Calix asked.

Lavrin shrugged. "I know they were displayed in Hightenmore in your honor. Auden created a memorial to all of you and to the battle in the great hall. But, from what you tell me about the mounting battles in the North, I would not be surprised if they found new soldiers."

Calix beamed. "I would not object to that. I'd be glad to see others continuing the fight in our place. We may not be able to see or protect our friends in the North for a long time now. I doubt our mission will send us north any time soon. It's a shame, out of everything I missed, I wanted most to help you save your father."

Before Lavrin could respond, Nadrian rode up beside them. "I've done a quick search through my book from the King, and there are many powerful weapons used in the past. Yet, most of them don't seem right for this journey. I have several guesses, but they are little more than that. For the King to specifically send us back just to find this single item, it must be very unique..."

"...And very powerful," Lavrin finished. "No matter the reason, I'm glad I get to see all of you again. I have missed you terribly, which you probably noticed from the Haven Realm. But I must ask you something, and please don't take this the wrong way. What has happened to all of you? Something has changed within you, something drastic. I can feel it. I almost feel like the four of you deserve new names, because you are so different."

Calix sighed. "The Haven Realm is the best place you can ever live. It is beyond perfect. Though we are happy to see you again, Amcronos seems a lot less beautiful than it was before. It seems... empty. Like it is a haunted shadow of the glory of the Haven Realm. The sad part is, we have not even reached the dark regions of the land yet. Since these joyful areas seem so dim, the darkness may seek to blind us from all light."

"Don't talk that way, Calix. You really have changed. What you have said is true, but need you be so downhearted? I am so glad you experienced the Haven Realm, yet I fear you have lost your humanity. Those who have remained in Amcronos will help you as you help us. You can teach us more about the King and his mighty honor. We can help you remember your joy and your humanity. Is that a deal?"

Calix reached out his hand. Lavrin placed his hand on Calix's shoulder. "My dear friend. I'm not sure how they act in the Haven Realm, but I think we are past the point of handshakes."

"Of course. My mistake. Let's just make sure to keep the mission before us first."

"I agree," Lavrin said. "This mission seems like it will affect more than just our lives. It might even alter the future of Amcronos. We must keep our quest secret, and find the weapon at all costs. For now, we must put aside anything that might hinder us. And I'm not talking about supplies. I'm hoping that we can keep our eyes not on the past, but on fighting for a bright dawn to come. As much as I hate to say it, things will never return to how they once were until this is over. I can only hope this messenger you've mentioned will point us in the right direction."

CHAPTER 5

THE MESSENGER

The open plains treated the nine warmly. Lavrin could see no enemies nor looming threats they would have to face. It was strange; Lavrin had always felt danger was nearby. Now he did not feel it. Everything seemed open. There were no trees, mountains or waters, only lush grass. Lavrin went over to Nadrian and asked her where they were. She flipped open her precious book and found a map. "The Hills of the Gorills," she told him.

"I've never heard anything about this place before," Lavrin replied. "What do we know about this area?"

"Not much," said Calix, always at Lavrin's side. "The only mention of it in the Haven Realm was of the barbarian camps in the area. They are not the most civilized people, but many of them lead honest lives. We only need to find the messenger and leave this area, since I doubt the weapon is here. The barbarians should do us no harm. Nevertheless, we should avoid contact with them if possible. If provoked, they could prove quite the adversaries."

"I agree. Barbarians sound like trouble, and we are still recovering from our desert pains. I, at the very least, am not feeling up for any battles. How are we supposed to find this messenger, though?"

Calix looked at Chan, who motioned for him to tell Lavrin. There was something they had kept from him. Calix slowed his horse and looked toward Lavrin and the others. "The King told us this messenger is living as a barbarian, trying to sway them toward the King's side. If his mission has been successful, we should not be ambushed, as they should be expecting us. We need to find this tribe, find the messenger, retrieve the message and leave as quickly as possible. We cannot anticipate how the messenger's mission has been going. We may be forced to fight or retreat if his efforts have been unproductive. I can only hope that he's at least alive."

"So, are we supposed to be avoiding these barbarians, or meeting up with them?" Lavrin asked.

Chan took off his helmet. "We will be ready to fight if necessary, but it should not come to that. We are meeting up with the barbarians, but should try to limit contact and conversation with them. They get angry easily, from what I hear. Angry with outsiders, at least. That is why I fear for this messenger. Hopefully, he is tactful and resourceful. The camp should be coming up in a day's ride. Maybe two if we continue at this speed."

"We can speed up. The horses seem capable, and there are no obstacles in our way except for a few hills. We are ready to fight if we need to. Let's hope these barbarians aren't very barbaric. One other thing… how will we tell the messenger apart from the other men?"

"He should give us clues or hints, if not come to us directly," Calix began. "This messenger will want to continue his task of influencing this camp, so he may try to meet with us alone. There is no exact way to predict what is going to happen, only that we need this information, and need to keep the messenger's identity hidden from the barbarians."

The group continued onward, following Calix and Chan. They were the only two who knew where they were headed. Yet, even they did not know exactly where the camp was located. They only hoped they would find it soon, and could get started on their quest. The mystery of this weapon weighed down upon them. Could they not serve the King better fighting with the armies of the Light? Did not the North need them? Somehow, this artifact was more important.

The journey over the hills kept the group headed northeast. They hoped to find the camp soon, because night had almost fallen. If they could find the messenger quickly, they could find the weapon faster. Lavrin, most of all, wanted to meet up with the army in the North. He knew nothing about what was happening at Srayo. The little information Chan had told him about the North left him wondering.

What if his father was in danger? What if this weapon could protect the army of the Light permanently? If the King wanted this item, no one had the right to question his judgment.

Calix stopped the group. "Do you see that soft red glow in the distance?"

Nadrian squinted her eyes. "No. I see nothing glowing or red. Are you playing a trick on us, Calix?"

"I know I see something about a mile away glowing red. It's a light, hazy red, but still. None of you notice it? It's right there near those bushes."

Kyra put her hand on his forehead. "You don't have a fever. I do not see anything there, Calix. None of us do. Are you sure you feel alright?" Then she had an idea. "Did you receive something in the Haven Realm that changes your eyesight?'

"I don't believe so." Calix paused. He grabbed his necklace and slowly took it off. The red flicker disappeared. He put it back on, and the light returned. "I think it's my necklace. That means there is a follower of Natas off in the distance."

They instantly went into high-alert. Chan whispered, "You said it was a faint red? It is probably one of the barbarians, since they are tied to Natas, but loosely. I doubt these hill men would have any real loyalty, except to their own camp."

"But they are going to be more hospitable to the minion of Natas than to us," Calix answered. "Wait. He is moving." Everyone scanned the horizon, trying to follow Calix's gaze. Then they spied him. Though he was off in the distance, they could barely make out a barbarian walking out from a cluster of bushes. He was heading over one of the hills, and the nine followed him.

Chan hurried them onward. "We can't lose him. He will lead us straight to the camp." They rode up to where they had spotted the man, then stopped. Reaching the top of the hill, they beheld a small encampment of wild men. No one knew what to do from there. Approaching these barbarians could be disastrous, but they would get nowhere without being in the camp. Grax dismounted and lay in the tall grass. He crawled closer toward the camp to the edge of the hill. He turned and motioned for the others to follow.

They left their horses out of sight, and inched their way up to Grax. He kept himself low. "I suggest we lookout here for a while," he told the others. "We will get a layout for the camp and what is happening inside of it. If we get lucky, we may even be able to distinguish the messenger from the others."

It seemed like the best option at the moment, so they watched the camp. The minutes dragged by slowly, but no one cared. Lavrin stopped scoping out the barbarians for a moment, and turned to his companions. A smile lit across his face as he thought back to the times they had before. How many times had they fought together and struggled past incredible odds? Now they were all together again. His old and new friends on a mission across Amcronos. Even as his friends surveyed the camp in angst, Lavrin felt surprisingly at peace. This was where he was meant to be. He could only hope this mission would be successful, like the ones before.

Lavrin had learned so much about his new companions over their trips through the mountains and deserts. He also remembered the many great times with his old friends in Northwest Amcronos. He was equally grateful to have all of them by his side. No matter what happened past this moment, he was filled with joy, knowing they had joined by each other's sides. With this joy in his heart, Lavrin doubled his efforts to find the messenger.

They had been watching the camp for an hour. Not much activity had been going on. The messenger could not be made out from the rest of the savages roaming around the camp. The nine knew as they watched the area, that the barbarians always carried their weapons with them. They seemed ready for a battle, though not many other camps were settled in the hills. No one knew who they were prepared to fight, only that they were prepared.

Though the barbarians wore animal skins, and looked unruly, nothing they did seemed out of the ordinary. Maybe the messenger had been influencing them in many ways. It was hard to tell their mindset as they went about their lives.

Kyra broke the silence after another ten minutes passed. "We could do this all day and learn little. Though we have not found the messenger, we know these barbarians do not seem very aggressive. They seem a little uncivilized, yes, but we can hardly hold that against them. I suggest we lay down our weapons and walk into the camp peacefully. If we appeal to their humanity, they will not kill nine unarmed people."

"Or we could simply attack them," Kasandra responded. "With four of us bearing the armor of the Haven Realm, they would not stand a chance. We would not have to kill any of them, just wound them until they surrender. Then the messenger will find us, and tell us to stop fighting them, which of course we will be more than happy to do."

Nadrian drew an arrow. "I could cripple five men from this vantage point."

"No. Don't fire." Calix shuddered at the thought of betraying the trust of the messenger and losing their mission before it started. "We absolutely should not fight them at all. If we send our entire group into their camp, they may take us for an enemy scouting party. Let me walk down to them. You can make sure I'm safe from this distance. I will try to negotiate with them, and slip a message to our ally that you eight are up on the hill."

"What if they attack you?" Lavrin said. "You've already died before once, you don't need to died again."

"It is worth the risk. It is better than any of the other options we have. Besides, the messenger will protect me."

"I suppose you're right. You are placing a lot of faith in this mysterious man, though. At least we know there is a follower of the King somewhere down there. Best of luck, Calix." Lavrin reached his hand out to his long-standing friend.

Calix smiled. "I thought you said we were past that." Lavrin nodded. Everyone encouraged Calix and said a brief word to the King to look out for him. They could not bear anything to happen to him.

He rose from the hilltop, leaving his sword and his necklace with his friends. He could not bear the thought of losing his gift from the King. As he neared closer and closer to the camp, he wondered what would happen to him. He did not have his sword, but did they know that he was peaceful? Calix decided he should raise his hands, just in case.

Why had they not confronted him? He had almost reached the camp, still no one met him. He realized they had not noticed him yet. Not one of them even looked his way. Should he call out to them? Should he let them know he was approaching, and meant no harm? Calix thought about sneaking his way around the camp, but decided that he would stick to the plan. Discuss terms, find a way to have peace. If everything falls apart, hope the messenger will settle things down.

He was just a few steps from entering the camp. His hands were still raised in a gesture of peace. Calix noticed several barbarians huddled around the fire pit. Stepping out of the shadows, he walked up to them. They were all looking the other direction. Calix suppressed his fear. This was too important for him to panic. "Hello, friends. May I speak with the leader of your people?"

Without hesitation, the four barbarians turned around, rushing him with weapons raised. Calix closed his eyes, but they stopped inches from him. He opened his eyes to see them staring intently at him, as if he was a threat. They held their weapons toward him, but he was glad that they had not attacked. The barbarians lowered their axes, and grabbed him by the arm. They forced him through the camp, until they reached a large building. It was rustic in comparison to the usual stone or brick building... rustic like the barbarians themselves.

They shoved him into it, and stood post at the entrance, making sure he did not escape. A few lanterns lit the room, but it was overall shaded. Calix could make out a throne of sorts at the end of the room, with a mighty warrior seated upon it. He was surrounded by a few elite guards, ornately dressed in animal skins and holding long bows.

A barbarian stood in the far corner of the room. He looked like another one of the guards, except he was shorter and did not hold a weapon. This man stepped toward Calix. "You face the ruler of our people. This tribe has lasted in these hills for generations. We are not a people to be trifled with. Our ruler wishes to know why you have come to us. Speak the truth and you will live; lie and you will be dead before you can beg for mercy."

"Why can't I speak to him directly?" Calix asked.

The stout guard relayed the message to the mighty warrior atop the throne. He uttered words in a language Calix could not understand. The guard turned to Calix. "I am his translator. He does not know your language, neither do many of the people of this camp. Our ruler wishes to know who you are, for we have not seen your armor or its markings before. Are you a servant of Natas?"

"My name is Calix. I do not serve Natas. I wish for peace, and only peace. Tell your master that I am from the West. I will be passing through your camp to find my way to the other side. I only desire to rest here for a few days, then to head on my way."

The translator relayed the message to the ruler, who answered harshly to the translator. The poor man bit his lip. "Calix, I am to inform you that we are not a people who take visitors lightly. My master sees you as a threat. He says no one from the West would want to travel to the East. He sees that you have no weapons, but wonders why you would enter our camp instead of travel around it. You are not a peasant, or even a common knight to be wearing such fine clothes. Your armor impresses my master. He says if you are nobility, then you should not have entered our land. No prince or lord should have dealings here. He wants you to…"

A scout ran into the room before the translator could continue. The scout looked alarmed, and babbled urgently about something. He kept pointing in the direction of the Southern hills. The ruler and the translator were deep in conversation. Eventually, the translator crossed his arms, and stared intently at Calix. "Why did you not tell us you had friends in the hills nearby? They are armed and hostile. Some of them wear clothing like yours. Our race has conquered many that have risen against us. Are you scouting for one of our enemies? Why should we not kill you now, enemy spy?"

Calix tried to remain calm. Things were looking grim. "My friends and I only wish to dwell here in your camp for a few days and then continue on our way. We are not spying on your people. You should know that we are not the same as your enemies. We do not dress like they do, nor do we talk like they do. If you have never seen us before, why do you take us as a threat? Please let us stay here. I promise that we will not harm you in any way." Calix paused. How could he let them know their intentions without revealing the existence of the messenger?

Before Calix could continue, the translator stepped toward him. "Enough of your meaningless words. We shall throw you in our prison. Maybe you can convince us better from there." The translator looked to his master, and the strong warrior motioned to the guards. They grabbed him and dragged him away. His instincts told him to resist, but he did nothing to stop them. Resistance meant hostility; hostility meant death.

The guards did not let up on him, brutally pushing him into the prison and tossing him into a cell. This jail was the most obscure that Calix had ever seen. It was not even a building. Rather, it was out in the open; the rooms were wooden polls forming walls and a roof. There was only one other prisoner amongst the rows of small cells. Maybe they were built this way on purpose, since there was no refuge for the prisoners from rain or snow. In winter time, no one could survive.

Calix was shocked. He had never expected to be thrown into jail so quickly. He had only been in the presence of the barbarian's leader for a minute, and they had rejected him. At least they had not harmed him in any way, or taken his armor. Apparently, they did not think things through, for they had not even searched him.

If he slammed into the side of his chamber, Calix reasoned he could break it in a few tries. But what would that do for him? If he showed aggression, they would get more aggressive. Calix decided he would try to make things as easy on the messenger as possible. He had to remain peaceful so the messenger could free him. Then he stopped dead in his tracks. What if the other prisoner was the messenger? Maybe they had rejected his ideals and imprisoned him?

Calix crawled to the edge of his cell. "Hello there. Can you hear me? What is your name?"

The prisoner was startled. He eventually gained his composure. "My name is not important right now. I assume you have a weapon on you? There are probably plenty of places to hide a knife somewhere in that armor. How long would it take you to break out of here?"

How long had this man been captured? If he was the messenger, he could have been locked up in this open-air dungeon for months. Calix could not blame him. He had always been slightly claustrophobic. "I don't think escaping is the best option right now. You seem tense. Tell me, why were you imprisoned?"

The man rubbed his neck anxiously. "Well, you see, I visited the camp one day. I was a little hungry, and was hoping to get some food. They found me in their camp and brought me in for questioning. I stayed with this people for a while, and got to know them. I learned their language, and almost became part of their tribe. Sadly, they never trusted me, and blamed me when someone tried to steal their supplies. Now, I heard your allies are nearby. We should escape and meet up with the rest of your friends."

It was all beginning to come together. His story made sense. All they had to do now was escape, but Calix realized it would be better to wait for his teammates. Nothing was worth causing a battle when one was unnecessary. Calix was fine waiting if he needed to. He was afraid, however, that his new friend would not be so patient.

*****

"They captured him!" Nadrian already had an arrow loaded in her bow.

"We can free him," Kasandra said. "All we need to do is circle around the camp, spring in toward their jail and get him out of there. They won't know what happened. We don't know what he said to them, but maybe he already has found the messenger. If we free Calix, we can get our journey going again."

"What if he needs more time?" Grax asked.

Nadrian continued to look through the camp. "I'm not sure what extra time in captivity will give him, except possibly torture."

Lavrin drew out his sword. "I cannot bear to lose Calix again. We need to get him out of there, I agree. We are forgetting, however, that if we upset these people, the King's servant could pay dearly. We need to think of him and his life, as well. If we ruin his chances to save Calix, we will have acted selfishly. What we need to do is free Calix in such a way that the barbarians remain calm, and we still find this messenger."

"This might be able to help." Grax brought out Calix's necklace from his bag. "We can find Calix and the messenger both by looking at the hearts of these men. He said that a follower of the King had a bright color emanating from them. I think he said it was a blue or white. Send someone in there alone, from behind the camp, who can find Calix and free him quietly. We will worry about continuing our mission later."

Felloni held out his hand to Grax. "I will. I'm the most qualified."

Everyone looked toward him. He had a point. He was the most silent. His skill in hunting made him perfect for the job. Grax handed the necklace to Felloni. He put it on and instantly covered his eyes. The array of color had stunned him. All other colors faded away except for the lights emanating from the hearts of his friends. It was stunning, far brighter than Felloni had expected. His hands remained pressed on his eyes for some time.

"Are you alright, Felloni?" Kyra had her medical bag ready.

He stood up and answered, "I'm fine." He did not tell them about the ringing in his skull or the sting behind his eyes. How did Calix deal with this? Under the cover of night, he bolted off to the far side of the camp. He made sure to stay behind the protection of the hills until he was directly behind the barbarian's prison. Felloni could not see Calix, but he could see his strong blue light.

Like a vapor, Felloni glided down the hills and hid behind a hut. He was completely focused on the flickering light of Calix's heart, like a long-lost treasure. Felloni knew he was close. He kept going closer and closer to

Calix's cell. Then he noticed the guard. There was a tall barbarian standing watch over the two prisoners under his care.

Felloni knew he would have to go through him to reach them. In a fraction of a second, he sprung upon the unsuspecting guard and clamped down on his mouth. The guard suffocated and collapsed. Calix whispered, "Felloni, did you kill him?"

"No. I only knocked him out." Felloni got to work cutting the rope holding the cell together. Calix was quickly freed.

"Free him, too. I think he is the messenger we were sent for." Calix motioned to the other prisoner. Felloni rushed over to him, and noticed his light was a muddled brown. Not the color he had expected. Nonetheless, Felloni broke down his cell and released him. The three left the scene in great haste, making their way back to the rest of the group.

Lavrin embraced Calix, and the others congratulated Felloni on his success. Felloni was more than happy to return Calix's necklace to him. Its bright flashes of light had not faded from his eyes. After everyone recovered from the initial excitement, they huddled together.

"Did you find the messenger?" Lavrin asked Calix.

"I believe this man is our messenger." Calix looked toward him, and noticed the mixed state of his heart.

"Messenger?" the man said. "What messenger?"

Calix could tell by the look in his eyes that he was completely confused. Clearly, this was not the one they had hoped to find. Then who was the messenger? Calix turned to the rest of his team. "We should return this man to the camp at once. I am certain now that he is not the messenger we are searching for. We can't let this incident escalate into something worse."

"I agree." Chan stood up and grabbed the poor prisoner by the shoulder. The man had no idea what was happening to him.

Before he could protest, a shout arose from the camp. "Calix, return our prisoner. We know you have him. If you return him to us, we will let you leave. He caused great shame and disgrace to our tribe."

Calix rose to his feet. He noticed a group ascending from the camp toward them. The translator was the one who had called out to him. Calix blinked hard. No, he was not seeing things. A blue light shone out amongst the group. One of the members of the force was the messenger.

The prisoner was brought forward by Chan and handed over to them. The two sides stood just a few yards from each other. The translator received a message from his master and said, "Thank you for returning this villain to our custody. Our guard took this from one of your men."

The translator approached them, holding one of Felloni's knives. Felloni was stunned. He felt over himself and noticed one of his sheaths was empty. Calix approached the translator and took the knife from him.

Then he noticed something he never expected. With the translator separate from the rest of the group, it was clear. The light from the translator's heart was a shimmering blue. Calix stood staring into his eyes in awe. He was the one who had sent him to confinement in their jail. He was the one who had threatened him. Of all the men Calix had expected, the translator was the least of them.

"I'm sorry for what I had to do to you," the translator whispered. "You seem like a very honorable man; I simply had to keep my standings in check. Here is the location of the first piece of the Titan's Heart. That is what the weapon you are looking for is called."

The messenger slipped a map to Calix. Not knowing what else to say, Calix replied, "May the King reign and His followers prosper."

Both nodded and went their separate ways. The messenger went back to his master, talking to him in the native tongue. Calix returned to his group, too stunned to even speak.

*****

"So, they just threw you in there?" Kyra asked.

Calix nodded in agreement. "Basically. They just took me out of the hall and straight to their jail. It was hardly even a jail, though. They had just planted poles in the ground and tied them together. They did the same thing for the roof, too."

"That's unbelievable. So, you happened to meet this other prisoner when you were thrown in?"

"He was the only other prisoner there," Calix replied. "Naturally, I wanted to find out what he knew, and what had happened to him. Though I was confused by his anxiety, his story matched up with the messenger's. He claimed he had entered the tribe and had almost become a member of it, before being accused of theft. Now, I see that these similarities were only a coincidence. I was so blind. The messenger not only fooled the barbarians, but completely fooled me."

Uminos hurried to catch up to the group. "So, Calix, what did the messenger give you?"

"He handed me a map with the location of the first piece of the Titan's Heart, which is what we are looking for. It is still so strange that he was the messenger. I mean, he was one of the main reasons I was thrown into jail in the first place. He did an excellent job covering his identity... almost too good of a job."

"Can I see this map?" Uminos reached out, and Calix handed it to him.

Uminos looked over the map for quite some time as the group continued northeast. He studied it, and then handed it back to Calix. "That is interesting. Apparently, the weapon is so powerful that five of its pieces have been spread throughout Southeastern Amcronos. Furthermore, this map only shows the first location. This makes it all the harder to find. We should travel lightly and carefully to find them all."

"Definitely." Calix handed the scroll to the others for them to see. "To find these five pieces, we will be going into the heart of Natas' lands. We must trust that the King is guiding us, because if he is not, we will perish. Now that we are together, we must remain strong to face the perils ahead of us."

"You're right, Calix," Lavrin said. "The piece we are headed toward now takes us close to Aphenter. I have heard of wicked things that happen there. I'm also worried that this map includes lands not far from Balyon. Hopefully, we can avoid too much exposure to dark forces in this journey."

"What do we know of this forest?" Kasandra pointed to part of the map.

Lavrin bit his lip. "Nothing, I'm afraid. I fear that forest is so secretive that no one knows much about it. That is probably because no one travels there to find out. I know I would never want to travel to such a dark place."

"A dark place," Kasandra asked. "I thought you said you knew nothing about it."

"I've heard stories. I don't know whether they are true or not."

The members of the team kept their hands close to their weapons, feeling that evil was closing in around them. Felloni felt this most of all. He was still shaken up from their time in the desert and the encounter in the barbarian camp. He realized how different his life had become after he had met Lavrin and Calix. He had been on journeys before, but none close to these. Never could had dreamed he would have fought an evil Seviathan king or a tyrannical leader of Saberlin.

None of their recent missions had been simple or easy. Even their time of diplomacy after the war in the Mazaron had been stressful. Each town in the mountains had seemed to hang in the balance of their every word. Felloni was ashamed that with such great importance placed upon him, he had almost betrayed the King in the desert. He had almost betrayed himself and all he cared about. Never again.

Now his long-lost companions had been summoned back from the Haven Realm by a sandstorm to help them find an ancient weapon. A weapon of seemingly great importance. He so desperately wanted to be strong. It was a lot to take in. So much had happened. This was the first chance he had had to truly dwell on it.

Little did he know, the rest of the group was thinking the same thing. They had fought beside each other for so long that it seemed like nothing could surprise them now. They had changed the course of history and of nations; what more could they face? Amcronos, however, had many surprises still to throw their way.

CHAPTER 6

A HIDDEN CITY

Mild. It was all so mild. The same scene unfolded for miles. The grass was long and reaching, and the hills had evened out into open land. Clouds covered the sun from all sides, as if it did not exist. Lavrin kept the small fire going as the group huddled around it. Its thin trail of smoke rose to the clouds above, joining in their troubled sky. They had been traveling north for two full days, and still did not know exactly where they were headed. The first piece of the Titan's Heart seemed to be in the middle of nowhere. The map showed it close to Aphenter, but outside of the city. The team did not know what lay near Aphenter, but there was no city in that region. There was nothing on the map... as if the piece was simply laying somewhere in the plains.

With hope in their hearts, the group had set their course based on the map. Though where the piece was shown seemed odd, Lavrin was glad it was not inside of Aphenter. The whole team knew they should stay far from that city. If the piece had been close to that malevolent fortress, they would have needed reinforcements, and a lot of them.

When they had journeyed far enough for the day, they enjoyed the chance to rest and share stories. Grax recalled the great festival of the King in the Haven Realm. He spoke of the gifts they received, and of the splendor of the gathering. Kyra talked about the arrival of the stone golems at the Seviathan fortress. She spoke of their heroic victory, but also included the freeing of the Seviathan people. Chan described the times spent in with the King and His angels. He talked mostly about training with the King's greatest warriors, and learning from his wisest scholars.

It was a tranquil time for the team to unwind and lay aside their cares. Even though they knew it could not last, they let the peace wash over them. Who knew what terror they would soon face? Everyone shared openly their excitements and anxieties. The time passed as the group bonded. It felt as if they needed to learn about each other for the first time; so much time had passed and so much had changed. Those from the Haven Realm had plenty of knowledge to endow to the others, and those of Amcronos had plenty of life lessons they had learned along the way.

They realized this might be their last time to connect before entering the heart of Natas' lands. If they could not enjoy their blessings now, how could they remember them in times of trouble? They were a strong, unified force and would need to rely on each other more than any of them knew. From this point on, there would be fewer and fewer followers of the King.

*****

The rain continued to surge. Nadrian did not like it. She used to love the rain, until she first experienced a refreshing downpour in the Haven Realm. Now the rain felt different... it was as if it clawed at her when it struck at her skin. She never expected that everything in Amcronos would become so lackluster.

Nadrian had always considered the land slightly shaded because of Natas' influence, but now it seemed utterly tainted. There had been so much kindness and hospitality in the Haven Realm; now it seemed like they were the only soldiers left of the King in Amcronos. The Northern army seemed only a distant hope. All the team had was each other and the King to rely on now.

With the memories of the past fueling them on toward the future, the group slugged onward through the rain. The mud clung to their boots, trying to drag them down. In the sky above, the dark clouds had blotted out the sun's rays. It was a bleak moment. How quickly the landscape had turned from hospitable to hostile. All they could do was walk on. The nine continued toward the first piece of the Titan's Heart following their precious map. It was their only guide.

The wind blew against them; the rain soaked them to the bone. It was as if the forces of nature were bent on stopping their progress. It was as if, even to the smallest detail, the darkness of the land hated them. As the team endured the onslaught of the storm, they began to slow. Lavrin, however, thought of his father. He was fighting for his father, he was living for his father and his King. With an inner shout of courage, he pressed on and the others followed. They rallied around his passion and battled through the elements by any means necessary.

*****

They were drawing close, at least from what he read on the map. Calix was desperately intrigued by the weapon they were pursuing. He had asked Nadrian about it, but she could only find stories. Stories not of the relic itself, but of the wars fought to claim it. So many dead. So many going before them, and their countless failures.

This only fueled Calix's wonder. The Titan's Heart, what an interesting name. The King himself had sent them to find it. Out of all his followers, the King had chosen this group. Clearly, he saw something in them. Of all the King's soldiers, were they really the best suited to find the Titan's Heart? Was it really the heart of a Titan, or was this a comparison of some sort? Titans were symbolic of physical strength; their great feats of courage were things of legend. A heart was symbolic of love; throughout history it resembled this most honest and resonating ideal. Calix was amazed. The King had sent them to find the relic of strength and love.

Surely this weapon was not one of darkness, but of the light. The light... the cause which they rallied behind. Without it, the team never would have been formed. Without it, there would be no resistance to Natas. In fact, without the light, Lavrin and Calix might never have met.

They had been bonded in brotherhood, being the only family each had for such a long time. Now Lavrin had his father, and Calix had seen his family in the Haven Realm. Ever since meeting together again, things had been different; their relationship had changed. They still had the memories they cherished, but now felt differently about the future. One day, Calix would have to return to the Haven Realm, and they would be split apart again. Brothers separate once more. It was inevitable. Calix nudged Lavrin and asked, "I never told you I got to see my parents again, did I?"

"I don't believe so." Lavrin scratched his head. "I'm sure they're amazing people."

"They are amazing. I hardly know where to begin. My mother was always caring and generous, giving to the poor. She took it as a mission to help everyone she met. My father liked strategy, and taught me how to always win an argument. He was very passionate about it."

Lavrin raised his eyebrows. "But, I've won arguments against you before."

103

Calix replied, "Yes. Well... I let you win. I suppose my mother's kindness comes out as well. It was wonderful getting to see them again. They told me they had been watching some of our times in the forest. They told me you were too adventurous for your own good." Calix had to hold back his laughter. "They even said they weren't shocked in the slightest when you were caught by Chan, Grax and Felloni."

"Did they, now?" Lavrin blushed. "They were probably right. Did you get to explore the Haven Realm with them? All these stories about it get my blood rushing. I can almost see it."

Uminos, far ahead of the team, stood on the rise of a hill. He peered out into the distance. "I see something," he yelled.

Everyone rushed up to him. They looked down on the scene in confusion. A short distance away, it looked as if there were thousands of water droplets suspended in midair. They seemed to curve around or away from an area, as if fleeing from it. The land beneath the spectacle looked still and dry, though the rain pounded the rest of the ground. The crystalline fragments pounded the valley with thousands of hammer strokes. Naturally, the group moved closer toward the area.

It seemed as if there was nothing there. Still, these miniscule dewdrops rolled down the side of the air till they hit the ground. Kyra reached to touch one. She instantly drew her hand away. Then she reached for it again, and felt a smooth surface. She felt along the invisible wall. What was it? Glass?

The others watched as she walked down the side of this see-through surface. Her hand ran along the nothingness; at least, that is how it appeared. She stopped. Kyra felt something sticking out from the side of the wall. After putting down her bag, she placed both hands around the object. She was able to turn it with little effort. Then she realized what she had found: a doorknob. Kyra pushed the doorknob and watched as the door opened.

Out of curiosity, the nine entered the doorway and were amazed. They beheld an entire city, teaming with life and people. There were shops, houses and buildings lining the streets. How had they not seen any of this from outside? The golden hue of the city was marvelous. Some of them felt almost as if they had returned to the Haven Realm. Yet they were not warmly welcomed. An armed escort confronted them a few seconds after they entered. They did not look happy. "How did you find our city?" they asked. One of the massive guards grabbed Uminos by the arm. Uminos gazed up at the behemoth and was alarmed. At least they hadn't used their weapons…for the moment.

The question was apparently rhetorical, because the guards seized the nine and led them off. Without a moment to assess the predicament, the team found themselves in front of an assembly. Hundreds had gathered, but they were focused on four men who sat at the head of this assembly in large thrones. These leaders were short and stocky, but dressed in fine clothing. They themselves did not seem impressive, but their thrones were incredible, fashioned of rare elements, each unique and strangely metallic.

Lavrin could not tell what these men were thinking; their faces were as emotionless as the walls around them. One of them, holding an impressive scepter, said for all to hear, "It has been a long time since we've had visitors." He turned his gaze toward Lavrin. "This city is run by its greatest minds. We pride ourselves on our inventions and technology, so much that our engineers and architects lead us. My three leaders and I, who are before you now, consider our city's concealment our mightiest achievement. This city has been hidden a long time, so long it has fallen off many maps. The four of us have ruled, undisturbed by the outside world. That is, until now. Now we face nine outsiders who have already managed to frighten some of our citizens. How did you find us?"

Uminos stepped forward. "The rainfall left droplets on the walls of your city. Out of curiosity, we investigated these drops of water that seemed to cling to thin air. Then we felt our way along the surface of your walls until we found the door."

"Fate has favored you, Seviathan. Your group was very fortunate to find the only entrance to our city. We will find a way to fix this problem in our defenses. I will assign my best men to making sure the rain no longer reveals us. In the meantime, I'm very interested to find one of your kind so far from home. I can tell your necklace was crafted in the Haven Realm." He pointed toward Calix, then sat back in his throne. "Clearly, you are a very diverse group. Almost too diverse... one that would not come together by chance. This is becoming a most interesting encounter."

Calix answered him. "We could say the same thing. We did not expect to find an invisible city today. I will say that your workmanship is marvelous. Truly, you must be a people of great wisdom. You must have some knowledge of the Haven Realm if you know its handiwork. Maybe it was the King's will that our mission brought us to you."

The rulers of the veiled city turned to one another. For the first time, they looked slightly worried. Then their faces looked back toward the group... very worried. "What sort of mission?" they asked after a pause.

If there was one thing Calix had learned in the Haven Realm, honesty went a long way. He knew if he spoke the truth, things would turn out alright. "We are on a quest for the King. There is a weapon that our King desires and this was the location of its first piece. Have you ever heard of this weapon?"

The four leaders averted their eyes. Eventually they replied, "Yes, we have. In fact, our ancestors helped forge that weapon with the smiths of the Haven Realm. That was many decades, if not centuries ago, and we are no longer allied with the King. We see the power of the Titan's Heart as one that neither Natas nor the King should have."

"What if we earned it from you?" Grax rested his great hammer on his shoulder.

"Earned it from us? We must discuss this proposal. Your arrival here has given us more than enough to think about. It may take us a while to come to an agreement." The four leaders, along with assembly, exited the room. The doorways swung closed and were sealed shut with impenetrable locks. These people were incredibly cautious. All the team could do was wait for an answer.

Everyone hid their anxiety as best they could. Had they ruined their chance to obtain the first piece? Could they trust these men? At the very least, they could tell they were brilliant engineers, as their masterful architecture was apparent. The tall arches and high ceilings gave the room a sense of splendor. The thrones were the greatest works of art, designed in an articulate fashion known only in this city.

At least there was still hope. There was a chance their proposal would be accepted, and they could earn the first part of the Titan's Heart. There was hope that these men would honor their alliance with the King, even if it was generations ago. The past always has a way of affecting the present. History decrees it.

Though he was dismayed both the hill men and these leaders seemed hesitant toward them, Calix was glad no fighting had occurred. He remembered his final thought before being taken to the Haven Realm- how much he hated war. Not only was war brutal, but it's after affects were costly. Deep in his heart, though, Calix knew he would enter many more battles before returning to the King's side.

*****

The doors opened. Without saying a word, the assembly returned to their seats. They did not even look in the foreigners' direction. Instead of drawn out strides, the leaders returned to their thrones quickly and quietly. It was not what the team expected from the once arrogant lords. Lavrin only cared about one thing. "What was your decision?"

"Typically, we do not consider outsiders trustworthy. On the other hand, we consider ourselves generous. Since we are so benevolent, we will give you a chance to earn our piece of the Titan's Heart. You will fail this test, however, and when you give up, we may or may not give you grace."

"We are ready for your challenge."

The rulers were not impressed by Lavrin's bravery. "We take great pride in our city and the safety of its people. Keeping our citizens away from danger is our primary goal. To this end, we created a labyrinth underneath our city that sits above our dungeons. It is the best prison ever created… sadly, we've only used it once before. All I will say is the man did not escape, nor is he with us any longer.

"We will lock you in this dungeon and seal the labyrinth. If you can escape alive and get out of the labyrinth, ring the bell atop the southern watchtower. We will give you until sunset to succeed. If either you die, or our guard in the bell tower rings it at midnight, you lose. You will need to complete the mission to receive the piece, because the fragment of the Titan's Heart is well-hidden. I assure you, you will not find it without us. I will let you know, that if our guards find you once the challenge has begun they will attack you on sight. There is no room for mercy until after sunset. I would wish you luck, but all the luck in the world would do you no good now.'"

A squad of guards entered the room. Lavrin felt his heart pumping. There was no turning back. The guards moved closer. Their first action was to remove all weapons from the nine. They then turned toward the exit. As the guards escorted the team out of the area, Lavrin noticed Chan's eyes darting about. He was concentrating, taking in every aspect of the town... the placement of the buildings, the direction the guards were taking them and the location of the bell tower. A lone watchman stood atop it, staring down at them. Lavrin guessed this watchman was counting down the minutes until midnight.

After several turns, the road ended at a large building. It did not look like any of the other buildings in the city. It had no windows and only one entrance. Approaching the doorway, one of the guards unlocked a series of mechanisms.

The door did not open as they expected; as gears turned and braced, the door slowly lowered into the ground. It sank as if drowning, yet followed by the harmonious ratchet of gears and levers. The guards hardly seemed to notice, and the group followed them into the structure. At the end of the dark hallway inside was an open door... an ordinary door. The guards forced the nine through it, then followed. One of the towering sentinels lit a lantern.

Calix was the first to step down the descending staircase. He turned around to witness a guard stabbing his spear in a machine next to the door. After twisting the spear several times, the door clinked shut. Now the only direction they could go was down.

Although they expected to get a glimpse of this labyrinth, the team was led down the staircase straight into the dungeons. They were guided into a row of prison cells. The cells did not have iron bars, but rather mechanical doorways that opened into each cell. These contraptions were extremely sophisticated, with gears, levers and bars spread across them systematically. They made the first door seem childish and rudimentary. How could anyone break out of these immovable doors? Lavrin shuddered. They had not even reached the labyrinth, and already they were in serious trouble.

One of the guards looked over the group and stepped toward Chan. All Chan could do was take deep breaths as the sentinel forced him into one of the cells. He could not see anything in the dark, tight cell. Even in front of his face, his hand was only a gray, undefined mass. Nothing was clear; everything was shaded and confused. What would happen to the rest of the group? How could they escape? How could he find them again? Chan gripped his dragon tooth necklace and let his emotions flow into it. The King was with him; the King was always with him, he reminded himself.

Chan stopped. If he could focus, then maybe… he felt something below him. Something was touching him on the floor. It was stirring around him on all sides. What was in the cell? He knelt down. No, it could not be. Water was rising out of the floor. He was going to drown.

CHAPTER 7

THROUGH SUFFERING

"It is time." His voice was firm but compassionate.

The others turned toward him and nodded. They had to continue with the plan, no matter what they had gone through. This tragedy, this death in the midst in victory, had to mean something. If they did nothing, the lives of their friends were lost in vain. They would continue, carrying their banners in their hearts.

The army had camped a small distance from Srayo, and was taking a final rest before the long journey ahead. The soldiers recovered both physically and mentally from the past few days. Lives had been lost, many close to their hearts. Such was war. Such was the price to be paid.

Auden knew it would be hard on the men to set out now, but it had to be done. Now that they had defeated one of Natas' armies, they needed to move out. It was time to strike back. He knew that with most of the soldiers, their emotional scars would heal in a matter of weeks. That was, except for the Xalaians, whose loss of their leader could damage them for a lifetime. Auden had no idea how important their dragon king had been to them, so he went to comfort them.

It was only a short walk to reach them. Try as he might, he could not read the expressions of their faces. He could tell something was not right, as he sat down beside them. "I know you are feeling a lot of pain and sorrow right now, so I came to comfort you."

One of the squid men answered, "He was our leader, but he was so much more. Since the beginning of our race, the dragons have guided us. The dragon who accompanied us to battle was the last of the water dragons. He rushed into battle with valor, but blind to his own fate. We now have no more guidance as a people. It's not only that our champion is gone, but that we will never have a water dragon by our side again. I suppose we will have to find a way to stand on our own. The only thing I can say is you may not be able to hold us back in the next battle. Our time at Xala Lake made us soft, but no more. We will unleash a fury that has been concealed for generations. We will divide the enemy as our ancient ancestors did, never looking to the right or the left."

Auden thought about answering, but decided it was best not to. This was not his place, nor his culture. He was glad to see one thing, however. The Xalaians were ready for war. He only hoped the rest of the army carried the same zeal out of the victory at Srayo.

He told the Xalaians it was time to set out, and they were standing before he could finish. Auden made out Denethor in the mix of soldiers, and headed toward him. Denethor noticed and met him halfway. "The men are preparing to move as we speak."

"That is good." Auden looked back toward the squid men. "I would give the Xalaians some space. They are still bearing the weight of their loss. What did you and the other leaders decide about our plan from here"

Denethor took a deep, cleansing breath. "Boranor assures us that the stone golems remaining in the West will protect our lands. Any attacks from Aphenter or anywhere else will be stopped. This will allow us to set that out of our mind for now. The towns of Fairfick are nearby, and may hold some resistance against us. Besides Aphenter, however, the most powerful locations of Natas' influence are Quoto, Wessnor, the Towers of Woe, Malstrate and the Southeastern cities. That is, of course, excluding Natas' capitol - the colossal fortress of Balyon.

"From what Quinn tells me, Dalto and Wessnor are locked in a struggle against each other at the moment. We cannot conquer all the darkness at once. We must let those remaining in Dalto deal with the North. Thus, we believe we should focus on the cities of the East. It would completely cripple their forces if we can conquer some of their massive castles. With that said, we believe that if we can locate Natas' troops and destroy them army for army, we will have a better chance. If these legions Natas has sent against us ever fortify themselves in a city, they will be twice as hard to defeat."

"That makes sense," Auden said. "You left out one detail, though; how will we find the armies of Natas before they find us?"

"That, sadly, is what we don't know. We may not be able to. Whatever happens, we must make sure our men have their swords close at all times." Denethor stroked the mane of his horse before mounting it. Auden followed his lead and climbed onto his own mount.

They rode to the front of the camp, and noticed how quickly the men had readied to march. Their training had already paid off at Srayo; hopefully it would continue to pay off in the battles to come.

The army formed ranks behind Auden, Denethor and the other leaders in a matter of minutes. Auden looked to his left and right, and discerned many familiar faces. Matthias seemed to have bonded with Lord Quinn, and still wore his Daltonian clothing. Auden had heard the stories of Matthais' time in Pelios and Dalto, but could not imagine how it would have been to be there.

There was also Boranor who was standing beside his fellow stone golems. Standing together, they were a sight to behold. They were talking with the leaders of Dreylon, who beheld the stone golems with the utmost respect and awe. Boranor appeared to be thinking ahead, as his distant look proposed. He knew the importance of his people in this war, and had no intention of letting anyone down.

Auden scanned the ranks of men and noticed many were gazing his direction. They were waiting for him to give the signal. "We move out," Auden called forth. "We head toward Lake Tibern, and shall travel in its direction unless otherwise occupied. We shall enter the towns of Fairfick only if necessary."

The army followed the lords without delay. They headed due east as they had planned. Auden glanced behind him after several minutes and spied Warren, who had fallen back into the middle of the army. He was talking with some of the soldiers. They were smiling and conversing with Warren as if he was another man in the ranks. He had become like a brother to them. That was how it should be. The lord and his troops, one and the same.

Auden decided to let the troubles of the war slip from his mind for a moment. He slowed his horse to a trot. Warren and the rest of the troops soon caught up to him. When Warren realized Auden was beside him, he stopped his conversation with the soldiers. "Is something wrong, Lord Auden?"

"Yes," Auden replied. "Ever since Srayo's attack, I've been trying to care for the men, but have never given them the chance to know me. As I can see by the laughter you have brought, I should spend less time focusing on the war and more on my companions."

Warren nodded and returned to his previous conversation. Auden, in turn, greeted a group of men next to him. "Hello there, fine soldiers. How are you feeling today?"

They were caught off guard. "We are well, sir."

Auden grinned. "Tell me, how do you think we did in defending Srayo?"

"We did decent, sir," one of the soldiers said. "It's difficult to judge, knowing that we were caught so off guard. From a technical standpoint, one could say that we had few loses and successfully held the castle. On the other hand, the loss of the dragon was disheartening and our men appear beat up from the fight. If we had known about the catapult, or about the acid, or even about the storm... men could have been saved. If only that scout had lived, he could have told us everything. I think we should treat scouts as the highest priority. The only problem is, most of our scouts are already injured."

"A fine judgment. Now that you mention it, you look quite injured yourself. Are you feeling alright?" After taking a closer glance, Auden realized the soldier had more than simply minor injuries. He had suffered worse than many in the battle. He only possessed one arm.

With a downcast gaze, the man answered, "Well, sir, I've been better. It's a nasty feeling, living without a right arm. The bruises I can recover from, and the cramping in my legs will wear off, but I fear the unbalanced feeling may linger. It was my good one, too. I'll have to train harder to learn to fight with my left. I can't be losing my balance in the fights to come. I need to be in top form to fight for you, sir."

A tear rolled down Auden's face. He could not even imagine what it would have been like to be crippled in such a way. He did not have to fight as they fought. He did not have to stare into the eyes of the enemy and raise his sword against him. None of his closest friends had died. How could he even hope to help his worn-down troops?

The soldier spied the small tear as it traveled down Auden's cheek. He realized in that moment just how much Auden cared for them. This was what set apart the forces of the Light from any battalion of Natas - the Light was driven by compassion, kindness and hope. These emotions were but distant myths to the side of darkness.

Auden wondered what he would want if he was hurting. Most of all, he realized, he would want others to care for him and encourage him. With drive, Auden led his horse to the front of the ranks. "Halt!" he proclaimed. At once the army stopped. Auden continued. "It has come to my attention that we are more injured from our previous battle than I had realized. Though some have scars and wounds, I believe our biggest wounds are inside of us.

Many of you may be hurting without anyone else knowing it.

"So, what I want you to do is place your arms around the men next to you and look them in the eye. Tell them you are there for them. We must help each other up when we fall, and help each other grow stronger when we are defeated. Though we were not defeated this time, unless we stand by each other's side, we may get defeated yet. Therefore, stand strong knowing you have others who care for you and who will help you at every passing moment."

At first, the soldiers complied simply to follow orders. This time was different, however. They felt the sense of brotherhood and loyalty that transcended their temporary aching inside. Their inner burdens were lifted as they looked their fellow soldiers in the eye and told them they would fight for them to the end. When the army continued, it marched on with arms wrapped around each other. The forces of Light had become more than an army; they had become a unified front against Natas.

*****

"That is one of the towns of Fairfick," the scout relayed to the lords. Denethor noticed the scout was pacing.

Denethor tried to comfort the frantic man. "What happened out there? Is something wrong, soldier?"

In a moment, the scout tensed up. Then he closed his eyes and breathed deeply. "It was not what I expected, that's for sure. When I was given the assignment to scout out the town, I was slightly relieved... not too far from Srayo, not that dangerous, or so I had presumed.

"The town is filled with many vile things. So much was happening there that I decided to write it all down." The scout pulled out a wrinkled piece of parchment from an inner pocket of his cloak. The information the scout had penned on the parchment was barely legible, and looked more like random markings than actual text. Apparently, the scout had written it down in a hurry. Somehow, the scout was able to decipher his message. "The villages of Fairfick have been preparing for war. Besides gathering weapons for their own braves, many wild men from the South have come north to reinforce them. Even with the combined forces, however, we should be able to defeat them easily."

Denethor raised an eyebrow. "Then why are you so worried about them?"

"I have not finished," the scout continued. "Gathering troops is not the only things they have been doing. They have been gathering powder with which they are making bombs. These explosives seem very powerful; I would expect Natas has been helping them create these devices. They could wreak havoc on us unless we disarm them."

121

"You said you witnessed someone set off one of the devices?" Denethor looked straight into the scout's eyes.

The scout was caught off guard. "Yes. Yes, I did. The explosion was quite large."

Denethor let out a small grin. He turned to Auden and Warren. "How do you men feel about getting our hands on some of Natas' powerful weaponry?"

Warren instantly knew where Denethor was going. "It would be dangerous. I have no doubt, however, that the right assault team could handle the job. We would have to have a way to safely transport the devices."

"I'm sure we could figure a way to do so. Getting our hands on their prized possessions may rouse them to attack, so we need our army to be ready when we retrieve it."

Auden joined in. "That could be easily arranged. We should leave our supplies here, so that we can reach the towns by nightfall and the assault team will not be in danger. I'm sure the Daltonians could recover these weapons silently and swiftly. They are more agile than the average man, and are very precise in their movements. I will go to Lord Quinn and assemble a team."

Denethor nodded. "Thank you, young scout. You have given us a sizeable advantage for the moment. You are free to rest for the night. Report back to me tomorrow morning and I will assign you to a new location. You scouts are our eyes and ears. We will need you throughout this war."

The weary scout walked away scratching his head. He had received the opposite response than he had expected. The lords had accepted the frightening news as promising and intriguing, instead of petrifying. This sent the scout away utterly confused. After thinking it through, he decided to accept it as it was and rest for the night. Apparently, he had done a great service, and that was all that mattered.

Auden reached Quinn without delay. This could be something the troops could rally behind. A successful seizure of these weapons would not only be tactical, but also practical. Auden only hoped Quinn would be optimistic toward the idea.

Quinn was occupied showing Matthais his sword. Matthais seemed fixated on the weapon. It was majestic, perfectly crafted down to every detail. Auden had heard the stories of Quinn's intense duel with Halithor, and how Quinn had both frozen and lit his blade on fire to gain an edge. Had Halithor captured Dalto, who knows what would have happened. Now Halithor lay in a grave at Srayo and the tide of the war was turning.

With ample patience, Auden waited until Matthais handed the sword back to Quinn. Auden approached him and said, "Hello, Lord Quinn."

Quinn spun and around and almost fell backward. "I did not expect to see you here at this time. You caught me utterly by surprise. What may I do for you, Lord Auden?"

After carefully deciding how to phrase his answer, Auden replied, "I need your help. You see, we have received news from a scout that the towns of Fairfick are preparing to fight against us. Though they have a fair number of warriors, more importantly they have crafted bombs, possibly using dark secrets from Natas. We need to capture these weapons so that we can use them against our enemy instead of being destroyed by them. We know that your men are swift, trained and determined. Could you assemble a team of your warriors that could handle this task?"

"This sounds dangerous. Do you expect most of my men will return from this endeavor?"

Auden responded quickly. "I expect all your men to return from this mission if it goes as planned. We will make sure they are prepared in every way. I have full assurance in the abilities of your men to carry out the undertaking."

"When will you need them to head out?"

Auden beamed. Things were really looking up. "I would expect within several hours. We will need to travel a little farther, then set up the army before they set out. The sooner we can claim the devices for our own, the sooner we can rest easy. Do you think your warriors are up for the challenge?"

Quinn paused. "I know they will be ready. I will gather my best soldiers and prepare them for the task. We will retrieve those bombs, no matter the cost. Let me know when we are moving out."

"We will be moving out as soon as possible. All that we have to do is leave the supply wagons with a small guard and we will be prepared to move."

Auden and Quinn separated and instantly began their tasks. Auden reached the back of the army in a few minutes, and started giving out commands. Soon enough, the wagons were unfastened from the horses driving them. Ten men were left to defend the resources, since as many soldiers as possible might be needed at Fairfick.

Before Auden reached the front of the forces, Quinn had assembled twenty of his fastest, most skilled warriors. He took them to the front of the army near Auden. They seemed determined, ready to complete their goal, like hawks ready to strike. Quinn's elites brandished their weapons with honor, already processing the upcoming endeavor. It was a challenge they would gladly accept.

With a melodious blast of the trumpet, Auden signaled the forces to head out. The caravans were left at the scene, and the army marched onward to the east. Both Denethor and Warren pushed Auden to keep the men moving onward, the thought of impending explosions pressing on them. In full compliance, Auden increased the pace of the army, and they sped across the woodland.

In breakneck time, the army reached the edge of the forest. Rays of light greeted them through the swaying branches. Everyone covered their eyes from the unexpected array of blinding light. The lords were instantly dismayed. It would be incredibly difficult to get the Daltonians into the town without alerting it. They could not afford to wait until nightfall, however, because the wild men could decide to attack them at any moment and they could not defuse a bomb once lit. If these enemies snuck upon them, they could arm their bombs and flee... leaving the armies of light in havoc.

Thinking through possible solutions, Warren found Boranor in one of the ranks. He approached him hastily, knowing that the stone golems were their best bet if a battle occurred. "Boranor, I need to know something of the upmost urgency. How far can you throw a boulder?"

Boranor looked down at his arms. "I have never tested my limit. But to answer your question, I will ask another. What would be the target?"

"If things go south, we may need you to barrage the enemy when they charge toward us. If your people could hit them from just outside the forest, that could be an incredible advantage. Make sure you are ready for a battle. We cannot be caught off guard."

After Warren finished conversing with Boranor, a thought entered his mind. It just might work. He prayed silently to the King as he rushed off.

Warren scrambled through his bag in a frenzy. He almost gave up hope until something caught his eye. The edge of a clear vial lay barely visible at the bottom of his sack. He allowed himself to grin and dug the flask out from his belongings. Warren read the inscription: 𝕿𝖍𝖊 𝕷𝖔𝖓𝖌-𝕷𝖆𝖘𝖙𝖎𝖓𝖌 𝕱𝖔𝖌. It was just the one he had been looking for. Maybe the mage would finally prove his usefulness.

Rushing to Auden and Denethor, Warren held out the potion as he breathed heavily. Auden read its label. He gazed at Warren and noticed his face was red and flushed. "This must be one of your mage's mixtures," Auden said. "The potion he used on the Pelios warriors practically saved them, so maybe we can rely on him for a second favor. How does this supposed fog work?"

"I'm not completely sure," Warren noted. "We left the mage at Srayo because he refused to accompany the army. Apparently, he has very strong views about war. Anyhow, I would wager that we should simply pour out a few drops and see what happens."

Auden shrugged and popped open the cork. The light blue mixture flowed to the end of the flask. With a delicate touch, Auden tilted the bottle so that a single drop of the liquid fell to the ground. Instantaneously, a mist arose that covered the three lords. As they stumbled out of the fog, they were at a loss for words. It worked perfectly, better than anyone could have expected.

Denethor knew they had a way to sneak in the Daltonians, but the army still needed to be in formation when the barbarians attacked. He found his troops talking and laughing. It was an encouraging sign. Denethor called them to attention nonetheless. "Soldiers, I am truly glad to see you bonding as a unit. However, we are at a point in our campaign where the stakes are rising. Therefore, we need to keep an uplifting yet prepared mindset. Since we must stay alert, form the scorpion formation with the Seviathans at the front of the south point."

In a short couple of minutes, the scorpion formation was formed inside the tree line. They were close enough to the plains that they could barely see out of the trees, but they could not be seen. The soldiers returned to their conversations, this time remaining in rank and focusing to the east.

Denethor headed back from the soldiers and felt the strong breeze sweep across his face. It was cool, with a tint of cold along the edges like a glass of icy water. When Denethor met back up with the other leaders of the King's army, he beheld a small group of soldiers standing beside them. Their sharp, bronze helmets clearly distinguished them as hawkers, elite members of the Daltonian army.

They had a look in their eyes unlike any other. It almost frightened Denethor how passionate and observant these hawkers appeared. He knew they would give their best toward the mission. They would do whatever they could to claim the bombs and thwart the malicious intent of

Fairfick's towns. Denethor only hoped their zeal would be enough.

News of the hawkers' skill had spread through the army, and now would be a major test of their reputation. Quinn looked at the team he had assembled with pride and honor. He knew they could accomplish great things. As Denethor entered the circle of leaders, he listened in to the discussion. "I spoke again with the scout," Warren remarked. "He informed me that the bombs are being stored in a warehouse at the southern end of the town, so your men must travel through the city at least momentarily to reach them."

"I know they can handle it," Quinn answered. "With the fog covering the area, the wild men will not be able to find or stop my group."

Warren thought of something - a problem the other lords had not considered. "What if the bombs are too heavy to carry?"

Auden pulled out a horn from his belt and handed it to a member of the assault team. "Sound this if something goes wrong, like the bombs are too heavy, or a large force attacks you."

Since everyone was content with the plan, they headed to the edge of the shadowy forest. They realized it was the perfect time to strike, as powerful winds were sweeping down into the plains. After being given encouraging words and final instructions, the Daltonians drew their weapons. Without a moment's delay, Warren found Boranor. He came to with Warren, who handed him the vial of the long-lasting fog. Boranor held it in his hand like it was a pebble. "You want me to throw this?"

"Make sure you get it as close to the town as you can. And don't get off track by the wind."

"The wind?" Boranor patted Warren on the back with his massive hand. "My friend, you really think the wind could stop me?"

Walking just past the tree line, the mighty stone golem launched the potion toward the target. It soared farther and farther. Warren watched its flight eagerly. He watched it shatter just in front of the town. It released its contents onto the swaying grass on impact. A cloud swelled up around it and flowed eastward, steadily pushed by numerous gusts.

The twenty or so hawkers flew toward the mist like stallions. Nothing could hold them back now. Luckily, the fog traveled at a speed even greater than they did, and enveloped the town before they could reach it. The sprint to the town might have winded other warriors, but not the hawkers.

Naturally, their first thought was to reach the bombs. Though the fog concealed them, the hawkers could hear the confused shouts and muffled commands echoing around them. How could they find the storehouse while practically blinded because of the mist? They replaced the troubling notion with determination; they had to reach it. It did not matter how they did, as long as they found the deadly devices.

The soldiers made sure to keep their footing as they treaded in the direction they believed was south. The hard ground gave them a sense of a stability compared to the lack of bearings around them. As they stumbled onward, a hawker suddenly grunted. He had collided headfirst with a wall. "I found something."

With a feeling of enthusiasm, the other Daltonians headed toward the sound and reached the building as well. They inched their way around the corner of the wall and down its other side. Suddenly, the soldier leading the others halted. He felt a door. Motioning to his allies, he directed them inside, and the team entered the room. It was not what they were hoping for.

They were confronted by four heavily armed men with broad shoulders and scowls on their faces. These brutes drew their axes forcefully and charged the Daltonians. Both sides had been utterly surprised and the duel started out incredibly uncoordinated. It got worse when the battle left the room out into the clouded town. No one could see who or what they were swinging at. Worse, the clashing of weapons ricocheted through the village, and warriors rushed to aid their townsmen.

A Daltonian took charge of the situation, and just at the right time shouted, "Hawkers, to me." They followed his lead. In the confusion, they escaped from their adversaries. The head Daltonian then whispered, "We must get out of here; do not engage in battle. Follow the sound of my footsteps."

The others did not hesitate. They rushed after him as he bolted toward the other end of the city. Breath for breath, step for step, the Daltonians shadowed their head combatant as if they were one person. Their training had paid off, for no one in their team had been injured in the small skirmish, and they were now closer to the storehouse. The men of Fairfick, however, had not been so lucky.

The assault team once again stopped. Their leader began to mentally place them as a unit. He looked around through strained eyes and noticed a well amidst the outline of buildings. They were only a short distance from the bombs. The yells of angered townsmen and savages rushed toward them. Time was slipping away. The assault team bolted to a locked structure, larger than the others. With precision and quick thinking, the group broke the locks and rushed into the storehouse.

There they were. Eight sizeable bombs, large enough to cause serious damage to any army. The black hue of the bombs, combined with their spiked edges, gave them a threatening appearance, and the men knew they were not to be taken lightly. The hawkers hurried up to the devices. "We need to get them out of here. Now!"

Before they could pick up the destructive contraptions, a voice sounded from behind them. They turned to see a large force of wild men. The looks on their faces were far from pleasant. "Where do you think you're going?"

The Daltonians instantly huddled together, readying themselves for the oncoming attack. They retreated to the back of the structure, hoping to find a way out. The mass of hostile warriors rushed toward them with weapons held high.

******

"That could only mean one thing." Denethor's brow furrowed.

Auden frowned. The long, clear blast of the horn rung in his ears. Their assault team was in trouble. Auden could only guess what had gone wrong and could only wonder what evil had befallen them. He refocused himself and called the forces to attention. They awaited his command. Rallying up his own courage, Auden proclaimed, "Army of the Light, charge!"

Both cavaliers and infantrymen, stone golems and Seviathans, Xalaians and Pelios' swordsmen rushed past the trees. The Xalaians led the army, bent on honoring the deaths of those fallen. The army left the safety of the forest out into the broad daylight of the plains, steadfastly driven to overcome their adversaries.

The fog had completely lifted as the forces of the Light were halfway to the town, and the warriors of Fairfick scrambled to defensive positions. They had barely assembled a front line as the warriors of the Light attacked them. Though fiery and zealous, the unprepared wild men native to the area were no match. The coordinated, precise strike against them unraveled whatever stand they hoped to make. With a sixth sense, the warriors of the Light expected every enemy attack and countered it masterfully. The town was besieged in a short time, and some of the civilians of the town had not had time to empty the streets. This defeat would send a message to other towns of Fairfick, and Auden knew these villages would not trouble them again.

While Auden checked on the status of the soldiers, Lords Warren and Quinn rushed to see if the hawkers had survived the battle. They reached the storehouse, and Quinn beheld a bronze helmet laying outside its door. Picking up the helmet off the dirt, he bit his lip. He turned to Warren with a look of dread. His face said more than enough… were they too late?

Warren placed a hand on Quinn's shoulder. "Maybe they completed their mission. We did not hear any explosions." Quinn nodded and gently pushed open the door of the storehouse, hesitant to see what horror lay inside.

What he witnessed inside shocked him. The Daltonians were seated on the floor, sharpening their weapons. Though they were slightly battered, they seemed to be enjoying themselves. Quinn dropped the helmet and ran toward them. They stood and greeted him. "We have something to show you, Lord Quinn."

They stepped aside, and Quinn beheld eight bombs, fully intact and arranged to form the letter Q. His first reaction was to fall to his knees. He ran his hands through his hair in disbelief. He tried not to look too stunned, but could not help it. Warren, on the other hand, returned the helmet to one of the soldiers. "I believe you're missing something."

The Daltonians helped their befuddled leader to his feet, and one of the soldiers thanked Warren and received his helmet. The hawkers turned to Quinn. "We were wondering when you were going to arrive. After we sounded the horn, the barbarians heard your battle cry and were instantly alarmed. Seizing the opportunity, we routed them from the storehouse. From there, they left us with panicked shouts as they rushed toward the army. We were simply sharpening our blades for the next battle. As good a time as any."

"Are any of you hurt?" Quinn asked.

"There are some injuries, but they will heal soon enough. You trained us almost too well, sir. I forgot, there was one casualty against the brutes." The head hawker held out the horn, if it could still be considered that. It was slice open and trampled. Quinn did not care. His face lit up and Warren had never seen him so jubilant.

After recovering from the shock, Quinn said, "I will call in some soldiers to help move these bombs."

"There is no need. We have enough strength left to carry them. We would love you to aid us, sir." Quinn did not reject, but helped his men carry the explosives toward the army. Luckily, they were meant to be portable, so moving them was no issue.

Everyone gathered together a short distance from the town. Denethor had told the citizens that they were not going to be harmed. They could bury their dead and continue their regular lives.

The army was glad to have a major victory with little to no fatalities. Talk spread about the heroic accounts of the battle amongst the ranks. The troops were merry as they walked back into the forest toward their supply caravans. Everyone heard the stories of the assault team and their triumph. The forces were glad to see that after the long months of training and hardships, things were finally looking up.

Birds chattered in the treetops in their usual manner, and the trees seemed more welcoming than before. Their bark did not seem as dark and tainted and their red leaves shone like joy instead of pain. The damages that had haunted the soldiers the previous days had dissipated like a subsiding flood.

Nevertheless, as if the will of Natas would not let them remain at peace, they caught the strong smell of smoke and burning timber. No one knew what to think. Could a forest fire happen so spur of the moment?

Reaching the spot of the blaze, they realized it was far from a random happening. It was sabotage. A massive fire was smoldering over a pile of supplies, torn down tents and wooden beams. It was instantly recognizable; the fuel for the fires was their caravans... wagons loaded with precious commodities such as food, blankets, water and medicine.

The backbone of the army of Light was slowly turning to ash. For a mere moment, the forces of Light let it continue, unsure what they could do to stop the powerful, sweeping blaze. Then Auden could stand it no longer. "Xalaians, surely there is something you can do to stop this. We need to salvage as much as we can and soon, before it perishes."

The squid men stepped out from the mass of troubled men and jetted a powerful stream of water. It hit the fire at its center, and choked it, causing it to die. Still, the damage had been done; they had been too late to save most of their resources.

Men hurried to dig out whatever they could from out of the ashes and embers. They tossed destroyed items aside in a frenzy to find whatever could be saved. Their heartfelt efforts brought little reward. They searched the rubble hopelessly.

Denethor approached the other lords who had gathered together. Auden spoke to him. "How bad is it?"

"It is horrible. Worse than we could have expected. We have salvaged three tents, a dozen blankets, a few bags of food and one barrel of water. Our caravans are beyond reassembling. Whoever did this knew what they were doing. We also found the guards we left to defend the supplies; it appears they did not stand a chance. When you add up the miniscule amount of food we rescued in addition to the food some of the soldiers carried along with them, we have enough to feed the army for two days on half rations.

"We have enough water to possibly last five days on half rations. Even if we cram three men to a tent, that is only nine men covered from harsh weather. They should only be used for the desperately injured. This could mean serious trouble for our allies from Pelios. If it rains again, we will struggle to protect them. In addition, I expect our endeavor will take us into the winter, and a dozen blankets is next to none for that time. We have been dealt a mighty blow, to say the least."

Warren replied, "It was those wicked savages of Fairfick. How could we not have left more guards? They completely ruined us. We have no hope for surviving unless something is done quickly. This is horrible. No, this is beyond horrible... this is cataclysmic!"

The others tried to settle down the infuriated lord, but realized what he said was true. It was a serious issue. It could ruin their endeavors against Natas permanently, causing them to fall back to Srayo after just beginning their campaign. No one could let that happen. Not now, on the verge of making serious steps against Natas.

Instead of letting themselves submit to the unyielding pressure of failure, the intuitive lords sought to fix the problem. They needed food and water above all.

Meanwhile, shelter and warmth for the winter would be crucial in the long run. How could you gain several months' worth of resources in a week? This was a battle no one expected to fight. A mysterious battle… fought without swords or armor.

They could not travel north to Dalto… it would leave the lands of the Light helplessly undefended, and would take them far off their determined route. A few cities lay to the south, all of them loyal to Natas and either too small for such supplies or too strongly fortified. This route would also take them far off their course.

There had to be an option, a possibility to the east that could aid them. Lake Tibern was a distance away, but they could reach it in good time if they kept a prompt pace. A few trading outposts surrounding it might be able to supply their needs. It was a slight detour from their original strategy, but such was unavoidable.

The lords addressed the army with their decision. It was one they could only hope would turn out for the best. No one opposed it; there seemed no other way to continue. A great defeat had followed a great victory, and everyone was left at odds with their scattered emotions. They could only cast those emotions aside and set their eyes for Lake Tibern. They could only hope it would be their salvation, not their downfall.

CHAPTER 8

DEPRESSION OF THE MIND

A weight had come over the army. Something tainted and undefined. It sank into them and found a way to drain their strength. This power, one that clouded the minds of the soldiers, was that of hunger. It was powerful... it was motivating... it was elusive.

The forces of the Light had been traveling five full days on half rations and, though still maintaining a sliver of energy, they were wearing thin. This was even though the beings from Pelios did not eat, and the stone golems consumed earth and rocks as their diet. The terrain had not been difficult, but the soldiers, already tired from two recent battles, needed sustenance to recover.

141

Denethor looked at the bottom of the sack with dismay. His own bag of food was now diminished to several crumbs. Looking up from his coarse, empty sack, he surveyed the state of the forces. Lowered heads, heavy laden feet and weary eyes told the story clearly. It had only been two days since the armies' celebrated cheers of victory had turned to despair.

The effects of war had laid this once empowered army low far quicker than anyone could have predicted. Denethor picked up his feet from the tall, dry grass and searched out Matthais, someone he knew could brighten the situation. "Matthais, how are you this day?'

Matthias brushed the burs and thistles off his clothes. "I am managing."

"That is good to hear. Do you know how are men are holding up?"

"It is hard to say." Matthais was slow to continue. "Allowing some of the men to take turns riding the horses has helped them rest to an extent. Many have tried to remain optimistic, singing an occasional song or speaking with the creatures in our ranks. I've heard Auden has been spreading stories from the King's histories which have inspired the troops. Nonetheless, they are overall weary and distraught. Many have been asking us about the upcoming winter, which shall be upon us in a few months. I fear that while our army is surviving, we are far from fighting condition."

"That is fair. We shall probably reach the nearest trading outpost in a full day's march. If we can only encourage the men enough to keep them going, we will make it."

Matthais considered the past few months. What had kept the army enthusiastic thus far? "You could rouse them with a passionate speech," Matthais said.

Denethor look down at his helmet clutched by his side, with the King's emblem outlined in gold. "Yes, but speeches alone cannot sustain a militia forever. I feel like we need to do something memorable and important. Not that speeches aren't important, but now does not seem the time or the place for one. I was thinking when we set up camp tonight, we could have sort of festival to cheer up our men."

"That is an excellent idea. I know of a few men who can play instruments. They have brought them for just this kind of occasion. I will have them ready to play tonight. This might be just what our forces need right now. One more thing, Denethor?"

"Yes?" he replied. He knew the question before Matthais asked it.

"Are we going to find enough food at Lake Tibern?"

"I hope so, my friend," Denethor said. "I hope so."

Denethor and Matthais parted ways, making sure to shake hands before they left. Denethor allowed himself to hope; maybe things could start looking up again. Maybe this festival would be a marvelous one, and Tibern would hold everything they needed. Was this too desperate of a prayer? He was determined to keep the moral high, so that the reality of hunger would not strain them any longer.

The soldiers felt their stomachs growing more and more empty, filled only by a half ration of water. That alone was little for a common man, let alone a warrior. Still, hope for a brighter day kept the men pressing on with each step. One more day, one more day and it might be better. With each heavy trod, the army heaved themselves up sloping hills and down winding valleys. It would get better. It had to.

Though the inspiration of Lord Auden and determination of Lord Warren fueled the men, many looked back on the past in despair. Watching the battles unfold in their minds was like self-induced torture on the soul. Try as they might, they could not stop themselves from thinking about the tragic deaths and brutal clashes that had progressed in the recent past. Even great victories like the ones at Srayo and Fairfick brought memories of distress. Why did they always remember the bad, and not the good?

In the deep crevices of their hearts, the soldiers grimly realized that they might not make it back from this war. For some, it drove them farther into despair. For others, it gave them a cause to rally behind, knowing the

King was watching over them and would take them to a better place.

Few men realized that they were traveling in excellent weather, and that the terrain they traversed could be much worse. Their thoughts were on the battles of the past and fear of the future. The autumn breeze and the leaves changing color on scattered trees was a sight to behold. The resolve of war, though, kept the soldiers from admiring the majestic view.

Even the occasional bird that passed above them whistling its gleeful song uplifted only those who looked upward instead of at the ground. It was a hard period for the army, but the lords realized it may be the first of many. As a unit, they had already gone so far. Auden remember how at one time Hightenmore had been threatened, and now they had pushed the lands of the Light to beyond the mountain pass.

Auden walked beside Denethor for a long while. Their conversation had begun around their homelands and the ins and outs of leading a city, but it turned to pressing matters. "When will our scouts be arriving to inform us on Lake Tibern? We need information about the region as soon as possible," Denethor remarked.

"They could come any moment now," Auden said. "We sent them off with the mission a week ago, and told them to return straight back to us with the news."

"I can only hope they shall arrive sooner rather than later."

Auden decided to change the subject momentarily. "I received word that you are planning an event tonight to encourage the troops. I am glad you thought of it. Though they remain loyal, and are pressing on in strength, it seems their optimism and hope are dwindling."

"Let's hope then that we can get supplies soon. Even without wagons we can load the resources onto the horses and the stone golems, if they are willing. If we can get our warriors revitalized tonight, I'm sure they can make it to Lake Tibern."

Auden agreed, but then felt his mind wander. He had not heard much about Lake Tibern, and had no clue what to expect from it. The only thing he did know was that it was massive - the only lake of its size in Amcronos. At least the lords had already readjusted their battle strategies.

Denethor watched as Auden stared off into the horizon. Denethor was not sure if he should awaken his spell-bound friend or let him continue his distant thoughts. Eventually, Auden's demeanor began to weigh on Denethor's mind. "Auden. Auden, are you there, my friend? Wake up. Come to reality."

Auden flashed out of his daydream and blinked hard. He rubbed his eyes, wondering what had happened. "I'm sorry, Denethor. My thoughts were on the future... to Lake Tibern and even past Tibern. I was considering the fate and the cost of our campaign."

With true heroism, Denethor replied, "No cost is too great to defeat Natas. Our soldiers are trained; our strategies have proven effective. Though they outnumber us, we have the hearts of lions. The King is on our side. We will not lose this war."

"That is very true, Lord Denethor. Thank you for encouraging me. I know that we can win this war. I simply forgot our potential due to our current circumstances. Thank you for reminding me of the heart of our calling. Never before has an army such as this been assembled against Natas, and it may never again. We must get our army back on its feet. Do we know if the villages surrounding Tibern will have enough provisions?"

"That seems to be the question on everyone's mind. They are trading outposts, so I would wager they have at least some resources available."

Auden and Denethor continued planning for the days ahead while the army lingered on toward the massive lake. Few had ever dreamed they would have been able to see the still waters of Lake Tibern. Then again, few had envisioned themselves fighting in the front lines against the dark forces of Amcronos.

As if second nature, every soldier kept a hand near his weapon. They could never know when an evil assault or wicked barrage would come against them. Whether out of fear or from proper training, the forces of the Light scanned the area every passing hour.

Uneventful hours of closing in on their destination faded away like scorched grass. There were few signs of life or civilization beside sporadic pillars of smoke ascending in the distance. Yet, even though little life was noticed, Warren spotted something flying high above them. It was like a bird, but a pale white. It was hardly noticeable in the sky above, camouflaging itself with the shifting clouds.

Suddenly, Warren watched as its wings seemingly split from its body. There was only one creature that could be. It was a fourwing. Warren remembered its kind from the festival at Srayo. He had used one to summon Boranor to the North. Now Warren watched as it swooped and dove above them with intricate movements. It seemed able to travel any distance at any height.

As it gazed down at the ranks with steely eyes like a hawk, it spied Warren. Recognizing him, the fourwing plummeted straight toward the lord. Warren was thrown off guard as the regal fourwing landed on his shoulder. He stood completely still, not wanting to scare off the creature.

The fourwing climbed down Warren's shoulder and curled around his hand. It let out a squawk as Warren stroked its leathery feathers. They were smooth to the touch, and incredibly as Warren touched them, they turned from a pearly white to a light brown. Somehow this creature had completely mastered the art of camouflage to the extent it could match whatever surface it encountered. No wonder no one had witnessed this creature before. The blacksmith had told him it could blend in with the night, but this was more than he had bargained for. Warren remembered his curiosity r toward the mysterious blacksmith at Srayo. How could anyone have discovered such a creature?

Warren continued to pet the soft down feathers of the fourwing, until he felt something on its back. He realized it was a rolled-up piece of parchment. Warren took the parchment from the fourwing and unraveled it.

Dear Lords of the Light,

I write to you now to give you my support. You have led us to great triumphs in the past, and though I do not know how the army fares now, I know you shall be there to care for them. I can only hope that you receive this letter and that it pushes you onward in steadfast zeal. To Lord Auden, Hightenmore has grown even more prosperous than before the war first began. Your victory there against Zekern seems so long ago, but its effects are still helping your city.

To Lord Denethor, your wife and daughters are living in the comfort of Vanswick and are kept safe. They miss you very much, and long for the time you shall come home victorious and hold them in your arms.

To Lord Warren, ever since you employed me as your temporary replacement, the high walls of Srayo have been strengthened. Supplies sent to us from the helpful villages of the Mazaron have aided our recovery. The friends you left behind tell me I have been running your position well. I only hope I am living up to your reputation.

To the rest of the army, the tall and the brave men, you are held in the highest regard. I only had the delight of knowing the new additions to our army briefly, but they are foreigners to us no longer. From Dalto to Hessington, we are one band of brothers. We are one militia, and we stand as one for all that we hold dear. An ambassador from the King greeted us a few days ago, and told me you should not fear. The King is always with you. This ambassador, who called himself Idrellon, soared back to the Haven Realm having given us his full support of the region. Aphenter remains quiet. If they come against us, be it at the mountains or at Srayo, we are ready to face them. We will not let you down. May the King reign and His followers prosper!

In loyalty,
Ekin, Caretaker of Srayo

Like a newborn child, joyful cheers came from Warren and he almost glowed. The fourwing looked to him, squawked in its usual manner, then flew back toward Srayo. Its wings returned to their white hue as it disappeared into the sky above.

The soldiers stared at Warren and the note he held, unsure what to say to their beaming leader. He rushed outside of the battalion and rocketed toward the front of the forces, clutching the note as if it was his life. He could not help himself from continuing to cheer as he hurried onward. Not one of the odd looks he received countered his blissful spirit. A leaping gazelle, his feet glided upon the surface of the plains as if he was weightless.

When he completed his sprint, Warren handed the letter to Auden with a glow that would make the moon envious. His inner conscience told he was overreacting, but Warren could not help but express the cascade of emotions.

Auden did not know what to think. It took him a long while to get over the unusual appearance of his friend, but then he read over the letter. He read over it a second time. He read over it a third time very slowly. All his mind could process was laughter, so laugh is what he did. They had finally received the sign of the King they had been waiting for.

With his hunger a forgotten memory and pain a long-lost nightmare, Auden handed the precious paper to Denethor. While Denethor's reaction was far more composed, he was glad to the bottom of his heart. It was the perfect thing to share with the troops. The King's timing was impeccable.

He decided to stop the army there, and gathered them around in a massive circle. The few tents they had were set up, and the soldiers' mood increased by seeing their lords so animated. Many of them lay aside their armor, finally able to enjoy the luxury of resting. Hundreds of eyes turned to Denethor, who stood in the camp's center.

Wasting no time, he began reading aloud the letter, and the words were repeated to those who could not hear. Thus, the content of the inspirational letter was heard by each of the warriors. It gave them great hope. They were not forgotten. They were not alone. Even from afar, their allies remembered them.

Denethor motioned to Matthais, who then called to the musicians among the group. They were common people from the militia playing whatever instruments they had carried with them. It was amazing how fluently they played together. The song they played was well-known to all the men, and many whistled the tune.

The fiddle and the flute chimed together in the harmonious melody. It was a beautiful mixture of clear sounds and sharp vibratos. The soldiers started to sing the words of the song and it caught on throughout the group. After a few minutes, the tune had reached its climax and many laughed as their fellow kinsmen tried to keep up with the flying pace of the fiddler.

As if on cue, the fire leapt at the peak of the melody. Everyone was mesmerized as its life filled the air. It was just what Denethor had hoped for. No one was forlorn or distraught. Nature did its part by cooling the men with the perfect humidity. It was a little thing but it brought lasting relief.

Like all things eventually do, the song slowed until it faded away. The musicians followed the lively harmony with a more peaceful tune. The weary men closed their eyes and let the soft noise wash over them. It drowned out all the other noises, and rested in the comfort of safety. The night drifted on, as the men enjoyed a break from the struggles of the war. The moon gently lit their camp and those guarding the camp were comforted by the soft light.

*****

Morning came quickly. Auden rose from his tent breathing in the fresh air. Today, they would besiege the enemy trading towns. He hoped they would not have to kill any of the civilians. He simply wanted to get the supplies, leave something to compensate the town for their loss, and leave. Auden had no specific plan in mind with Lake Tibern, but had heard the people surrounding it were friendlier than many of Natas' other followers.

He stood several feet from his tent, glad to see his soldiers already awake and ready to face the day. After packing up the camp, the army set out toward Lake Tibern. The entire mood of the forces had changed for the better. Faces were no longer downcast, and spurts of lively conversation filled the ranks. The men were finally starting to look like their old selves.

Tibern was only a short day's march from where they had camped, and the army zigzagged through clusters of trees toward their destination. Ever onward and not looking back, the forces of the Light made excellent time toward the lake. Each soldier saw his companions not as warriors, but more as brothers. The tension between the Xalaians and the men of Pelios dwindled, and the Seviathans no longer viewed the stone golems as threats.

Eventually, Lake Tibern could be seen close by. It was beautiful, a shining gem. Neither Warren nor Auden could find any other way to describe it. Lily pads clung to the borders of its tranquil waters. Dragonflies danced between the reeds which stood above the waters with pride and stature. Even in the daylight, the glow of torches and candles could be seen in the trading towns. An occasional boat would row in from a surrounding town, though most were docked. There were three towns they could see. Two were distant, farther past them on the lake's shore.

Auden noticed that in the closest town, men and women were unloading a boat full of barrels. Barrels meant food, or at least some sort of resource. The soldiers watched the lively scene and waited for their orders. Auden did not know what to tell them. They desperately needed food, water and supplies. On the other hand, they could not simply go down and raid an entire village. That was the way of Natas, not of the Light.

Deciding he needed help on the matter, Auden summoned the lords. Their opinions were divided, however. Denethor felt the tradesmen were simply citizens of Natas' lands, and that their provisions were far too important to be negotiated for. Warren and Quinn felt they should address the town and try to convert them to the Light or barter for the supplies. Auden was torn; both sides had valid arguments. How far were they willing to go to continue this quest?

Auden came to a decision. "We will sneak into the town and take the supplies we need, but only what we need, and leave a gift in exchange. No one will get hurt or killed."

"What are we going to give them, exactly? A horse?" Warren asked.

"Actually, that is what I was thinking. A horse or two would seem a fair trade. Hopefully, they shall not despise us for it."

The lords agreed, and everything was prepared. Two horses were readied to be taken, and the Seviathans volunteered to carry the supplies back with them. They were by far the most logical choice, stronger than men but quieter than stone golems. Auden felt he should go with them, so they set off with the horses toward the town.

As they approached silently, they found the stables were one of the closest buildings. That was fortunate. Auden sneaked the two horses to them. With nimble fingers, he tied the two steeds to a tall post. He left a simple letter, thanking the townsfolk for their hospitality and hoping they would understand.

Softly stroking the horses for the last time, Auden whispered, "Farewell, noble Frostear and Silverfoot; you did your kingdom a great service. I hope you have blissful lives here."

Auden rejoined the Seviathans, who had already begun loading the provisions into bags. If only they could have reasoned with this town to join the Light. The people in it might be decent and honest. Now was not the time. Maybe one day they would know the truth.

After several minutes, the Seviathans had retrieved enough cargo to last the army many nights. No one was in the storeroom, so gathering the necessary items was relatively simple. As the Seviathans were loading the bags onto their shoulders, a voice came from the far side of the building. "I heard a new shipment of pearls from Quoto will be arriving in the next few days. I have been saving up money to buy my wife a necklace. The look on her face will be worth more than gold."

A second voice entered the conversation. "That would be nice. Have you heard about what happened to the towns in Fairfick? I was told they were raided by the forces of the Light. While I would never join Natas' army, even if they pointed a spear to my face, I hope we never have to deal with those maniacs."

Suddenly, the door of the storehouse opened, and the two men walked in. They continued their conversation as they laid down a large crate in the corner of the room. Both Auden and the Seviathans hid behind the various barrels stacked around the room. The Seviathans had reacted instantly, covered by the shadows, while Auden barely hid in time.

From the raw, pungent smell, Auden instantly could tell the crate was full of fish. Definitely something they did not need to bring along with them. The two men chatted about their views on current events as if they knew everything about the world. Their conversation headed farther and farther south, and grew even more heated. Auden almost enjoyed hearing the two civilians argue like jackals, but he also was saddened by how little they understood. They had been blinded, and desperately needed the blindfold taken off.

Once the villagers left, Auden helped the Seviathans gather and carry the load out of the town. They placed the supplies in the center of the camp just as they heard a ruckus coming from the trading town. Apparently, the villagers had found the horses, and seemed overall confused about the matter. Nevertheless, to make sure nothing surmounted, Auden ordered the army to head southeast, away from Tibern. He did not want the lives of these tradesmen taken as well.

Both Auden and Warren knew they would miss the tranquil atmosphere of Lake Tibern. It was somewhere they hoped they could visit again, somewhere they could enjoy without danger looming over them. Not all the lords thought this way, however.

Denethor was thinking five steps ahead. His thoughts were on battles to come… for they would indeed come. He wanted every angle of this war thought through, because he knew Natas' advantage over them was extreme.

How could they account for the layered defenses of Quoto? Could they continue to leave Aphenter unattended on the border of their homelands? Was Natas centralizing his forces to spearhead the army of the Light directly? Or, was he instead trying to capitalize on the defenses already built, and waiting for them to be attacked? Denethor had to stop himself dead in his tracks. It was too much for any one man to handle. Breathe.

Denethor slowed his horse to a trot and called to one of the Seviathans. "How many supplies were gathered?"

"We found enough food to last the army for several months," the Seviathan replied. "That is, if we remain on half rations. The water barrels we gathered should last that long, as well. Sadly, there was only a few stacks of blankets. Hopefully winter does not hit us hard, sir."

"Thank you soldier, I'm sure the King will keep us safe from winter's wrath."

Once a safe distance from Tibern, the army had its first true meal since before the raid on Fairfick. The warm soup delighted the warriors. Nothing tasted better to them in all the world in that moment.

While the men broke their weeklong fast, Warren decided to ride out a short distance away from the army. He did this on his own merit, not telling anyone he was leaving. A nagging suspicion had been bothering him for some time, and he had to put his fears to rest. Warren led his thoroughbred into a section of woodland. There he tied up his steed and silently drew his sword. He did not even know why he did this, except for the same suspicion plaguing him.

A bush rustled a few feet away. Warren flinched. Drawing closer to the shrub, he lost his grip on his nerves for a split second. He pounced on the bush. To his surprise, a rabbit bounded away from the bush at top speed. Warren realized he had gotten worked up over nothing.

Moments later, he heard another rustling noise. Warren kept his sword in a striking position. Suddenly, out of the corner of his eye, he noticed something moving in the shadows. Without thinking, Warren attacked the shaded figure, who retreated instantly.

Warren continued closer to the man, who had his back to a tree. Before he could reach him, Warren watched three other men walk out from behind the trees. He had fallen into a trap.

Keeping a level head, Warren readied himself in a battle position, holding his sword like a gladiator. The four enemies drew their blades and surrounded him, one on each side. Warren took a deep breath; he could tell by their stances and circular formation that they were trained. Deciding to make the first move, Warren advanced to his right and swung at his opponent.

The warrior was prepared. He stepped to the side and parried the attack. Warren continued assaulting the man, intent on not losing the ground he had made. After several thrusts and slashes, Warren had his opponent right where he wanted him, until he heard someone charging from behind. Warren spun and blocked the downward slam just in time; had it come a few seconds sooner, he would have been finished.

A cornered lion, Warren engaged both foes simultaneously while watching the final two soldiers close in around him. Using all his strength and training, he was able to successfully counter two different attacks and found a window of opportunity. He pounced toward his enemy with claws extended and a mighty roar. The clang of his sword meeting chain mail was clearly definable. One down, three left.

Looking at him with piercing hostility, the other warriors took several steps away from Warren. He could tell they hated him, but they also did not seem hungry for a fight. For the first time, he noticed a hint of fear in their eyes. This sent the remnant of fear remaining in Warren scattering to a distant land.

Warren stroke straight at the heart of the trio. He kept his blade in constant action, swinging furiously. He parried a thrust, then drove a foe's sword into the ground. Meanwhile, the final combatant came at him with an arcing slice. This pierced Warren's flesh, causing him to grimace in agony. Still, the battle was far from over. Warren focused on the man who had harmed him, since the other two were temporarily reeling. A kick to the stomach after a well-timed block sent his adversary to the ground. There was nothing he could do to stop Warren's strike.

The other soldiers took flight. Warren chased after them. All three pairs of feet pounded over the scattered brush with ease. Nevertheless, as one of the soldiers sneaked a glance back at Warren, he tripped over a thick root.

Warren caught up to him before he could blink. "Go ahead and finish me off," muttered the exhausted soldier. "My friend will reach safety and they will send an army to hunt you down."

"An army, you say? No, I will not kill you. I will take you back to my camp, and you will tell me a little bit about your friends and this army."

Not a word came from Warren's adversary, and Warren took his weapons. He promptly threw them into a thorn bush. From there, he forced his prisoner to his feet and escorted him toward the wonderful place of interrogation.

When Warren entered the camp, everyone stared at him and his captive in disbelief. One minute Warren had disappeared, the next he came back bruised and worn. Auden was the first to rush up to him. "What happened to you?" Before Warren could answer, Auden continued, "Someone call a doctor at once."

"I don't need a doctor. At least not now. I found this man with three other spies in the forest nearby. I can't know for sure, but I think they've been watching us for at least two days. Please do with him as you will. I desperately need to lie down."

Warren had not been exaggerating. The moment he finished talking, he collapsed. Several doctors carried him off while relaying various commands to each other.

The lords and the men turned their attention to the enemy spy. Without hesitation, some of the soldiers bound the spy with ropes and took him to the center of the encampment. Some of the men whispered to each other that the spy should be tortured for what he did to Warren. The lords, however, settled the warriors down. Auden approached the spy, now bond and on his knees. "I can wager you're an intelligent man. You probably already know what I am going to ask you. Still, you can at least be decent enough to look me in the eye."

The man looked up, straight into Auden's passionate eyes. He said nothing.

"I guess I can do the talking then," Auden continued. "As I was saying, you seem like a smart soldier. If you had all the facts, I would bet you'd see us in a much better light. Let me give them to you. You probably can tell by the way your fellow soldiers and the civilians talk about him, that Natas is feared. This is because he rules by deceit, power and anger. Yet as powerful as Natas is, he is nothing compared to the strength of the King of Light."

"I'd like to see your face when your entire army is ground to dust by Natas' forces."

Auden remained unraveled. "Natas' armies are weak. They have no strength. They have no hope of standing against us."

The spy spat on the ground. "You are too foolish to see your own demise. The armies of Natas have enough spears to stab every one of your men clean through the heart. They have you cornered, surrounded on all sides. Your blind old eyes deceive you. You think you're safe, but you would rather have drowned in Tibern than face what is coming against you."

"Let them come. There's no way they can reach high ground by the time our cavalry run them through. Natas is a fly we will step upon. We shall smear his face in the dirt."

If he could have, the spy would have punched Auden straight in the mouth. "You naïve, arrogant toad. Shut your slanderous mouth. Your cavalry will be overrun by ours. Our forces are mounted atop sturdy horses bred for war. We will take the hilltops any day now, and you will be pushed back to Srayo faster than a…" He paused. Then he started anew. "The South will not save you, Tibern would have you slain, and the East brings the strongest men of Balyon up your throats. The North could not protect you, Wessnor will defeat Dalto soon enough. Flee west before you see enough blood to fill your nightmares for decades!"

"Thank you, sir. You have greatly helped the forces of the Light." Auden turned and walked away.

The spy furrowed his brow and his mouth hung agape. What could he have possibly meant? He had mocked the forces of the Light; how could he have helped them?

Auden had a smile as wide as the moon. He met up with the other lords soon after. Warren joined them, though weak and bandaged. Auden turned to Matthais. "Write this down." Matthais dipped his quill in his personal ink jar. He then readied his paper on the hard back of one of his books.

Auden started out slowly, then began to talk faster and louder. "Here's what we now know. The spy said there were armies. That means plural. Natas has split up his forces against us. He told me the South was not safe for us, that Tibern would slay us, and that some of Natas' greatest men came up from the East and from Balyon. Thus, there are probably three armies: one to the south, one coming from Quoto toward Tibern, and one rising directly toward us from Balyon. This army from Balyon is the strongest.

"We must claim the high ground, because the spy said Natas' forces had a large cavalry. He claimed their armies had enough spears to stab through the heart of everyone in our army. We can guess Natas' generals are using spearmen to reinforce their cavalry. He mentioned that it would have been better if we had drowned in Tibern. That means Natas knows where we last were. That is probably the general region his armies are now converging on."

Quinn was the first to reply. "Brilliant. Auden, your interrogation skills are second to none. I have never

164

seen such a clever way to draw out information. Then again, I never had to watch many interrogations in Dalto. Do not worry about his threat toward the North; Dalto shall hold strong to the end."

"I know what we need to do," Denethor remarked.

CHAPTER 9

ONE MAN'S PLAN

Everyone listened intently to what Denethor had to say. "If they are going to split up forces, we need to be ready for attacks from multiple angles. You are right, Auden, we do need to claim high ground. The area near Tibern is defensible. I say we meet the northern force of Natas' army head on. We should set up defenses on the hilltops south of Tibern. They will come at us, expecting their other two armies to be on their way. Being forces of Natas, they will most likely attack quickly. That will give us a greater chance of defeating them as they rise up the hills."

They agreed to the plan, and the army prepared to head out, knowing the faster they could reach the hills, the better. Their few tents were rapidly disassembled, and the stone golems willingly placed the supplies on their capable shoulders. Each man grabbed what he could carry, and kept his hand a little closer to his weapon than before.

Thousands of feet marched onward toward the southern edge of Tibern, drawing themselves ever closer to the battle they knew would soon come. It was a battle in the heat of a war to decide the fate of Amcronos. It was lot of weight for one army to carry.

"I would wager there are plenty of boulders around the hills that we could use," Denethor said to Auden. "If not, we could always harvest some of the trees on Tibern's border, and use those for barricades."

"The more defenses we have, the better prepared we will be. I say we do whatever we can to make the hills even more fortified. There is a fair chance we will only have a day or so to set up battle positions and raise whatever battlements we can. Our soldiers must work swiftly."

"The stone golems could probably cut the preparation time in half. It seems we will always have need of their strength," Denethor added.

Light showers flickered on and off as the forces of the Light strode toward the pleasant hills. Pleasant hills to be made pleasant no longer. Droplets clung to the cold iron of the resilient armor the men wore. Chills ran down their spines as invading bits of frosty rain snuck past their chain mail.

Hardly anyone conversed on the way to the battlefield; every mind turned toward their own responsibilities. They had been trained and prepared for moments like these, and knew what was asked of them. To fight with honor to their last breath to make Amcronos a better place. A land like it had once been, free of turmoil, free of strife, free of evil and darkness.

Even the swordsmen of Pelios, who had once despised the King for seemingly abandoning them, now viewed him as their master. It helped that their fires were bright, for the rain threatened to kindle those fires. Luckily, the tents that they carried helped cover them.

*****

They made it. The gentle slopes of the hills cascaded across the horizon. Warren admired the view more than anyone else, even more than Matthias did. He could make out the small form of a scavenging hedgehog in the grass below. It scurried about without a care in the world. Warren envied the small creature. Its only task was to care for its family; predators could not follow it into the safety of its burrow.

The border of Tibern was visible to the north; nothing lay south except a single river that streamed in the direction of the ominous Balyon. It flowed its course unwillingly; nothing would ever willingly travel to that place.

The river wound around the hills like a serpent, unhindered by its surroundings. The view was perfect in its

169

own way. Warren did not want to see such innocence tampered by the polluted hands of havoc and destruction. Still, Natas had forced them to violence, and if war was demanded of them, they would raise their banner ever higher.

Before the army had even reached the slopes, Auden, Denethor and Quinn began relaying orders. In fact, each lord was preparing his men… except for Warren, who was recovering. No one doubted their leadership.

When Auden told the stone golems to gather large stones on the third hill to the right, they left at once. When Denethor commanded the Pelios soldiers to travel to Tibern and harvest trees for battlements, they complied. Quinn advised his men to scout out the far parts of the area, claiming the hills as their own. The forces of the Light continued east to set up at the center of the scene.

It was not harmony, but not chaos. Orders sporadically flew from commanders to their ranks. Each man simply did as he was instructed.

Ranks were formed, barricades constructed, and the defensive strategies were dispersed to the soldiers. Everything was set in place. With the preparations going swiftly, Auden had time to think of another objective. He knew just the people to ask. He found the Xalaians as they finished setting up a blockade. He spoke to them briefly, and they were happy to comply. Their mission was to travel through the waters of Tibern to search out Natas' army. They left toward the lake as evening began.

The battalion of twenty Xalaians reached Tibern in excellent time, leaving the rest of their group with the army. Nevertheless, they would have to sneak past the traders on its edge to get to the waters. It would be difficult, for though late in the evening, villagers still roamed the streets with lanterns lighting the way. Apparently, it was commonplace to work into the night in this town.

The Xalaians snuck like foxes into the town, hiding behind buildings or bushes. They decided there was no way they could make it to the waters as a group. There were too many people - too many prying children and cautious parents. Their watch scanned the streets.

They decided to send their fastest warrior to reach the safety of the waters. From there, he could distract the civilians. The lone Xalaian set off toward the center of the town. He crept down an alleyway, and watched the villagers walk by. He had to time it just right. A fraction of a second could make all the difference. After waiting for a short while, a cart came rolling out near him. It stopped a short distance away, and several men started unloading it. The Xalaian instantly dove underneath the cart. He took a deep breath; no one had noticed him.

Eventually, the men were done unloading the cart, and hooked it up to a horse to be sent back. Of its own accord, the horse began drawing the cart, and the Xalaian noticed it was taking him straight toward the dock. The cart stopped directly next to the edge of the dock, and the horse grunted. Taking his leave, the Xalaian dove into the water without a splash. He rose out of the lake to see the horse. He recognized it instantly as one of the horses Auden had left.

"Silverfoot." The Xalaian quietly called out to it. The horse turned toward him and neighed softly, then left with the cart. For the first time in many years, the Xalaian found himself praising the King.

Now for the distraction. The Xalaian knew exactly what to do. He swam under one of the boats and began to shake it. He heard mutterings and a few shouts. The Xalaian peered out of the water to see he had gathered a large crowd. He then began shooting out streams of water. Several citizens felt to the ground from the impact. The bombardment of water continued to stun the unsuspecting villagers.

This not only provided ample time for his fellow men, but almost the entire town had gathered near. The Xalaian wondered if he had gathered too much of a crowd. Luckily, no one could see him. He was safe if he was hidden… right? Nevertheless, his fears were confirmed when someone pulled out a bow and fired arrows into the water.

The Xalaian fled like a dart. He met up with his companions, and they continued toward their destination. The travel through the lake toward its eastern shore put their minds at rest. To finally be able to swim again felt miraculous. Since they were so overjoyed to be in cool waters again, the Xalaians traveled at an unbelievable pace, racing each other at incredible speeds. The massive lake would have taken several hours to cross in a boat, but it took them only twenty-five minutes to reach the eastern shore.

They bid farewell to the waters as if parting with a friend. They had no time to dwell on the matter, however, because they spied campfires on the horizon. Campfires not of a town or city, but of a massive gathering. Who else would be gathering in such droves but the forces of Natas?

Of course, they had to investigate to be sure. With utmost caution, they moved closer to the distant fires, creeping from tree to tree. As they drew near, they could not believe their own eyes. Not only was it an army of Natas, but a tide of dark warriors filled the hillside. Now that they had drawn near to the enemy camp, they noticed at least ten different campfires, spread throughout the mass.

This was horrible. Natas' army was closer to the forces of the Light than expected. They needed to get back to the others and warn them. As they retreated toward the waters, an arrow flew out of nowhere and struck one of the Xalaians in the back. He fell down dead instantaneously.

More arrows shot out toward the group, and a battalion of angry, dark figures charged toward them with swords raised. They had been discovered.

With all haste, the Xalaians fled back to the water, the only place where they would have the advantage. Several died before they could reach Tibern, but most of them dodged the oncoming attacks. When they descended into the water, they instantly began to strategize with the few moments they had.

Natas' men were cautious as they slowly advanced toward the waters. They held their weapons high, ready for something to spring out of the bushes or the lake. Still, they were not prepared for the lightning quickness of the Xalaians. As the men drew near to the water, the creatures flashed up from out of the lake and pulled them down. Meanwhile, far off Xalaians shot jets of water at the archers, stunning them.

More and more enemies approached, and soon they were firing arrows and jabbing spears into the lake. They could hardly aim, but stabbed wildly hoping to get lucky and find their targets. Most of the projectiles were avoided by the swift Xalaians, but a few hit their mark. The Xalaians continued to swim up to and stab any enemies that drew close enough.

After the shoreline was stained red, the soldiers of Natas stopped venturing near the lake and simply shot into the water. Soon enough, this tactic forced the Xalaians to retreat, and they headed straight back to the forces of the Light. They now knew the soldiers of Natas were expecting them, and would be upon the army soon enough.

With speed faster than even before, the Xalaians rocketed through the depths of the waters with increased purpose and drive. When they reached the far border of the lake and snuck past the townspeople, they regrouped for a brief moment. Counting their men, they realized they had lost ten of their twenty. This realization was beyond painful - it was excruciating. Every Xalaian was a brother, and their family was falling fast.

Somehow, they found the strength to hurry back to the forces. When they burst into camp, everyone gathered around them. They got out the words as best as they could manage. "Natas' army is on the east. The east side of the lake. It is large and powerful. We lost half our group when they found us. They know. They know we are close. We will need to be prepared for battle. I doubt they will be here tonight, but we should be ready just in case."

It was not long until the lords went to their troops. They had them set their ranks in the predetermined locations and readied their battlements. These battlements were strong and durable, but no one knew how much they could rely upon them. The lords dispersed among the ranks, making sure every soldier had his weapon and every archer had his bow.

Torches were lit, but hidden behind the barricades. It was a precaution so that the enemy did not see them or their formations before the battle began. Every spear was readied, every heart ablaze with passion. They knew their enemy was coming; there would be no surprise attack this time.

All that was left to do was wait. They had to stand, waiting with weapon in hand and sweat dripping down their necks. After minutes on a blade's end, Auden returned to the recovering Xalaians. "How far off were they?" he asked.

"They were not far. I'm not sure if they will come directly at us this time. That is what I had expected. Maybe they are going to wait until daybreak; their camps were fully set up when we arrived. All I know is they know we were spying on them."

"I suppose they will come when they come. Thank you for your support. I'm sure you did all you could."

The Xalaian nodded, then lay back down. Auden left him and relayed the message to the other lords, making sure they and their units stayed alert. They remained on the lookout for any sign of the enemy. They would be ready as well, Auden could feel it. Whether they came now or later, one thing was clear, they would be prepared. Finding the army of Natas unaware would be almost impossible. They may have before, but not this time.

Matthais remained at the back of the army. There was no way he would be able to fight. In fact, he was one of the only ones never to have fought. Humble ambassadors were not entrusted with weapons, and he was fine with it being that way. He was not the strongest nor the most capable, but his heart was large and his mind was always open. Sitting in the tent, he waited to hear the first sounds of battle. Instead, he heard footsteps approaching.

Gevnor entered, looking distressed. Matthais could tell something was wrong. "How are you feeling, Gevnor? Do I need to get a doctor?"

Gevnor sat down beside him. "No, it's not that kind of problem. It's much worse. I realized that this whole time I have been worried that my son would die and I would never see him again. I never even considered what kind of state I would leave him if I were to die in this war. He would be crushed. Surely, I would be in the Haven Realm, but I would not be able to stand letting him down."

"Lavrin is strong," Matthais said. "He gets that from you. You are a valiant man. How you continued to hope through your horrible slavery in the Mazaron is a mystery to me. I would have lost all sanity after a few weeks."

"Thank you for your kind words, Matthais, but I fear I will do little good worrying and wondering. How am I supposed to be ready to fight thinking like this? I need closure. I need a sign that will help me to let go of my anxiety. Somehow, I need to know that Lavrin is alright."

Matthais closed his eyes. "I once felt the same way. When I was in the North, recruiting the people there to join us, I lost a dear friend. Over and over I asked myself how to forgive myself for not saving him. I eventually thought back to what Lord Quinn told me. He said that someday I would see my friend again. It is as you said. You would travel to the Haven Realm, and he would one day see you there. You will eventually live out your lives there together. Either way, you and Lavrin will never be separated. The only difference is how long you have to wait. Patience may be hard, but it will be worth it. If you struggle with this again, ask yourself: Would you rather live with Lavrin in Amcronos as it is now, or a free land? Surely, you would prefer Amcronos at peace."

Gevnor chuckled. "Thank you, Matthais. You have cleared things up for me. I imagine Lavrin and his friends are laughing and having a wonderful time right now. They've probably gathered on some hillside and are feasting on a good meal."

CHAPTER 10

THE LABYRINTH

Chan struggled. He fought against the cold metal walls like a caged animal. Caged and ensnared with no hope of escape. The water level slowly rose from below. It was half-way up his boot.

He slammed against the door to no avail. Nothing happened. Neither did he hear any noise from outside his cell. Chan shouted, "Lavrin, Calix, Kasandra! Does anyone hear me?"

No response. His prison caught his screams and stuffed them in a bag. Chan looked down. Though it was too dark to see, he knew the water was there. He felt it… it was so cold. A thought exploded in his mind. The gears spun out of their mental shafts. What if he could stop the water? Chan bent down and ran his hand along the floor of the cell. He instantly pulled it back up. The floor was grated and sharp. There were far too many holes to cover. The water continued to rise from beneath him.

What else could he do? The water reached the top of his boot. He felt like screaming. Instead, Chan calmed himself, steadied his breath, shut his eyes and thought. Not as if to remember something, or to apply one thing to another, but to solve this problem. His entire body was dead still, as if he was applying every ounce of his soul to this single task. There had to be something he could use to save himself. Boots... no. Teeth... no. Foolishness. No, not foolishness... brilliance. He would use his teeth.

Chan pulled out his dragon tooth necklace. He thanked the King over and over. Feeling his way over the massive door, Chan tried to find a keyhole. His captors were smart - no keyhole. What had they not thought of? He considered driving the dragon tooth into the grated floor. He had no idea why, but he went along with this notion. He did not have much time, and it was worth the shot.

Suddenly, the poison on the tip of the tooth reacted with the water. The water began to sizzle and bubble. Chan noticed the water starting to dissolve like acid. It was acid. He had somehow formed acid.

While the acid burned through the bottom of the door, he realized the entire water around him started becoming acid. His legs began to burn hotter than stars. Chan finally let out the scream he had been holding in. Raw, undefiled pain shot up his nervous system. Chan braced his back against the wall and climbed up the cell with his legs. Though this got him out of the acid, it caused his legs to throb even more.

"A little longer. A few more seconds." Chan continued to talk aloud to himself, until the acid died down and the water returned to normal once again. The water began to stream out of the hole and onto the prison floor. Chan collapsed momentarily. Everything went black; luckily, it was only temporary.

He soon managed to crawl out of the cell. His eyes darted about. With decent effort, he found the lever that controlled the contraption and cranked it backward. It took him several tries to operate the mechanism, but eventually he caused the cell doors to swing open. Water flooded out from the cells and the others gasped for air. Apparently, they had been near death. That would have been the end, right then and right there.

After recovering from the initial shock of almost drowning, the friends embraced Chan and thanked him for saving them. At that moment, they realized he had paid a dear price for their salvation. His legs were deeply scared by the acid. So much so that he could barely walk. Uminos lifted him onto his shoulders, and they continued to the next part of the labyrinth. That is, after they heaved in musty dungeon air as if it were gold.

The path away from their cells was narrow and hard to follow. It took them precious time to navigate. At the path's end, they found the entrance to their next challenge.

As if they had not experienced enough danger already, they stood before a literal labyrinth. They had expected it was only a name... it was not.

The team faced a massive maze, too complex to plot a way through. On the other side of the underground expanse was a spiral staircase rising to the surface. Above anything else, the group was lured by the exit. All they had to do was make it there. It was so easy, yet so impossible. So close, yet farther than the moon. There was nothing else to do but journey down into the maze and hope to find their way out. They had no idea what time it was, but they needed to reach the tower before the sunrise.

Lavrin led the group into the labyrinth. He reached for his sword, and realized to his regret that it was gone. He remembered they were without protection. This was going to be hard. Hopefully, they would not have to get into any battles. If so, they would have to rely heavily on teamwork.

The team arrived inside the endless twists and turns that made up the maze. "Should we split up?" Chan asked.

"No. We need to stay together." Lavrin turned to his friends and motioned for them to follow.

They headed down a thin corridor and made a sharp turn... a sharp turn into a dead end. Their first reaction was to turn around and head back, but a wall stood in their path. Lavrin expressed what everyone was thinking. "Where did that come from?"

All of a sudden, the magically appearing wall started to move toward them. The team continued to back up away from the opposing barrier. Uminos pushed against it. He used all his might but it did not stop. He called to Grax for support. Not even the two strong warriors could halt the path of the wall. The whole group rushed up to help... to no avail.

There had to be some other way out. Once again, the team was trapped in a death cell. While the other teammates fought the steady movement of the wall, Kyra ran to the other dead end. It was not moving toward them. Kyra ran her hands over the wall. It was smooth. She searched for some stone to turn or brick to push that would trigger an opening. No luck.

Kyra shifted her perspective and got down on her knees. She pressed her ear up against the bottom of it. Knocking on it, she realized it was hollow. What could that mean? Finally, Kyra stepped back and kicked. The wall crumbled at that point and a small box was inside.

The approaching wall drew close to its counterpart, threatening to crush them by brute force. Kyra undid the latch on the box and brought out an intricate metal ball. It had some glowing substance held inside its elaborate outer rim. Kyra could only think of one thing. She shouted to her friends, "Get away from there."

They obliged and retreated. Kyra threw the sphere at the encroaching wall. It broke open, and the liquid burst out over the rough gray bricks. Amazingly, the substance continued to spread over the wall, stretching across like a cloud. By the time it neared even closer to the team, it hardened and formed a web-like structure. A sigh of relief left the exacerbated companions. They had made it.

Now to get out. They were trapped in a narrow lane of space, barely enough for them to fit. Budging and squirming, they soon were comfortable enough to attempt escape from their predicament. The more they searched for an exit, the more it seemed their trap was full-proof. Kyra reexamined the hole she had found, but to her dismay nothing else was in it.

Calix turned to Uminos. "Could you climb out?"

"The walls are very high. I could attempt it, but even if I did get out, what good would that do?"

Calix frowned. "I don't know. I'm just trying to find a way out of this mess."

"Everyone, we need to remain calm," Lavrin said. "Everyone search the area you are in. Look for keyholes or loose stones. Find something… anything we can use to escape."

Each of them pressed on the walls beside them. As he pushed on several rocks to see if they would budge, Felloni noticed the floor below was uneven. He knelt and looked at the ground. After studying its layout, he noticed a small crack barely big enough to put his finger into. He pulled up on the stone beside the crack and one of the walls began to move.

Felloni received proper congratulations from his relieved friends. The team found themselves in another series of hallways. How many more traps lay down these corridors? After one left turn and two right, they neared a small opening in the labyrinth. Before they could reach it, they were cut off by a curved wall that slid into the opening. At that moment, they realized the labyrinth was trying to kill them... trying to lock them in and throw away the key.

Reaffirming this notion, the vines running down the walls beside them began to stir. At first, the group thought they were seeing things, but it happened again. Starting slowly, then rapidly, the plants reached out to grab them. At first, they considered this mere chance that they had run into the plants, but it was the opposite. The plants had run into them. Uminos clawed the vines apart as they twisted around his arms. As he was about to break free, they went for his legs. Chan could tell they were in trouble. "Run! We need to get out of here!"

They bolted away from the vines until they heard a startling cry. Turning about, they witnessed Kyra being grappled by the vicious plants. She lay on the ground, consumed by the carnivorous vegetation like a rabbit in a snare. Without any contemplation, Lavrin dove into the entanglement and clung to Kyra tighter than any of the vines. He wrestled with them, but there was no overcoming their sheer mass.

They grew and grew as though they would never stop. Uminos rushed into the chaos and began slicing through the overgrowth. Grax and Calix headed in moments later, tearing leaves and ends of the foliage. They had almost freed Lavrin and Kyra when the plants changed tactics and went straight after them.

As the vines switched targets, Lavrin grabbed several of the stalks and yelled for Kyra to run. She forced her way past a few other outstretched vines and ran to safety. Nadrian and Chan stood with her, unsure if they should rush in or remain out of the way.

The battle against the ever-growing foliage continued. With no blades to aid them, the warriors looked like they were losing the fight. Eventually, Grax yelled, "Lavrin, you have to get out of there! Quickly! There is no way we can get you out."

Lavrin grunted loudly. He kicked and wrestled until he found a small opening. Diving through the hole, Lavrin crawled away from the plants, continuing to thrust off any outstretched vines.

Uminos was caught at the center. He was almost completely surrounded in an encasing of leaves and greenery. It was as if he was being placed inside a spider's web or a caterpillar's cocoon. Uminos realized he had other weapons beside his claws. He bit the thick vines with his razor-edged teeth and slammed into them with his spiked tail.

The vines were apparently more life-like than it would appear, because not only did they continue their assault, but they also hissed loudly. Thorny fangs grew out of their venomous buds. In the heat of the moment, Uminos almost forgot he was fighting plants, not snakes. Everything was becoming dark. He found it harder and harder to breath. Suddenly Grax ripped out a large vine wrapped around Uminos' face.

The flash of light and air rejuvenated Uminos and he tore apart his attackers. With the help of Grax, they were able to break through and retreat to the rest of the group. Before even taking a breath, the group bolted down a hallway taking them north. At least, what they thought was north. Every hallway looked the same, adding to their confusion and misery. Surely the makers of this labyrinth had known what they were doing. All the prisoners knew was that they had to get away from there.

Calix already prepared himself for the next obstacle they would face. His imagination ran away from him as he envisioned giant statues climbing over the walls to attack them. A shiver ran down his spine. They are not real, he told himself. Calix was not the only one readying himself. "What will we have to face next?" asked Kasandra.

"Whatever we face next, we will conquer," Calix replied. He tried to sound brave and heroic, though this was the first time since Hightenmore he had been truly terrified.

Kasandra, however, was more grounded in reality. "I wish I had my spears. I would have chopped those vines down in seconds."

"There will be time later to consider what we have gone through," Chan remarked. "Until that time comes, we need to keep moving. I think we are heading in the right direction. We must reach the exit at all cost. The King sent us to claim the pieces of the Titan's Heart. This is the first step. If we cannot claim the first, how can we expect to find the others?"

No one… no one wanted their mission to be for nothing.

Moved by Chan's statement, and remembering that the King had sent them, helped the group press onward. One turn led to another in silence. No one spoke for a time, letting their thoughts circulate. The dim torchlight made their eyes weary. The stone bricks seemed to press upon them at every angle. At least they did not see any more vines.

After making their way through several passageways, the group entered an opening in the maze. It felt incredible to have space to move about. Nonetheless, the team was disheartened as hallways spread out in all directions. There was a stand in the center of the area, and the team naturally headed toward it.

The stand was incredibly detailed, crafted out of various shapes and designs all made of bronze. Only Kyra took the time to fully admire its uniqueness; the others were too focused on the writing inscribed on its top:

You Will Never Make It

That was not what they wanted to hear. They wanted a sign telling them to turn right to reach the exit or something encouraging. The letters stuck out from the stand in bright gold. "Everyone search the entrance to each passageway," Lavrin said. "See if there is anything we could use to know which way to go. There must be a clue somewhere."

They obeyed and went to survey each entrance. While most of them focused keenly on the markings on the walls and searched for footprints or layers of dust, Kyra was distracted. She could not help but be drawn back to the stand. She stood above it, gazing at it as if it was see-through. Sliding her fingers over the letters, she felt that the word "never" seemed different from the others.

Kyra pulled it downward, and it left its place with a resounding clink. Then the other words seemed to be drawn toward each other. They mechanically shifted to fill in the gap, and formed a new sentence:

𝔜ou 𝔚ill 𝔐ake 𝔍t

A loud noise began to sound, like many machines were working and firing in unison. She had started some chain reaction resounding through the whole labyrinth. The rest of the group instantly ran up to her. "What did you do?" they asked.

"I just pulled it down. I must have triggered something."

There was no time to discuss anything else, because the ground beneath them started to move. Sections shifted, exposing pools of lava below. All the tunnels were inaccessible except for the third to the left, which had an uneven path heading toward it. With increased caution, the group stepped closer and closer to their destination. They felt as though the ground may shake again and they would plummet into a lava-filled grave.

Luckily, through steady footing and focus, they made it to their destination. They looked back at the pits full of lava. One wrong step would have been enough. This was getting serious. With every obstacle, the stakes were raised. With every obstacle, the danger grew greater, and the time they had left diminished.

Deciding there was no hope in contemplating the past, the team knew there was nothing to do but continue forward. Forward... the way all lives headed and dreams pointed. The way lords desired and kings considered. There was nothing Lavrin and his companions could do but hope to outwit the labyrinth. It was the first of many steps on the road toward the Titan's Heart.

The team was delighted to see a long, straight hallway after the numerous turns they past. Then they paused. A long hallway meant something was going to happen, since they had not encountered one yet. Uminos slowly inched his way past the group and down the path. He kept himself alert. He had to, a trap could be sprung at any moment. Surely the straightaway was there for a reason.

As best he could, Uminos tried to step quietly. Nonetheless he felt something was going to go wrong. He turned back to the others, and they motioned for him to continue. Uminos decided that neither going slowly or going fast would change the trap, so he headed down the straightway faster.

It seemed like the path never ended, as if it stretched for miles and miles in front of him. His feet grew weary. He felt as if there was a weight on his shoulders... a massive weight that could not be lifted. How long had he been walking... hours? Suddenly, his eyes closed. He forced them open, but they sunk back to where they had been. Why was he so tired?

He looked down at his arms and noticed layers of sweat forming over his scales. It was too hot. Too hot for him to think or to breathe. The last thing he heard was voices calling to him. Then all went black.

*****

Lavrin stood there, stunned. Uminos lay collapsed on the ground in front of them, a mere throw's distance away. Lavrin turned to Calix, who was just as shocked. "What happened to him, Calix? I don't see any smoke or gas that could have knocked him out. In fact, I don't see a trap anywhere."

"It's like he fainted simply by reaching a certain area." Calix stared at Uminos. "We can't go back. Our only choice is to rush through that area, pick up Uminos and take him with us. Maybe he wasn't going fast enough."

Listening in on the conversation, Nadrian added, "We should protect ourselves in case there is a gas that knocked him out." She took her sleeve and tore off a section of it. She wrapped it around her face, covering her mouth. She nodded for them to do the same.

They agreed, and soon everyone had their own makeshift mask. It was noticeably makeshift, but they hoped it would at least give them an edge. Taking a deep breath, they waited for someone to take off first. Felloni, unafraid of any obstacle, was the first to bolt in Uminos' direction. In a split second, the rest of them followed and reached the seemingly lifeless form of the Seviathan.

"He has collapsed from heat exhaustion," Kyra remarked. "His cold blood must have spiked from the rising heat in this area. We need to get out of here before we get boiled alive."

They heaved Uminos onto their shoulders and sprinted onward. His heavy frame made it hard to continue in the rising temperature. It kept getting hotter and hotter as if trying to make the sun jealous. Still they continued forward, motivated and driven. Each step drove them onward. Right as they felt as though they would not be able to keep moving, the temperature started to fall. They were almost out. They were almost free of scorching air that seized them by the throat.

Finally, they rushed on a few more yards, then collapsed. They were mangy dogs, panting for water and breathing heavily. Kyra got up and placed her palm on Uminos' temple. "He's going to survive."

Lavrin was about to reply, when he looked up and beheld the spiral stairway to the surface. He rose from the ground in delight. Had they really made it? No, what if it was a mirage or some form of the cruel trickery? Lavrin asked Calix, "Do you see the staircase, too?"

He gave Lavrin an odd look. "Why would I not see it? It's right in front of us. Are you okay, Lavrin?"

"I'm fine. I was just making sure it's not another trap."

In a matter of time, everyone left the stone floor and headed toward the stairs, Uminos being the last of them. Grax supported him along the way. Lavrin ascended slowly, mindful anything could trigger a trap, but was soon passed by Kasandra who burst up the steps. Chan stumbled behind her, but Nadrian picked the weary soldier up. "Come on, Chan. We're not far."

Kasandra rose into the cool evening air blissfully. She found herself laughing; an incredible relief washed over her. There was the watchtower on the far side of the city, much higher than any other building. Its light canvased the area, illuminating the city enough to remove the groping shadows.

Nadrian came out of the underground moments later, and almost shouted in joy. The soft glow of the distant tower and the orderly houses of brick reminded her of the Haven Realm. She remembered the constant light that would stream out of the King's hall and the beautiful white stone and colorful marble houses. The Haven Realm had changed her... made her altogether a new and better person. Now she had to prove she was different, and that her bitterness had been left behind in her past.

Chan was not feeling as strong as his teammates. He sat beside the exit, exhausted. "Go on. My legs are killing me. I'll be fine here. We don't have time to be slowed by my injuries." Nadrian would have argued against it, but knew he was right. At least Uminos was recovering and could continue with them.

The team wasted no time heading toward the watchtower. They sprinted closer to it, until they realized a band of soldiers stood in front of them. It was a large group, at least a hundred strong, armed to the teeth with sophisticated weapons. These weapons were crafted out of rare materials and designed in fashions never seen before; surely the craftsmen of this city were greater than any in Amcronos.

Grax knew that the armor of the Haven Realm could withstand the masterful blades and bows, and that Uminos was also protected to an extent. He feared, however, for his allies without Haven Realm armor or thick scales. They were not nearly as protected.

Lavrin watched the enemy archers draw back their bows. He whispered to his companions, "Split up. Everyone head toward the watchtower a different way. One of us is sure to make it."

Each of them snuck into separate alleyways moments before the archers fired. Lavrin realized how close his team had been to death once again. The numerous paths, side roads, and alleyways soon became channels that the warriors of the Light used to lose their trail. Within a minute's time, each member of the team was on their own.

The darkness of the alleyways covered them. It protected them until they would sprint into the open to reach safety once again. They had armor, but no weapons, or chance of fighting a battalion of trained, enhanced guards. Their single chance was to ring the bell atop the top and claim victory. Then the guards would stop.

Lavrin crept to the edge of the building. He stared into the large street, and found several men posted in his way. Lavrin felt for his sword, then remembered. No weapons. He hated himself for relying so much on his blade. He scanned for any way to bypass his foes. Nothing.

There was no horse he could mount to ride past them or weapon he could attain to fight them off. Lanterns were spread through the area so there were no shadows to hide in. He could try to dash across the road to the other side, but it looked even less promising than his current location. As Lavrin looked down the street, he suddenly heard footsteps from behind. He turned around and could tell guards were coming. He leapt to the ground, lying as flat as a rock. They walked past. Lavrin was about to get up, but one of the sentinels returned to the alleyway.

Lavrin held his breath. The guard drew his weapon and began to walk his direction. His eyes were at the far end of the path, but if he looked down, Lavrin would be caught. The guard had a determination in his gaze, as if he could face an army of a thousand and still fight with valor. By this time, the guard stood right beside Lavrin. His foot had almost crushed Lavrin's hand. Lavrin's heart was in his throat. He could not think. He forced himself not to make a sound.

"Soldier, return to your post." The call came from behind him. The soldier spun to find his commanding officer. He immediately complied and Lavrin was left. His joy was indescribable, though his nerves were fluttering. That had been far, far too close.

Lavrin arose, making sure to remain concealed. Anxiety rushed through his system, until he heard a soft noise coming from his left, like the cawing of a crow. He tried to match the sound to its owner. His eyes met those of Felloni. Of course it was Felloni; who else would climb onto the roofs to signal him?

Felloni motioned to Lavrin that he was heading toward the tower. Lavrin nodded. Felloni took off, gliding atop the dark rooftops with ease. It was as if he had lived his whole life leaping from house to house. His focus was on the mission, but he was ever watchful for his presence to be detected.

Closer and closer Felloni drew. He was going to make it.

As if in spite, the moment he thought this, an arrow whizzed past his face. They had spotted him.

He was not far from the tower. He tried to move to the far side of the rooftop, but ended up losing his footing. Felloni found himself dangling from the edge of the roof, held on only by willpower. Shouts echoed from below as more archers took their shots at their suspended prey.

Felloni clenched his teeth as the sharp point of an arrow embed itself into his leg. Looking down, he realized it had gone almost completely through him. Exerting all necessary strength, Felloni pulled himself up onto the roof. There was no time to think. No time for pain.

He stared at an archer down below. This soldier had the perfect angle to snipe him straight in the chest. Felloni closed his eyes. Nothing happened.

Below, Grax had dragged the guard to the ground and had taken his crossbow. He tossed it to Nadrian who stood a few feet away. She fired several shots quickly, though unaccustomed to crossbows. Nadrian was a fast learner. She adjusted the crossbow, and her shots apprehended several guards.

Felloni realized his friends had stopped trying to reach the watchtower, and were now preoccupied with protecting him.

As if readying for flight, Felloni sprinted for the end of the building and jumped. It was fate that the watchtower was not far from the rooftop. He flew in the air until grasping the edge. He pulled himself onto it, but was met by a massive guard. This protectorate was a muscular giant who carried a sizeable halberd, ready to slice him to shreds. Felloni found himself shuddering.

The mammoth charged at him, and Felloni was knocked backward and slammed into a column. The impact would have given him a concussion, had he not had the armor of the Haven Realm. Nevertheless, with an arrow in his leg and ringing in his ears, Felloni was in no shape to fight.

To make matters exponentially worse, Felloni heard Nadrian shout out, "Chan. No!" as Chan was being dragged away by a host of guards.

"It seems you have lost," Felloni's adversary said. His voice was deep, deeper than a cavern. His eyes reflected not anger, but resolve. Resolve that would net let himself be defeated.

"Not yet," Felloni countered.

He drew the arrow from his wound and shakily rose to his feet. He held the arrow like a knife and stumbled toward his opponent. His opponent took a step backward out of shock. The wildfire inside Felloni's eyes made the impressive soldier stop dead in his tracks. "Why are you doing this? You can't defeat me. I will have to end you if you continue to resist. Give up and you may live."

"I'm not here to fight you," Felloni answered. He dropped the arrow and grabbed the sides of the large bronze bell. He shook it with all his might. It rang violently and the noise permeated the city. The civilians awoke in a stir. The guards sheathed their weapons and Nadrian rushed to make sure Chan was alright. She held him in her arms. No, he could not be dead.

Chan cracked a small grin. "Let a man fake his death in peace."

Nadrian shook her head and threw her hands into the air. "You scared me to death. I can't believe you would do that to me."

Meanwhile, the scene had completely changed atop the watchtower. Felloni's enemy was now helping him up and placing him on his shoulders. The man opened a hatch in the floor and carried him toward the bottom of the tower. Before descending to the surface, Felloni beheld the first light of sunrise coming up from the horizon. Victory.

*****

"Felloni, my friend." Lavrin stood above Felloni, who was resting.

He opened his eyes. "Lavrin."

199

"Yes, Felloni?"

"This is the most comfortable bed I have ever slept in my entire life."

Lavrin laughed heartily. He sat back and thought about all they had been through yesterday. They had almost been drowned, crushed, eaten by vines, thrown into lava, boiled alive and assaulted without means of defending themselves.

It was now morning, and the group had been allowed to rest in an abandoned house in the city. Although it was abandoned, it was in fine condition, and the team had slept better than they ever had before. The citizens of the city had also been kind enough to supply Kyra with the medicine she needed to patch up both Chan and Felloni. She also made sure Uminos was properly cared for.

Lavrin returned to the present when Felloni asked, "Where's Grax?"

"He is collecting our weapons from the guards with Uminos. Why?"

"He saved my life."

"I will let him know you wanted to speak with him."

Felloni lay back his head and returned to his slumber. Lavrin entered the kitchen where the rest were.

The wooden floor creaked, alerting them of his presence. "How is Felloni?" they asked.

"He is doing just fine."

Everyone sighed in relief. They continued with their conversations as if all was right in the world. Kasandra had prepared breakfast for them. The roasted sausage, buttered toast and hearty soup more than satisfied them. Even Grax had been filled. Nadrian claimed it was almost at the level of feasts of the Haven Realm.

Acting upon this notion, Nadrian filled two bowls with soup and loaded two plates with the meat and bread. She headed first to Felloni's room. She found him asleep. Gently, she left the meal on the side table beside his bed.

She then headed for Chan's resting place. She found her companion awake, and she sat on the chair beside his bed. "How's the leg?"

"Mostly recovered. That acid hacked away at me with a vengeance. Luckily, my leg was not in it for too long. Whatever Kyra was given to treat the burn is working."

"That is a relief. I'm surprised you made it so far when we emerged from the labyrinth; no one even had to help you along."

Chan paused. "I'm surprised too. I guess I was driven by the desire to claim the Titan's Heart. When will we receive the first piece?"

Nadrian had been wondering the same thing. "All I know is we will need to move on once you and Felloni have healed. I wonder what trials will await us at the next location. This Titan's Heart must be one of a kind, to be protected by invisible cities and who knows what else."

She knew Chan needed to rest by the drooping of his eyes. She placed the food beside him and left him in peace.

As she left, she heard Grax and Uminos entering the building. She rushed to meet them, and was handed her shimmering bow crafted with rare wood found only in the Haven Realm. Little did her captors know, but her bow was beyond priceless. She took it with delight. Though it was light, it was marvelous to feel the weight of her bow on her back. There was a wholeness found in returning a weapon to its master; both were far better off together.

The team gathered around the center table beside their injured allies. The table had been cleared of dishes, and now held a map which stretched from one side of it clear to the other. As if struck by lightning, some of the teammates stopped dead in their tracks. They remembered the treehouse. This was how it had all started. They had gathered around a map discussing plans for the future as they were now.

Like all moments of reminiscence, this instant passed in and out of existence, drawing them back to the task at hand. They had all but secured one of the five pieces. They had learned from the leaders of the invisible city that the next piece was located far to the south. It was held inside the Forest of the Unknown, a region notorious for being dark and haunted.

Lavrin pointed out the obvious. There was little they could do to prepare for the Forest of the Unknown except be ready for the unexpected. He continued to talk about how their supplies had been returned to them, and could last them for some time. While they conversed, the door swung open to reveal a short man dressed in the clothes of a squire. "Our leaders want to see you."

The team gathered their weapons and exited the building, leaving Felloni and Chan to sleep. Their escort guided them back to the same building where they had started. This time, they were no longer amazed by its incredible architecture. Instead, they were fully focused on the leaders, awaiting the prize they had earned.

The men, seated upon their thrones, gazed at the victors with keen interest. "You defeated our test. It was a marvelous showing; rest assured we were watching you the entire time. You conquered some of our challenges in ways we never expected. We were surprised how far you were willing to go to claim the piece of the Titan's Heart. Follow us."

They arose and headed toward a large hatch. They descended into it. Lavrin was the first to follow them down.

The team found themselves in a massive room. It was full of blazing furnaces, metal slabs and smiths pounding in unison. The noise was deafening. Unusual tools crafted other unique devices and weapons. It was a forge beyond comparison. Channels of water flowed past each smith's section, allowing him to easily cool off his masterpieces after they had been torched. Large supply carts were loaded with the creations and hauled out of the forge systematically. Everything had a purpose and completed its job to perfection. Lavrin recalled his father's smithy so long ago, but nothing could have prepared him for this impressive display.

The leaders walked onward and took the group to the back of the forge. They opened a massive circular door that was covered with numerous chains. No thief could have stood a chance against its advanced protection. The leaders motioned for the team to stay.

Lavrin gazed into the metallic room and noticed the only thing held within the vault was a block of solid iron. This block was taken out of the room and handed to Lavrin. "The piece of the Titan's Heart is inside. It is up to you to get it out." Lavrin's heart sank… another problem.

"Have we not done enough for you?" Kasandra asked. "Didn't you promise to give us the piece once we passed your test?"

The leaders were not amused. "And there it is."

The city's assembly left the followers of the Light standing there.

Grax reached for the block. "Where is the nearest chisel?"

Lavrin stepped back. "It cannot be that simple. We can't risk damaging it. There must be another way."

"Let's melt the iron off. We will be left with the piece," Calix offered.

"Now we're getting somewhere," Lavrin said. "We would have to make sure we don't lose the piece in the fire after we melt the iron. We can give it a try."

They went over to a furnace that was not being used. After stoking the fire to life, Lavrin found protective gear and told the others to back away. Lavrin grabbed a long pair of tongs and clamped the block. He carefully lifted the block and placed it in the fire. The flame flashed bright white and started melting the metal. In less than a minute, the block started to melt. All of a sudden, the block fell from the tongs and into the fire. Lavrin realized the tongs were melting. Lavrin had never seen a flame hot enough to melt tongs. He took them out and threw them into the nearby water. Steam arose right as they met the water. Soon enough, water ran over the tongs to submerge them completely. Grax bent over and picked them up from the stream.

The team turned their attention back to the fire. A clear sharp stone was left where the metal cube had been. It was bright blue and gemlike, beckoning them to claim it. They had to find a way to get it out of the blazing furnace. How? He looked for a way to shut off the furnace but to no avail. There was no hatch to choke it or lever to cut its fuel. Suddenly he had an idea. "The fire is too hot. It may burn the piece if we don't act quickly. Everyone run and get a bucket."

While the other teammates gathered the water, Lavrin found another set of tongs. The fragment was still there, taunting the fire to try to melt it.

"Run up the fire just close enough to toss your water into the furnace. It won't be enough to put it out, but it should give me enough time to grab the piece."

The smoldering ashes brushed up against the gemstone; luckily it was invulnerable to the fire's heat, and awaited its deliverance. Lavrin nodded to his friends, and they ran up close to the fire and threw their water into the furnace. A chaotic eruption filled the entire area in a fog. Lavrin had not prepared himself for this. He rushed up to the furnace and groped about with the tongs. Eventually, just as he felt the heat rising again, his tongs braced onto the piece and he flung it out. He scrambled to get as far away from the furnace as possible, even with the protective suit on.

It took far too long in Lavrin's opinion for the steam to clear, but soon it passed. The team claimed their bounty with zeal. They had done it. Calix held onto it tightly. The group left the forge and reentered the hall where the leaders of the invisible city sat talking. "We have completed this challenge," Calix called to them. "We would now like to leave your city in peace, unless there is another trial you have for us to face."

"You have done well," one of the leaders answered. "You defeated challenges that were meant to end you. Your team has not even lost a member, which shows your resolve and promise. We will not hinder your travel anymore. Go now in peace. If you cannot protect the piece on your journey, bring it back here and we shall protect it once more. It is far too valuable to fall into the wrong hands. Otherwise, do not bother our people any further."

CHAPTER 11

ONWARD AND ON

The team left the hall proud. Proud of what they had accomplished, and their compliment from the proud ruler. They headed straight back to their dwelling, disregarding the odd looks from the townspeople. Clearly, no one in the city was glad of their victory. No one except for the team itself.

Inside, they found Chan sitting at the table. "Welcome back. Is that the artifact we came for? It is beautiful." Calix handed it to Chan, who held it with reverence. He glowed as he inspected the piece. He could only dream about what the final, complete Titan's Heart would look like. It would be quite a sight.

"How is Felloni?" Kasandra asked Chan. "We need to get moving before we are attacked by another squadron of guards."

Chan rose to his feet, then cringed from the ache in his leg. "We're going to be attacked again? I will wake him at once."

"No. I was exaggerating. I doubt we will be attacked again. We claimed our treasure rightfully. We will tell you all about it once we leave this place. I have an odd desire to leave immediately."

"I feel it also," Calix said. "It is as if we are being driven onward by the hand of the King himself. We may have plenty of time, or we may not have enough time. All I know is we should not risk wasting it. Can we see Felloni?"

Chan motioned for them to enter his room. They beheld Felloni laying on his bed. His sleep looked like a deep, comforting one. They hated to wake him, but he looked much improved. Kyra rested her hand on his shoulder and whispered, "Felloni. Felloni. We need to move out, Felloni."

He stirred, and rubbed his eyes. It appeared his dreams had been so deep he no longer knew where he was. Luckily, it lasted only a moment. He gained his bearings and stood up. "We won," he said.

"How did you know?" Lavrin said.

"You're not dead."

Everyone stood with eyebrows raised as Felloni left the room.

The team later gathered their provisions and weapons and were ready to set out. Chan had gotten to the point where he could walk on his own, but Felloni had wrapped his arm around Grax for support. They headed for the doorway out of the city, and before leaving, they turned back and looked at it one last time.

Turning their focus back to the mission, they left the city only to find it storming outside. They realized the brilliant mechanics of the invisible city had already fixed their problem with the storms. The rain no longer clung to their invisible dome, and the city vanished from sight like a vapor.

Lavrin gathered a handful of stones. The others looked at him, wondering was important enough to hinder them from finding shelter from the downpour. They noticed he was forming a pile out of the rocks. "So we can always find our way back here again," he said.

Once the pile was sizeable enough, the team sped off toward the woods in search of some form of covering. They found a cluster of maples with thick leaves to protect them from the deluge. As dreary as it was, it was pleasant to be back in the world, and not in an underground dungeon.

They pulled out their blankets and rested against the trees. Traveling on in the rain would be pointless. It would tire them out by the time they had gone half a mile. The conversation turned to what they were all thinking. "Did that really just happen?" Kyra asked.

The group was silent. Had it? Had they just wrestled with man-eating plants? Had they debated with rulers of an invisible city to claim a piece of a mysterious artifact? It was then that the group realized how crazy their lives truly were. Crazier than those of lords, spies or even adventurers. There were hundreds of people living in peace, having never left their homes or the ones they loved. Those were the ones they were fighting for.

The rustling of the leaves laden with rainfall was mesmerizing. The droplets splashed around them, yet not on them. It was as if they found the one place it was not wet. The hand of the King was over them; it had been this entire time.

As the downpour died to a sprinkle, the team hastily gathered their supplies. They started off again, heading south. Their journey was slowed by the fresh mud, but they managed to keep a steady pace.

The terrain was rough, full of scattered rocks and steep inclines. Several times the team had to double back when coming to the edge of a cliff. At one point, they came to another cliff and started down into the ravine. The drop was not a long one, but would nonetheless not be survivable. A river flowed along the bottom of the chasm, ready to sweep away any unfortunate victim. "Have we been here before?" Kasandra asked.

Lavrin looked at the surroundings. "I don't believe so. Why?'

212

"Because I'm beginning to feel more and more that we've gotten ourselves lost."

Lavrin turned to Calix, hoping for some sign that they were not lost. Calix in turn looked down at their map and bit his lip. Lavrin did not know what to say. "We will find our way to the Forest of the Unknown somehow. In the meantime, we must keep our spirits up and try to make sense of this region."

This was no small task. It was a landscape unlike what they were used to, and the ups and down made it hard for Felloni to keep up. His legs betrayed him. He told himself he was letting his teammates down and thus pushed himself harder and harder. Of course, this simply increased the flaring pain in his legs.

The team zigzagged through the area making slow headway, but headway nonetheless. There was little life surrounding them... no rabbits scurrying about, or creatures hiding in the grass. The grass itself seemed stiff as if tainted by frost. Life had been sucked from the region as if a tornado had whisked it all away.

Kyra twirled her hair unknowingly as she contemplated the path she had found herself on. What if she had stayed in that dungeon in Saberlin? What if she had never been freed? It would be miserable beyond compare; she might not even be alive. She owed everything to the King. He had saved her and given her a drive. No force, not even death, could stop her from following Him because death only meant to see Him, face to face. Kyra decided not to let her fear of captivity haunt her forever.

Kasandra too thought back to her origins living a meaningless life in her village in the Mazaron. That is, it had seemed meaningless until she and Rowan rebelled against the Seviathans. If only Rowan was here now. She realized she needed his shoulder to cry on and his comfort and kindness more than ever. Her eyes focused on Uminos, the very Seviathan who had caused her so much grief, walking amongst them as an equal. She cast aside that thought. Uminos had changed, he was a better person now. Instead of resentment, she remembered that the mission was above her emotions, and the King above this mission.

The air was unnaturally dry, and the team made use of their canteens. Life had even vacated the sky above. At least there was still life in the followers of the Light. After making sense of where they were, they finally were sure they were headed the right direction.

No one felt it necessary to be ready for battle since the land was so empty. No one that is, except Felloni, always ready to be on the defense. Such was his outlook on life - that a battle was always a moment away. He had to be ready, whether or not anyone else was. His eyes surveyed the horizon. Natas could have spies watching them. Even at a time that most would consider peaceful, Felloni was poised, his knife in ready to launch at an adversary. No taking chances.

Chan and Calix were deeply engrossed in conversation. "Why would the King not send his warriors to claim this Titan's Heart?"

Calix did not answer for a while. "Maybe he is the one who hid it there in the first place. Maybe the King set these guardians to protect it."

"Would it not be safer in the Haven Realm?"

Once again, Calix carefully sorted through the catacombs of his mind to answer. "It is hard to say. Maybe he hid it even before Natas' rebellion. It would have been logical to scatter the pieces in a relatively unpopulated Amcronos at that time."

"Then why not send a squad of warriors from the Haven Realm to reclaim them once Natas took control of Amcronos? Surely not every soldier in the King's army has been fighting against Natas' minions for the last few centuries." Chan's eyes showed it all. Calix could tell he was passionate about the subject.

"Maybe they have been. Maybe this whole time Natas has been sending wave after wave of dark enemies against them, keeping them occupied."

"Well, that is unlikely," Chan stumbled.

Calix looked Chan in the eye. "What is the point of this, anyhow? I know it is a very interesting concept, but why does it matter why the King has not claimed this

Titan's Heart? We are going to get it for him, and then we will go back to the Haven Realm."

"That will be wonderful," Chan remarked.

"What do you mean?"

"I cannot wait to return to the Haven Realm. I thought I would love to come back to Amcronos, and in a sense, I do. Overall, though, I have found myself desperately longing to be in the King's presence again. After tasting perfection, everything here seems bland."

"I know it's hard," Calix replied. "Everything I remember about Amcronos is not the same. But, we must do this for our friends and for the King. He wanted us here for this purpose. We have to finish this task to the best of our ability, and strengthen our friends for the missions they have yet to complete."

"Have you told Lavrin yet? That we are going to have to leave?"

Calix exhaled deeply. "No. How can I? I couldn't bear to give him such a burden. So much has happened and changed between us. I miss the times it was just us and our little dog running around the forest. Now everything is so different. I wasn't even there when my best friend found his father after years of searching."

He looked ahead and noticed Lavrin far past the group, scouting out the area. If only. If only he could go talk to him like he used to. No. Calix knew that life would never be how it was, and maybe something better would emerge from it all. Maybe one day they would look back and laugh about these hectic times.

Until that day, Calix was content letting their quest take Lavrin's focus. They were still the best of friends, but Calix could tell it was more like they were soldiers than companions. Nothing had gone wrong between then, and nothing had torn them apart. It was simply the nature of life; time changes a man.

Calix nodded to Chan and rushed to catch Lavrin. Lavrin did not even notice him. "How are you Lavrin?" Calix asked.

"I'm fine. Why?"

"Well, I suppose I was just curious. I remember after I came back from the Haven Realm, you told me I need to become human again. How've I been doing?"

"Better." Lavrin smirked. "You have matured far beyond your years. Yours eyes tell it all. I don't know much about the Haven Realm except what you've told me, but I can see the shimmering light of the star lanterns you described."

Calix chuckled. "I'm surprised you remembered those. I don't even remember telling you about them. Guess it never crossed my mind."

"Why did you come to me, Calix? I'm glad to have the company but... no matter, whatever it was we can discuss it in due time. For now, I should keep my attention on the present. We must claim this artifact. This... how should I put it... treasure seems to be calling out to me. There is no other way to describe it.

"It is more important than every other journey combined. Now that I think about it, this is the only task we've ever received directly from the King himself. From what Nadrian tells me and what I read in Matthais' histories, this is a very rare occasion. The King has only given missions in person two or three times before."

"Then let's do it. Let's claim this thing and get it back to the King before we can blink. No power can stop us. We have enough potential to slay any forces trying to kill us before getting the Titan's Heart. We are strong together, never to be shattered apart."

"Calix?"

Calix noticed Lavrin had stopped, so he stopped as well. "Yes, Lavrin?"

"You're beginning to sound like a human."

Calix wrapped his arm around Lavrin and they walked on.

CHAPTER 12

VILLAGES AND JOURNEYS

It was small… a quaint little village. The task was utterly simplistic. Go in, fill their canteens and return to the group.

Grax had been chosen because he fit in with the tall, strong woodsmen of the area. He had no clue why there were shivers running down his spine. It was the simplest task he had ever been given; pretend to be a villager long enough to reach the well, then leave. Maybe that was just it - it was far too simple. Why couldn't it be a heroic duel against a swarm of troops? For the first time in his life, something made him wish for war. All this nonsense over such a trivial job.

Grax was dressed in long leather breeches and a green tunic that smelled of pine. He was perfectly fit for his role. The team had camped just a half-mile away, hidden by the hillside. Once again, Grax found himself without his cherished hammer, and felt off-balance without it resting on his shoulder.

He continued the descent down the incline and neared the village. It was a brisk afternoon, cold enough to make a bird migrate, but not enough for a bear to hibernate. Grax had planned everything; Chan had made sure he had. These people were in Natas' domain, and likely followed him, as well. Grax had asked for Calix's necklace to know friends from foes, but Calix assured him no villager would own such an item.

His first step into the town calmed his senses. It was homely beyond any place he had seen before. People were chatting vigorously, and there was no sign of brawling or hostility. They looked like honest people, not followers of Natas. Grax walked along the small street past the villagers. A young boy with wavy black hair ran up to him. Grax could tell the boy was out of breath and had worked up a sweat.

The little child said to Grax, "Excuse me, sir, but my sister is caught under a cart. Please come quickly. She needs help."

He followed the boy who looked back at Grax longingly. "Help her," he kept saying, even as Grax began to lift the cart. The tiny girl, only about seven, crawled out from beneath the cart with tears streaming down her pale cheeks. Her first action after arising was to run up to Grax and hug him. She wrapped herself so tightly around his leg that he could do nothing but stand there.

Grax called the boy to his side. "What happened?"

"I was guiding the ox until he went off the road. He led the cart straight over a rock which caught onto the wheel. The cart tumbled and there was nothing I could do. My sister was riding in the back on top of the cabbage. I tried to lift it, but I wasn't strong enough."

"I see. Well let me see if we can salvage any of those cabbages." Grax and the boy bent down, and found several that were not crushed or dirtied.

The boy glowed with thankfulness. "Thank you, kind sir."

Grax nodded. "It was nothing. Tell me, though, why were you guiding such a large cart?"

"We're orphans, sir." The child looked down to the ground and twiddled his thumbs, ashamed to be brought low before his new hero. "I sell whatever I can to make a life for me and my sis. My aunt helps. She is nice. She wants us to move in with her, but my sis is so terribly afraid of our uncle that I couldn't bear it."

"I see. Well I'm very sorry for what happened to your cart."

The boy brushed his hair to the side. "It's alright. I'm sure my aunt will convince our uncle to fix it. Anyhow, what brings you to our town, stranger?"

"How could you tell I'm not from around here?"

"You talk different." The boy went on. "Is there anything I can do to help you?"

Grax bent down to get on the boy's level. "Could you direct me to the well?"

"Better yet. I'll take you to it."

The child grabbed his sister by the arm and bolted off down the road, making sure Grax was following. The little girl had to exert herself to keep up. Grax kept a steady pace behind the siblings. His long strides kept him from falling too far behind.

They reached the well soon enough. It was clearly run down, but Grax drew near to it with the canteens ready. No one else was near the well, which left Grax stumped. How could no one be drawing water at this time?

Grax took hold of the crank, ready to draw up a bucket full of water. He turned it several times, and the clinks and clanks let him know it was working. Yet when he looked inside the bucket, there was no water.

"That well has been dry for some time," said a voice from behind him.

Grax turned to see a middle-aged woman with long brown hair. She wore simple clothes and little distinguished her from other women except her kind smile. "Then where do your folk get their water?" Grax asked her.

"Usually from the nearby streams, but those are also dwindling. We barely have enough water to last."

Grax's heart dropped. "Where would be the closest place I could go and get water? I'm a traveler and need to fill my canteens for a long journey."

"Tell me your name first," she replied.

"Of course, how foolish of me. My name is Grax. What is yours?"

"I'm known as Ressa. These children are under my care. I'm their aunt."

The young boy ran up to his aunt and motioned for her to kneel. "We already told him about you." He whispered.

"Oh, I see. Well, did you tell him your names?"

In the rush of saving his sister and escorting Grax to the well, the little lad realized he had forgotten his manners. Instead of fessing up to his aunt, the boy turned to Grax. "My name is Tylo and hers is Rylo. I'm terribly sorry we have no water to offer you. We might have some bread."

"I have plenty of food, my dear boy, but thank you for your kindness. However, I'm afraid I must ask again where I could find water."

Ressa frowned. There was nothing she could do for him, Grax knew it that moment. Though he knew he must move on, he could not help but accept her invitation to their home. His compassion overwhelmed his focus.

Grax followed Ressa, who took both Tylo and Rylo by the hand. After walking a short distance, Ressa opened the door of a tiny cottage. She motioned for the little ones to go off and play. Grax had to catch his breath as he entered.

The house was atrocious, not suitable for a cockroach to live in. Cobwebs clung to the ceiling, the floor was covered in dirt, and dust plagued the few pieces of furniture they had. The ceiling had sunken in the middle, probably due to the damaged roof. Crumbs clung to the edge of the miniscule table, which Ressa promptly dusted off before Grax sat down.

The chair almost collapsed under him, but luckily it held. Grax tried to hide his concern, but it was of no use. She knew the conditions she was living in, and could tell he was stunned. "What really brings you to this town?"

"What do you mean?" Grax replied.

"No one would simply come into this sinkhole for water. This place is beyond desolate. You haven't scratched the surface of its poverty. Either you came here knowing literally nothing about us, or are here for something other than water."

Grax shifted on the rickety chair. "What do people come here for?"

"Slaves mostly. There are no businesses here, no livestock or farming. I suppose there used to be lumber, but most of the trees are dying. This is a town without hope."

Grax could not respond. His heart was broken beyond anything he had ever expected. His mind was completely tossed about, and his perspective shifted from getting back to his assignment to the mission of saving these people. He did not tell himself it was not his place, or that he had far better things to focus on, he was too consumed with the poverty before him. It was even worse when Ressa brought out half a piece of old bread from her pantry and gave half of it to him to eat.

What could he do? What could he say? He dared not reject the bread, but on the other hand had no desire to eat half of a moldy loaf. Grax pushed the plate aside. "I ate less than an hour ago. How about you tell me how I can help this city. I may only be able to stay a day or so, however."

"If you could help this city in one day, I would give you all the water in the world."

"I will do the best I can." Grax rose and headed toward the door.

Ressa did not try to stop him. She had seen travelers like him come and go. None of them lifted a finger to save this desolate village. She figured they were too small, too out of the way for anyone to care. Little did she know, Grax felt quite differently on the matter.

He headed straight to a cluster of trees just beyond the village, and drew his hand axe. It was not as magnificent as his long hammer, but it was still Haven Realm quality and sharp enough to pierce through chain mail.

The first tree fell to the will of his muscular arms, which pounded the axe into its trunk with vigor. Thump, Thud, Thump. The wailing of the axe laid low another small willow. Bark crackled and wood splintered as he began to fasten planks out of the fallen branches.

A few villagers noticed him off chopping wood and were instantly curious. They dared not near him, seeing he was fully absorbed in his task. Soon enough, word reached the alleged mayor of the town. Alleged, because he held as much authority as a dog over a pack of wolves.

Still, the mayor stomped over toward Grax, demanding him to stop. Grax did not even notice him approaching. "Stop this instant. As the mayor of this village, I order you to cease this action. What right have you to chop down our trees?"

Grax halted his work. "I'm doing what should have been done a long time ago - rebuilding Ressa's home. If you could assign some of your men to help me, we could possibly reframe that stable of yours. It was built so poorly that if I was a horse, I would kick it down and run off."

The mayor clenched his fist. "How dare you insult my town! I will do with it as I see fit. I will not let you take my hard-working men and put them to lumberjacking."

"Put it to a vote, then."

The mayor stopped dead in his tracks. "What do you mean?"

"You heard me," Grax continued. "Put it to a vote. Ask your men if they want to help rebuild this town or if they would rather fold their hands and eat dust, and sleep under roofs that can hardly be called that."

The mayor stomped off. He held a brief meeting with the townsfolk. Within ten short minutes, the men of the town had gathered what little tools they had and began helping Grax. Some took the wood and stacked it in bundles next to houses to be hammered into place, others tore out old boards.

The little boys made a fire in the center of the city. They found whatever straw they could and used it to thicken their roofs. The stable was restructured, and the horses would have shouted in approval if they could. The townsmen did not consider their throbbing hands, only kept on chopping down trees and hammering boards into place. Practically every tree along on their border was turned into planks to repair the town.

The stubborn mayor was the only man in the whole city not joining in the activity.

Grax had naturally become the leader of the operation, directing men to go to and fro, carrying and hammering. Hours passed as the sweat of a hundred produced the reward of a revitalized community. They worked until they ran out of nails.

As the sky grew dark, the community gathered in the center of town around the ever-flickering fire. Ressa was the merriest looking around, seeing hope she had not witnessed in ages. One man had changed their entire society for the better. In the grand scale, what Grax did was minor, but the hope he brought was extraordinary.

Grax sat around the campfire sharing stories of the King's ways, and everyone listened with intent. Every word he uttered clung to their minds like sap. Many confessed they would love for their village to join the side of the King.

As if on cue, rain began to pour down from the sky, and everyone rushed to grab buckets. So much was collected that three barrels were filled with the bounty. The community gave Grax enough water to fill all his canteens to the brim, and he thanked them kindly.

Grax had to leave in far more of a hurry than he would have liked, but was glad to know his impact had ranged further than a few sturdier buildings. His trip back to the team was not a long one, and he found them waiting for him. Everyone asked him where he had been, and he told the story as they gathered their supplies to embark once again on their crusade. They were a day behind, but Amcronos had been made better because of it.

*****

"There are scratches all over your axe," Kyra said. "Were you really cutting down that much wood?"

Grax shrugged. "I suppose so. The time passed so fast that I have no idea how many trees I chopped."

"I think what you did was very kind. They could not have asked for a better man to help them."

Grax did not reply. He was far too humble.

Kyra turned her attention to Nadrian who walked beside her. Nadrian was utterly consumed in her book. She stared intently, as if there was nothing else in the world. Kyra watched her read. Every few seconds Nadrian would flip a page, and then all would return to normal.

After this cycle continued for several paces, Kyra asked, "What are you reading about, Nadrian?"

She jerked her head up and looked at Kyra, then looked back toward her book. "I'm trying to find any mention of the Forest of the Unknown. Even for a book from the King, it has very little information on the subject. In fact, I have been able to find plenty of material on almost any other subject, except this. It is quite puzzling. It only says that no one journeys into the Forest of the Unknown intentionally, and no one leaves it unscathed."

Kyra tried her best to swallow the lump in her throat. "I guess we will be the first, then. That is, to willingly enter that place. I'm confident the combined experience and weaponry of this group can fight off whatever we find in there."

"Agreed." Nadrian was already back to scanning her book.

Kyra shook her head. She thought Felloni was the quiet one.

*****

The path they followed twisted and winded enough to make a snake envious. It was hard keeping the course as the dry air thrashed them and the scattered bushes all looked the same. There were no markers to tell one place apart from the next.

The hazy blue sky did not change. The coarse grass preparing for an upcoming winter was no different. The animals that occupied the region continued with their lives expecting nothing.

This continuous stretch of grassy plains began to wear down on the team. Not because it was too much for them to handle. Nor because it exerted them to their limits. Rather, it made them miss the intriguing landscapes they had now passed. The lack of any civilization upset them. Was there really no one who lived here?

It made sense, however. What a better place to hide a piece of the Titan's Heart than in the woods far from any villages. The team did not know what that something was that guarded it, but legend told them it was very dangerous.

Conversations lingered, but dwindled as quickly as they had begun. Little noise spread through the small band, save that of Uminos sharpening his claws on his scales. A sharp and piercing sound, it continued for several minutes until Uminos was content. He looked around the bleak surroundings in discontent. Mundane. That was the word he was looking for.

Finally, like the discovery of a buried treasure, the sore eyes of the group gazed upon a forest. A forest known only as 'unknown'.

CHAPTER 13

THE FOREST OF THE UNKNOWN

They had made it. Was that a good thing? No one was sure. At least they were one step closer to claiming the Titan's Heart.

The trees were very peculiar - twisted and bent into knots. They formed a row like a wall, blocking their entrance. Lavrin approached the wall of limbs and branches, trying to find a way past it. Eventually, he turned himself in such a way that he slid through a diagonal gap between two branches. "Pass me the supplies," he said to the others. "There is enough space here to store them."

They unloaded their packs and handed them to Lavrin one at a time, who set them down in a large pile.

Kyra was the next to wedge her way through the space, and Lavrin took her hand to help her along. Chan followed into the forest.

As he entered, Calix noted, "I don't see any signs of life in the area with my necklace. We are alone, at least for now."

Everyone had entered the forest except Grax, who stood sizing up the narrow opening. He drew his axe and began chopping. The tree branch fell and he entered his newly formed hole, glad he had not tried to squeeze through.

"Why didn't we have you do that at the beginning?" Kyra thought aloud.

The team reloaded their gear and found everything drastically different inside the forest. These trees were no longer bowed, instead a sense of darkness clung to them. Dark leaves on dark branched in a shadowy place... it was enough to dishearten any man.

A lone crow cawed at them from nearby. It flew off, spreading its black wings. It did not appear again.

Calix was the first to shake off the foreboding omen and headed deeper into the thick woods. The others retained their focus on the bird a moment longer until returning to the task at hand. Chan drew his sword, already feeling like he was being hunted. The team made headway through the intense darkness. They devoted themselves completely to their survival.

They were surviving, though not in danger. They stuck close together, though not under attack.

Past occasional cobwebs and slimy moss, the team ventured toward what they believed to be the center of the forest. At one point, they stopped to gain their bearings, and heard a snake hiss behind them. They jumped back, and beheld a massive snake. It had a pattern of black and red diamonds running down it, and searing red eyes gazing straight at them. This snake was far too large... and menacing.

The chase began. Darting through the entanglements like gazelles, they took flight. The snake began to gain ground, for it was used to the area, and could weave in ways they could not.

The group bolted through the forest until they reached a clearing of grass. They turned with weapons drawn, but the snake remained in the trees, unwilling to venture into the open. Lavrin was the first to turn around to see an eerie building in the middle of the expanse that glowed haunting light toward them. They began to feel sleepy... more tired than they had even felt before.

Their eyes sagged and their bodies drooped until they fell to the ground. Lavrin fought the spell as long as he could, until he spied several hooded beings towering above him, forcing him into the sleep. He could not overcome it.

*****

There was a smell of smoke in the air. It saturated everything around him. The evening sky was fading. Not a star shone upon its canvas, and no wind rustled across the grass. Lavrin looked around for any sign of life. There was none. Where had he gone?

He stood there in a daze. His mind was clouded and his senses numbed. After what felt like a hundred years, he took a step forward. A soft crunch beckoned him to look downward. Ashes. Piles and piles of ashes lay heaped on the ground. What fire could have caused such a thing?

Lavrin looked back up. In front of him stood a house, if it could be called that. It was charred on all sides. Lavrin shuddered as he noticed a massive hole blown into a side of the wrecked building. The roof of the house was nowhere to be found. It must have been engulfed in the flames. The remaining sparks of fire dimly lit what was left of the house.

Drawn out shadows extended from the scene in every direction. It was unnaturally eerie. It was impossibly mysterious. Yet Lavrin was drawn toward it. He felt every notch and every detail calling out to him as if they knew his name. Then Lavrin stopped. Something was calling him. It whispered to him with words of poison. "Lavrin. Lavrin. Do you not remember?"

Lavrin felt his stomach churn and his hairs stand on end. The polluted sky. The lingering traces of a raging storm of fire. This was no new sight. This was... his home. Lavrin felt like crying out in agony, but nothing came.

There was nothing left for him to do but move closer. That did not stop him, however, from asking himself a myriad of questions. "How did I get here? Why am I here?"

The mysterious voice from within returned. "You are here to suffer."

Lavrin wrestled with the thought for a moment, then decided to move in closer once again. He found himself standing within the wreckage. The voice from within talked Lavrin through the rooms, although he had not forgotten them. "There was the kitchen. Your mother would stand right over there as she cooked. And that there. That is where your father would lay down his winter coat still covered with snow. Your mother hated when he would do that."

Lavrin tugged his hair angrily. "Get out of my head! Whoever you are, you do not belong here."

"Oh, that is where you are wrong. I belong here as much as you do. I am your conscience. I am here to remind you of all you lost. Here to show you what you could have saved. Come with me."

Lavrin suddenly found himself outside the house. He was standing above a trivial patch of dirt which held three wooden crosses, lined in a row. Lavrin knelt and examined the crosses intently. "What are these for?"

"They mark the resting places of your father and mother."

"What about the third cross?" Lavrin looked behind him, feeling as if there was a man standing nearby.

"It is the burial marker of Kyra. She too is dead."

Lavrin rose and stepped away from the graves. "That's impossible. She is alive. My father is alive. And I will never give up hope that my mother is still out there somewhere."

With a stinging pain growing in his heart, Lavrin fell before the crosses and began to dig up the dirt with his hands. It was abnormally cold, and his hands felt blistered. Lavrin continued to shovel fistfuls of soil until he found part of a bone. It could not be. After a few more seconds of work, Lavrin scrambled away from the hole. He had seen a skull.

Nothing was making sense. Lavrin held his head in his hands and breathed heavily until his lungs stung. This did not relieve the pain. He pounded his fists on the ground and moaned loudly. This did not relieve the pain either. Eventually, Lavrin was too worn out to fight any more.

He found himself feeling alone, betrayed by his own self. Was this his fault? Had he lost everyone he loved?

It felt wrong to ask these questions, but how could he stop himself? Lavrin shook himself from the grip of his emotions and got up. He went to wipe the tears from his cheeks, but decided to let them flow. They were doing no harm. Lavrin stood above the three graves, unable to speak.

Then, just like the first stir which starts the tidal wave or the first drop that starts the storm, a power grew within Lavrin. He felt it was a power, but it shifted and developed until he felt it calling out to him. Lavrin could not tell what the source of this wellspring was, until it began to speak. "Lavrin. You are not alone. You are not forgotten."

His first thought was to fight against it, to yell at it with all his might, but then he realized this voice was not the same. The first voice, the one that had taunted him, did not sound like this one. This simple calling was one of tranquility, honor and decency.

It continued to speak to him, and this time the voice echoed all around. "Lavrin. Remember what I have done for you. Remember how you fought for me at the gates of Saberlin. Remember how you climbed mountains and crossed deserts for my name's sake. I am here for you. You know where you are. You are with Kyra and your friends. She needs you. Your father needs you."

"Thank you, my King." Lavrin turned his back to the haunting graves, knelt on the soft earth and closed his eyes. He allowed no thought to penetrate the defenses of his will, save those of the King, Kyra and his father. They were the reason he had to fight on. His friends had not given up on him, and he would never give up on them.

Lavrin remember the warmth in his father's eyes after they had reunited. It was the same warmth his mother had shown him every day. She had always been so hopeful. Lavrin knew her hope remained within him, as well. "This is not real," he whispered to himself. "The King is with me, and I have all I need. I must wake up and find my friends. This is not real. I must wake up."

*****

Why was it so dark? Lavrin opened his eyes slowly. Above him stood ten beings. They were unlike anything he had ever seen before. Their long faces glowed with radiant light. In contrast, their eyes were large and dark, as was their flowing hair. At first, Lavrin thought they were very beautiful, until they stepped out of the light into the shadows. Their faces grew dark, and their eyes became a staunch white. Their hair turned bright, but their skin was darker than the deepest crevice of the most remote cave.

Lavrin stumbled to his feet and drew his sword. He rushed forward and stabbed one of them in the chest. The being grabbed the hilt of the sword, and it dissolved at his touch. The sword then reformed in the hands of the ominous being. "Do not make a fool of yourself."

Lavrin stepped back. The beings looked him over several times, then turned to each other. He only heard bits of their conversation. Something about honoring their promise. A note about something's value. A remark about giving him another test. Lavrin was glad they made him wait. It gave him time to think.

For a moment, Lavrin forgot about the creatures who had huddled together. He looked around. His friends were strewn about like fallen branches, still in their deep sleeps. Every so often, one of them would twist or turn, trying to ward off their nightmares.

"We have never seen someone overcome our illusions." The assemblage of robed beings walked toward him. "Then again, few even continue into our forest after facing our snakes. You need not fear them; they are of little danger. They are another one of our illusions. This belongs to you now. If you ever find you can no longer protect it, bring it back to us and we will hold it for you. It is one of many artifacts we protect." The living shadows, as Lavrin later decided to call them, held out a piece of the Titan's Heart and his sword.

Lavrin reached out and took them. "What about my friends? What will happen to them?"

"They will remain in their fearful dreams until they conquer them. That, or they die from lack of food and water. It should not concern you now; that relic you hold is worth more than their lives."

"No," Lavrin said. "Their lives are worth more to me. How can I save them?"

The living shadows looked at each other with wide eyes. "Well, you could enter their illusions and try to help them overcome them. I will warn you, however, if you get trapped within one of their nightmares, you will die with them."

Lavrin put the piece of the Titan's Heart into his supply bag. "How do I begin?"

"You should reconsider. The lives of your friends are no reason to…" Lavrin stopped listening and placed his hand on Kyra's shoulder. He yelled out in pain and felt his strength drain away.

*****

Lavrin grinned. He was greeted by warm lights, rose bushes and spreading elm trees. The smell of honeysuckle was faint in the air. "What a beautiful place," Lavrin said. He walked around the garden taking in the aromas and pleasurable sights. What could possibly go wrong here?

He had not seen Kyra, until he heard her nearby. He found her on an elegant stone bench on the edge of a tranquil lake. She was seated with three other people. Lavrin walked up to them, but they continued talking. Soon enough, he was right next to them, but they did not notice him. He was about to say something, when he noticed Kyra was crying. He went to console her, but his hand passed right through her. That was when he remembered, he was in her dream; it was only real to her.

"You are mistaken, my dear, if you think we would ever turn from Natas to the King of Light. Natas has given us this majestic area all to ourselves. What has the King ever done for us?" the tallest of the three said. Lavrin, in pure ghostlike array, passed through the bench and those upon it. The two closest to Kyra resembled her strikingly. Lavrin realized these had to be her parents.

Kyra had told Lavrin many times how she longed to save her parents from Natas' clutches and bring them to the King. He knew she thought about them often. Lavrin stopped himself mid-thought when he heard Kyra starting to reply. "Father, how could you say that? I've been telling you again and again what the King has done for me, yet you say he has done nothing for us. He could do amazing things for you too, if you let him."

Her father shook his head. "Natas has warned us about people like you. You see what you want to see and hear what you want to hear from this King of yours. You should get as far away from him as you can. If you don't, you will be no daughter of ours."

Kyra's face stiffened. "Mother, will you let him speak to me that way?"

Her mother sat motionless. "Why don't you ask your friend what he thinks? I'm sure you will listen to him over anything I might say."

"Yes, Lavrin. Please let my parents know about the blessings of the King."

Lavrin stepped forward. So, they could see him after all. Before he could say anything, however, the man at the far end of the bench stood up and began to pace. "I once thought of the King as noble and just," he said. "He used to be the one I put all my trust in. But that path was a dangerous one. I abandoned him many years ago. He failed to help me in my time of need, and I was forced by his negligence to cast him aside. The King of Light is no friend of mine. He will end up costing you everything, Kyra."

Kyra got up from her seat with a fire in her eyes. "You are lying. Whoever you are, you are not Lavrin. You are... well I don't know what you are, but I hate you."

Kyra stormed off to a cluster of trees nearby. Her mother went to follow, but Kyra's father stopped her. "Give her time. She will see the true glory of Natas soon enough."

"Now is her time of weakness. Now is the best time to convince her to join our cause."

Kyra's father stopped his wife once again. "All in due time. She is close. She is very close."

Lavrin looked intently at the false version of himself. He had the same face, same demeanor and same voice. Lavrin felt like vomiting. This was getting too strange. Never in his wildest dreams had he thought he would see a copy of his own self.

He realized he had to go and help Kyra. He had to save her, now more than ever. Was she really going to join Natas? She had been betrayed by her parents, who Lavrin now considered to be pure evil incarnate. Maybe her real parents were decent people, but these dream-inspired parents were bent on destruction - destruction of Kyra's faith in the King.

Lavrin ran to find Kyra, but could not see her anywhere. He then remembered what had happened in his vision. Maybe he could find Kyra another way. Lavrin wished he could have seen the beginning of her nightmare. He cleared his thoughts, dwelling only on his longing to get to her. "Get to Kyra." His mind echoed his heart.

Lavrin opened his eyes and there she was. She was beyond miserable and past distraught. She covered her face with her hands to hide the torrent of tears. Lavrin knew how emotional Kyra could be at times, and how large her heart was. This was beyond anything he thought her capable of, though. She seemed broken beyond repair, and almost to the point of mental abandonment.

Lavrin could stand it no longer. "Kyra. Can you hear me, Kyra?"

She looked up, but saw no one. "Get away from me, Lavrin. You have abandoned all that you have ever stood for. You are a wicked soul. Don't come anywhere near me."

"Kyra, I am not the Lavrin who sat with you beside the lake. That was not the real me, and you know it. I heard what you said to that man, and it was completely true. He is not Lavrin. I am Lavrin. I…"

"Prove it."

Lavrin went to reply, but cut himself off. He searched himself for a sign. Something to prove his character. "Do you remember when we stood looking into the horizon at Saberlin?"

"Yes," she said. Lavrin could tell there was a reluctance in her voice. It troubled him.

"Well, before they let you go free, you asked me why I had chosen to free you. I dwelt on that question long after you escaped, hoping you had reached safety. You were what kept me going during the long days of slavery. The King guided my steps and reminded me how much I wanted to see you again, free and protected. I would not have changed my decision for all the money in the world. The King saved you for a reason, Kyra. You have been the peace in the chaos of our adventures and have centered our team on hope and loyalty. I need you to wake up from this, Kyra. I need you to wake up."

She smoothed her dress. "How can I?"

"This is a dream. An illusion. Focus on that. What you see around you and what you've been told are lies. You need to go and confront your fears."

She left the woods and headed toward her parents. She was invigorated, even though she doubted if the Lavrin she heard was real.

Kyra readied herself. In front of her were her three targets. She had to face them. She had to overcome them. The world around her suddenly felt cold, and chills clung to her like the first frost of winter. The trees no longer appeared jubilant and the birds no longer sang. Every step took great effort. Every breath was sharp and thin.

Kyra caught herself just before she fell back into despondency. She stopped, closed her eyes, and moved on. Lavrin had told her to focus. He said that was how he went through his trial. She trusted him, and set her mind to facing her fears. By the time she was a short distance from her parents, Kyra knew exactly what to say. "You need to understand something."

Her parents, who had been talking with the alternate Lavrin, spun to face her. "Yes, what is it, dear?" Kyra no longer found her mother's voice soothing, or even caring.

"I will continue to insist upon your acceptance of the King, and will not stop until I have enough evidence to prove to you that he is worth it. He is worth every bit of trust I place in him and every ounce of faith I hold in him."

Kyra waited for her parents to respond, but was appalled to hear Lavrin answer instead. "What about what I told you? The King abandoned me and left me for ruin. He took every ounce of faith that I had placed in him and left it to rot. Don't you see that..."

247

Kyra was all too happy to interrupt. "I don't care about you or what you say. You are not the real Lavrin, and you have no part in my life. I can tell by your words and your character that you are sputtering more lies than anyone I have ever known. I will not listen to a word you say. This is between me and my parents. Get away from us."

At that exact moment, the wicked Lavrin was vaporized into dust and ashes. He was nothing more than a cloud of smoke, gone to haunt her no longer. It was that supernatural display that reassured Kyra that nothing she had seen was real. She looked her parents over. Would they disperse, as well? Kyra waited for them to mystically disappear, but they remained unchanged.

In fact, they seemed completely unaltered by Lavrin's banishment. Kyra was thrown off guard by her parents' display. They appeared utterly emotionless, with faces of stone and eyes of steel that did not look anywhere but straight at her. Were they even human?

It struck her as fast as lightning. They were not human. They were not even real. More than ever, Kyra wanted to get out of the bewildering scene. She wanted out. She kept in mind what Lavrin had told her, what the real Lavrin had told her. He had escaped by concentrating on the fact that nothing before him was real, and by facing his fears. Those were not her parents. That was not her father. That was not her mother. She tried to calm her pounding heart, but it continued to pulse rapidly. "Mother, Father, I need to tell you something. I no longer care what you think about me, or if you shun my love for the King. I will never stop trying to win you over to the light, but I will stop letting what you say affect me. You have no hold on me."

*****

Kyra jerked up from the ground and gasped for air. It took several seconds before she felt she could breathe. The first thing noticed were the darkened trees. Their black limbs stretched out toward her, hoping to grab her by their fingers.

Kyra could not control her unruly nerves and adrenaline. She felt a hand on her shoulder. She spun about to see Lavrin, who whispered, "It's alright, Kyra. You're free now."

She was about to flee, but this was not the Lavrin from her nightmare. This one had the gentle gaze and kind words that she always remembered. Kyra embraced Lavrin and began to weep. "It was too real. You were there, but you were not. Now you are here, but…"

Lavrin held her up from collapsing. "There, there," Lavrin began as if consoling a frightened child. "It's going to be fine, Kyra. I'm here for you. It's okay." He let Kyra pour out her distress until her anxiety subsided.

Lavrin gently laid Kyra down and approached the living shadows. "How dare you do this to her! You are monsters. Wake up my friends, or else I'll…" Lavrin stopped. What could he do to such powerful beings?

"How dare we? We are the protectors of sacred treasures that should never fall into any hands but our own. If you did not want to see your friends in agony, you should have come on this journey alone. The Titan's Heart is a powerful tool, and should not be dealt with lightly. We commend you on saving your friend; no one has been able to do so before.

"We have seen some warriors defeat their own fear, but fall forever asleep at the hands of their allies. They knew how to deal with their own fear, but not the fears of others. She was strong and her fear was weak; you were lucky to have such odds in your favor. We will let you know, however, that the longer your allies lay in their torment, the harder it shall be to waken them."

Lavrin stomped away from them. "You clearly have never met followers of the Light." Somehow, he knew they heard him. Lavrin knelt again beside his friends. Right as he was about to place his hand on Nadrian, Kyra said in a weak voice, "Wait, Lavrin. You're not going to leave me with those creatures, are you?"

"I must save the others. You need to rest. I will always be with you." He placed his hand upon his chest. "I will always be in your heart." He looked down at Nadrian. She was tossing about, her eyes clenched tightly shut. He had to save her. He had to save all of them. He could not live with himself any other way.

*****

A deep red and purple sunset stretched out over the horizon. Its majestic colors bewitched him. Lavrin took a step closer, focused on nothing but the sky. Suddenly, he felt the ground beneath him shift. He looked down. Nothing but sand stretched across for miles. He was in a desert. Not again. It seemed so real. He knelt and ran his fingers through the grains of sand. How could this be? The living shadows possessed a power Lavrin could not fathom. They cast their dreams upon people, preying upon the terrors already inside of them.

Suddenly, a scream pierced the evening air. "Nadrian?" Lavrin whispered. He took off toward the sound. He hardly noticed the tents he passed or the moans of nearby camels. It took far too long to reach Nadrian, but when he did, he cringed. He remembered hearing about her life growing up in the desert, but had never imagined anything like this.

Nadrian was stumbling backward, trying to ward off the thrashes of the whip. "It was an accident," she yelled. "It was not my fault." Yet it was to no avail.

Cuts ran across her face, and her arms were streaked in lines of crimson. A mob of desert nomads with whips in hand and malice at heart kept her surrounded. What could she possibly have done to deserve this? Lavrin ran closer, and pushed several of the nomads to the side. Nadrian looked up at Lavrin with blood-shot eyes. "Help me."

The words barely escaped her mouth and Lavrin sprang upon Nadrian's attacker. The coarse man stumbled back. "Get out of my way. You know nothing of our traditions."

"I don't care what your traditions are." Lavrin clenched his fist. "Let Nadrian go."

"My daughter must pay the price for her actions. What she has done cannot go unpunished."

Lavrin wanted to fight back with a sharp comment, but he was aghast. This was Nadrian's father? Her own father was beating her? Lavrin turned to Nadrian. "What did you do?"

Her eyes glared, two furious suns of emotion. "I did nothing." Her words came out slowly, emphasizing every syllable. "I was attacked. I defended myself. I tried to run away, but he gave me no other choice. I did not want to kill him; I was not even trying to."

It was at this time, Lavrin realized how different this illusion was from Kyra's. Nadrian seemed much younger, maybe fifteen. Every aspect and detail down to the clothes of the nomads seemed taken directly from one of Nadrian's memories. He would have to convince Nadrian that something that had once been real, no longer was. Lavrin knew that would be extremely hard. He did not let the word impossible enter his mind, but it crept around him, trying to find its way in.

Lavrin knew, above all else, that he would never be able to save Nadrian while the threat of pain was standing before her. The lashings of whips would only feel more and more real as time progressed. He had to get her somewhere safe. Maybe then he could help her understand. He had no time to plan beyond that, because Nadrian had been thinking the same thing. She was now on her feet, looking for any gap from which to escape. Lavrin could tell she was desperate.

Nadrian took another step toward the edge of the circle, and the nomads drew their spears. They were pointed straight at her, warding her from escape. Nadrian knew this was coming. "By law you are not allowed to kill me. You must honor our sacred traditions."

She bolted straight at one of them, barely avoiding a lash from her father's whip. The unsuspecting nomad was slammed to the ground and Nadrian fled toward the center of the camp. The other desert warriors turned and chased after her, including her father. They left Lavrin, as if he was nonexistent. He, however, was not content being left behind.

Lavrin sidestepped tents and rushed past barrels trying to keep up with the mob of angry desert dwellers. At least they had not caught Nadrian yet. Lavrin stopped himself. He turned around. Nothing. Maybe his nerves were getting the better of him. Before he could take off again, a hand covered his mouth and he felt himself being dragged downward.

Struggle as he might, Lavrin could not break free of his captor's grip. He tried to scream to no avail. Suddenly, he stopped fighting when he realized his captor was none other than Nadrian. She motioned for him to stay silent before releasing him. "Lavrin, something is terribly wrong with all this."

Lavrin lay silent. "This is exactly how I remember it happening," Nadrian continued. "I remember being whipped by my father. I remember finally being able to escape. Every one of those people who surrounded me back there were faces I had known for years. You are taking the place of my brother. He stood up for me, just as you did.

"On top of all that, I distinctly remember my brother and I hiding in this tent. I will probably be stealing a horse soon and riding off to the North. No matter what I do, I cannot stop myself from being impacted by emotion. You must stop me, Lavrin. You must find a way to stop me from leaving. The pain is too real, and I'm afraid I will not be able to endure these feelings much longer."

Lavrin realized he had been looking at this the wrong way. Nadrian knew this was not real, but felt helpless to stop it or the reactions it brought from within her. She had seen all this... felt all of this before. At least Lavrin now knew he was fighting with her, not against her. Nadrian rose to leave the tent. Lavrin grabbed her by the arm. "You told me not to let you leave."

"I have to go. Tell mother that I was always innocent. Good luck, brother."

Nadrian freed herself from Lavrin's grip and opened the tent flap. Without even knowing what was happening, Lavrin found himself saying, "May your future be bright, sister." Nadrian drew a small knife and left.

Lavrin ran his hands through his hair and shook his head. Why had he said that? This was serious. They were falling deeper into the dream. The words of the living shadows came to Lavrin like a nightmare. The longer they spent in the illusion, the harder it would be to escape. It was time for action.

The horses were not far from the tent, and the violent sun beat down upon Lavrin as he reached his destination. There was Nadrian, almost ready to gallop away. Lavrin charged in front of the horse, stopping its departure. The horse reared and Nadrian yelled, "Get out of my way!"

"No."

Nadrian grabbed the reigns. "Then I will have to run you over."

"You won't. I know who you are inside, Nadrian. You are someone who sticks to what they know is right, no matter the cost. Nadrian, you are my friend. Do not do this to me. You have to overcome this."

"It's too late, brother. I mean it's too late, Lavrin. I..."

Lavrin could tell Nadrian was struggling with her inner self. He walked up to her, hoping to get her off the horse, but she gripped the reigns tighter.

Suddenly Nadrian's father ran out in front of the horse with whip in hand. Nadrian succumbed to the terror of the moment and took off. Her father was helpless to stop her as she pushed her horse faster and faster. Lavrin, in one final effort to save Nadrian, called out, "Wait. Chan needs your help."

Lavrin watched her ride out of the camp at breakneck speed. He only hoped she had heard him. She faded into the distance. Lavrin felt a hand grab his shoulder. Before he could react, he found himself surrounded by a host of nomads. They chained him and threw him to the ground. He struggled to get back on his feet, but they shoved downward once more.

Spears pointed down toward him from all angles. Nadrian's father brandished his whip. "I should punish you instead of your sister." He held the whip so firmly that his knuckles whitened. He raised it above his head, ready to lash out at Lavrin. As it descended toward him, Lavrin readied for the worst, but it never came.

*****

The dim light of the glade was welcome compared to the sweltering rays of the desert's hot sun. Lavrin felt his brow. It was laden in sweat as if he had, in fact, been in the desert. Everything had been going wrong. How had they gotten out of there?

Lavrin sat up to see Nadrian rubbing her eyes. "You had me worried." Lavrin could hear the agony in his own voice as he spoke.

Nadrian used her bow as a crutch to help her stand. She walked toward him and helped him get up as well. "I'm glad you called out to me. I would not have wanted to stay for what happened next. Promise me one thing."

"Anything."

Nadrian's eyes grew cold and her face dimmed. "Never tell anyone about what you just saw."

Lavrin did not reply. "Why save her?" a voice from behind him said. "She does not seem very grateful."

Lavrin spun around to see none other than the living shadows who ominously began to speak in one voice. "You barely escaped. How lucky are you, Lavrin, son of Gevnor?"

Nadrian drew an arrow and aimed it toward the shadows. She moved close to Lavrin, as if to protect him. "Who are they? How do they know you?"

"They know everything about us. I call them the living shadows. They are the ones that put us in these illusions."

Nadrian fired her arrow straight at one of the shadows, but it passed through him. She drew another shaft and fired it through his head. It was a perfect shot, but the shadow was unfazed by the attack. The shadow came into the light, turning ghastly white, and stared at Nadrian with dark spectral eyes. "You cannot kill me, mortal. But I can kill you any way I desire."

Nadrian drew back. She dropped her bow and took off toward the forest. "Nadrian, no!" Lavrin yelled.

She stopped and returned to him, seeing she was not being pursued. After picking up her bow, she stood beside Lavrin, still as a rock. Lavrin made her focus on him. "Listen to me. They shall not harm you. I need you to look after Kyra. I helped her waken, but she has a serious fever."

Nadrian walked over to Kyra, making sure to stay far away from the living shadows. She bent beside her and began to help her. Suddenly, Lavrin heard Chan scream out. He rushed to his side. Chan was shaking vigorously. Lavrin grabbed his arm to try to calm him, and found himself dragged into Chan's vision.

*****

Lightning pierced the dim night sky. It thundered in disapproval of the manslaughter it had just witnessed. People fled to and fro, screaming while fires blazed. Disarray and turmoil erupted as women and children tried to evade their armed pursuers. Fiery light of the blazing pyres once called houses illuminated the area. Menacing soldiers with spiked axes and maces trampled down civilians and dragged them into captivity.

Lavrin watched the brutal display, utterly appalled. He eventually had to look away. That was when he saw Chan. He was beaten half to death and chained to a large wooden pole. Lavrin wanted to help him, to ease his suffering, but he too found himself held back by many lengths of chain. Chan wrestled with his restraints like a wild ox or a bear robbed of her cubs. Chan was more animal than human as he fought with all he had to break out of the chains. Lavrin felt Chan's agony as if it was his own.

Lavrin called out, but found his voice drowned by the torrent of noise. He tried again, but with no luck. The noises of evil and of destruction were deafening.

A man approached Chan, dragging a little girl behind him. She was too scared to cry. The brute threw her down near Chan. "Tell me where it is." Somehow, Lavrin heard those words perfectly.

"I don't know what you're talking about," Chan answered. At first Lavrin thought it was a threat, until he realized Chan had no idea. Of course, the enemy soldier did not accept this answer, and called to one of his fellow pillagers, who seized the little girl and carried her off. Chan closed his eyes as if to wash away the panicked screams of the poor soul.

When Chan opened his eyes, his interrogator had left him to help put down a small band of men. These men had armed themselves with simple farming tools to fight against the invaders. They knew they stood no chance, but could not allow their town to be ransacked without a fight. They were utterly overwhelmed by their foes.

It was too much for Chan. Lavrin heard him scream out, "Marvelous King of Light, if you hear me now, kill me please. I cannot endure this. Take my life and spare theirs."

It was after this that Chan spotted Lavrin. Lavrin wanted to help him, but did not know what to say. He whispered, "Chan," knowing there was little chance Chan could hear him.

Chan, however, received the message. Maybe he had read Lavrin's lips. "Lavrin? Are you alright?"

"Yes. Chan, what you see is not real."

Chan did not reply for some time. He pressed his head against the wooden pole and watched the destruction continue. There was no one to stop the oppression. There was no defense for the innocent. Finally, when his heart had enough, he turned back to Lavrin. "Where are the others?"

At that moment, a burly man approached Lavrin. The malicious warrior brandished a double-sided axe which he pointed toward Lavrin's neck. Chan received the message without a doubt. "I will tell you whatever you want to know."

The warrior lowered his axe and approached Chan. The area began to quiet as the rebels were put down. Lavrin knew this was his chance. With all his strength, he cried out to Chan. "This is not real! You have to wake up, Chan."

Chan stared blankly at Lavrin. Lavrin could tell he was consumed with misery. He wanted vengeance… vengeance against these mercenaries at any cost. That was an emotion too powerful to conquer with words alone.

The sharp tip of the warrior's axe pressed itself gently against Chan's neck. "Speak."

Chan bit his lip. Eventually he complied. "You have ransacked my town, killed my family and destroyed everything. What else could you possibly want from me?"

"You know."

It struck Chan between the eyes. He knew exactly what they wanted from him. Lavrin listened to Chan reveal the location of something - he did not know what. Each word was a fight, but Chan soon finished, and the brute left him and began dishing out orders to his subordinates.

Lavrin surveyed the village under a new light. This was Chan's home; this was where he had spent his childhood. Every house he had once known and every path he had traveled before. All that was left of his village now was a burial ground of hopes and dreams, and the smoldering remains of lives once cherished. Now hundreds were being hauled into slavery, helpless before their oppressors. Lavrin watched them loaded onto ships as cattle. He felt his heart race. Was that his father?

No. Lavrin shut every door to his mind. This was not real; he could not get consumed by it. This was all lies, every aspect and every moment. Lavrin wanted out, and wanted out now. He kicked and struggled, hoping to find some weakness in his imprisonment. There was none. He did not even realize that the dream was capturing him, as well.

Rain began to blanket the island, drowning out the fires and sending the nearby seas into turmoil. The blood from his beating ran off Chan's face. His entire body was scourged and afflicted. If he was not killed, he would die from the blood loss alone.

Lavrin looked down and realized he too was beaten and battered. He was at the point of death, just as Chan was. A single tear, lone and desolate, slid down Chan's cheek as he watched his enemy draw near once more. In his hand, he held the Titan's Heart, glowing majestically. Its majesty, however, spelled only wrath.

"My master shall be pleased." Chan's persecutor clutched the Titan's Heart tightly and its aura turned black.

Chan looked away. Once again, he shouted to the King, "Why must you do this to me? Why must you strip me of all I hold dear? I thought you cared for me, my King. I thought you cared for me!"

"Chan," Lavrin called to his friend through the rainstorm. "You know this is not right. The King has not done this. He has not abandoned us."

Chan paused, and caught his breath. He looked at Lavrin, then at his chains. He began to laugh. It was not a laugh of joy, but of revelation. Something had sparked. He had begun to understand the truth Lavrin had spoken. Chan nodded to him.

The evil warrior closed in on Chan and raised his axe. "Now you die."

"So be it."

As the axe fell, Chan remained smiling, and let his arms fall limp under the restraints. He closed his eyes and listened to the drizzle of the rain and the soft patter of the wind for what felt like an eternity. Then his eyes opened.

*****

"I was so blind. You helped me see." Chan wrapped his arm around Lavrin.

Lavrin was too overcome with emotion to answer. Chan helped him to his feet, but Lavrin struggled to stand. It was then that Chan noticed Lavrin's wounds had followed him from the vision. Lavrin was bloodied and bruised. His inflictions ran down both arms, and his face had drained off color.

After several attempts to remain upright, Lavrin's feet gave way, and he collapsed. Kyra, Nadrian and Chan surrounded him instantly. Kyra ran her hand over his forehead. "He needs rest," she said.

Lavrin reached up and grabbed Chan's arm. "Your home is safe."

"It never was in danger. Thanks to you, I can know my family is not in harm's way."

"You must save the others," Lavrin said before releasing Chan and laying back down.

Chan's expression grew stern. It was a daunting task. He watched his bewitched companions shivering and cringing as if they were in a blizzard. They were helpless, fighting giants too powerful to comprehend.

Chan would not be given the chance to fight beside them. When he neared Calix and placed his hand on him, nothing happened. A living shadow came up beside him. "No. You will not be allowed to save them. We shadows as you call us, are a curious race, and your friend's determination has intrigued us. He alone will act on their behalf. If he dies in the visions, the Titan's Heart will return to us once again."

Chan looked to Nadrian for support, but her gaze was downcast. "These shadows are the ones who enslaved us to these dreams, and there is nothing we can do against them. They cannot be harmed and cannot be reasoned with. We have to listen to what they say."

"Kyra, is he able to go on?"

Kneeling over the fallen hero, Kyra surveyed her patient once again. "It would not be a good idea."

Hearing this, Lavrin sat upright. "Have you so little faith in me?" He crawled up to Uminos. He stared at the living shadows who surrounded him threateningly. "You want to see determination? I will show it to you."

CHAPTER 14

FIGHTING FEAR

The blood moon showered the heavens in broken petals of light. The vibrant red contrasted the night sky - the colors of Natas. The colors of red and of black. As ominous as it was, no one cared. They focused on the living shadows, who towered above Lavrin.

Apparently, they did not take threats kindly. They drew their swords and readied to kill Lavrin where he knelt. As they went to stab him, he placed his hand on Uminos, instantly pulled into his reality.

The living shadows paused, then pulled away. As they had said, they were a curious race. Moreover, they were proud. Surely, he could not save another. Surely, in this condition they would have their relic returned to them.

Kyra watched Lavrin close his eyes as he entered Uminos' vision. She knew Lavrin should not have been the one to try to save him. Lavrin needed to recover. She hated the living shadows for forcing him onward. It was the first time she had hated anyone in a long time.

*****

Lavrin was instantly calm. He knew exactly where he was. He was in the Mazaron Mountains, in what appeared to be a Seviathan village. Lavrin could feel the tension that was weighing him down as his senses grew weary. The thin mountain air and the crowded atmosphere did not help. He found his way to the side of a building, and rested against it in its cool shade. He would find Uminos after he regained his strength. His cuts and wounds were gone, but Lavrin was nonetheless weary.

He was not the only one sitting in the shadows. Lavrin heard a voice coming from down the alleyway. "I am not alone. I have friends. They will find me. I am not a mistake."

Lavrin turned to see Uminos with his face in his hands. He was shaking as he rocked himself back and forth. It was as if he was having a nightmare inside of this nightmare. Lavrin went to his friend and sat beside him, wondering what had happened. Then Lavrin knew. On the other side of Uminos sat a living shadow, whispering destructive words.

The living shadow had physically entered the vision as Lavrin had, but Uminos could not see him. Is that what had happened beside the graves? It must have been. The voice from his own nightmare was the same voice torturing Uminos.

This had to stop. The longer Uminos listened to such things, the more likely it was that he would believe them. "Uminos, don't listen to him."

"Get away from me, Lavrin."

Instead of being stunned by the harsh comment, Lavrin became even more determined. That voice had sounded more like a living shadow's than Uminos'. Uminos was being taken over. "Whatever he is telling you is not true."

Uminos looked to Lavrin with disdain. "That's just it. Everything he is telling me is true, I've just been too blind to see it. He's told me what I need to hear. He's shown me where my trust really belongs."

"I don't understand."

Uminos scoffed. "Of course you don't. For all my life I've been the outcast, running here and there, stealing whatever I can. I have never had anyone look out for me. I thought that when I joined your team it would be different, but now I see that none of you have ever been my friends. I expected you to watch my back, but you look at me as if I'm some weapon to throw at your enemies. You've never asked what my dreams are for the future."

"Uminos, don't you see? That is because out of everyone on team, you are the one I am surest of. I know you are steadfast in your desire to make up for what you did in the Mazaron, but you have no need to. You were not yourself at that moment and…"

"Yes, I know you have forgiven me of that. That is a burden I left behind in the desert. What you are too blind to see is how the others look at me. For all my years living in the worst of conditions, those who should be the most kind turn a deaf ear.

"Kasandra looks at me with bitterness, still holding Rowan's death over my head. Kyra looks at me with fear, unsure what I'm capable of because I'm a Seviathan. Chan views me as someone who needs to be watched, lest I lose control of my mind again. Felloni views me as a weapon, something that could do a lot of damage if handled right. Nadrian sees me as a stranger. Shall I go on?"

"No." Lavrin looked downward, his hands folded together. The more he thought about it, the more he realized what Uminos was saying was true. "I give you my word that I will make this right."

Uminos was not content with this answer. "Do not make promises for someone else. There is no way you can change what is already in their hearts. Besides, I haven't mentioned how you look at me."

"How do I look at you, Uminos?"

"How about you ask yourself that."

There was a hostility forming between them; Lavrin could feel its icy presence in the air. Lavrin's word would be of little use if Uminos did not believe him. He knew he had to keep trying. "Whether or not the others realize it, you are an incredibly important member of the team."

"That's the question, though. Why am I important? What am I useful for besides being thrown into the heat of battle?"

The living shadow stood beside Uminos, continuing to whisper words of discord. Uminos did not fight against him, but listened to him as if he were a friend. Lavrin could tell now that the shadows wanted revenge, and would do anything to get it. If anyone deserved freedom from this captivity, it was Uminos. For so long, his mind had not been his own, and once again chains were wrapped around his conscience. Uminos was being imprisoned all over again.

"When we first arrived in the desert, and everything seemed to fight against us, you held us together. You bravely came to rescue us and remained loyal to the King, even as civil war almost broke lose. You stood beside us in the labyrinth while our limits were put to the test. Without you, we would not have made it this far. I know that the King will use you in many ways.

"Don't focus on what others think of you; focus on one day being in the presence of the King. Picture him thanking you for the stand you have taken. Picture him thanking you for carrying the banner of the Seviathans into a brighter Amcronos. Is that not enough?"

Uminos paused, and color returned to his eyes. He replied with a sense of honesty and sadness. "How am I to take a stand if no one sees me as their ally?"

"Uminos, I have watched you grow in your faith even when the rest of us were struggling. In the desert, you continued to persevere through more trials than I could count. You gave me the courage to fight on, and now I'm trying to do the same for you. If that is not friendship, I don't know what friendship is."

The living shadow that had plagued Uminos retreated to a mere afterthought. Now in the light, Uminos approached Lavrin and reached out his hand. "I will come back with you. I have had enough of this nightmare."

Lavrin shook Uminos' hand firmly. "You knew this was an illusion?"

"Yes. The shadow told me everything. He really told nothing but the truth. He just twisted how I saw the truth, as Jafer once did. I told myself 'never again,' but it seems I have once again fallen for the same lies. They were so captivating, and got me thinking down all the wrong paths. My curiosity got the better of me. I could not leave while I had that voice inside my head. You never did answer my question, though."

"What question was that?" The two walked into the open square, and watched the Seviathans who lived there.

They seemed more real than anything Lavrin had seen in the other dreams. In the other visions, the setting was real, but the people were ever so slightly fake. Too edgy. Here they were perfect. The living shadows were improving in their horrifying ways. For Uminos to have known this was a vision... Lavrin knew there was more to Uminos than met the eye.

He scratched his scaly neck. "What am I good for besides fighting?"

"I tell you what," Lavrin answered. "Whenever I have time, I will tell you all that I know about being a blacksmith. I think you would quite enjoy the trade. Maybe when this war is over, you could start your own shop."

The village around them faded, and a bright light pierced the horizon. "I will hold you to that," Uminos said with a smirk.

"You had better," Lavrin replied.

*****

Without so much as a cringe, Uminos got up from the ground and reunited with his companions. Something about his Seviathan endurance had prepared him to awaken. He had been ready to return to the glade, and had no trouble adjusting to the light.

On the other hand, Lavrin appeared almost unearthly. His pupils had faded from a sharp black to a pale gray, and white marks ran down his arms and face. They looked like scars from a great battle, only without a trace of blood. Their ivory white and steel gray stood out upon Lavrin's skin like the plague. Only they were not sores, but almost engravings on his very skin.

When Kyra asked the living shadows about his condition, they told her it was the price of being in too many dreams for too long. Lavrin had been inflicted with a poison of the mind, which would grow worse the deeper he went into the visions. She continued to pester them about this illness, until they told her that, like scars, the white marks may last him the rest of his life. If Lavrin entered another dream, he could go blind or have trouble breathing for years to come.

Lavrin pulled Kyra aside. He had been listening to their conversation. The living shadows did not follow them as he had expected, but watched from a distance. Kyra could not look Lavrin in the eye, for the sight of him was horrifying. "Lavrin, we need to get you out of here. This place is cursed, and I will not watch your condition get any worse."

"What if I'm not even sick?" Lavrin asked. "These beings are masters of illusion. For all I know, this is a trick to get me to leave our friends as their prisoners. I feel completely fine."

"What if it is real? What if the moment you come back from saving someone you are blind for good? Lavrin, I cannot bear to see you like this."

Lavrin went to comfort her, but she pulled back. She buried her face in her hands as Lavrin had watched Uminos do moments before. Lavrin could do nothing to keep her from running away. He knew there was nothing he could do. He needed guidance.

He went to Chan, but Chan could not look him in the eye, either. Lavrin knew whatever was happening to him was serious. Lavrin needed answers. "Chan, I trust you as a friend and a leader. I need to know if I should try and save someone else before it is too late. The longer they stay in there, the worse their odds."

Chan ran his hand across his temple. "If you go on, it might mean your death. There is still a chance that the others could overcome their own fears and awaken. I agree, however, that we cannot sit by and do nothing. We should try and bargain with these living shadows. They said they are collectors of rare artifacts. We could offer them everything we own to get the others free. We have armor from the Haven Realm, and even Calix's necklace if we are desperate.

"I say we leave this place as fast as we can. Nadrian is angry, Kyra is clearly distraught, I am trying to hold myself together and you look half-dead. Uminos seems like the only one who is alright, probably because he has experience with this kind of thing. What do you think we can afford to give the shadows?"

"Anything but the other part of the Titan's Heart. I doubt the shadows are in the market for weapons. They want something of value. I have an idea."

Lavrin approached Felloni, and carefully removed the book of the King's histories, making sure not to be drawn into his nightmare. He took the precious book to the living shadows. It contained hundreds of the most valuable stories to the followers of the Light. It was one of a dozen or fewer in all Amcronos. After Lavrin proposed the trade, one of the living shadows took the book and scrolled through it. "This Matthais... the one who wrote this. He was a friend of yours, yes?"

"Yes, he was. He helped my friends in a time of trouble and gave this to them. I did not get to know him as I would have liked, but I will not forget what he did for my team."

The shadow looked at the book once again, then handed it back to Lavrin. "That is the problem. Neither you nor your friends knew this Matthais for long, and do not have a deep connection with this book. We only collect items that hold a special importance to their previous owner. That knife, for example, the one from your childhood, is something we would be interested in."

Lavrin brought out the knife and held it in front of him. For the last time, he felt its smooth case and gazed upon its exquisite emblem of the King. Though the handle had since worn out and the blade had started to rust, the knife retained its former beauty. It was one of the only

remnants of his childhood he had left. It was one of the
only things left from before the fire. Lavrin handed it over
to the shadows. The past was worth losing for a better
future. This mindset, however, was not one the living
shadows held to.

They received it with pleasure. "We shall heal you
from your sickness so that you can try to save your other
friends. Keep in mind, they have been under our control
for some time now. There is one relic greater to us than all
others. That is the relic of human lives. We will not part
with them easily. I would leave now, lest you lose your life
and your Titan's Heart."

Already feeling his spectral scars disappearing,
Lavrin returned to the place where his friends lay battling
their own selves. He could tell Grax was relatively calm
and seemed in the least danger. That is, compared to the
others. Lavrin decided that if anyone had the strength to
outmatch his fears, it was Calix. With that in mind, Lavrin
walked toward Felloni and Kasandra. From what he could
tell, Kasandra was struggling to remain in the fight. Felloni
would have to wait.

*****

He had been expecting a battle on a mountainside or
a rebellion tearing through a village. Instead, Lavrin was
greeted by dark expanse, lit by nothing save a single
candle. The candle was on a pillar or column of some sort
which seemed stable, though there was nothing for it to be

set upon. Lavrin knew that if the candle's light failed, the darkness would envelop everything.

Lavrin doubted Kasandra was afraid of the dark. There was something else going on. As he moved toward the candle, he began to hear shouting. There was anger and distress in both voices, but the sound was distorted by the darkness. With some effort, Lavrin made out Kasandra's voice. The other voice he recognized, but could not quite remember.

Soon enough, he found Kasandra. Whoever she was shouting at, he could not see. "Kasandra, what is going on?"

She turned his direction, but looked past him. Apparently, he was as invisible to her as the other voice was to him. "Who's there?" she asked. "Rowan, did you hear that?"

That was other voice... Rowan. It made sense now. Of course, Kasandra would think of Rowan. His death had likely been on her mind ever since he passed at the Seviathan fortress. Lavrin listened as Kasandra and Rowan returned to their argument. It took Lavrin a few moments to piece it all together.

"I did everything I could to save you," Kasandra said.

Rowan's words were anything but forgiving. "You may have done everything then, but you have let my memory fade so very quickly. You buried me, then ran off with your new friends as if I was no longer important. As if leaving our village to rebuild itself was not enough, you joined a group with my very killer."

"He had no choice."

"That's what he wants you to believe. You have no idea when he will turn on you. He is a wild beast that you have allowed to roam freely. He should not even be alive at this moment. You should have stopped him from shooting me."

Kasandra could no longer stand upright. She fell to her knees. Lavrin watched the candle's flame weaken. Kasandra looked at Rowan, terrified. "What could I possibly have done? What do you want me to say?"

"It's not what I want you to say, it's what I want you to do. I want you to honor the creed we formed long ago. Do you remember it? We said we'd watch each other's family if anything happened. Well, something has happened. I expect you... no, I demand you to make sure my family is safe. You owe me that much. What is this team to you, anyway? They're nothing more than a group of ragtag adventurers, seeking glory by chasing whatever they fancy. They should mean nothing to you."

"They are much more than that to me."

"I want you to listen to me very carefully." Rowan acted like a father, correcting the wrongs of a wayward daughter. "The first thing you must do to ensure my family's safety is kill Uminos. If he killed me, he may want to hurt those around me. Then you must steal the piece of the Titan's Heart from Lavrin. It will be useful. After that, you must leave the group somewhere they cannot escape, so that they do not follow you. Once you return to my family, tell them that I love them and that I will try to be with them shortly. I have been planning to return to Amcronos for some time. The Haven Realm is nothing more than a prison to me."

Kasandra drew one of her spears and extended it toward Rowan, threatening to stab him straight through the heart. She pulled it back; she could never hurt him. "Rowan, this is madness. You cannot seriously expect me to betray my friends. They have done nothing but take me in."

"They may be your friends, but I am your cousin. We are united by blood and by heritage. When I see you in a few months, I will make sure we rebuild the Mazaron to the glory it once was, with our village as its capitol."

Lavrin did not speak, knowing that until the conversation settled, he would not be able to say anything to Kasandra. She continued to battle against Rowan's comments, which gave Lavrin hope.

The candle's light was growing stronger. "Why would you possibly want to escape the Haven Realm?" Kasandra asked. "We were raised on stories of its majestic cities filled with beautiful sculptures and glorious paintings. You yourself told me about how much you longed to see it.

I will never, no matter what you testify to, believe that the Haven Realm is a prison."

"I was wrong. It's my tomb. Trust me, if you were here you would want to escape as well. I thought you were my friend, Kasandra. I thought you would help me get out of here."

Kasandra paced the empty space. "Rowan, it's just not that simple. I want to help you, I do, but how? It just doesn't make any sense."

"It will make sense if you help me. Why do you not return to the Mazaron now? You will die if you continue on this fool's crusade. Turn back. You have no quarrel with me. Your mission is already accomplished. We freed our homeland, that is enough."

She almost wavered. "If this quest fails, our homeland may not stay free for long. I have to keep going."

Enraged and utterly engulfed in fury, Rowan's voice shook the ground. It did not sound human any longer. "You shall not defy me."

As the tension reached a point of no return, Lavrin saw his chance. "She shall stand." Lavrin heard his voice begin to rise with the eerie power present in Rowan's. "She shall tear down the walls of your deception and break through your defenses. Kasandra is a follower of the King, and shall always live to defy you and your tyranny, Natas. For now, I see you as you are, and you shall fall to the ground begging for your life before the tip of the King's sword.

"You are not Rowan, but you are the Lord of Balyon himself. I will not let Kasandra listen to you any longer. You have seen the Haven Realm before, but you shall never see it again until taken there in chains."

What had once been a candle turned into a blazing wildfire which could have made any forest shake. It leapt toward the voice of darkness and consumed Natas in its attack. Lavrin had thought the fire was the symbol of Kasandra's will. As it turned out, it was not a symbol of her will, but of his own.

*****

He did not awaken to the soft glow of the glade, or to the frightened faces of those he held close. He awoke to a cage of dark iron, knotted and twisted as if it had grown out of the ground like an unruly weed.

Lavrin realized his clothing was torn on all sides. It was as if he was a criminal, and he was not alone. Felloni also sat in a cage, dressed in shambles. In his usual manner, he was utterly still, but Lavrin could tell he was dying on the inside. There was a tint in his eyes he had only seen once before.

Felloni was angry, terribly angry, there was no denying that. But why? That was the question Lavrin needed answered. It was the first thing he asked whenever he entered someone else's nightmare. Why?

It did not take Felloni long to notice Lavrin. "Don't look down."

Lavrin, of course, was curious, and looked down. Now he could see why that was the first thing Felloni had said. Lavrin could barely make out the ground hundreds of feet below, and what he saw did not encourage him. They were on an island of sharp, grey rock surrounded by roaring waves. There was no possible way of escape. The coastline of the island was littered with dead men's bones. Violent waters stretched out in every direction. It was mesmerizingly terrifying.

Felloni waited until Lavrin took his gaze off the distant ground and back at him. "So, have you come to mock me, as well?"

Up to that point, Lavrin had been too confused to hear it, but now he could tell there were shouts coming up from the tower to which they were chained. They were aimed toward Felloni; apparently, they wanted him dead. They echoed and chanted desires to torture him. They did not stop shouting his name, nor did they stop taunting him. "Who are those men?" Lavrin asked.

"They are enemies of my past. They have imprisoned me here and haunt me with memories of things I should have done. There are so many, I can never prevail against them." Felloni moved to the edge of his cage and shook it violently. "You win," he shouted to his enemies. "You locked me up like a wild animal. Go ahead and get it over with."

283

They spat at him and drew their weapons, as they looked at him with disgust. Had Felloni not been in his cage, they might have killed him then and there.

"Felloni," Lavrin said. "They have not defeated you yet. I don't know what happened in the past, but I do know that no wrong you did to them matters now. We are on a mission to save Amcronos. Our mission shall more than make up for any missteps of long ago."

"I admire your spirit, but these men are of the worst kind. They were murderers, swindlers and thieves, and no doubt still are. I could have stopped them. Their sneers and jests are only barely louder than the crying voices of those I should have saved. I do not know which I find worse. You do not know the things I have done."

With the plethora of threats and jeers slung at Felloni, Lavrin found it hard to focus. How much did he really know about what Felloni had done? Could it be that... no. Although he and Felloni had not always seen eye to eye, Felloni was someone he could trust.

He had only ever seen him do what was right. The past was the past, and Lavrin knew there was nothing that would change that. "Then we will hunt them down."

This was the exact opposite of what Felloni expected to hear. He had presumed Lavrin would wonder what had happened between him and his enemies or how they had captured him. Instead, Lavrin seemed not only forgiving of his past, but willing to help him fix it. The only thing Felloni could think of to say was, "It will be hard."

"When this is over, I'm sure we will find a way."

"You're not at all curious?"

"Of course, I'm curious. But the truth is, what you did before does not matter. What matters is that you strive to serve the King. Maybe someday I will tell you about times I wished I was stronger or wished I had chosen a different path. It's not what you do to your enemies that matters; it's what you do for your friends."

"Please do not tell the others." Felloni's eyes were bloodshot, the inner wounds he relived left him feeling all too vulnerable.

"Trust me, I have plenty of things I would not want to share either. You must make up for your mistakes and own up to the consequences. That will be a challenge enough. No man should have to face that while his companions wonder about his loyalties. I would not do this to you. Although we bickered in the desert, that was the moment above all else when I could tell that you stick to your values. I believe these values hold true to the King's ways. That is enough for me."

Felloni mulled over each word Lavrin said. "You would still trust me after seeing how many enemies I have? I was not always a good man. Before I met Nadrian and Chan, I did some terrible things."

285

Lavrin was unwavering. "And since then, you have more than changed from those ways. I could tell in Hightenmore when you chose to stay in Amcronos, that you were a man of honesty. Decisions like that do not go unnoticed. They are remembered for generations. Whatever battles you still need to fight after we claim the Titan's Heart, you must go on and fight them.

"You were lost, confused and untrained. Now you are strong, passionate and talented. You will find those battles will look much less intimidating when you face them one at a time. I don't know who you used to be, but I know who you are now. I trust that the man I see before me will not stop, will not rest, until he has done what must be done. Just remember one thing: do it all in the name of the King."

Felloni nodded.

He knew what he had to do, and he could not do it in a cage.

*****

There was no rest, no relief for Lavrin. How greatly he could have used it. How sweet the rest would have been. Alas, it was not to be. He decided that the shadows were trying to overwhelm him by sending him from one vision to the next without delay. There was nothing he could do but go on.

He did not feel the physical strain of these events now, but knew that when he did awake, all their weight would collapse upon him. He could only hope that the weight would not be too heavy. There were only two of his friends left. This had him wondering - was he in Grax's dream or Calix's?

Thundering applause echoed down the hallway, as if a triumphant speech had just finished. Lavrin first noted the smooth stone walls and the torches lighting a path directly toward the noise. Obviously, that was where he headed.

He made his way there, all the while thinking about his two remaining friends. Out of all the group, he had the least idea what they feared. He had always known Grax as someone who was strong and sure-footed. His honesty and loyalty were all but impossible to rival.

Grax seemed impervious to fear. Likewise, he had been with Calix for as long as he could remember, and had seen no trace of a hidden fear in him. Lavrin felt like he would have known Calix's secret by now, if he had one.

As Lavrin turned the corner toward the noise, he beheld hundreds, if not thousands, of warriors clad in the black armor characteristic of Natas' army. Some even wore red capes, a sign given to those who stood guard for Natas. Lavrin entered the massive hall and saw many of Natas' generals, but not the dark lord himself. Some of them he even recognized, and shuddered.

There was Zekern, and Jafer was not far away. Each malevolent leader seemed to be giving a speech, directing their comments toward a man on the far end of the podium.

The recipient of the high praise was blocked from Lavrin's vision. After some effort, Lavrin worked his way to a place in the crowd where he could see Grax seated on a bronze throne. His fists were clenched and pressed against his forehead. Every word seemingly said in his honor he hated, and Lavrin could tell why.

He at last made out a comment. "It has been encouraging to witness how brutally Grax has fought against the ways of the King. We will soon not only see him clad in a red cape, but possibly as Natas' right hand man. He has truly earned this right. He has helped us murder those who stand against us, and for that we are truly grateful. Thank you for all that you have done, Grax; with your malice and cold-hearted greed, we are closer than ever to killing the King."

Grax tried to scream out, but somehow his voice had been taken from him. Although this was supposed to be a grand ceremony, to him it was more of an execution. Lavrin knew he had to get to him, before his mind deceived him and he believed this was reality. He wanted to get Grax out of here quickly. He felt as if an executioner stood beside his friend even now.

Lavrin fought his way through the crowds. He bumped and shoved, but no one noticed. Soon enough, however, he had snaked his way to the stage. The speeches heralding Grax's commitment to Natas continued without pause, and Lavrin wondered how long this had been going on. Had Grax been listening to this for minutes? Hours? At least he was with Grax now. At least he could try and repair the damage that had been done. "Grax, I'm here. Can you hear me?"

Grax did not look his way. Everything Lavrin tried failed to get Grax's attention. It was as if he was deaf. That was when Lavrin realized that all Grax could hear was the speeches and their ensuing applause. To him, those noises were the only real ones.

Lavrin rushed to center stage and violently shoved the speaker off the podium. The crowd gasped. "What has been said of Grax is not true," Lavrin said. The crowd met him with hostile glances.

He was afraid they might rush the stage and kill him. Nonetheless, he continued. "You have said Grax is an evil man, bent on destroying the King and his followers. This could not be farther from reality. I have watched Grax stand against the forces of evil, not for his own glory, but for the glory of the King. How anyone could think…"

Lavrin's speech was cut short when he looked away from the crowd and at Grax. Grax's eyes were consumed with grief, as if had just lost someone he loved. Although he could not speak, his gaze told Lavrin all he needed to know. "This is what I could have been," Grax's expression told. "This is what would have become of me. How can I be sure that it's not still part of me?"

"It's not still part of you." Lavrin screamed both at Grax, and at the situation. "You did not choose to take this path, and that is what matters. You decided to commit your life to the service of the King. I've watched you conquer both the enemies around you and the enemies within you, time and time again. Every time you succeeded, you knew that it was not your strength that brought you the victory. The strength of the King caused your victory. The only reason I am here today is because of the courage I saw in you. You helped me survive when I should have died. Now let me help you live."

Lavrin expected the scene to fade and the glade to reappear, but this did not occur. He hoped at the very least for someone to answer him, but no noise was heard. Should he keep talking, or wait for the lull to end?

Once again, Grax seemed to speak to Lavrin in words unspoken. "I have been here for weeks. Where were you all that time? They have never stopped. Their words have never stopped."

Still nothing happened. It was as if they were waiting to see if the masses approved or disregarded Lavrin's call. The crowd did not yell foul words or gruesome remarks toward Lavrin, but rather a small quiet voice hovered over the room. Everyone heard it, but no one knew who said it. It was a living shadow, audibly interfering in its own illusion.

"Grax is mine," it said. "He has been in this hall for days on end. To him, weeks have gone without reprieve. He is destined to stay here forever. I shall never surrender him." The message was meant for Lavrin, and he received it with utmost clarity. For the first time, Lavrin felt hatred, raw and powerful, for the living shadows. They had started out as mysteries, but now they were enemies.

"Have you no morals?" Lavrin asked. "You weave traps for your victims, and then jab at them while caught in their cages? Leave Grax alone! He is my friend and brother. I will do anything to save him. You may be undefeatable in the real world, but here I have conquered you time and time again."

Instead of the shadow's regular objective nature, sounded bitter, if not enraged. He promptly changed the subject with acid in his words. "We will give you Grax if you let us have Calix."

"No! Let me have my friends back and I will give myself in their place. What you are doing to them is wrong, and they do not deserve such evil. Take me, for I am the one you have wanted this whole time. You said you were curious about me? Then claim me and release my friends."

"We will not accept you. That is not how it works."

Lavrin turned to Grax. The mighty man was clad in the finest robes, and precious gifts littered the hall about him. He hated them all. He muttered to himself inaudibly. His lips moved for himself alone. Lavrin could not read them.

"It's fun watching him beg for it to stop, isn't it," the living shadow taunted. "Oh, you can't understand him? Let me translate: 'Is this where I belong? I am a monster. How I started is how I will end. I fought so hard to remove this evil from inside me. Maybe I've been fighting it because I'm afraid. I don't know. I don't even recognize myself anymore. Who am I? What have I become?'"

The living shadow stopped just as Grax did. Lavrin and the shadow watched as the hordes of Natas' followers rushed forward. Not toward Lavrin, but toward Grax. They tore his robes and cast him to the floor. They surrounded him, punching and kicking him from back and front, left and right. Grax did not even fight back. He lay on the floor and took the beating, void of emotion.

Faithful to the end, Lavrin rushed the scene and tried to take the blows in Grax's place. They passed right through him and found their target. Lavrin turned to his friend. "Get up, Grax. Stand up."

"He cannot," the living shadow mocked. "Soon he will have even forgotten your name."

"That does not matter to me. There is one thing he will never forget. Grax, listen to me. You were given a letter from the King. You have cherished that letter ever since it was handed to you. What did it say, Grax? What did it say?"

The living shadow was irate. "It said nothing, Grax. You have forgotten it. It is lost to you now."

Grax disagreed.

*****

Lavrin's teeth were clenched, ready to verbally attack the living shadows. It was at that moment, however, that he found the soft glow of the sunlight breaking into the glade. Was he back in the glade?

The aftereffects of the visions no longer bothered Lavrin, especially when he saw Felloni and Grax reunited with the rest of the team. That moment made everything worthwhile. It was short-lived, though, because the living shadows had gathered in front of Calix and motioned for him to join them. Lavrin could tell the living shadows were not pleased. Lavrin turned to his teammates. "Get out of here now."

"You were in there for hours, Lavrin. It's now morning. What happened?" Kasandra asked.

Lavrin sighed. Time had passed very strangely. Had it been Felloni's dream which kept him? Or had he lost himself for that long in Grax's? Either way, it did not matter. "I cannot explain right now. All I can say is you need to get out of here. Leave this forest at once."

"Wait, Lavrin. You can't expect us to…" Grax was cut off.

"Yes. I expect you to leave this cursed place right now. You are not safe. These living shadows have been plotting against us, I can feel it. They may kill us all if they decide we've gone too far. I won't see you die by their swords. I will see that Calix is returned to us. We will meet outside of the forest. Get as far away from this glade as you can. Go…now!"

The team gathered their supplies and weapons, but still could not believe that they were leaving. It felt horrible, as if they were abandoning Lavrin to a cruel fate. Before departing from the glade, Chan felt Lavrin grab his arm. He pulled him aside, and handed him the piece of the Titan's Heart. "If we do not come out of the forest, you must continue on with the mission. Promise me."

Chan struggled to get the words out. "I… I promise."

He turned to leave, but Lavrin still had hold of his arm. "One more thing," Lavrin said. "If Calix and I don't make it out of here, it is up to you to comfort the others, especially Kyra. I fear these nightmares will haunt our team for years to come. Don't let them grow despondent. There is too much left to be done."

The two locked eyes and shook hands. They went their separate ways, knowing what they had to do. Chan led the group away from the glade and into the forest. Lavrin remained. He was the only one of his group left, save Calix. As Lavrin went to enter Calix's illusion, the living shadows stopped him. "You do not want to continue on this path."

"I cannot let Calix die here," Lavrin said.

"You will not survive. We are a proud race above all else, and you have threatened our power and dominance. You have taken our piece of the Titan's Heart and many of our victims. We have had enough of you. If you try and take Calix from us, you will die with him. He holds a presence that we have grown to desire. He is our greatest prize, and if you try to restore him, you will be our second greatest."

The living shadows all knelt beside Calix and laid their hands on him, as if ready to enter his nightmare. Lavrin was stunned. Did he have any chance against their combined power?

Ten of them, one Calix with Lavrin by his side. They had faced worse odds before, but not like this. Not with Calix dying. Not with foes such as these. Lavrin knelt next to his friend as the shadows had. He tried to gather himself, but instead felt the sickness returning. His head ached while his lungs seized. The shadows had only healed him so far. Maybe they had planned it this way. They must have planned it so he had no strength left for Calix.

There was only one glimmer of hope. If anyone was strong enough, it was Calix.

CHAPTER 15

NO WORDS TO EXPRESS

No fire was lit; no light shown from the heavens. It was almost completely dark, but there was just enough light for Chan to see the mortified look on each face. There was not a single person in the camp who remained joyful. Not a single word had been spoken for over an hour. It was as if only dead remnants of the once thriving team were left.

Chan tried to guess their thoughts. He hoped to catch a downcast glance or hopeful manifestation - neither came. He could hardly tell if they were breathing. They were lifeless, frozen to the point of becoming statues. It had been thirteen hours since they left Lavrin; Chan had counted. The Forest of the Unknown was still viewable from where they sat, but barely. From the hillside, the trees seemed more like blades of dark grass than tall pines. Nothing they could see gave them hope.

Although the group tried to remain focused on Lavrin's return, their thoughts returned to their visions. What if they had been real? What if the others knew about the darkest parts of who they were? Could they ever be accepted again? These questions tormented each of them, but no one had the courage left to tell the team. They were too embarrassed to speak, but too destroyed to go on without help.

After so many close calls and encounters with evil in the past, there had always been a few who tried to lighten the mood. Usually, someone sought to take the pain and transform it to something better. Not this day.

No one was hungry. Sleep was not an option. No one cared to plan the next length of their mission, or find inspiration in the King's histories. Nadrian despaired over what she had done. Uminos wondered if he would ever again find acceptance. Grax feared the inner evil that once resided in him. Felloni remembered each of his past enemies. Kyra doubted whether her parents would ever be receptive to the King. Kasandra wrestled with the thought of letting down those she loved.

Only Chan kept his mind off his fears long enough to see a torch lit in the distance. The light was barely noticeable, but it was an instant joy to him. It was simply a firefly's light now, but Chan knew that as it approached, Lavrin would appear, as well. Surely enough, through the swaying grass and heavy air, came Lavrin. He held something in his arms.

As Lavrin drew near, Chan realized that it was not something he carried, but someone. It was Calix. Chan rushed over to help Lavrin, but the rest of the camp was oblivious to his arrival. Their trances had them locked away in deep places. Places a mind never explored, and for good reason.

Before explaining anything, Lavrin laid Calix down. "Why is there no fire?"

"What happened back there? Is everything..." Chan was cut off.

"Everything is fine. Get a fire going right now."

Chan gathered the remaining firewood and stacked it in a pile. He tenaciously searched for any rocks he could find and formed the base of the pit. Lavrin threw his torch into the branches and logs, and the fire consumed the dry grass below. No time was wasted as Lavrin took Calix and put him beside the fire. "That should help."

"Help what?" Chan asked.

"I'll explain later. In the meantime, we need to get him something to drink."

Chan found his flask after a few seconds and handed it to Lavrin. He watched Lavrin give the water to Calix in short spurts. At first Calix rejected it, but eventually he was able to drink. No one else in the camp budged. Did they even see him? Lavrin unraveled his blanket and laid it on top of his friend. Once everything had been set to Lavrin's standards, he pulled Chan aside, and they walked away from the camp.

It was some time before Chan heard about Lavrin's final confrontation with the living shadows. Chan had to piece together Lavrin's broken sentences. His words were filled with pain. "It was… how could I never have known. My best friend and… maybe the living shadows forced him to think that…"

"Slow down, Lavrin. Tell me exactly what happened," Chan said.

"When I entered Calix's dream, everything was wrong. Calix had gone far deeper in his nightmare than I had guessed. An unnatural sense of evil clouded the vision, probably because of all the living shadows. What I saw in there is something I should probably not tell anyone, but for your sake, and for Calix's, I will. The vision took us to many places, and we only stayed at each one for a few minutes. Where we went was not what troubles me, it was what happened there.

"Death. Over and over Calix was dying, right before my eyes. At one time, he was in a lake, chained beneath the waters; in another, he was falling from a cliff. In battles, he was one of the fallen. In another instant, disease captured him in its snare. The hours I spent trying to stop Calix from his fate were to no avail. It felt like days on end. I only just released him less than an hour ago."

Chan expected Lavrin to finish the story, but he never did. He appeared on the verge of a breakdown, toying with his fingers and staring hard at the ground. "How did you escape?" Chan realized that if Lavrin did not focus, he may fall to a fate worse than that of the others. He was on the brink of destroying himself.

As Chan had hoped, Lavrin righted himself. "It was as if something snapped. There was a loud crack, as if glass had shattered. It distracted the living shadows, and gave Calix enough time to free himself. Or enough time to listen to me... I don't even know if he heard me... but something changed after that. I can't explain it, but it seemed as if some force pulled us from the dream. When I awoke in the glade, Calix was shaking tremendously, but I knew he was awake.

"I got him out of those woods as fast as I could. The living shadows chased after us, but I dove out of the woods before they reached us. I'm afraid I might have taken too long. Calix's muscles have seized, and he looks on the brink of freezing to death. It's not even cold. He may still be recovering from it all, but I..." Lavrin's voice snapped. He barely had enough left in him to say. "I hope he can recover."

"He will recover. I'm sure of it." Chan hated telling Lavrin something he himself was unsure of. One thing Chan did know: Lavrin had not told him half the horrors that had occurred in Calix's nightmare. Lavrin was hiding something. Maybe a lot. Chan knew it was not his place to ask. "Now we need to get back to camp so that you can get some sleep."

"Absolutely not. I will take the night shift."

"You need to rest."

"I need to help Calix."

Chan had nothing to say against that. It was not long before the two returned. Tents had been set up; that was a good sign, but it was all too clear that no one would sleep this night. They were far too tired to sleep. Lavrin found himself a comfortable spot near the fire and thought about the new weight on his shoulders. Not only had he battled his own darkness, but now he had to carry the darkness of every other member of the team.

Did he even have the right to see what he had seen? Some things were better left unknown. He sacrificed knowing their greatest secrets in exchange for their lives. He longed to share everything with someone. If he could have someone else see what he had seen and feel what he had felt. Maybe Chan…

No, as much as that would help, he owed it to his friends to cherish their secrets. Lavrin told himself that the only place and the only time he would share this knowledge was as a team in the Haven Realm. Maybe then, but not before. In Amcronos, secrets were too damaging to share. Across the crystal sea was different.

He could never see his friends in the same way. When he looked at them he would see their darkest fears and greatest regrets. Though he hated everything about it, this was not what troubled him most. Lavrin was most afraid of how the others would look at him. Would they hate him for the things he had witnessed? Would they want him to help them, or to forget it had ever happened? Most of all, could they still trust him?

The morning could not come soon enough, but every second seemed to span a decade. There was nothing to do but wait. Lavrin thought about the living shadows. As much as he longed to, he could not focus on the present or the future, only what he had witnessed in the glade. It was as if a part of him was still there. He realized it was his innocence he had forfeited, and instead he now had a responsibility beyond anything he had ever shouldered before.

Lavrin knew he would have to help keep this team going at any cost. Their mission would help the forces of Light triumph over Natas. Lavrin's thoughts turned to the forces of the Light in the North. Were they facing enemies as great as the living shadows? He did not know what trials they may be encountering, but could only hope they would continue onward.

They had to continue onward; Amcronos was at stake.

CHAPTER 16

THEY COME FOR WAR

They had seen the enemy mounting on their doorstep. War was coming. For the last few hours, they had watched Natas' ranks take up positions against them. Both sides knew a battle was coming, and both were taking every measure to gain the upper hand. Auden, Denethor and Quinn went back and forth over every aspect of the battle plan. They had already planned everything, but they had started second-guessing their decisions.

The keen eyes of Quinn's hawkers had already mapped most of the army mounting against them. Reports were coming in to the lords from the hawkers… and they all said the same thing. The forces they were facing were almost four times as large as their own, but the hawkers had seen no signs of dark creatures on their sides. It was an army of men, and men alone. No matter how many of them there were, Auden knew they could challenge them. The only issue was how to maximize their creatures without risking loss.

Back and forth the discussions went. Denethor would say one thing, and Quinn would propose something else. Auden would counter one idea, just to have his own countered. The three lords wished they had Warren with them. A fourth opinion could mean everything. They almost called for him, but he needed to heal. Eventually, the plan had been revised, and the three left the table to instruct the men. It was a risky strategy, one that might fail or might succeed based on every action the enemy made.

The forces of Light could not attempt a frontal assault on an enemy with such numbers; they would be overrun without question. This left them one option - bring the enemy to them. They owned the high ground, meaning Natas' troops would have to charge up the hills for an attack.

Auden made sure that every man who could wield a bow had one in his hands. The stone golems could hold off most of the frontal assault, so they would not have use of shield bearers. Every spare bow and quiver was handed out, and the stone golems were spread along the eastern and southern perimeters. Between the stone golems, swordsmen of Pelios brandished their longswords. They stood tall, ready to uphold the honor of their people.

Everyone accepted the formation willingly, everyone except for the Xalaians who were not content being in the reserves. Their blood ran hot from the loss of their leader, and they longed to avenge him. It took much longer than the lords would have liked to convince the zealous race their time would come.

"You must understand the situation we are in," Denethor began. "You have done your part. Because of the information you gave us from Lake Tibern, we are not caught off guard. Please understand that we cannot send you into the heat of battle when you are tired from your mission and away from the waters. If we need you, you shall be the first to strike from the reserves. Until that time, rest."

"We won't argue," they said. "Only don't forget us in the heat of battle."

A hawker burst into the group, cutting off the conversation. His helmet did not hide his angst. "They are coming."

The lords followed the scout as they drew their weapons. However, there were no cries of bloodshed in the air, nor ricochet of weapons. Maybe it was a false alarm?

No, it was no false alarm. Quinn was the first to reach the front lines, and stood between two swordsmen of Pelios. Something was different about their enemy. The evil henchmen of Natas did not seem so... evil. They had formed orderly ranks and carried the same weapons in the same manner. Each regiment had a captain, and each soldier looked to him for instructions. Their armor was well-polished, though still as black as night. The soldiers seemed disciplined and focused.

Quinn turned to Auden. "Since when have the forces of Natas been so…" He searched for the words. "…so structured?"

Auden scanned the enemy lines. "Never. I do not see the same hatred in their eyes, or sense the same bloodlust in their hearts."

"They are trying to trick us," Denethor said. He seemed convinced, but the other lords were not so sure. Even though the sun shone like a glittering diamond, chills ran through them. Auden felt as though his stomach was being wrenched from him.

Before anyone could stop him, Auden stepped past the front lines. "What is your purpose here?" he called out to the nearest enemy captain.

No one knew why he did this, except Auden alone.

He expected a brutal reply, but instead, the captain motioned to one of his soldiers. No matter how hard he looked, Auden could not make out the signals. He took a step closer to the enemy, preparing to call out again. Suddenly, a lone arrow shot out from the regiment and embedded itself in Auden's shoulder. The command of the captain, so cold yet precise, had been for his archer to kill Auden. He scurried back behind his front lines as fast as he could. That was not how he had imagined it going.

Everyone on the side of the Light was in shock. The medic rushed to Auden. "Can you walk?"

"Yes, I can walk," Auden said through clenched teeth.

"Come with me, sir." The medic escorted him toward the medical tent, just as footsteps thundered from below the hills.

The army of Natas advanced. It was not charging with fiery passion, but slowly nearing within formation. Thousands of footsteps. Thousands of footsteps marching in time. The heartbeat of metal boots thundering against the hillside was far more terrifying than any battle cry. No soldier broke out of line, and no rank advanced faster than the next. The army was one, breathing as one, advancing as one.

Denethor took charge of the army of Light as Quinn tried to shake off his fear. The strongest of all the army, the stone golems and the Pelios swordsmen were on the front lines, Denethor had made sure of that. He was confident that they could hold off any attack if they remained together.

The captains of Natas' army had planned for this. Denethor watched Natas' army break off into four separate groups. Two of the groups neared the western side of the hills, two of the groups neared the eastern side. They trapped the army of the Light in the hills, and marched toward them on both sides. Denethor would either have to spread the stone golems and Pelios swordsmen to a thin line, or leave part of the army without these elite units. Rushing to prepare for the oncoming assault, Denethor commanded the stone golems to guard the eastern flank, and the Pelios swordsmen to brace the western. Each race knew how to fight as one. The army of Light could not afford to be less unified than their enemy.

Every instant, the forces of Light waited for the army of Natas to charge. The enemy soldiers would have to charge against the stone golems and other mighty creatures while running uphill. The army of the Light had every advantage as far as the terrain.

This did not sway the meticulous eye of Natas' captains. They each turned to their rank and gave the command. Over half of their army drew their bows and unleashed a barrage of arrows that soared in the sky, only to coming crashing upon the forces of Light like a downpour.

As the archers prepared to unleash a second volley, the soldiers under Denethor panicked. "We can't sit here and let ourselves be killed," a soldier cried out to Denethor. He could not respond. His focus was on the second barrage blackening the sky. The arrows sped through the air, setting their aim on any unfortunate soldier who stood in their path.

Each man cowered beneath his own shield.

Quinn almost fell to the will of three black shafts, but one of his faithful hawkers stepped in their way. As he fell to their bloodlust, the soldier looked back to his lord.

He had no time to say it, but Quinn could see it in his eyes, "For the honor of Dalto, for the name of the King." Something had to be done, but Quinn did not have the influence to command more than his people. He sought out Denethor with a holy vengeance. He found Denethor trying to organize his archers for a counter-volley.

This did not satisfy Quinn; he was thinking along much more drastic lines. "We need to charge them. We cannot sit here and let ourselves die by the hand of their archers."

"We cannot lose this position. We have to hold our ground."

Denethor resumed his command, and the archers of the light readied their longbows and crossbows. Their counter-volley would have been equally as devastating, but the forces of darkness hoisted long shields forged out of a metal stronger than iron. Only a handful of them fell. Natas had spared no expense for this regiment.

"They will sit back there and destroy us, while we watch it happen." Quinn was no longer the calm lord focused on honor and diligence. He now had only one goal: to see this enemy perish. "We have enough force to break through while their front lines are thin."

The fear in Quinn's eyes sparked a longing in Denethor he had never felt before: the longing to flee. It took a mighty effort to keep his focus on the task at hand. "That is exactly what they want. Can't you see they are tempting us? Here we have the high ground and our barricades. They would take much fewer casualties in an open field battle. We must hold. I don't know how, but we have to find a way."

"They will kill us. They will kill all of us."

"They will run out of arrows."

Quinn turned his back on Denethor and left. He did not trust Denethor's plan, but there was no time to argue, and no place for doubt. He left before his emotions could destroy him, and went to unify his men. Denethor rushed throughout the southern flank and gave the command to fortify against the barrage.

Before either lord could stop him, they watched Warren limp into the fold of the army. He took Auden's place and did the same for the eastern flank. They had no energy in them to stop him; they needed his help.

Warren was the only lord left in the army who felt confident in their victory. His hope and vigor could only be explained by his youth. His young heart had not seen the desperation the other lords had. His mind was not yet burdened by the blood of many wars. This was his greatest advantage. He had watched Auden be taken away. He now watched Denethor and Quinn shake each other's confidence. Warren felt a massive weight upon his shoulders to inspire the army at such a dire hour. This weight he did not refuse, but ran toward.

As he lifted his voice, it was drowned out by the third barrage. This time the men had been ready, and were as protected from the volley as one could hope. Warren tried once again to rally the forces, and this time, all near him heard his valor. "Men of the Light. Soldiers under the King's banner. Hold fast no matter how many arrows come our way. Find strength in those around you, and give strength to those who need it. The battle may seem lost now, but when they are forced to charge against us, that is when our victory may be found."

No longer did the army of the light scramble in disarray. Formations were resumed, and with them came the passion to hold once more against the enemy. The fourth volley came with the same bloodlust as the others, but now the arrows did not find their marks. The evil shafts hit little more than dirt. It was hard set that the soldiers of the light would hold through a thousand nights and swelling storms if they had to… but they did not have to. The ranks of Natas had run out of arrows.

The captains of the dark army ordered each archer to cast aside his bow, and they formed a great pile. They had fulfilled their purpose and were cast aside. Every soldier now carried a new weapon, ready to charge. Without a moments delay, Denethor and Warren ordered their men to drop their bows, as well.

If it was a battle of swords and spears the enemy wanted, then that was what they would get. The time of emptying quivers had past, and the moment turned to shields and axes.

The dark army kept in formation as they approached with swords at the ready. Little did they know that the army of the light had more than barricades protecting them on the hill. Denethor watched the forces of Natas begin their charge. He readied to give the command, but whispered, "Not yet. Come closer. Closer."

When the dark army first clashed against the barricades, Denethor gave the command. The army of the light sprang into action. The stone golems confronted the western flank, the swordsmen of Pelios attacked the eastern flank. On the southern flank, the hawkers allied with the other soldiers against Natas' men.

Against the stone golems, the enemy gained no ground. The golems towered over them, and attacked them with a rage that could have challenged mountains. They were impervious to most of the weapons used against them, and fought with a zeal that they had never known. These were not simply stone golems; they were empowered by an elixir of great strength from Warren. He had kept it with him since Srayo for a time such as this. The stone golems overwhelmed whoever stood against them. The western flank of the dark army retreated.

The eastern flank suffered the same losses. Although they were not afraid of the flaming swords or molten armor of the Pelios warriors, they did not know how to fight against it. Their spears were shattered and their tactics useless against the skillful attacks of fiery soldiers. No shield could block the fury of strikes that came upon

them. The eastern flank fled down the hill they had
charged up.

Those remaining in both divisions joined the center
of their army. This, the southern rank, seemed to be
gaining the most ground against the forces of the light.
They, the dark army, had broken through the barricades and
forced their way into the heart of the hills.

Though it seemed like a victory, this proved to be
their downfall. Warren had spared no expense in using his
potions to gain the advantage. He had used every trick and
scheme he could muster against this foe. He had given
both the Seviathans and Xalaians, creatures not in the heat
of battle, an elixir of invisibility.

It only lasted a few short minutes, but that was all
that they needed to charge the unsuspecting dark army from
behind. Their silent attack assaulted the enemy from the
one place their formation was weakest.

Trapped between the combined forces of the
humans and their allies, the warriors of Natas were attacked
on all sides. Both sides fought till the bitter end. The battle
did not end until every soldier of the darkness had been
finished. None fled or were taken prisoner. They fought
with misplaced honor. The hills were stained red.

A victory was won for the army of the light, but
once again there was no joy in the triumph. Few of their
creatures had fallen in the battle, but the arrows had done
their damage to the likes of men. Warren's potions had
helped save many, but the battlefield was devastated with

lives taken, nonetheless. The southern flank of the light was saved only by their allies, but still suffered greatest.

The lords gathered together as was their custom after battle. They left the men to tend to their wounded. It did not take them long to find each other, and they left the battlefield to talk privately. Instead of discussing how to recover from the battle as they often would, they spoke about their enemy.

Warren was on the verge of grimacing in agony but he did not know why. "I feel as though we have done something wrong."

Quinn cast his somber eyes once more over the hillside. "Maybe we have."

There was an air of regret about them, as if the victory was a horrible thing. "How could an army of Natas fight with such stature and heart? Why did they not shout at us or mock us with their threats? It is as if they are not of Natas at all."

Denethor's thoughts caught ablaze. It came to him, clear as a night pierced by moonlight. "Say that again."

"It's as if they are not of Natas at all."

"This whole time we have seen the legions that come against us as evil. They used to be merciless in their brutality, and altogether savage. This is the first time we have fought against men trained by Natas himself. The dark lord does not want brutes; he wants men bent toward loyalty even over being bent toward hate. Natas has not trained these men to be wicked; he has simply trained them to be submissive. This whole time we thought we were facing thousands of enemies, but in truth we are only facing one."

Denethor was going to continue, but he stopped as his words reached his own ears. One enemy. He locked eyes with his friends. They were all thinking the same thing. Never had they considered such a feat, but now the lords set their eyes on Balyon. One enemy.

Warren stood, ran his hands through his hair and shook his head. "It's impossible. We cannot journey toward Balyon. Natas likely has enough men on that route to stop an army ten times our size. What you are suggesting is suicide. I know we just had a great victory, but if we charge the gates of Balyon..."

"Then we go around." Denethor's words were sharp but not aggressive.

Neither of the lords answered him, so he continued. "Natas will not expect us to head east. We can continue past Tibern and toward Quoto. If we can liberate that city, we will not only deal a great blow to Natas' empire, but give ourselves a direct route to his capitol."

"What about the dark mist?" Quinn asked.

"Or the fact that we are leaving our own lands open for attack?" Warren continued.

Denethor wished Auden were with them, for he was confident that Auden would support his position. "I'm sure that both of Natas' other regiments will follow us east if we continue in that direction. If a threat comes upon our homelands, there is little we can do now. Take heart; the men we have left at Srayo, and the stone golems remaining in the Mazaron shall ward off any attack of Aphenter or another dark city. As for the dark mist, we shall either have to find a way through it, or hope that the King grants us favor and destroys it.

"There is only one way to free Amcronos, and that is to cut off the source of this deceit. The only way to free Amcronos is to end Natas' tyranny. I feel as you both do about today's battle. The King longs to see the followers of Natas released. They fought with bravery and intelligence, because they are men just like us. They are men who believed what they were doing was right, only they have been so greatly deceived that there is little hope for the other soldiers under his banner.

"Only if the source of their deception was to end, could we hope they would remember the light, and remember the King. Never before has there been an army such as ours to stand against Natas. We have gathered together every follower of the light that we could muster. We represent the Mazaron and its strength, the Northwest and its prominence, Pelios and its power, Xala and its majesty and Dalto and its honor. If we do not risk it all, then we have not risked enough."

318

No words could be said against his argument, so Quinn and Warren agreed with Denethor. For better or for worse, there was no turning back. The lords went to share everything they had decided with Auden, but first Quinn said to Warren, "It seems like your potions have been quite useful. That mage of yours was quite the find. First, he saved the men of Pelios at Srayo, and now his potions have saved us all. Do you have any more secrets we should know about?"

"Just one, and I'm not going to share it until absolutely necessary."

CHAPTER 17

ABSOLUTELY NECESSARY

"I will not do that unless absolutely necessary."
Lavrin would hear no more of it.

Chan tried to make himself as clear as possible.
"We need to keep moving."

Something shook inside of Lavrin. The feeling that
there was no way to win, no matter what you do. "I know
we have to keep going, but look at them. They are trying
so hard to be strong, but they are dying inside. I'm just as
afraid as they are that I must face my nightmares again.
The only thing keeping me from becoming like them is I'm
more afraid that what those shadows did will force us to
stop. How are we going to keep going on like this?"

321

There was nothing but agony on the faces of their friends. Chan watched some try to hide it, while others struggled to catch their breath or bit their lip. No one was worse than Calix. He was shaking where he sat, and whispering frantically to himself. Chan turned back to Lavrin. "What else did you see when you helped Calix?"

"I have told you enough."

Chan tried not to let the words sink in too deep. It was a hard time for himself, how much harder must if have been for Lavrin? Lavrin bore not only his own weight, but the weight of the entire team. Chan tried again. "You have no right to let this eat away at you. This will kill you if you don't let me help."

There was a pause. A long pause that turned suspicion to panic.

"Death."

This time, Chan could not help but be taken aback. "Sorry?"

"Death. That is what I saw in Calix's nightmare. That is what I told you. He was dying, and then dying, and then dying again. I had to watch my best friend drown and get stabbed and..." Lavrin choked on his own emotions.

Chan placed his arm around Lavrin's shoulder. There was little else he could do. Chan, who had thought he was so strong, was brought back to the horrors of his own vision. His people, the villagers of Hessington, were slaughtered before him and he could not save them. Unspeakable death. He looked to Calix... he knew what he was going through. Chan wondered how he would have fared for hours longer in his torture.

The living shadows had put them through revolting torment, just to guard one piece of the Titan's Heart. If this artifact was that powerful, then why had Natas not tried to claim it for himself? Chan realized that maybe this artifact was so hidden and protected that not even the dark lord could obtain it. Why were they trying to claim the Titan's Heart, if Natas himself thought it was better to leave it alone?

He knew exactly why; the King had told them to. The King wanted them to find it, and that was what they had to do. Once again, Chan felt the fire in his soul to charge onward toward the next piece, but it mattered little.

No matter how greatly he longed to keep moving, Lavrin had a point. The team was shattered, barely holding onto whatever fraction of peace and hope kept them from returning to their fateful nightmares. It was as if they had not even left the glade at all.

Lavrin already knew what he wanted to do. "Chan, you have known most of the team longer than I have, so tell me if I'm wrong. I believe that those who were in the Haven Realm have enough strength within them to keep going. Except maybe Calix. Uminos has been through torment even worse than these nightmares, and Kasandra was shown a struggle she has already been facing for some time. I fear that Calix may never fully heal, but the person that I am most scared for is Kyra. She has always been our bright light. She is the one who sees the best in every situation. Now, I fear that she has changed. I think we should pull her aside and try and help her."

Chan shook his head. "No."

"What?" Lavrin asked. "Well then, what do you recommend?"

"I think you should go talk to her, just the two of you."

"Why is that?" Lavrin asked.

"You already had a deeper bond than most of us before this, but now you have shared in her deepest fear. It would be a hindrance for me to go with you. You're on your own with this one, Lavrin."

"I see what you are saying. Thank you a hundred times, friend."

Chan said nothing. He let Lavrin go and do what needed to be done.

Lavrin approached Kyra where she was seated by the fire. "Kyra, we should talk."

At first, she looked away, but when she turned to him, her face displayed a thousand sorrows. "I don't feel like talking right now."

"Kyra, we should talk."

She realized that it had been a statement, not a question. Against her emotions, she submitted. "Alright. What do we need to talk about?" She knew, only she hoped Lavrin had something different in mind.

"Come, there's something I wanted to show you."

Curiosity numbed her frostbit heart. She followed him.

Lavrin took her away from the camp and up a nearby hill. The grass swayed beneath their soft steps. The moonlight cascaded the hillside in a cool array. Fireflies danced in the scattered bushes. Lavrin led Kyra to the highest stretch of the hill. There he sat, and he motioned for Kyra to do the same. Intrigued, she followed his example.

Finally, after letting the silence run its course, Kyra had to ask. "What did you want to show me?"

He took a deep breath. "I think you have a right to know. Do you see the camp?"

"Yes." It was illuminated by the campfire, which was bright even from this distance.

"When I was shown my vision by the living shadows, I saw my house. Not the treehouse where I lived most of my life, but my first home. It was lit ablaze, and the smoke rose to the skies. Imagine the destruction of the small campfire magnified ten or more times. There was nothing I could do as I watched the smoke billow and the smoldering walls turn to rubble.

"I walked on ashen ground and wandered through the wreckage, not knowing what to think. It was far too real for me to keep my composure. I would have sunken into a mighty despair right then, but it got worse.

"I suddenly found myself a short distance from the house, probably closer than we are to the camp. Below me, I found three markers. They were burial markers. One of the living shadows was whispering to me. He told me that I was there to suffer, and that the first two crosses marked the resting places of my father and mother."

Kyra found herself immersed in Lavrin's story, imagining every detail. "Who was the third marker for?"

"That is exactly what I asked him," Lavrin continued. "You know what he told me? It was there for you. When I heard that you were laid in the third grave, something inside me snapped. I felt as though everything was lost. I could not live with myself if I lost both my parents and you. It was at this point that the King entered my vision and helped me escape. But I feel as though a part of me remains there, and now I know why.

"The question has haunted me since that nightmare. Why did the King not save me sooner? Looking back, I'm confident that I have the answer. He wanted me to see my greatest fear. It was not going back to that fire. It was not even watching my house burned to ashes. My greatest fear is losing those I care about most."

Kyra chocked on her own tears. They were both joyful and sad. "Lavrin…"

"No. I need to finish. I'm afraid… no, I'm terrified that I might lose you. Not while I can still fight am I going to let you be defeated by your fear. Ever since I met you in the dungeons of Saberlin, you have been a bright light to me.

"You helped me see my purpose when I struggled to find it in those prisons. You continued to look at life with innocence and hope, even when we faced the Seviathans in the Mazaron. You kept our team from destroying itself in the desert. You have been the most important member of this group, not because of anything you have done, but because of who you are. You are the hope of this team. You are my hope.

"If I had not quit at Saberlin, then I would have quit at the Mazaron, or at the desert, or at the first challenge of the Titan's Heart. The King wanted me to see that. The King wanted me to see that it is my duty to see your shining light thrive amidst the darkness we have encountered. You have saved my life many times; please let me save yours."

Kyra was lost in a tidal wave of emotion that she let carry her out to sea. She remained in the blissful ocean for she knew not how long. It was not until Lavrin whispered her name that she returned to the shoreline.

"Kyra," he whispered again. "You don't need to say anything. I understand."

She opened her eyes, and gave Lavrin a quick look that told him everything that he longed to see. The very next moment, she stood atop the hillside and rushed toward camp without saying a word.

"Where are you going?" Lavrin asked as he rushed after her.

"I need to talk with Nadrian."

Lavrin stopped. He thanked the King a hundred times over. He had restored Kyra to the ray of sunshine that Lavrin always knew her to be.

*****

When the group saw that joy had returned not only to Kyra but to Nadrian as well, the atmosphere of the camp changed. Conversation sprung up once more, and though not always on lively matters, it was a step in the right direction. Kyra had returned to being a wellspring of hope. Although her fears remained hidden in the back of her mind, at least they stayed there.

Lavrin and Chan no longer feared an end to their mission. They still doubted their ability to remain focused, and wondered if the pain would ever leave their team, but at least the wounds were healing. Scars were expected, but the bleeding had begun to stop.

The only two who had conquered their own nightmares, Lavrin and Chan, watched life return to both Kyra and Nadrian. If only this was the case for the rest of their companions. The many promises Lavrin had made to them plagued him.

He saw the loneliness that haunted Uminos, and the regret of Felloni. Lavrin noticed the fear that Grax battled, and the confusion that penetrated Kasandra. These emotions were like shattered glass - clear but sharp. The fate of Calix took a much darker form, polluted and muddled.

Lavrin knew how he felt about Calix's vision... terrified. What Lavrin longed to know, however, was what was going on inside Calix's head. Though obviously not well, he did not go to anyone for help.

Instead, he had not spoken to anyone since the living shadows, but curled himself into a ball and whispered indecipherable words. The white in his eyes made his dilated pupils all too ghostly. It was as if he had never left his horror.

For the first time, Lavrin wondered if Calix should have returned from the Haven Realm. It was not because Lavrin did not long to see him, and he still did not want to say goodbye, but the thought weighed on him. If Calix had remained in the Haven Realm, he would never have endured the torture that was destroying him on the inside. Would Calix be a liability to the mission? Should they leave him behind? No, this was one matter on which Lavrin would not budge, even though he saw these same questions in Chan's expression.

Lavrin gave Chan a look that said more than a thousand words. The one thing that overarched even the quest, even the journey itself, was loyalty. Hardship did not sway him, neither glory nor fame mattered, even love could not be as important as the mission. But loyalty trumped even that. If Calix would have to be left behind, then Lavrin would not take another step.

Chan could not stand the silence. "What can I do to help, Calix?"

"I don't know. I don't know if even I can help him. His limbs shake as if he has had a seizure. Kyra assures me that he is healthy, but something deeper must be attacking him. He will heal, he must. The King will heal him, won't he?"

"I hope so."

Lavrin, so desperate for hope, found none in Chan's reply. "I will strap him to my back and climb over the highest mountains if I must. He will continue with us, and he will recover."

"He can have half of my rations, and I will carry his load."

"Thank you, Chan. I fear that if you were not here, my grief would have overwhelmed me, and both Kyra and Nadrian would not be recovering. You are more than a friend - you are a brother. But, as a brother, I expect you to help me keep this team alive, and nothing less."

"I understand," Chan replied.

"We leave at sunrise."

*****

Sunrise came quickly, bringing with it the peace of the morning breeze. The peace in the air did not descend to the anxious and weary souls of the travelers, however. They were in a land not their own, incredibly far from home. What lie ahead hid in the shadows, while what remained behind left them scarred. There was no rest for their desolate minds, and their spirits could not lift their hearts.

Beckoned on by a fleeting sense of urgency, Lavrin hastily spurred on his companions, who packed up their supplies in a short time. They submitted to Lavrin's leadership and left the area faster than they ever had before. Faster for everyone except Calix, who barely kept up, even though Chan carried his burdens. The team carried on, helping Calix however they could.

Soon, they had left the place far behind them. Their focus was on the next challenge for the Titan's Heart, and they wondered if it would be as devastating as the last. This question would linger with them for some time because, as they knew from Lavrin, the next location of the Titan's Heart was a long journey away.

The living shadows had told him of its location, but had also given him a stern warning. "Believe it or not, we showed you mercy compared to your next challenge.

Although you consider us wicked and cruel, at least we negotiated with you. Do not expect this luxury there." Lavrin had kept this detail from the rest of his team.

For the first time since leaving their homeland, the group found themselves in familiar territory. Long stretches of open grassland with hills and scattered groupings of trees reminded them of the Northwest.

Though the distance to their next location was long, Lavrin was glad that they had plenty of time to recover in open land. His heart returned to the Northwest, not only his home, but where he had left both his father and Vin. He had left his entire life there… in exchange for a mission.

The hours slipped by as the team walked in silence, enveloped by their own memories. No one even noticed how quiet they had become again. Lavrin, most of all, lost himself in his daydreams. He pictured the plains surrounding Saberlin and Dreylon, so similar to the ones he now crossed.

In fact, everyone from the Northwest remembered those grasslands, some longing to return to them and others longing to know if they were safe. The team had not received any news about the North or their homeland for far too long. The only thing they had to go off was the vague memories Chan had from the Haven Realm.

Chan had not forgotten the wonders of the Haven Realm, but they had started to fade amid the chaos of Amcronos. When he had first heard from the King that he and those with him could return as the King's ambassadors, he was thrilled. At that time, his hopes and dreams of saving the land were grand, but they had since been replaced with reality. The reality was that there was only one being with enough power alone to save Amcronos, and that was the King himself.

Though Chan wished the King would cleanse the land of Natas once and for all, he figured that the King had loftier plans in mind. All that Chan knew was that Amcronos had become much darker than it had seemed from the Haven Realm's glorious balconies, and only the King knew when he would return to that splendid place. It may be days or years until he saw the golden cities again.

Chan motioned to Lavrin, and they drew themselves ahead of the team. "Where is the next piece of the Titan's Heart?" Chan asked.

"We are headed toward Malstrate," Lavrin said.

"I've heard of Malstrate before. What do you know about it?"

Lavrin pulled out a map. "I got this map from Matthais back home. I know where Malstrate is, but very little about it. What have you heard?"

"Nothing good, to be sure. It is not far from Balyon, and thus is one of the most loyal cities to the dark lord's cause. I hear that it is a beautiful city, but that there is great evil hidden beneath. I hope that our path takes us back south quickly, because from the streets of Malstrate one can see the edge of the dark mist protecting Balyon.

333

We should avoid getting close to that wicked shadow and the fortress of evil within it."

"I hope we can leave the city quickly," Lavrin answered. "The living shadows, mysterious as they were, did not actually tell me where the next piece is. They only told me that there is one man who knows where it is, and that he lives in Malstrate."

"They told you nothing else about this man?"

Lavrin tried to not sound despondent. "No, nothing. They simply said that he will make himself very hard to find."

Chan hung his head. All good fortune seemed to fight against them. "I figured it would be like this, but the rest of the team needs hope, not bad news. I say we go into Malstrate just the two of us. We can tell the team that we will have better odds that way. If we go alone, then we will keep the team farther from Balyon and farther from bad news."

Lavrin did not know what troubled him more, that Chan was suggesting such a thing, or that Lavrin found himself agreeing. "In any other circumstance, I would have disagreed with you, but we have been placed in a situation more dismal than before. Journeying so close to the dark mist is dangerous in its own right. I have a feeling claiming the next piece of the Titan's Heart will be impossible if our hearts have not recovered from the living shadows' spells. There is only one thing… we will need

Calix's pendant. Without it, we will not be able to tell who is for the King, and who is against Him."

"We should go to Calix, then."

The two waited to ask Calix for his pendant until camp had been set up that evening. The moon struck its pale face upon the dim canvas of the night. The stars followed its lead, and sparkled in the reaching abyss that tried to hide their glow.

The campfire shifted from brilliant array to the brink of sputtering out. Calix sat alone, far from the fire, shivering, though it was hardly cold. His eyes were wild, as if looking at a hundred things at once, afraid of them all. He seemed afraid even of Lavrin and Chan when they approached him.

Chan stopped a few steps away from Calix, afraid to frighten him further, but Lavrin continued forward. "What's wrong, Calix?" Lavrin asked.

"You want it from me."

"What do you mean?"

Calix gripped his necklace with both hands. "You want my gift from the King. It's mine. You have no right to take it from me."

Hoping to calm him, Lavrin sat next to Calix. "We need your pendant, Calix. We need it to help us find the next piece of the Titan's Heart."

"I need it. It helps me fight the voices."

Although Lavrin did not understand, he did not protest. If something was helping Calix, he could not take it away. There was only one option left for Lavrin. "Calix, where we are going, we may not return from. If you come with us, I need to know that you can stay focused and prepared for whatever happens. Can you promise me this, Calix?"

"Will going to this place help me fight the voices?"

Lavrin knew better than to lie to Calix. "I don't know. All I know is I need the pendant that the King gave you. I will not force you to give it to me. Come on, Calix, we should tell the others we are leaving."

Chan, Lavrin and Calix approached the rest of their team with their packs already gathered. The others could tell something was going on, and were not pleased.

They had a feeling what Lavrin was going to say before he said it. "Friends, our mission takes us toward the city of Malstrate. This mission requires stealth and speed, as we try and find someone in the city who knows the location of the next Titan's Heart piece. We should leave within the hour."

"Of course, you only mean the three of you," Kasandra replied. "For all our quest, we have remained together, as one unit. We have never split up before and should not start now. What are the rest of us supposed to do? Sit here and wait?"

"Actually, Kasandra," Lavrin said, "before the Mazaron Mountains, our team did whatever was necessary for the task at hand. We would split up whenever we needed to."

"Kasandra's right, Lavrin," Nadrian said. "What are we supposed to do while the three of you go to Malstrate? Yes, we have done whatever was necessary to get the mission done before, but I don't think it's necessary now."

Tension that filled the air. "I need you to stay and heal. If we are to continue past Malstrate, we need to be ready for our next challenge."

Nadrian and Kasandra were far from convinced. "What if we are healed?" Kasandra replied. "Who gave you the right to decide if we are fit to fight? The fact that you would make a decision that should be for everyone is not only wrong, but selfish. You should have come to us before making this decision. I know for sure that I'm not letting you go into this battle without me."

"Who said this is a battle? The three of us are going to sneak into Malstrate, find who we need to, and get out of the city, hopefully without a sword being drawn. This is exactly why I'm afraid to bring the team into this mission. There is too great a risk that a battle will break out. If swords are drawn, then there will be ten for us and a thousand against us. At least if three of us go and we are captured, then the rest of you are safe. If we die, the rest of you will live to carry on our quest."

Kyra's eyes lit up, not with joy, but with distress. "You're not planning on dying there, are you, Lavrin?"

"Of course not. If everything goes as I hope it will, then no one will even know we are there. Sadly, we must prepare for the chance that things will not go as I hope. It seems that the farther we journey, the less things seem to go our way.

"Sometimes I long for the days where the threat of Natas was a distant shadow, and my life seemed secure. Now I feel as though my life is far from safety. Maybe one day, when I set my eyes on the Haven Realm as some of you have before me, I will once again be at peace. May that day come quickly."

Lavrin expected someone to continue the argument against their departure, but it never came. Instead, Grax said, "If this is how it is going to be, then there is no point delaying you further. If you believe this is necessary, then we shall wait for your return. We will put every effort into preparing for the battles that await us. The King keep you, all three of you. Protect each other with a mighty passion. May the King reign and His followers prosper."

Goodbyes were said in haste, not because it was necessary, but because the three wished to return to their team all the faster. They carried with them only the minimum to get them to Malstrate and back. They sprinted into the spectral shade of the night, and turned their feet north, closer to Natas than they had ever been before.

CHAPTER 18

HOW TO FIND HIM

The clouds spread their wings across the sky with their silver bodies hiding the stars from the wanderers. Wanderers they were, in a land far from home, stumbling over scattered rocks and running through paths never taken before.

Lavrin and Chan found their way with little difficulty, but Calix's feet betrayed him, and he struggled to keep up. His mind remained encaged by the living shadows. He tried to hide his distress as much as he could from his companions.

In truth, Lavrin worried for him greatly. He had seen Calix's torture, and knew that he may never fully recover. He hoped that this mission would restore Calix in some way. Hope was one of the few things Lavrin had left.

It was something he could control, the only thing that the King had given him to rely upon. It had not failed him yet, and he believed that it would not fail him at Malstrate, either.

Lavrin did not know how long it would take to reach Malstrate. He trusted that, as the first night fought the coming morning, they had made fair progress. He had no way to measure the distance they had traveled, since they passed by no landmarks of any kind.

There were no villages in these parts, and neither had there been since they had left the Hills of the Gorills. In some sense, Lavrin was glad they would be reaching civilization soon; he only wished they would reach some city closer to the King, and farther from the darkness.

This city's reputation was notorious, second only to Balyon. Inwardly, Lavrin wondered what would happen if the man they looked for said the next piece was in the hands of Natas in Balyon. That would be a great and mighty horror.

Unlike Calix, who hoped to find solace and zeal in this mission, and Lavrin, who wanted promise and clarity from this quest, Chan thought ahead, past Malstrate. In fact, he thought past the Titan's Heart to the end of their journey. Chan was wondering when the King would call him back to the Haven Realm. Moreover, he questioned whether he would be able to leave his friends when the time came. It was hard to leave them once; to do it again would be far worse.

What if the King called him back when the team needed him most? What would happen if, in the heat of the battle, Chan was taken from the fight? Although this was a great burden, he had too much trust in the King to let it trouble him. Chan knew he could not change the King's timing, only fight on in Amcronos for every hour he had.

Breaking the silence that permeated the air, Lavrin said to Calix, "Did I ever tell you that I sat by your graveside for many hours after your death?"

"Yes. In fact, I watched you sit there."

Lavrin smirked. "Did you hear what I said?"

"I did," Calix replied. "You were glad that I had died an honorable death, and wanted a full tour of the Haven Realm when you reached it."

"That would take a very long time," Chan remarked. "At least a week."

"It would be worth it," Lavrin said. "Both of you have told me many stories about the wonders of that land. Remind me again why the King chose to send you back to Amcronos."

"For this exact purpose," Chan said. "To help claim the Titan's Heart. The King wanted a group to assist you through this rough time, and had planned for us to return, even before we left Amcronos. I am glad that he did, because the desert tribes would have sprung into civil war if we had not intervened."

"We could have handled it."

"Of course you could have, Lavrin. Of course you could have."

Lavrin nudged him on the side and laughed. Chan also laughed, and their conversation continued for an hour as Calix listened from behind. The terrain became easier and easier to cross, which was surprising since they were heading in the direction of Balyon.

They soon found themselves on a broad path of smooth stone heading northward. The path was straight and open; it had been traveled many times before. Luckily, no travelers occupied its way today. If any had, the three would never have traveled on the path at all.

As they headed closer to Malstrate, the trio passed single wooden poles on one side of the road or the other. After coming toward the fifth pole, Chan stopped. "Lavrin, what do you make of these?"

"My guess is they are markers, showing us how close we are to Malstrate."

"We cannot be too far off," Chan said. "If we hurry, we may reach it as the sun is rising."

"I hope we don't reach it too quickly," Calix answered.

Chan and Lavrin were both confused, but Lavrin spoke first. "Why would you say that, Calix? We need to get to Malstrate as fast as we can."

Calix's expression grew somber, more despondent than Lavrin had ever seen it before. He almost did not reply to Lavrin, but after weighing the silence, he decided to answer. "When the King told us we could return to Amcronos, I was not excited to see the land again, nor was I excited to see Kyra, or Felloni, or anyone else. The only reason I was thrilled to return was because I knew you needed my help.

"I longed not only to see you again, but to save you from the dangers I knew were heading your direction. Now we are going to the very footstool of Balyon, the edge of the dark mist. Even with my pendant, I cannot help but see visions. Even this very moment, I'm reliving my nightmares. Already I feel the burden of my visions clouding my eyes. I'm watching myself die, over and over, and the only thing that keeps me going is you.

"Lavrin, if you go into Malstrate and die, I will never forgive myself. You are more than my friend, more than my ally; you are my brother. Don't go in there. Chan and I can manage it, the two of us. All that we've fought for together means nothing if you don't make it out of there alive. I may fear my own death, but I'm mortified of yours."

Calix's hot tears glowed in the starlight. The night did not cover the devastation he felt or the terror he harbored. Lavrin was stunned at the sincerity of Calix's plea. Chan instantly realized that he needed give Lavrin and Calix some time. He went ahead of his friends to scout the path.

344

Lavrin found a place to rest and motioned for Calix to sit behind him. "Look at how far we've come, Calix. Think about how many challenges we've fought after leaving the Forest of Torin. I know you remember the years we spent, hoping for opportunities just like this. We could only dream of living for the King; now we are making a difference for his cause that can be felt throughout Amcronos. I don't plan on stopping all that we've worked for at Malstrate. I will not die in Malstrate."

"Lavrin," Calix answered. "It's exactly because of the dreams we had and the difference we've made that I can't let you go into Malstrate. You are too important to the cause of the light to recklessly throw your life away."

"Even if I die in Malstrate... even if I do not make it out, I will go to the Haven Realm and the forces of the light will continue to drive back Natas."

Calix rubbed his pendant. "As a friend and a brother, I want you to live out all that you have desired. I have already experienced death, and relive the sting of my nightmares a hundred times over. I don't know when the King will return me to the Haven Realm, but you have a chance to live out your life here. Even more than that though, as a follower of the light, I know how the King talks about you. His plans for you stretch far beyond me and the rest of the team, for that matter."

"Then the King will be with us in Malstrate. If he has plans for me, then he will protect me, even at the footstool of Balyon. Our mission is the King's mission, and he will help us succeed. Take heart, my friend, we will not go into that city alone. There may be many friends of the King in the city, hiding their allegiance for a time such as now. As I have told you before, we are only going in to find who we need to find and then leave. We are prepared for anything Natas might throw at us."

Although Calix was far from convinced, he conceded to Lavrin's desire. As concerned as Calix was, he did not want to dishearten him. He did, however, decide that if anything went wrong in Malstrate, that it would be his life, not Lavrin's, that would be spent.

*****

There it was. The city of Malstrate lay before them. It shown in the light of the risen sun with splendor. Even from far away, Malstrate looked massive. It seemed to tower above the placid grasslands that surrounded it. If it appeared this immense from a distance, then clearly it would be more impressive when they reached it.

The trio could have stalled, studying the tall, proud buildings from afar, but they remembered their purpose. Get in and get out. Besides, they could behold the city much more clearly at its gates.

They followed the path ever closer to Malstrate, until it combined with another road heading toward Balyon's footstool. Chan dove behind a cluster of trees, grabbing Lavrin and Calix as he did so. The three hid and watched as a battalion of soldiers, two hundred strong, marched past them. Lavrin turned to Calix. "What do you see?"

"They follow Natas. Every one of them."

"Should we hold off entering the city?" Chan asked Lavrin.

"No," he replied. "The city will open the gates for these men. When they enter, we can go in behind them. Let's follow them. Make sure to stay quiet and out of sight."

With the stealth of thieves and the silence of shadows, they stalked in the bushes and amongst the trees. Like tigers they crept, waiting for the perfect moment to pounce. Everything was going just as they had predicted. The battalion was oblivious to their whereabouts, and it continued its approach to Malstrate's southern gate.

The distance between them and the city closed faster than anyone expected, mostly because the trio was far too focused on the soldiers they followed. It worried Lavrin that, at the very least, two hundred guardsmen of darkness were going to be patrolling the streets. Of course the city would be protected; fate never let the journey be easy.

"State your name and business in Malstrate," the call rang loud and true from one of the gate's watchman.

"Sir Traxius of Natas' thirty-first division. We have little business in Malstrate, save to pass through it," he called in reply. "We are to reinforce the forces of the North because of the light's recent victory over the highland rank."

"Do not talk of victory or of defeat. The army of the light gained a temporary advantage, but is in far over its head. Now that we have learned its strengths, Natas will find its weaknesses. There is no need to stretch things out of proportion."

Traxius scoffed. He had no quarrel with this watchman. "I simply was stating our 'business in Malstrate' and I'm sure we will be spared nothing, as you put it. Now let us enter. My men are hungry."

The watchman said nothing of their accommodations. "You may enter."

With great effort, the heavy bars of the gate began to lift. The clinking of its chains made a vexing noise. This fortress had stood for Natas for centuries, and the mighty dark iron gate was just one testament to this fact.

Lavrin, Calix and Chan were thrilled to finally hear news of the war in the North. They had not expected to hear it from such a source, but they did not care. They had not heard word of it since half their team had arrived from the Haven Realm. Not only were they now hearing of the war, but they were hearing of victory.

It seemed the army of the light had won a great battle, and for that there needed to be celebration, but not yet. Lavrin was most excited to hear the words of the watchman; his father was in that war, Nadrian had told him as much. In fact, it was one of the first things she told him after they left the desert. Of all the regrets Lavrin held, not remaining with his father stood out above the rest. All in time... in time he would see his father again. He was sure of it.

"We are going to miss our window." Chan watched as Traxius' soldiers filed into Malstrate.

"Not yet," Lavrin replied. "We need to wait until all the troops have entered the city. If the gate takes as long to close as it did to open, then we will need to go when the gate is half-way closed. We should be able to run under it. By then, the soldiers will have moved on, and the watchman may be preoccupied."

Chan bit his lip. "That is, if the gate does not close faster than it lifted."

"It's old, rusted almost to the point of uselessness. I'm sure we could climb a mountain before that gate hits the ground."

Soon, the last of Traxius' men entered the city, and the watchman called for the gate to be closed. It began its descent. Chan almost sprinted out, but Lavrin caught him. "Not yet. The watchman is still watching."

Closer and closer to the ground the massive gate came. It soon passed half-way. Chan had been nervous before, but now he became desperately worried. "We're going to miss it."

"Not yet," Lavrin said again. His eyes were fixed on the watchman. Turn around. Turn around. It was as if Lavrin was trying to whisper in his ear. Look into the city. Lavrin knew all he needed was a moment, a flicker. The gate was three-quarters of the way closed. It continued its descent, and Lavrin grew more and more desperate. How were they going to enter Malstrate any other way?

Then, about two feet from the ground, the gate stopped lowering. A loud screeching sound came from inside the wall. The noise was horrifying, as if something was dying.

The call from several men inside Malstrate confirmed Lavrin's hopes. "Something's wrong," they shouted. "The gears are jammed. Someone give us a hand!" The watchman not only turned around, but completely left his post to go assist them. Lavrin almost laughed; instead of giving them a window, the King had gone a step further and fixed them a door.

Chan did not even wait for Lavrin's signal. He knew what Lavrin would say. Lavrin and Calix rushed after him to slide under the gate. Chan took off his pack as he ran, and threw it under the iron bars before he crawled beneath them.

Lavrin was the next behind him. He handed his supplies to Chan through the gate before dropping to his stomach. He slid under the heavy bars as fast as he could, trying to make room for Calix. Then, as Lavrin rose on the other side, he heard a fateful sound; the gate was working again. Slowly but surely, it started its descent. Calix dropped to the ground in a complete panic. His room to maneuver grew smaller and smaller. Luckily, the watchman was still focused on the gears of the gate, hoping they would not break.

Calix watched the sharp teeth of the iron bars draw closer to his chest. He pushed his body underneath them with haste, rolling to the side just before the gate sealed shut. With a sounding report, the gate finished its task. Calix was shocked to see that his pendant, his gift from the King, lay just an inch away from one of the bars.

Had it fallen differently, it would have shattered into too many pieces to count. As if it still was at risk, Calix snatched it and clung to it. Lavrin and Chan helped him to his feet, and the three disappeared into the crowds just as the guards looked their direction.

After making sure they were far enough from the gate, the three stopped and surveyed the city. Each had a strikingly different view of Malstrate. To Lavrin, it was magnificent, at least in its architecture. Huge buildings towered on both sides of the busy street.

Each structure was adorned with unique designs. Some had massive pillars - columns with wreaths etched upon them. Others had arrays of arches over each doorway, glimmering as if made of pearl. Balconies opened from the sides of houses, and some had statues of rare marble atop them. How could this be Malstrate? It

351

seemed so vibrant. Was not Malstrate supposed to be an evil city?

Chan was not nearly as impressed as Lavrin was. He compared Malstrate to the vast and magnificent cities of the Haven Realm, and compared to them, this city fell mightily short. There was no laughter of children in the streets. No golden light reflected off crystal waters in the elegant fountain in the town square. Although Malstrate's magnitude was great, Chan also sensed a hidden darkness about it... as if behind the curtain of its exterior lay something foul and decaying. He had no idea how right he was.

As the two surveyed the city, Calix fell to the ground, still clutching his pendant. His breaths were short and gaping, as if he had been poisoned. Truly he had been, but not by a vial or fog. He had been poisoned by what he had seen.

Lavrin called to Chan, desperately watching as color drained form Calix's face. His eyes grew so dark that Lavrin almost retreated in fear. It was as if a sunset had fallen over him in wake of a tormented night. He looked to Chan, but Chan had no answer.

They both noticed that they were starting to draw attention from civilians, so they picked Calix up and carried him into an alleyway. Unlike the street corner, the alley was all but forsaken - the perfect place to hide, at least for the time being.

When they set Calix down, his knuckles were ghostly white and his eyes were tightly shut. Lavrin knelt beside him; the only time he had seen him this bad was with the living shadows. "Calix? Calix, can you hear me?"

To the utmost relief of his companions, Calix opened his eyes. They were no longer blackened, but nonetheless still in anguish. It looked as though he was going to speak, but Calix found himself void of any words. His eyes left and right in a whirlwind, as if looking for someone. "What's wrong, Calix?" Lavrin asked. "We are safe, my friend."

"I have seen it."

This time, Chan looked to Lavrin. Neither could make any sense of it. "What have you seen?"

"You have not seen it? You have not seen the power of Natas in this place? I..." his voice faltered. He tried again. "I have not witnessed such corruption, such deceit, such... it is as if I am face to face with Natas even now. Everywhere I see his presence, as if his cursed hand holds this city in its grip. There is no heart void of loyalty to his commands here. All I see are shadows. Shadows of pain, shadows of pride, shadows of lies.

"If this is the footstool of Balyon, then truly Balyon must be darker than the deepest cave on the stormiest night. I have witnessed the full power of Natas in the hearts of these people, and I'm stunned beyond words. I had been a fool to think I knew of evil before, for now I see it for what it really is. This city is his spawn, his child in wrath and in

353

ruin. If souls like those here stand against the light, then any army we could muster ought to be afraid. Where can I go to hide from these fallen ones?"

Lavrin felt too ashamed to answer. He had first seen the city as beautiful, while beneath its façade, its layers were wicked. It was the people, not the surroundings, that defined this city, and according to Calix, this city was far more devious than it appeared. Not only did Lavrin fear for his friends, but he feared for the armies of the North.

From what little Lavrin had heard, they had pushed the dark forces back, but for how long? The soldiers of Natas were surely more deceived by his lies than these people. "Calix, you do not need to bear this burden any longer. Let me have the pendant; maybe I can find the man we are looking for."

"I would not wish such a horror on anyone, save Natas himself. Besides, this is my gift from the King, and he must have some reason for letting me see these terrifying things."

"Did you see anyone who might hold the answer we seek?"

"I must keep looking," Calix replied. "I only hope we leave quickly, because the longer I watch these people throw themselves toward the pursuit of evil, the worse I shall become. Remember that we are only here to find who we need to find and leave. If I never return to this place, I will not complain."

Chan looked around the filthy alleyway, then looked back to the luminescent glow of the market square. His disgust was obvious. How shallow the wealth and splendor of Malstrate really was. Nevertheless, its size was not to be lessened. "Where are we to start? This city seems to stretch on and on in all directions. To walk its streets until we find our man could take days."

Lavrin grinned. This was one of the few things he had accounted for. "That's why we won't be searching in the streets. Calix was right when he said that his pendant has been given to him for a reason. We need to take him somewhere high. Higher than any other building. From that altitude, he can find our man; I'm sure of it."

"We all know which is the highest building, but reaching it will be incredibly challenging," Chan replied. They had seen the mighty tower at the center of Malstrate when they entered. It loomed over the surrounding buildings with a stature that was unmatched. The heart of the city revolved around its structure.

To make matters worse, its purpose was to be a military lookout to aid the guards of the city. This lookout was positioned right next to the barracks, where the soldiers they had followed into Malstrate would now be staying.

This was where they were headed, into the heart of the furnace. The center of the blaze where the silver was purified was this lookout nestled beside the guard's keep. It would have been hard anywhere, but in Malstrate, on the border of the dark mist, it demanded their utmost attention.

They respected the fire's playful wrath, but also sought water with which to destroy it.

Lavrin, Calix and Chan also respected this dangerous task, for even if they could ascend the tower, what then? Would they kill the lookout? How long would it be until the city and its soldiers were alerted of his death? No, if they killed the watchmen then they would never escape Malstrate, but that would be a later challenge. Before that, they had to reach the tower, and before that still, they had to reach the city's center.

Calix rose from his resting place and stood beside Lavrin and Chan, whose eyes were fixated on the single spire that seemed to boast against the sky. Its height would have seemed even greater, if the buildings around it were not as high as they were. Lavrin once again had to remind himself that the majesty of this town was a trick of Natas, trying to sway them from their path.

Before attracting too much attention, the three blended into the crowd right as a guard's scrutinizing gaze turned their direction. The guard was looking for someone, that much was clear. Luckily, there were too many people for him to find his target, and the three outsiders scolded themselves for not being more careful. That had been too close, but it would not happen again.

They scuffled through the people, trying to act natural. This was difficult, as they were nothing like the bickering civilians around them. Calix did not look anywhere but at the ground in front of him, trying not to see the wickedness around him. Each man he passed was thinking only of himself, not caring who he trampled in the process. This sickened Calix. He clutched his stomach.

The only relief he found was in following Lavrin and Chan closely, so that whatever he saw besides the ground was his friends' pure hearts. How little they both knew of the deeper happenings around them. Calix knew this was a blessing, allowing his friends to focus on the task at hand. Indeed, they were more focused than the commoners of Malstrate could ever know. The citizens were not watching Lavrin and Chan, but Lavrin and Chan were watching them.

On they went, folding into the current heading toward the market square. It was not long, however, before they realized that Traxius' men, the ones they had followed into Malstrate, were roaming the area. They were in more casual attire, but were still identifiable as soldiers, especially because of the longswords strapped to their backs. Furthermore, this square was not a place of trade or bargain, but of perversion and slander. No good thing took place here; even Chan and Lavrin easily perceived this. They could not take Calix into a place that would harm him further.

Shifting along as best they could, the three found an alcove away from the commotion. After stopping for Calix to regain himself, the three decided to take a less direct approach. They walked down several side streets, passing fewer and fewer people as they went. It seemed everyone was heading for the center of the city. Why was everyone gathering in the heart of Malstrate?

Lavrin knew they would not be able to reach the tower that day, but maybe they could learn something valuable instead. He knew they needed a vantage point from which to watch the disorder. Lavrin motioned to Chan and Calix, and they ventured as close to the center square as they dared. Every person in the city was dressed in dark red. They would stand out like grass in a desert, and that was not what they needed. Maybe there was another way.

The first to notice the tall wooden ladder was Chan, but Lavrin followed his gaze. They slowly carried the ladder behind a massive building. From there, they scaled up to the roof with ease, and positioned themselves just out of sight. Besides, who would look for them on the rooftops? As the sun started to hide itself behind the cloak of the horizon, the throngs of civilians robed in fiery crimson surrounded a single podium.

The sight was impressive, but also terrifying. The hundreds that gathered covered every inch of the massive square. It was clear they were waiting for something. Lavrin turned to Calix. "Do you see the one we are looking for?" It was a long shot, but maybe he could be seen amongst the masses. Maybe there was one sparkling gem amongst the soot and coal.

Calix grimaced. He clenched his eyes and looked away. "No. He is not there."

"You're sure?"

The look on Calix's face said it all. Lavrin did not mention it again. They would have to continue with the plan.

Chan was studied each face in the crowd below. He wondered who they were waiting for. Then he found him - Traxius. He was mighty in form and stature, but it was clear, even without Calix's pendant, that he had a heart far darker than those around him. Yet it was not Traxius who ascended to the podium.

Alternatively, a man rose onto the podium who was unimpressive in stature but wore costly furs and golden rings. He cleared his throat, and addressed the crowd with a thunderous voice, shocking from such an unexceptional man. "Citizens of Malstrate, I have led you in the ways of Natas for more years than I can remember. This city has been a fortress against the King of Light and a thorn in his side for generations. Now, rumors have spread about the recent battles of the North, but I assure you that Natas has not looked past the armies of the Light.

"That is the reason that we are gathered here today. Natas has called for new soldiers to be recruited from among the most loyal of his cities. Not only will these recruits be given the honor of crushing our enemies, but they will have riches and land, as well. Their families will also be given prominence in the eyes of Natas himself. I will not waste your time this evening. Who will join the ranks of Natas' army?"

Lavrin's heart was wrenched as he watched families practically throw their sons at the registration tables. They were willing to give up their children merely on the promise of respect from Natas. They were so deceived by the lure of riches and gain that would probably never materialize. There was no inspiration to join, only a call to fight to crush the light, and earn fame and land as a reward. This was all that was needed to register new soldiers to Natas' ranks.

Chan turned to Lavin. "How vile is this? How much damage have our friends caused in the North?

"Apparently enough," Lavrin replied. "I wonder if my father is in any of those battles. If we were not on this mission, I would give everything to be with him right now. How many soldiers do you think they will enlist today?'

Calix cast his gaze over the square. "What does it matter? What are we to do against the endless resources Natas has under his rule? If he can call up thousands of soldiers simply by asking, what chance do the forces of light have? I don't think our armies can ever challenge him alone. We need the King to help us now more than ever. Where is his mighty hand to save us?"

Lavrin bit his lip, deep in thought. "Maybe that's the point. Maybe Natas is afraid of the forces of light because they have the King's blessing. I agree, Calix, that is the only hope that we will have in this fight. I may not have spoken with the King as you and Chan have, but I know that his love does not cease, no matter the circumstances. Maybe... I don't know..."

Lavrin's weary and afflicted mind battled against what he knew to be true. "Maybe we are the King's mighty hand. This Titan's Heart may be the answer Amcronos has been waiting for. For hundreds if not thousands of years, our lands have kept the hope that the King will always be there. This mission, this quest we find ourselves upon, may be that prayer answered. For now, let's leave this place. There is nothing more for us to learn, and we will never reach that tower with this many soldiers on alert. We need to rest for the night."

As Chan descended the ladder, Calix grabbed Lavrin by the arm. "I don't think I'm going to be able to find this person, Lavrin," he whispered. "What happens if I fail?"

Calix's honesty and humility touched Lavrin. It had touched him many times before, even back to the day they first met. Of all the things that Lavrin had missed about Calix, this was the greatest. "My friend, you don't need to trouble yourself with that. I'm sure a good night's sleep will rest your mind and your conscience. If the King wants us to succeed, we will succeed. If he has other plans in mind, then we will be ready to carry them out. He will help you to see."

The three made good use of the open streets before the people flocked back to their homes. It did not take them long to find an ideal spot to rest. Not ideal in the sense of comfort, but it was somewhere no one would search. It was an old, likely-abandoned storehouse. There were a few empty barrels and crates lining the walls. Dust clung everywhere, and spiders fastened their homes to each ceiling corner.

After searching through the storehouse, Chan pushed aside a barrel to find a half-broken door to a back room. He motioned for the others to follow him inside, and before they did, they threw several wooden planks and two barrels in front of the door. They figured they could not be too careful.

Inside the back room, the three unpacked what few items they had brought and set up for the night. They were glad that this area of the storehouse was in better condition, so they would not have to sleep amidst shattered pieces of wood. Although the evening had not given way yet to night, Lavrin and Chan were too exhausted to stay awake. They fell asleep quickly, and their dreams turned to their friends, and to the war for the North.

Calix, the one who needed sleep the most, could not find it. He wrestled with the nightmares that haunted him, and just as he thought he might escape them, he would awake in a terror. It took all he had not to scream out when he was jolted back into reality. Beads of icy sweat clung to his forehead every time he thought of the thousands of souls held captive to evil in Malstrate.

Even more, there were the souls captive across Amcronos. Malstrate was just one city that followed Natas with the same devotion. How many more hearts had been lured by one man? How many more would be killed if they did not follow him?

The night drifted by slowly for Calix, as he searched for something to ease his nightmares. The thought lingered that the living shadows had not only showed him his deepest fear, but also his future. Calix hoped that he would return to the Haven Realm without experiencing cruel death once again, but he could not be sure. Of all the deaths he had seen, which one would claim him?

These agonizing thoughts continued, until he fell to sleep simply out of exhaustion.

*****

"I don't know which will be harder, reaching the tower, or escaping it unseen afterward," Lavrin said as he watched guards enter and exit the barracks.

Chan was equally uncertain. "With all this focus on the war against the King, we will be killed the moment we are found."

"We'd better not be found, then. Come on, let's get a closer look."

Leaving their hiding place, the three ventured as close to the barracks as they dared down the side street. They were approaching it from behind, which allowed them to be bolder than they otherwise would have been.

The morning sun welcomed their mission, as the guards of Malstrate were more focused on escaping its bright rays than watching the back alleys. This was exactly what Lavrin had been counting on.

From the cool of the alley's shade, they watched the armor-laden guards struggle against the wrath of the sunlight and the heat it brought. They did their best to remain diligent, but soon they were taking off their helmets and placing them at their sides. Typically, the captain of the guard would have sternly disciplined them, but he was nowhere to be found. He was called to train the new recruits from the day before.

As the day progressed, Lavrin had to plan less, and watch more. The four guards in front of the barracks soon became two, as the guards decided they would shift active duty. This fortune continued as the three lookouts atop the watchtower dropped from three to two, and then to one. In their minds, Malstrate was far from the turmoil in the North, and the only threat they faced were rebellious citizens. Yesterday's display had shown that they were anything but disloyal.

Although there were many soldiers inside of the barracks, Lavrin's hope continued to climb, as he now only had to worry about two barrack guards and one lookout. The King was with them. "We need to distract them. Not enough to have them leave their posts, but enough to have them preoccupied. Something that would seem natural, but annoying. Convenient - that's it. We need something convenient."

To the delight of both his companions, Calix spoke up. "I have an idea."

After finding some commoners' clothing, Chan dressed himself as an average Malstrate man. He circled the market square to enter it from a central road... the road a citizen would usually approach from. He made his way toward the barracks in no hurry. At first the guards looked past him, but when he got close enough, the guards drew their longswords. "Halt, peasant. Why do you approach Natas' barracks?"

"In the commotion last night, I was unable to register for Natas' army."

The guards bit the bait, and directed him where to go to register. Chan was a particularly naïve commoner, who made the guards' job harder than normal. All the while, Lavrin and Calix made their way to the watchtower. Lavrin slid his hand over the doorknob, and much to his surprise, found the door locked.

He shot a glance to Chan, who doubled his efforts. Lavrin looked left and right to find the sentry with the keys, but spun back to the door when he heard it open. Calix stepped inside and signaled for a befuddled Lavrin to follow him. As Calix began ascending the staircase, Lavrin asked, "How did you do that? I was sure that the door was locked."

"It was," Calix answered. He allowed his first smile inside of Malstrate's walls. "You should try this sometime." He tossed a long, slender dagger to Lavrin.

The side of its blade had notches and curves that Lavrin had never seen before. It was a beautiful weapon, but with its many grooves, it did not seem like a conventional dagger. "What is it?"

Calix continued up the stairs. "It's called a hatch breaker. Macrollo showed it to me in the Haven Realm. In fact, he didn't let me leave without it. It has a variety of uses, the primary of which is picking locks."

Lavrin tried to catch up to Calix. "Why didn't you tell me about this?"

"I never thought I would need it. Looks like Macrollo was right, after all."

Before Lavrin could answer, Calix stopped. They had reached the top of the stairwell, and right above them they heard pacing footsteps. They had to move quickly; who knew what Chan was going through below? Hopefully, he had gone to wherever the guards told him to and sneaked away when they left.

Calix did not waste any time. The plan was simple: catch the lookout off-guard and knock him out. There was no need to kill him; besides, maybe someone checking on him would think he fell asleep. That would buy them extra time.

With sword ready, Calix quietly opened the hatch and rose next to the lookout. He thrust the hilt of his sword on the lookout's temple, knocking him out cold. As he collapsed, his body started to fall over the side of the tower.

Calix jumped toward the man and caught him by the arm. He carefully took the fallen lookout and laid him next to the overhang. That was close, he thought to himself.

"Find our man, Calix," Lavrin said, just a few steps behind.

Knowing the gravity of their situation, Calix brought himself as close to the edge as he dared, and surveyed the north side of the city. He inspected every street and balcony, every building he could see. He forced his eyes to stay open, no matter how wicked the city was. Nothing.

He shifted his view to the east, and beheld the same sights. Though he was not able to see into the buildings and houses, he could see glimmers of the hearts within them, as if their souls were candles. These brought him no comfort, either. There was not even a spark of glistening blue or dazzling white in the east. Calix nearly knocked over Lavrin as he sprinted to the west side of the tower.

He critiqued every street corner. Where was their man? A passing yellow glow glinted at the corner of Calix's eye, and he immediately focused on it, desperate to see any heart not black. No, this was not who they were looking for; it was only the distant glow of a torch someone forgot to put out. Calix was almost furious. If this man had the information for them, he should make himself available. What else did they have to do to find him?

In desperation, Calix threw himself at the southern portico. Maybe they had missed this man from where they had entered. No, he was not near the gate. He was not in any central road or rooftop. Calix turned his gaze to the market square. Could he have hidden himself in the center of the city?

Calix fell to his knees. He shot a defeated glance at Lavrin. "I don't see him," he said. "I don't see him anywhere." Calix took off his pendant and extended it toward Lavrin. "Maybe you should try."

To hide his despair, Lavrin took the pendant from his friend's shaking hand. The moment Lavrin's hand touched the pendant, he released it. He grabbed his chest, a sharp fire shooting through his veins. His vision fogged over, and he braced himself against a pillar. "My friend, you were right. Don't let me touch that again. The King must have blessed you mightily to bear such a pain."

Calix's smile was more acknowledging than joyful. "It's a beautiful feeling in the presence of thousands of the King's followers in the Haven Realm. Here, however, it has brought me great grief. It is the memory of hundreds of shimmering hearts lifting the song of the King in harmony that helps me bear this darkness. This gift is said to have been formed by the mightiest of the King's servants. You have, however, seen it at the darkest possible time. Maybe I will have you wear it one day when you leave Amcronos."

"We cannot stay up here any longer. I don't know how we are going to find our answers, but we will need to meet with Chan. Let's go find him."

They hurried down the stairwell, almost tripping down its stone steps. They reached the door not long after, not even thinking to look out before leaving. Much to their regret, they were greeted by the two guards Chan had distracted. There was no sneaking away this time - the sentries were looking straight at them. When Lavrin and Calix sprinted away, the guards gave chase. "Stop," they yelled. "What are you doing?"

Their voices attracted other soldiers, who alerted the rest of their forces. There were intruders in Malstrate. Some rushed after Lavrin and Calix, but others ran toward the walls to alert the watchmen on the city borders.

Lavrin and Calix would not be easily caught. They burst through side streets and bolted alongside buildings much faster than their pursuers. It was at times like these that they were glad they were not wearing heavy armor. After sprinting past wagons, dodging onlookers and running out of breath twice over, Lavrin and Calix lost their pursuers by diving into a concealed alleyway. The guards rushed past.

After a few minutes of recovering, Lavrin and Calix were ready to find Chan. They had told him to head southward if he escaped after his distraction. Lavrin and Calix had desired to sneak through the alleyways to find him, but after a couple turns, they realized that the only way back was on the main road. Of course, this was the exact opposite from what they had wanted to do.

Against their better judgement, they edged their way to the end of the shadows and looked onto the street which was starting to become busy again. Luckily, it seemed the soldiers of the city were searching all Malstrate, which meant they were spread thin.

When the crowds were at their busiest, Lavrin and Calix abandoned their safe place. They blended in as best as they could with the flow of people, making sure to head ever southward. As they walked, they noticed several guards searching the area, with swords drawn and on high alert. The road was not as clear as they had thought.

Lavrin and Calix tried to thrust themselves into the busiest part of the road, much to the dislike of those around them. Amid the chaos, the soldiers missed their targets, but Calix suddenly felt a hand grab his shoulder. He would have fought back, but he heard a voice saying, "Keep your focus on the people in front of you. Don't look at the guards. They will be searching for anyone acting suspicious."

Calix recognized the voice instantly. Instead of finding Chan, Chan had found them. "We are going to head down this road to the right; it will be about a quarter of a mile until we reach the southern wall. There are many soldiers coming up soon. They will be looking for two rangers. I am still in my common clothes, but you two are going to need to be especially careful. We should split up, but stay on the same route. We will gather back together at a narrow, tall building near the southern wall. It is a tanner's shop. No one will expect us to need some shoes."

Acting in haste on Chan's instructions, Calix made his way forward, ahead of Lavrin and Chan and to the right side of the road. Lavrin veered left, traveling at a slower pace. Chan allowed himself to drop behind both his friends, positioning himself specifically so he could watch Lavrin, Calix and the soldiers on patrol.

At first, it felt like everything was going too smoothly, until Lavrin watched the guards drag a ranger from the crowds and throw him onto the ground. He walked away from the scene, hoping to appear uninterested. Or should he have appeared interested?

Lavrin gained distance from the encounter as fast as he could, only not too fast. He told himself over and over to act natural, until he felt like everything he was doing was unnatural. To his relief, Lavrin spied the tanner's shop ahead. Even better, he watched Calix safely enter it.

Lavrin's sole desire at that moment was to enter the tanner's shop, though he did not know how much safety it would bring. Within a few moments, he had made it. Chan waited to make his entrance seem unrelated.

The shop was neither large nor grand; in fact, it was mostly empty. It was the perfect place for them to avoid suspicion, at least for the moment. Chan went up to the tanner and purchased a set of boots. He had to make his appearance there not seem unordinary. He then met up with Lavrin and Calix toward the back of the room. "Well done, Chan," Calix said. "You may have just saved our lives."

"I'm only sorry that I couldn't have distracted the guards for longer. We can't worry about that now. We have to go to our man and then leave the city."

Lavrin lowered his gaze. "We couldn't find him, Chan. Even from the great height of the tower, we couldn't see him. I wonder if he is real at all, or if the living shadows tricked us in the worst of ways. I fear that with Malstrate's soldiers looking to find and kill us, we should try and escape now, and hope the King has another plan. Maybe there are others out there who know of the piece."

"In most cases I would argue against it," Chan replied. "But I think you're right. Our lives are not worth it. Who knows? Maybe you're right about the living shadows. They could have been lying to us all along. I know the King will show us another way to find the next piece. The real question is, how do we escape?"

"They are going to heavily guard the gates. That is where they expect us to go. There must be some other way out. Cities as large as this have other exits. We could try their aqueduct..." Lavrin shook his head.

"What's wrong?" Chan asked.

"I doubt it will work," Lavrin said. "I remember seeing it from atop the tower. It was in plain sight from all angles. We would have to be incredibly lucky to even reach it. That's not even planning for how we get out of it."

Chan remained optimistic, despite Lavrin's lack of enthusiasm. "We must make it work. If we are going to try it, we should try it now. Soon, the guards will widen their search and we will have nowhere left to run."

They knew that their time to escape was dwindling and they had to act now. Thankfully, the tanner had been too preoccupied to notice them. They headed toward the aqueduct. Lavrin and Chan had almost reached the end of the street when they realized Calix was not with them. They turned around to see him just a few steps outside of the tanner's shop.

He seemed to be fascinated with something. Lavrin had almost reached Calix when he saw several soldiers turn his direction. He quickly folded into the flow of the crowd, crouching behind those around him. To his luck, the soldiers were confronted by their captain, and thus momentarily detained.

Lavrin reached Calix within an instant and shook him. "Calix? What are you doing? Once those guards turn back our direction, we will be dead men."

Calix was calm. Far too calm given the fact that he was in serious danger. "Don't you see it, Lavrin? The soft glow of star-like blue light? I've found who we've been looking for."

He walked down a filthy alleyway beside the tanner's shop, more of a crevice than an alley… far more dirty than any of the others. Calix did not even notice the foul stench in the air or the shattered glass under his feet.

He stepped over the waste and onto what little clear ground there was. His two companions watched the street behind them, weapons ready in case the soldiers had followed them. They looked out while he searched within, captivated by a single glow.

Calix reached down and picked up half a broken table. He tossed it to the side like the wreckage that it was. Beneath it, a little boy lay wrapped in a soiled blanket. His sympathetic hazel eyes searched Calix cautiously. He stood up and tried to look tall.

Despite his attempt, his scrawny arms and legs stood out. He took a deep breath. "Sir," he said. "Please… please put my home back…. That's my home…" The boy spoke with a lisp, but Calix did not mind. What did it matter how he spoke if his heart was so honest? He followed the boy's frail finger as it pointed to the piece of wreckage that had once been a table.

Calix knelt beside the brave boy. "Why are you out here all alone?"

A crystal tear trickled down the boy's face, but he wiped it away as fast as he could. "My parents… they don't like my talk… they say I'm strange… I don't know how to help it, sir." Once again, the child's handicap was evident. For such a small detail to cause this boy to have been abandoned wrenched Calix. He did not doubt, however, that these people were capable of it.

Calix tried to contain himself, both from his joy and from his overwhelming sympathy for this child. "What is your name, son?"

"My name is…" he stopped, as if trying to gain the courage. Calix realized he was trying to pronounce it without his lisp. "Andw… Andreu…" The boy grew frustrated. "Andreas. What is you?"

Watching the boy's sky blue heart, Calix almost forgot to say his own name. "I'm Calix. Andreas, you are a very kind and gentle young man. You should be proud of who you are."

The boy's response gripped Calix to his very core. "How can I be proud of myself if my parents aren't? How can… can I… how can I be proud of myself when I cry too much. I'm supposed… to be strong so they will love me again."

A burning inferno of passion rose within Calix. He wanted to hold Andreas tight and let nothing happen to him again. This boy had inspired him so much that his drive would challenge earthquakes. Calix approached Lavrin as if Andreas' father. "I don't care if I have to kill the entire army of Natas with my bare hands, I will not rest until Andreas is safe outside of Malstrate."

Lavrin's answer was short, but nothing more needed to be said. "I would expect nothing less."

"Who are they, Calix?" A tender voice rang from behind them. Calix rushed to Andreas, who had tightly wrapped himself in his dirty blanket.

Andreas took Calix's hand, already trusting him as if he was his hero. Calix took him to Lavrin and Chan, who had both listened in on the conversation. "Hello, Andreas. My name is Lavrin. I'm Calix's friend. We are going to get you out of here."

After Chan had been introduced to Andreas, the three took their charge to escape Malstrate with a renewed vigor. This boy would tell them where the next piece of the Titan's Heart was, but he could not remain in this wicked city. This boy could be the most important person they ever were tasked to protect.

They argued back and forth on plans of escape, getting nowhere. With the four gates heavily guarded, allowing no one in or out, they had few options. Lavrin had himself dismissed the aqueduct, but no better solution was presented. That was, until Andreas spoke up. "Why... you should... why don't you start a fire?"

Lavrin almost rejected the suggestion, but stopped. He allowed the thought to boil long enough to consider it. Something about it made sense, but he could not figure it out. "Why would we need a fire, Andreas?"

Andreas smiled widely, showing several teeth were missing. "Everybody... they all... run to fires. They run to catch the bad guy who made the fire... if they running to the fire ... they not running to the gates."

The three rangers were astounded. Were they protecting Andreas, or was Andreas protecting them? It was a brilliant idea. One each of them had wished they themselves had thought of. The best part of it was that they knew an old building made of wood, with a stable right beside it for straw. The team made their way back toward the abandoned storehouse.

They dodged through side streets, but even the side streets were becoming less and less safe, especially for a group their size. Nonetheless, the King was with them and they reached the abandoned storehouse unscathed.

On their approach, they had already decided upon their course of action. Calix, Chan and Andreas began to take straw out of the nearby stable and pile it into the storehouse. Lavrin snuck into the back door of the blacksmith's. He treaded as lightly as he could.

He waited until the blacksmith was preoccupied with a customer and went into the back room where the smith kept his furnace. With all haste, Lavrin picked up the long black tongs and grabbed a burning coal from the hearth. He snuck out the back door with his prize and reached the storehouse just as his friends finished filling it with straw.

Lavrin dropped the coal into the center of the storehouse, and rushed back to the blacksmith's as his three companions sprinted back toward the gate. From some ways off, Lavrin threw the tongs to land just beside the back door of the smithy. Confident that everything was set,

Lavrin followed his friends. Moments later, they heard shouts coming from all around them. Everyone was rushing to the storehouse. Lavrin thanked the King that the storehouse had not only saved them at night, but had saved them this day, as well.

Soldiers rushed to the scene, only to find the building engulfed by towering flames. They called in every direction for water to be brought. There was not nearly enough water in the area, so buckets had to be hauled from the aqueduct on the far side of the city. Soon, more and more help was needed against the fire's rage as it spread from the storehouse to the stable beside it. Horses trampled down whatever kept them from fleeing.

The four followers of the light reached the southern gate faster than they thought possible. Calix had carried little Andreas, for his thin legs were in no shape to run that far. Calix set down his new friend and immediately burst toward the southern gate with sword in hand. Lavrin and Chan followed, unable to match Calix's speed.

The guards of the gate hardly had time to draw their weapons before they were engaged by the three warriors. Warriors desperate for victory... warriors desperate to escape. Although the guards outnumbered their attackers four to one, they were little match for the experience and zeal of Lavrin, Chan and Calix. Each of them fought like mighty lions, turning every defensive move into an offensive attack. Their three swords, one of Amcronos, two of the Haven Realm, swung with a furious agenda.

Reinforcements rushed to help the fallen sentries. Calix rushed to raise the gate as Chan and Lavrin protected him. The gate usually took two men to raise it, but Calix was hard pressed, and running out of time. He lifted the gate just as high as it needed to be, then called to Lavrin. Lavrin threw him a small dagger, and Calix pinned it into the same gears that had bid them entrance into the city.

The gate was jammed in place, just as Calix had hoped. He called for Andreas, and the little boy ran to him as best as he could. Soldiers poured into the streets surrounding the southern gate. Calix picked up Andreas and bolted out of the city without a second thought. It had been their plan for the two of them to leave first, so Calix wasted no time in escaping. Lavrin and Chan bought them as much time as they could, before they had an opening to duck under the massive gate and make their getaway.

Faster and faster they ran from the city, trying to put as much ground between them and Malstrate. They did not look back to see if they were being followed. All they knew was that they were safe if they could get away from that place. The three invaders had escaped Malstrate, and the city's last pure heart had left with them.

CHAPTER 19

FROM THEN ON

They had been waiting for the return of their companions from Malstrate for four days. No one had dared express their doubts aloud. Finally, Kyra rushed into camp. She was obviously flustered, her breaths swift and sporadic, but that was not what caught her friends' attention.

In her arms, she carried a young boy who was thin and pale, a boy none of them had seen before. Kyra rushed into the center of the camp and began to shout orders. "Kasandra, bring me my supplies. Felloni, give me your blanket. Nadrian, wet as many cloths as you can find and bring them to me. Uminos, put out that fire."

Though they had no idea what was happening, they knew Kyra was desperate, and she was only desperate when she had a good reason to be. The once quiet scene flew into action, and Kyra soon had the weary boy resting on Felloni's blanket, with several cloths upon his forehead and chest.

Kyra unwrapped several herbs from her supplies and began to crush them into a powder. She mixed them together and poured them in water. She then called for Nadrian. "Lift him up slightly." Once again, Nadrian obeyed, and Kyra slowly gave her patient the medicine.

Finally, Kyra relaxed. "What is going on, Kyra?" Nadrian asked.

"He has a severe fever," Kyra answered. "One of the highest I have ever seen."

"Who is he?"

From outside the camp, a voice said, "His name is Andreas." Calix appeared just a moment after. He was followed by Lavrin and Chan. The three were ravaged by exhaustion, but nonetheless strong. They had been through trying times before, and had the fortitude to last through them, but poor Andreas had little strength in his frail body.

Calix approached Kyra first. "Is he going to be alright?"

Kyra paused. "I have done all that I can for the moment. I'm sure he will recover soon enough, and he can have a warm meal. You're lucky I found you when I did. If I had not been out searching for herbs, who knows what would have happened. In the meantime, you three can tell us why it took you almost two days longer than expected."

"And why we were not allowed to go with you," Kasandra quickly added.

Lavrin, Calix and Chan sat beside their fellow warriors and saw the pain in their gaze from Kasandra's remark. Clearly, it was something they all had been thinking about.

Lavrin searched, but could find no real answer. "On that account, I must apologize to you all. When I had heard that we were to journey to Malstrate, my heart was gripped with fear. Instead of trusting the King fully, I doubted whether we would make it out of Malstrate alive. For that reason, I decided to only take Chan and Calix. The King worked past my blindness and allowed us to escape Malstrate with Andreas, though it was much harder than it might have been with you at our side."

"You are right to apologize, Lavrin," Kasandra said. "I did not leave the Mazaron to be treated as though I was unnecessary for the King's cause. We could have helped you. We should have been there with you to…"

"Enough, Kasandra," Kyra remarked. "Can't you see that Lavrin knows that? He did what he thought was best for the team at a time of great crisis. What is done is done." She turned to Lavrin. "Now, Lavrin, how does Andreas fit into all of this? Why did you bring him out of Malstrate?"

Calix answered before Lavrin could. "He is the reason we went into Malstrate. He is the messenger we have searched for. I'm confident that when he awakes, he will share with us the next piece of the Titan's Heart."

Grax had been watching the boy since he had entered their camp. "He is the messenger?" he said. "I expected..." He cut himself off. "Well, I suppose it does not matter. What matters is that you are safe, all of you. I look forward to hearing from the boy. For the moment, however, there is someone the three of you will be happy to see. We have not been alone while we've waited for you."

As Lavrin, Calix and Chan looked around, they saw no one else. Although they still could see nothing, they heard a mighty sound coming from the sky above. It was like a rushing wind, like the beginning of a tornado in the air.

They looked upward, but were blasted backward by a fierce gust of wind. Then, landing in front of them, they beheld the majestic form of Idrellon. His graceful wings folded in as his silver and purple body came into view. No longer invisible under the sun's light in the sky, the mighty eagle bowed before the three.

"Idrellon!" Lavrin almost jumped with delight. He had to restrain himself not to rush upon the eagle and hug him. "It has been far too long. In fact, we have not seen you since the battle for the Mazaron. How greatly I have longed to see you again. Why have you come to us now?"

"Because a far greater war is raging now, and still greater it will grow. Its repercussions across Amcronos will make the battle for those mountains seem minor. I have been watching the armies at odds in the North, reporting to the King all that has happened. I have come at the King's personal request, as your companions here already know. I have come to warn you, and to instruct you. I will be blunt. The war in the North is on a blade's edge.

"The forces of the light have done well to even the score against the massive numbers under Natas' banner. This will not stop Natas, however, from trying to turn the odds in his favor once more. This mission you are upon, this quest for the Titan's Heart, is the only way for the army of the light not to fall to the forces of darkness. You must take haste, and make every measure to claim this ancient relic quickly, for the longer the North remains on a blade's edge, the more desperate they will be for a sign of the King's deliverance. You will be that sign."

Amidst the weight of what Idrellon said, Lavrin remained fixated on one point. "The King himself sent you to us?"

Idrellon nodded his head long and low. "He would have it no other way. He told me himself that I was to bring this message to you and then wait until the boy told you what you seek."

"So, he knows of everything? He knows not only of our quest to Malstrate, but of Andreas?"

Idrellon looked to both Chan and Calix who were standing beside Lavrin. "How much you have yet to see Lavrin, son of Gevnor. When you enter the Haven Realm, I'm sure you'll be amazed at how much he has known all along."

Chan chuckled as Idrellon continued. "You will be glad to know that the King has kept special attention on your father, who is likely helping the lords of the light plan their next attack as we speak. Kyra, is there any way we could wake the boy? Although it has been an honor to see you all again, I am eager to complete the King's next task for me. Besides, I have several friends in the Haven Realm who are eager to hear about your progress. Rowan will be the most interested. He always is."

Kasandra glowed as she thought of her cousin, but Kyra turned toward the sleeping Andreas. "His symptoms have worsened. I would prefer not to wake him, but if you are desperate, then I can."

The eagle's soft heart and compassion fell upon the little child. "We will give him an hour. I'm sure we have more than enough to discuss."

Idrellon was bombarded with questions, mostly about the Haven Realm and their friends in the North. The King's servant did as best as he could to answer everyone, and did not mind their eagerness. He had expected as much. For how long they had been without contact with the rest of Amcronos, the team soaked up information with an appetite. The hour disappeared faster than anyone would have liked. Soon enough, however, their hunger subsided, and they realized the time had come. With Idrellon's instruction, they too were now interested to hear from Andreas, and everyone turned to him as he yawned.

With tiny hands, he rubbed his eyes gently as he awoke. He stretched out, showing to a greater extent his boney arms. It was obvious that he had not had a good meal in a long time. When his eyes refocused, he was terrified. He scrambled out of his blanket and dove behind Calix's knees.

Calix knelt beside him. "What's wrong?"

Andreas clutched Calix's shirt. "Why are there... who are... who are these people? I'm scared, Calix."

With the love of a father, Calix carefully lifted Andreas up and sat him on his knee. "These are all my friends. They would never want to hurt you, Andreas. Actually, they want to protect you very much."

"Even him?" Andreas stared at Uminos in wonder.

Calix motioned for Uminos to come closer. "Yes, even Uminos. He may look tough, but really he's very nice."

Andreas cocked his head and studied Uminos with curiosity. He focused on Uminos' large yellow eyes which seemed to interest him even more than his scales. Then, out of nowhere, Andreas said to Uminos. "I like... I... you have a nice tail."

Uminos blushed and grinned widely. He did not
even realize that he was showing his sharp teeth to young
Andreas, who once again tried to hide behind Calix.
"Thank you," Uminos said, realizing his mistake. "Would
you like to touch it?"

Getting Andreas' focus off his teeth and back onto
his tail calmed him. Andreas slowly crept from behind his
safety net and reached out and felt Uminos' tail. He
giggled with delight. He looked back at Calix, searching
for approval. Calix beamed, and motioned for Andreas to
return to his lap. "Andreas," Calix whispered to him. "I
have a very important question to ask you."

Andreas was instantly curious. "What is… what…
what is it?"

Speaking up louder, so all could hear, he asked.
"Andreas, do you know of a place, a very special place you
want to tell us about?"

Andreas thought for a moment. Suddenly, he
looked much older and smarter, like he did when he helped
them escape Malstrate. "My home… it is not very
special… I do know… I have seen a special place… does it
count if a friend told it to me?"

"Who is this friend?"

It took Andreas longer than it usually took him to
answer. "He was… he took care of me… I loved him very
much. He told me about the King… I liked his stories… he
had great stories about the King."

"Why was he not with you in the city, Andreas?" Calix asked.

Sorrow welled in the boy's eyes. "Bad men... they... they took him away. I wanted to... I never saw him again. I miss my... the favorite story he told me."

Calix's heart was broken, but he did not want Andreas to be sad any longer. "Tell us about this story."

"He... it was about...it was a special place. It is very big... it is this big," He extended his arms as wide as he could in both directions. "It is... the place is... a very... a very fast river. The river... the river is skinny on one side... but the other side... the other side is also skinny... but in the middle, it is very big. In the middle, it runs very fast. There are rocks... there are rocks that stick up out of the water in the middle. In the... in the story I... I am always playing in the skinny part of the river... playing with someone... maybe I'm playing... playing with you, Calix?"

"Yes, maybe, Andreas. Thank you for telling us that."

Idrellon, with his tall frame standing above even Uminos, stepped forward. "I know the place. There is a river, the Longland River that runs north to south out of Malstrate. If you follow it toward the mountains southward, you will find the place. Funny, I have been there at least twice, and have never seen anything. Hopefully, you will find something that I did not. Now, my mission here is complete, and I must return to the Haven Realm with all haste."

Before the great eagle could leave, Calix stopped him. "Wait, Idrellon. I beg of you, take Andreas with you. He cannot remain with us here. Have him set up in my personal quarters, and set Macrollo or Rowan to care for him. His heart is as pure as any I have ever seen, and it belongs nowhere but the Haven Realm."

"It is a special request, Calix. I do not doubt this child's innocence. Normally, I would say no, simply because the King is the one who grants entrance into the Haven Realm, but now that I think about it, he already has. I wondered why he did not have me inform you and then leave, but now I see why he had me wait for this boy. I will take him, and I will make sure the best of the Haven Realm is not spared him."

Calix turned to Andreas with tears falling like fresh snow. "Andreas, I'm sending you to a very special place. Somewhere called the Haven Realm. There you will never be in danger again, and will have lots of good food to eat and a bed to sleep in. You will make many new friends there. You may even get to talk with the King when you are older."

Andreas smiled. "That sounds like fun. The King sounds… he is… he is a very smart person. I will… I want to eat the good food with you, Calix."

"I will not go with you, Andreas. Not yet. I will meet you there soon. You will meet friends there who will love you just as much as I do. Idrellon will take you there."

"I wish I was going there with you, Calix." Andreas pouted, but then turned to a grin once again. "But… if… I will go because you say it is good. I want… I will see you there soon, right?"

Calix melted. "Yes, you will see me there soon."

The two embraced. Calix knew he would miss that gentle spirit, that burst of hope in the otherwise evil Malstrate. The light in the midst of darkness. Andreas ran to Idrellon, who lowered his wing to allow Andreas on. The last words Andreas said in Amcronos were, "You… you are the… you are a very soft eagle. I like your feathers."

Idrellon took off into the sky, with Andreas cradled between his strong wings. The silver and purple body of the eagle soon blended in with the sky, becoming invisible as the sunlight passed through him. The team did not know if they would see him again, but what they had heard from the King's messenger gave them hope to continue. They would find the next piece of the Titan's Heart; they had to.

There was nothing more to be said, at least not for the moment. Their focus was on leaving this place and heading southeast until they reached the Longland River. They were on their way soon enough. Calix thought of his newest reason to return to the Haven Realm.

They were all quiet except for Kyra, who asked Lavrin everything about the mission to Malstrate. Lavrin was glad to answer her questions, but the more he said, the more he realized how hurt the rest of the team must have felt. Nonetheless, Kyra wanted to know everything about the journey, and was especially enamored with Calix's Haven Realm dagger from Macrollo.

Her heart was kind, Lavrin knew, and though she did not say it, Lavrin could tell she longed to ease his conscience. He was grateful for the attempt, but his thoughts were on the future, not the past. How to keep the team whole rivaled how to keep the team safe. What was best for his friends' lives rivaled what was best for Amcronos.

The allies he needed beside him were the ones he hated to take into battle. Kyra most of all. How was she supposed to protect herself in the heat of war? She was the greatest of friends, and an incredible healer, but the battles would only grow tougher from here. Lavrin accidentally whispered, "What am I supposed to do?"

Kyra's carefree spirit turned serious. She looked him straight in the eyes. "Let me help you. That is what you are supposed to do."

Lavrin covered his face with his hands. "I don't think you can help me with this one, Kyra."

Now she knew she had to help him. She decided to press harder. "Lavrin, please." She tried to search his expression, but Lavrin turned away.

At first, Kyra thought she would not hear of it again, but Lavrin turned back to her. "For just a moment in Malstrate, Calix allowed me to put on his pendant from the King. Seeing into the hearts of men was terrifying. Every single soul in that wretched place was evil, and Calix watched their shadows for the entire time we were there. I only saw them for a moment, and was horrified. It was then that I realized how greatly Natas' deceit has spread.

"We are traveling into the heart of his territory, to claim artifacts from guardians who have protected them for centuries. This is a band of warriors, many with armor from the Haven Realm itself. Those who do not have it, still have been training in battle for most of our lives. Them I do not fear for. I fear for you, Kyra. Am I supposed to take you into the heart of battle with no way to protect yourself?"

"That's why I have you, isn't it?"

Her courage was unwavering. Lavrin would have paid anything to see her heart with Calix's gift. "I couldn't bear to lose you."

"That's why you won't," she said. "I lasted just fine in the battles we've been in thus far. Lavrin, I know that you have much more important things to worry about than me. I understand. I talked with both Uminos and Felloni about their nightmares with the living shadows. They both told me the same thing: 'without Lavrin I would not have made it.' They told me off the promises you made to them. I would focus on those if you want to get your mind off the mission. I can handle myself just fine. Now go, you should be talking to them far more than you should be talking to me."

Lavrin marveled at her determination, but did not question it. He went to speak with Felloni. The two went ahead of the group, speaking mostly of Felloni's past, but also of the future. Lavrin realized that these enemies of Felloni's had not always been his adversaries; rather, they often were men who had abused him and taken advantage of him in past.

Especially when he was young, Felloni had been trapped under their authority. That was why when he helped Chan and Nadrian learn the ways of the forest so long ago; he had not wanted to go back. The light of the King had been far better than the wickedness behind him. He only wanted to go back now because of the evil they had done to his family. Lavrin saw it not as a desire for revenge, but as a love for his family. Felloni wanted to do it for them, not for himself.

Though Lavrin carefully took note of what Felloni said, there was little he could promise him. What he could say, however, was that if they were still alive, their end would be swift if the forces of darkness were stopped. If Natas could somehow, someway be stopped, the evil in Amcronos would flee.

Lavrin remained by Felloni's side, and they talked of many more things before they reached the river.

*****

Its current was strong, rushing with the strength of an ocean tide. This would not have been surprising if its banks were shallow, dashing over rapids that clung close to the surface, but no rapids were in sight in Longland River. It was incredible to see a massive river traveling at such speeds.

The team specifically looked for the wide center with narrow straits on both sides as Andreas had described. It was not to be found; the whole river seemed wide as far as they could see. To Lavrin, this meant only one thing. Since the mountains to the south were not yet visible, as Idrellon had mentioned, they were too far north.

No one doubted him. Although they were unsure how they went from traveling southeast to heading northeast, they doubled their efforts and turned their thoughts south. With the river as their guide, they would not get lost this time. It was a rare feeling for the travelers, knowing they had direction.

The longer they trekked by the side of the river, the more time they had to dwell on the coming challenge. Would the next piece of the Titan's Heart be even harder to claim? Would their team get out of this danger again unscathed? Even without knowing the opposition they may face, it was daunting. The only thing they knew for sure was that these guardians had been placed over their relics for centuries, and would not quickly part with them.

Ever thinking as a leader, Lavrin wondered how many guardians they would face this time. Little did he know this was not the only adversary they faced. Little did he know that he and his friends had been followed out of Malstrate.

CHAPTER 20

LET IT BE THREE

They had searched three days for their next location. Although the Longland River curved and bended, it never narrowed like Andreas and Idrellon had described. Now, the team was nearing the southern mountains, and was wondering what they could have missed. As the snow-topped peaks grew closer, the group became more and more worried.

Nevertheless, they continued to head south, following the river as their guide. Eventually, with the mountains only a half-day's travel away, the team found what they were looking for. The shimmering waters funneled into a narrow strait, then widened into a sort of pool. The same type of narrow strait continued on the other side. This was the place. This was where they were supposed to find the next piece.

The only problem was that although the scene was beautiful, it was too quiet. The evergreens that clung to both sides of the pool cast their shadows upon it. The pool seemed isolated from everything around it. It was as if nature was trying to cut it off from the rest of the world. The waters rushed and foamed as if breaking through rapids, but there were no rapids to be seen.

Grax stated the obvious. "This has to be the place, but how can the Titan's Heart be here?"

Felloni was unfazed. "So, I'm probably the best swimmer."

Everyone in the group looked at him, confused. He continued, "It's obviously not anywhere on the surface. That is, unless someone just threw it onto a tree branch. Maybe it's buried at the bed of the river."

Before anyone could say anything, Felloni had set down his pack and dove into the river. He rushed with powerful strokes against the current toward a large rock that jutted out from the surface. Although he fought against the strength of the river, he reached his destination. He clung to the rock as if his life depended on it.

The team set down their supplies. They were fixated on Felloni and his endeavor. After taking a deep breath, he plunged into the racing torrent… into the unseen depths of the Longland River. His companions held their breath with him as they wondered the mysteries of this place.

Far sooner than anyone expected, Felloni returned. He claimed his fill of air and dove once again. For a second time he returned, and snatched the rock with both hands. "There is something down there. It's too big for me to move. Come, help me out here."

Without hesitation, Lavrin jumped into the river and headed toward the rock. Though he was not nearly as graceful as Felloni, he reached the rock soon enough, and was surprised at how much he needed it. Without it, they would have been pulled down the Longland instantly. Felloni could tell that Lavrin was worried. "Don't worry. The current is not nearly as rough down there. Follow me."

Lavrin disappeared beneath the river, following Felloni as best he could. Underneath the surface was nothing like Lavrin expected. From above, the river looked cloudy and dark, but beneath it was breathtaking. The haze that gathered at the top of the waters dissipated a few feet down and gave way to clear waters.

It did not take Lavrin long to see what Felloni was heading toward. It was the largest bolder on the lake bed. It was massive, but not too massive to be immovable. He could see why Felloni had chosen it. It seemed impossible for any single man to move. The perfect place to hide something.

Soon, Felloni had reached the right side of this mighty but smooth stone, and Lavrin swam to its left. Lavrin nodded to his friend and they both pulled against it. It hardly moved at all. They gave it a second effort, determined to find what treasures it covered. The bolder was stubborn. Its size kept it from sliding either direction. Lavrin and Felloni waited until they could not hold their breath a moment longer, and scrambled for the surface. They reached it just in time, panting like dogs for all the oxygen they could cram into their lungs. They were so desperate they almost forgot to grab the rock.

When Lavrin had finally mustered enough breath, he called to Grax. "Grax, we need you."

"I'm not very good at swimming," came his reply.

"You're going to have to be today."

Grax frowned. He did not like that answer. Nevertheless, he kicked off his boots, and took off his inner chain mail coat. He needed any advantage against the river he could get. Unlike his friends, he first waded as far as he could into the current before beginning to swim. His mighty frame was challenged by the current. Though his swimming was nothing to admire, he got just close enough to the rock for Felloni and Lavrin to grab him by the arm. They pulled him in, and he was safely beside them. "Now for the hard part," Lavrin said.

Grax was not pleased. Clearly, he had hoped that had been the hard part. "What are we dealing with down there?"

Lavrin smirked. "Nothing you can't handle."

This time, Lavrin dove before Felloni, and found his place on a side of the massive stone. Felloni went to the same spot he had taken before, but this time they had Grax in the middle. The trio pushed and lifted with all they had, and the bolder began to budge, but it was not enough. This angered Grax. No one wanted to be on the opposite side of an angry Grax. He dug his feet into the bed of the river and powered through his granite foe. Lavrin and Felloni hardly had to lift as their resilient companion shoved the rock from where it lay. The two returned to their awaiting friends with their champion.

"You are not going to believe this," Lavrin called out to the rest of their team.

"Try us," Nadrian answered.

"I don't want to ruin the surprise. Just get over here."

Nadrian was the first in the water, but was quickly followed by the rest of the group, all except Uminos. The team reached the refuge of the outstretched rock, and another rock beside it. They were drenched but otherwise fine. They looked to Uminos. "What's wrong?"

His response was short and to the point. "Seviathans don't swim."

"They don't swim at all?" Lavrin asked.

"Not if it can in any possible manner be avoided. You cannot imagine how hard it is to swim with scales."

Lavrin was unfazed. "How far can you jump?"

At first, Uminos looked to his leader in confusion. Why did that matter? Then he caught on. He dropped his scimitar beside the rest of their possessions, and stepped several feet back from the river. He readied himself in a running stance, and then rushed toward the river faster than anyone had seen him run before.

He leapt with such incredible power that at first the team was afraid he would collide into them. Luckily, he fell just a short distance from the others and stretched his hand into the air as he sunk. Grax caught the Seviathan with the same strength that caught him when he had entered the Longland.

Grax lifted Uminos out of the river to let him catch his breath. "We are going to let you go first, friend."

He shook the water from his eyes. "Why?"

"So that no one can get in your way. Don't worry about swimming. You just have to sink in its general direction."

Uminos shot Grax a look that said more than enough. What general direction?

"You won't miss it," Grax said.

He dropped Uminos into the water without warning. At first, Uminos struggled against it, but then he turned his eyes to the river floor and noticed a hole, just big enough for a person to fit through. He aimed toward it, and fit

401

himself into the gap. Suddenly, he felt himself moving faster and faster, as if he had been flying but was now falling. He was terrified. He looked for something to grab hold of, but the rock around him had disappeared. It was then that he realized he was in a great expanse, being turreted downward by something that resembled a waterfall. It was happening too fast for him to take it in.

All he knew was he had been falling for too long. How far would this drop take him?

Finally, he felt his body collide with waters below. The impact was sharp, but the pain subsided quickly. Uminos might have drowned if his feet had not met solid ground. With a mighty effort, he pushed off and shot up toward the surface. As he neared the top of the pool, he saw a hand reaching out toward him. He stretched for it, and it pulled him out of the waters. Uminos turned to thank Lavrin… but it was not Lavrin. It was someone he had never seen before.

The soldier wore full body armor, black like coal but outlined in crimson red. Each piece of his commanding armor was expertly crafted, displaying his authority. His helmet was the most ornate piece, and he held it in his other hand. It was unlike anything Uminos had ever seen. It seemed to display a dragon's head, even down to the realistic flames. Uminos was afraid they would burn him.

This warrior, who had mysteriously helped him out of the waters, turned to help the rest of the group. Instead of asking anything, Uminos also went to pick up his friends who had fallen into the underground pool. It was only then that he could see the torrent he had fallen down. It climbed up to the hole above, a staircase back to the Longland and to all the lands that they had known. It poured out toward them like rain, and filled the pool he had come out of. This pool was much bigger than Uminos had first thought. It stretched on so far that he had to squint to see its other side. How many times had the stone been lifted before?

Soon, the rest of the team was out of the water with the help of Uminos and their unknown friend. Kyra rushed to check on each member of their group, making sure everything single soul was safe. Now with everyone accounted for, the Seviathan turned to the soldier of black and red. "Thank you for helping us. I must know, who are you?'

"My name is much too long for anyone to remember. What you probably are looking for is my title. I am called Commander. You would probably rather call me that."

"It would be rather strange to call you Commander when you are not my leader."

The man put on his helmet. "I may be soon enough. Anyway, you and your team will want to follow me. Trust me, I'm not like the living shadows, and this is no trap. Those things come later."

Uminos looked to Lavrin, and he too was infinitely puzzled. Those things come later? Nonetheless, the man had helped them, and there was nowhere else for them to go. They followed him, not completely sure it was the right thing to do. Why had this man helped them? Was he going to help them claim the Titan's Heart? Or was he trying to deceive them by gaining their trust?

The Commander had, by this time, gone ahead several lengths. He rounded a corner that had formed in the massive cavern wall, jagged and dark. Uminos wondered if the Commander's armor was fashioned out of the same ore; both were black, menacing and held something unknown. When the team rounded the outstretched arm of the cave, they stopped all at once.

The buildings in front of them was massive. They filled the entirety of a large chasm in the cave. It was unlike anything they had seen before. Their structures were wide and reaching, but every column and wall had masterful artwork upon it. Marble dragons wrapped around corners, and paintings of rising suns lit up the planks of mahogany and rosewood.

At first, the foreigners thought it was some sort of temple, but the Commander turned to them and stretched his arms out wide. "Welcome to our home. We call it Sanctuary because it is all we have known for many years." He paused, thinking back to times long ago. "Too many years."

He resumed his march toward Sanctuary, and Felloni watched the Commander's armor glisten under the ruby lanterns. He more than belonged in this place. He resembled this place, and it resembled him. This was

Felloni's thought before entering Sanctuary; once inside, he knew it to be true.

The Commander led them down a beautiful path lined with star lilies. It led to a garden of incredible awe, with thousands of colorful flowers intricately woven together. There were, in fact, hundreds of colors displayed in this garden. Surprisingly, no lanterns hung over this garden, for the flowers themselves glowed to light the way. Although the team would have stopped to admire the scene for hours, their feet obediently followed the lead of the Commander.

Past the garden, a mighty building twice as high as most stretched in front of them in both height and width. Its calm redwood frame was illuminated by paintings of immense battles. These tributes to forgotten wars were highlighted by the sleek black ink which formed them. A door of solid gold slid smoothly open by the Commander's firm hand as if bowing to his authority. He stepped aside to bid them enter.

They scarcely could hold their breath. The room was massive - a banquet hall that was an open expanse of the entire building. Columns of ivory and marble, white as starlight, rose from the ground to hold the towering ceiling as they had done for decades. In the center of this hall, one that reminded them of Hightenmore, were seven tables of stone. These tables held shimmering tablecloths of gold and white, and upon those tablecloths were rows of decadent food.

Although they all longed for the feast, Grax had dreamed of this meal for weeks in advance. His stupor was only stirred with the heavy sounding of the door closing behind them.

"Go enjoy yourselves," the Commander said.

The team approached the tables eagerly, but as they sat down, Felloni stopped them. "Wait," he said, and picked up a single grape from the table. He slowly sunk his teeth into it, ready to pull it away at any moment. When he finished it, he nodded to his friends.

The Commander watched him with intrigue. "Quite resourceful. You have no need to test for poison, however. We at Sanctuary believe that is a very dishonorable way to conduct oneself. Like I said, we are not the living shadows. For now, eat, and we will talk after."

Felloni looked to the Commander suspiciously. "You say 'We at Sanctuary.' Where are the others?"

Instead of answering, Commander turned back toward the golden door. "Break rank, men. Come and meet our new friends."

For a second time, the golden door beckoned the entrance of a large group. Soldier after soldier filed into the banquet hall, and took their seats at the six tables unoccupied by the foreigners. The Commander sat beside Felloni and Uminos. "There they are. Now, I see from your faces that you have many things to ask of me. I in turn have things I would like to hear from you. For now, I am hungry, and I would wager you are far hungrier than I."

Grax did not hesitate, and Kyra followed suit. Their hearts were open and eager to the Commander's generosity, seeing him already as an ally and a friend. Some in the group were not as optimistic, but started eating after a time. The last to begin was Kasandra, and she served herself only small portions, and did not touch the drink in front of her.

The Commander set down his fork and knife. "Are you not pleased with the food? We had the finest of all we have prepared for your arrival. Please understand the situation you are putting me in by doubting me. I am trying to be a gracious host."

Kasandra stopped eating also. "A gracious host who wears his armor to the table and has his warriors surround us where we sit."

The Commander's cheerful mood dimmed. "I see that you also come to the table with your weapons. I hope that you are not planning to do something rash."

Nadrian stopped eating and glanced harshly at Kasandra. Kasandra tried to relax, and served herself an extra portion as a sign of goodwill. Nadrian, even more than Kasandra, was glad to see that the Commander accepted it.

It was not till halfway through the feast that each member of the team realized the food they were eating reminded them of their home. Each had a meal which was unique, and each was perfectly reminded of their upbringing. Chan was brought back to roast mutton on the Island of Hessington. Nadrian ate food of the desert tribes that were her people. Kyra was reminded of life before Zekern's reign so long ago. Truly, the food was more than the finest Sanctuary had to offer; it was handpicked for each of them. Could the Commander really have known that much about them? Another question added to the ever-growing list.

No one spoke again until the meal was finished. The Commander stood. "Come with me," he said.

The team followed him out of the dining hall. They exited out a door at the far side of the room, also made of pure gold. How this place had acquired this many riches, no one knew. They seemed to throw around gold here as if it was wood, using it to fashion doorways and other constructions.

The Commander led them along a short walkway that branched out to many buildings almost as magnificent as the dining hall. They passed these buildings until they were close to the cavern wall. Built just beside it was a quaint pavilion atop which hundreds of ivory birds were carved.

Each bird was unique, and many of their species Lavrin had never seen before. "From the Bay of Cunon to the fortress of Wessnor, from the city of Robas to the castle Hightenmore which you well know, these birds fly. There is not a species which we have not carved. The only shame is that some of them were much too large to craft to scale. For example, that eagle you met with not long ago we had to make significantly smaller. Enough of that for now, I don't want to bore you."

He once again courteously opened the door into the pavilion. The team entered, and wondered how the Commander knew of Idrellon.

They were even more surprised when they saw, in a straight line of armor racks, all their armor. Each set was perfectly matched, and the racks even had the name of each warrior upon it. Chan was the first to approach his stand, and found there was no piece missing from his set. Not only was their armor completely intact, but the rest of their supplies lay neatly in a corner of the room. Chan turned to the others, who were just as stunned. "How did you get our armor?" they asked at once.

The Commander's pleasure was all too noticeably. "There are other ways to and from the surface than that waterfall you found. Actually, I have not seen that way used in a long time. For now, all I will say is that I don't want to ruin the surprise. That is how you put it, isn't it, Lavrin?"

The color rushed from Lavrin's face. "You were watching us on the surface?"

"Of course. You don't expect me and my men to be crammed in this cavern for all eternity, do you?"

Lavrin's expression darkened. He cast serious eyes at the Commander. "Speak to me truthfully. How long have you been watching us?"

"Actually, I haven't been watching you at all. My men are far stealthier than I. I prefer straight combat... but I digress. My men have been watching you since you left the invisible city with the first piece of the Titan's Heart. To be honest, half of my scouts in that region returned to me faster than I deemed possible. They approached me in a daze, sharing of a team unlike any other that had claimed one of the five sections of the Titan's Heart. When they watched you further in your journey, I had no doubt that you would best the living shadows, as you call them. Yes, I rather like that name for them. It describes them well. Lavrin, you were quite clever to think of it."

Lavrin barely whispered, "Thank you." His mind was in a daze, as if it was his first time seeing the sun. Watched? This whole time? His thoughts became cluttered, and he could not find the words to say. He wished he could have said thousands of things, but none of them came.

Uminos spoke up instead. "You mentioned the waterfall earlier. How does the whole river not pour into the cave?"

The Commander looked as if he had been asked this question before. "This place, Sanctuary, was founded in the ancient days of Amcronos, generations before Natas established Balyon. The same is true of the invisible city, though its glory has far increased now. Though I cannot answer your question, I would expect you of all people to understand. There are many mysteries about your people left to be answered, Seviathan."

Uminos lowered himself, as if ready to strike. "Do you have ill will against my people?"

The Commander unsheathed his sword and threw it on the pavilion floor. "I have neither ill will against the Seviathans nor against your friends now. If I wanted you dead, why would I bring your armor from the surface?"

"Speaking of armor," Lavrin said, "why do you wear the red and black of Natas?"

"Trust me. I am no follower of Natas. Neither am I a follower of the King. I wear these colors for three reasons. They represent the hardships Sanctuary has endured. They help me to blend in with the cavern walls, and finally they help me to kill any soldiers of Natas who think I am their ally."

Kyra felt the tension rising. "Thank you for showing us kindness, and for the excellent meal. I must ask, though, why are you helping us?"

The Commander took a deep breath, long and low. "Finally, someone asking a question I'd love to answer. The truth is, although in the future I may help you, I am not helping you now. I am studying you and preparing you at the same time."

"Preparing us for what?"

"You're here for the Titan's Heart, I already know," he said. "We all once were. Yes, that's right, I too once tried to claim the relic from this place - though for different reasons. I came because I was afraid, actually. I was running from great evil, and thought it could protect me. It's ironic, really; I thought the piece could protect me, and now I protect it. When the last Commander died, I took up his mantle, and now wear it with pride."

Though intrigued by this story, Kyra remember her question. "Commander, what are you preparing us for?"

"I asked a lot of questions too once. Long story short, I'm preparing you to help me defend it."

Kasandra, who had retained her suspiciousness, was quick to ask, "Why would we ever help you defend it?"

He bent down and picked up his sword, returning it to its rightful place. "Because I'm a man of intelligence and honor. I know you came here to fight for what you believe in. I could use warriors like you, especially those clad in Haven Realm armor. Your passion intrigues me, and I only look for soldiers who give their all.

"Make no mistake. We will fight you, we will defeat you and you will fight under my banner in turn. It's not such a terrible proposition. Getting to fight against the darkness of this world with some of the most elite warriors in Amcronos. Answering questions you never knew existed and living a life of both purpose and adventure.

412

One day I may even let some of you return to the Haven Realm. In the meantime, I will also protect you from the evil men that followed you out of Malstrate."

A long silence tightened the voices of the followers of the light… a silence that the Commander had expected. Lavrin felt unwoven by the Commander. This man knew not only that they were being followed, but also that they were oblivious to their danger. Lavrin wanted to punch himself. How had he not known? Why had he been so sure they were not followed past Malstrate? Or was the Commander lying to them?

The Commander waited for someone to speak, but when no one did, he continued. "It has put me in a difficult place, actually. I had to delay them in unorthodox ways. I could not have them learn of my scouts, but I didn't need two groups coming to the Sanctuary. I have no desire to add them to my ranks. On the other hand, I do not have men or women like you with me, yet."

Kasandra was the only one bold enough to confront the Commander openly. "You are lying. You have been lying this whole time. You want our trust, but the next pavilion you lead us to will have our graves beside it."

"If you were not so brash and stubborn, I would consider having you lead this team instead of Lavrin. Alas, he has something you do not. Tact. To answer your accusations, I have given you a feast and brought you your armor instead of keeping it as my own. I might have fancied Grax's hammer in particular. Can you not see that you are too valuable to kill? Burying you would be like burying diamonds.

"I have mentioned the living shadows before; let me mention them again. They collect relics, and I train soldiers. I too have goals I am trying to accomplish throughout Amcronos. You will help me complete them. You see, those star lilies you saw when we entered aren't star lilies at all. They are raven furrows, and they possess the most effective poison in all the land.

"It is effective, not because it will kill you, but because it can put you or any creature into a coma for a whole day. It could even knock out a stone golem. I've heard you're familiar with them. For now, my patience has run thin. I will retire to my quarters while you put on your armor and debate if you can trust me. My guess is Kasandra will say no, but for the rest of you, that's something even my spies could not wager."

The Commander silently closed the door behind him, so quietly that it sounded like nothing had happened at all. A whisper lingered in the room. "But for the rest of you..." it mocked. To make matters worse, the team's armor remained on their assigned racks, perfectly intact... almost too perfectly.

Did they dare to put it on? It seemed as though one man had put a spell over the entire pavilion, beckoning them to all sorts of doubt. Lavrin found the doubt the loudest. It seemed as though everything he was as a leader had been questioned, though subtly. Maybe the others had noticed it, maybe they had not. All Lavrin knew was he should have known everything that the Commander did.

They had been watched since the invisible city? He had not known.

They had been followed out of Malstrate? He had not seen it.

Maybe the Commander was right to question having Kasandra as leader instead of him. She had stood and said what they had all feared to say.

No. Now was not the time to doubt himself. Maybe that was what the Commander wanted. It seemed only he knew what he wanted. One thing was for sure: Kasandra had not witnessed the fight against Zekern, nor had she helped rebuild Hightenmore. She may be brave, but she did not have the experience that Lavrin did. Experience... maybe that was what made Lavrin a good leader. He would have to think about it later. Now was the time for action.

Lavrin turned to Kyra, his solid rock in troubled times. "Have you heard of these raven furrows?"

She blushed. "I... I thought they were a myth."

"If we have learned anything on our adventures," Lavrin said, "it's that the legends of Amcronos are often much more than legends. What do these myths say?"

Kyra ran her hand across her forehead. "Well, mostly what he just told us. That the raven furrows nectar

415

can be boiled to become a powerful poison that can render even the strongest creature disabled for hours. If you got enough of it in your system, you might never wake up at all."

"Looks like we're definitely going to need as much armor as we can get."

Lavrin approached the armor rack with his name on it, and reached for his breastplate. "Wait, Lavrin," Kasandra called from behind.

He was resolute. "Fear is what he wants."

Lavrin lifted his armor from the stand and began to fasten it. The others watched at first, and when no ill signs showed, they took to their own stands. They expertly readied themselves for battle, positioning each piece of armor with firm determination. They had done this many times before.

Lavrin watched his team prepare. He especially watched those who put on their Haven Realm armor, realizing he had not seen their new weaponry in battle. He figured he would see it soon enough. Now with the Commander having explained the nature of this Sanctuary, how to claim the Titan's Heart was clear. Fight for it. Earn it. Defeat them.

Though Lavrin had no idea how many 'them' was, he knew it would take the blessing of the King to accomplish such a feat. This did not worry him; the King's blessing had rested upon them since the beginning of their quest.

Everyone looked to Lavrin now, waiting for their next move. He could tell that though they looked prepared, inwardly they were far from it. They did not know what they were fighting against; none of them did. What Lavrin did know was that he needed to help his team however he could. He surveyed each of the warriors, garbed in the mightiest of armor and bearing weapons of strength. They could hold their own against the greatest of foes. All of them, save only Kyra.

Lavrin saw her caring eyes, her soft flowing dress amidst soldiers of chain mail. She was a fawn beside lions, and he realized something had to be done. Not only for her sake, but for the sake of them all. He had to even the odds any way he could. Now was not the time to hold back, but to ask anything and everything he could to gain whatever ground he was allowed. He needed to meet with the Commander.

"We need to return to the banquet hall." Lavrin did not need to say anything more.

They left the pavilion and walked down the narrow path that returned them to the hall. Once again, they entered it; once again to sit at the table. No longer to eat, but to decide the fate of the battle to come.

As if reading their thoughts again, none other than the Commander was there waiting for them. Though he sat at the head of the table, there were three warriors on each side of him, standing guard. Lavrin was unfazed, and sat beside him as if they were the only two in the room. "I thought you were going to retire to your quarters."

"I changed my mind," he said. "I decided I'd rather sit and think, and I see I will not be thinking alone."

Lavrin got right to the point. "If we are going to have this battle, we're going to do it my way. I have certain... requirements that I will not be denied."

"You don't need to prove that to me. I see the passion in your eyes, and I know that you will not leave here until you have what you want. Do you want to discuss this alone?"

"I have nothing to hide. They can stay."

The Commander clearly had nothing to hide either, for his men remained at his side. "What do you want?"

"Do you have a healer?"

"Yes," the Commander answered. "But he fights as one of us."

Lavrin figured as much. "If we are going to use the raven furrows, then I want this to be a battle where no wounds will be healed. Take your healer out of the fight, and I will take mine out as well."

The Commander was looking at Kyra as Lavrin spoke, and watched the displeasure across her face. He knew Lavrin would hear of it later. "You want a desperate fight? Where there is no thought of retreat? I will surely not deny you that. Though I wonder if you have other reasons behind that request. Go ahead and tell me the others."

"I only have one more request. We claim our victory if one of us holds the Titan's Heart in our hands, and you must tell us where you are keeping it."

"That's two requests."

Lavrin held fast. "I changed my mind."

Removing his once serious nature, the Commander grinned until it turned into a laugh. The guards behind him remained stoic - the masterpieces that were their helmets hiding their countenance. The Commander continued to laugh. "I'm looking forward to this battle. I don't think I've ever faced foes quite like you before. I will grant your desires. If you hold up the Titan's Heart, we have been defeated. It is in the throne room, the building farthest from the entrance, with the ivory tiger on its crest. The podium is center stage behind the throne."

"When will this begin?" Lavrin asked.

"Whenever you want it to. My men are always ready."

It took fierce concentration for Lavrin not to lose his confidence. The Commander seemed to tower over him as an intellectual and a leader. He knew how to answer every question, and answer it effortlessly. Although Lavrin had first admired this leader of Sanctuary, he now viewed him only as an adversary. "Let me go speak with my companions. We will sound the horn when we are ready."

"Good. I hope I will not be waiting long. First, coat your weapons in the raven furrow poison."

Before Lavrin complied, he asked. "What about yours?"

"I had a feeling battle was coming today. My men went ahead and tipped their arrows and coated their swords already."

Lavrin motioned to the rest of his team, and they followed him. He in turn followed the Commander, much to his dislike. He was tired of following him, but did not know the way. The Commander took them into the heart of Sanctuary.

The building, right next to the throne room, was also impressive. It was long and low, with the same care and dedication put into every piece of art decorating its frame. With the fierce ivory tiger prowling beside it, this building's crown was its single massive flower. It hung just above its doorway, with all the colors of life, and the span of three men.

The smell was pungent within, but no one could decide if the aroma was sweet or acrid. Nonetheless, they were almost overwhelmed by it. They approached the cauldron where they were asked for their weapons. The guards of Sanctuary skillfully dipped every arrow and spear, sword and hammer in the green toxin. Even Uminos was taken up and had his tail and claws dipped in the serum. The assassins did not miss a single weapon. The Commander released them, saying simply, "You can find your way to the front of Sanctuary. I need to speak with my men."

With that, the two leaders parted, not to meet again until the fighting began.

CHAPTER 21

WAR IS WHAT WE CAME FOR

From the front of Sanctuary, out and beyond its golden halls, the foreigners gathered. Before Lavrin could say anything, Kyra was ready and waiting. "What are you thinking? How dare you just…"

"Kyra," he whispered calmly.

"No, no 'Kyra'," she replied. "There is no answer you can give that will explain this to me. I have always been with this team, and am just as valuable as anyone else here. Maybe I can't fight like you, but you have no right…"

"Kyra."

She was irate, but Lavrin's soft tone puzzled her. "What?"

"It's not that you're invaluable, it's that you're the most valuable. I need you out of this battle for more than one reason. Firstly, you will hold the other two pieces of the Titan's Heart, keeping them safe while the battle ensues. Second, if we were to lose you, I, along with every member of this group, could never forgive ourselves. Your strengths are many, but you know that they are not for this moment."

Her flaming emotions were dimmed, but she was nonetheless questioning. "You may need me out there more than you know."

"We do; I know we do. You haven't let me get to the final reason why I made that request. If we sound our horn, run toward the throne room. You saw it when we had our weapons tipped. We may be hard-pressed to win this fight, and having someone who could rush straight for the throne room might bring us the victory. If you hear the horn, do not veer left or right; go straight for the Titan's Heart. Be ready for the call. Now, have I given you enough of an answer?"

"I don't like it," Kyra said. "I don't like it at all, but I will follow your lead."

Lavrin would have said more, but he had to turn his attention to the rest of the group. Each one was fully prepared to give their all. The scars of former battles wore upon their minds. How many more scars? How many more bruises, dark marks of cruel war, would they receive today?

"We have never faced an enemy like the Commander, but that doesn't mean we let him dictate this fight. We must rise higher than what he expects from us. Do not be deceived; these warriors are as battle-hardened as we are. Their steel is forged out of the same metal as our steel. They outnumber us and know the terrain. This does not mean we are without advantages. We can outmaneuver, outthink, and use our skill to overcome them.

"This enemy has prepared for this moment for a while now, but we have been preparing for this our entire lives. I do not doubt your resolve, nor your courage, for we have revealed these things to all Amcronos with our victories. The King is with us, and his hand has led us to these triumphs. We have the will of the King himself behind us; he will not fail. Some of us have even trained at his side, an advantage that outweighs them all.

"What you have probably wondered is how we will attack this stronghold. I have been thinking about the layout of Sanctuary, keeping a mental picture of every building. It is more wide open than a castle or fortress, but nonetheless has many places to hide and ambush. To be successful, we need to do the unexpected. The Commander has fought here many times, but will not be ready for this. He will be looking to take me out first, to take out the leader. I'll give him what he wants."

Nadrian, who had been silently readying her bow, spoke up. "You're going to surrender?"

"Far from it," Lavrin continued. "I'm going to create an opening for the rest of you. I will enter the far side of Sanctuary, acting as though help were on the way. You will sneak in the near side, then disperse in small two-person groups. Each group will lead itself. After they defeat me - if they defeat me - they will search for the rest of you. Get deep within Sanctuary and ambush them while they are expecting to ambush you. Do not go for the Titan's Heart until they are all defeated. That is what they want, to attack you while you are claiming the piece.

"Nadrian, you will ascend to the top of the great hall and unleash fury upon them. While they rush to defeat her, the rest of you will sneak attack them. Take out a few of them, then return to the shadows to take out a few more. From there, exploit any weaknesses you see."

As Lavrin was speaking, a noise came from within Sanctuary. At first it was unclear, cloudy waters to their ears, but then it clarified. It was a war chant, haunting and unified, rising like an ocean storm. It swayed over Sanctuary with a life of its own, a life that would have terrified most... but they were not most. They had heard battle cries and deathly cheers from numerous enemies before.

They refocused, the only thing they could do when a foe rallied.

As the chant filled the majestic halls of Sanctuary, the warriors of the Light readied their weapons. Grax slid his hand over the smooth leather and resilient iron of his commanding hammer. It was forged by the King's own smiths, crafted by the forges of the Haven Realm. He was blessed to carry such an item, and he knew it. He did not plan on submitting his might to the Commander any time soon.

In the meantime, Lavrin went to each of his soldiers... his friends... powerfully encouraging them. Not simply encouraging them - he feared that would not be enough. He mustered words of great strength... the most noble and mighty words he could find. Still, they seemed lacking. There was only one noise, clear and true, that would rally their hearts above all. The sound of it beginning. The sound of a horn.

Wasting no time, Lavrin pulled the horn from his sack and blew it almost angrily. He was tired of waiting, tired of thinking of the things that could go wrong. He wanted to claim the Titan's Heart, surely, but even more he wanted to defeat the brilliant Commander.

The blast of the horn rose far above the war chant, a feat not easily accomplished. The chant fell to dead silence when the sounding ended. Moments later, every light and lantern across Sanctuary fell. The Commander had been thinking as well... he decided they would fight in darkness.

The last to draw his weapon, Lavrin brought out his sword and held it in front of him. He went right, toward the far end of Sanctuary, the others went left, just as they had planned. Lavrin had kept the plan simple on purpose. He knew once the heat of battle began, there could be no more relying upon it. There could only be cunning and determination to carry them through the day.

*****

His sword no longer glistened, for the shadows covered it. Although Lavrin had not expected the darkness, he realized it might help his cause in the end. If he wanted his team to sneak in undetected, that was the way to do it. In trying to surprise them, maybe the Commander had helped them in the end.

Lavrin knew that he was who the Commander would come after. To take him out as fast as he could. Even more frightening was that Lavrin was heading straight into where the chanting had been the loudest. Where that lingering war cry had begun. He turned his thoughts to all he had learned in the art of war. Every sword stroke, every counter and block. Each combination taught to him in Hightenmore, each attack he developed in the Mazaron. He marched toward the east end of Sanctuary with purpose.

There was no sign of the enemies yet, but his eyes were peeled. Lavrin had to find them before they attacked, or he would be defeated too soon. He needed to give as much time as possible to his teammates. Every second for his friends was an advantage.

As the light had gone, Lavrin felt the shadow of death pressing upon him. Its burden was heavy, and though the Commander had said they would not die, something felt wrong. Maybe it was not death he was feeling; maybe it was terror. Lavrin decided that he had had enough of fear, and would not let it make him weary.

Think of all you've accomplished. Think of the battles you've won. What was this? This enemy may be unknown, but they would fall like the rest. The King had too much planned for them. He had to have more for them than serving the Commander the rest of their lives.

A quick rush of the wind. A whisper of a heartbeat. What had he heard? Lavrin wondered if he was deceiving himself. No. There it was again. It was like a thrush's wing, pushing against the air. It was something small, but it gave Lavrin what he needed. He changed from his defensive stance to one of full offense. He lunged toward the noise, only to find his sword embedded into a wooden plank. It was a building.

Lavrin heard the noise again, only this time coming from behind him. With a might he had never used before, he pulled out his sword just in time. He expertly blocked the jab meant for his shoulder. Lavrin could only make out the silhouette of a figure, but the warrior in front of him looked thin and agile, taking a stance he had never seen before.

This warrior did not advance, so Lavrin used the opportunity to gather himself. He took a mixed step position, allowing him to quickly change directions. He had a feeling this enemy was fast. Very fast.

He was not wrong.

As if waiting for Lavrin to ready himself, the assassin sprung at him with his twin blades. After narrowly deflecting the attack, Lavrin decided to draw his second blade as well. Though he could not tell for sure, he thought he saw his enemy step back and smile. Lavrin showed no delight in return.

Instead, he advanced, not rapidly like his opponent, but slowly; he calculated every step, waiting. Waiting for his foe to attack. Instead, the assassin perfectly matched Lavrin's fighting style and gradually approached. That was why he had smiled; he knew Lavrin's form.

Lavrin could only hope that he knew it better. Now it was his turn to advance on his enemy. He brought his right sword downward, while slashing with his left. It was perfectly blocked. From that point, Lavrin and the assassin were locked in a fast-paced skirmish of thrusts, parries and counters. They were incredibly close to each other considering how fast their swords were moving.

The tip of Lavrin's left sword was all that stopped the swing from cutting into his arm. All that stopped him from losing the fight. This gave him an advantage, though. Instead of simply striking toward the assassin's exposed chest, he lowered his shoulder and plowed straight into him. As the warrior fell backward, Lavrin brought up both swords, each barely scratching his sides.

The assassin struggled on the ground, trying to get back up. He dug one of his swords into the earth, trying to use it as a crutch. Suddenly, he fell as the raven furrow worked into his bloodstream. He could not overcome it.

Lavrin had no time to revel in this minor victory. He had to act his part. He carried two things with him, the first was the horn, the second was a torch. He lit the torch. The fire flickered to life. Small noises echoed to and fro like the shuffling of feet. Lavrin tried to look afraid, afraid enough to sell the ruse, but not too scared to destroy it. "Show yourself."

More out of instinct then intuition, Lavrin ducked. An arrow flew just above his head. An archer crouched atop the building. An archer drawing another arrow. Lavrin reached for a dagger. He launched it toward the archer. Luckily, he had two. The archer dove to the side and fired the second arrow. Lavrin spun, dodging the arrow and sending his second dagger into his foe's leg.

The archer had, in a sense, not lost but won. Although the raven furrow finished him, the archer had bought precious time. Lavrin was surrounded. Those sounds had definitely been the shuffling of feet. He was now away from the support of the building, and in open terrain.

On every side were assassins, now apparent by the torch light. Lavrin dropped the torch and picked up his other sword. He would need them both. The glow of the fire continued from below, and he watched his enemies draw in closer.

*****

A scream pierced the air. Not a scream of fear, or of desperation, but of a soldier giving his final effort. They knew what it meant. Lavrin was giving his last stand. They did not have much time. This was the part where they split. They had already taken care of two border guards simply by overwhelming them. This luxury would not be afforded to them again.

Felloni would be protecting Nadrian as she ascended the great hall. He would then climb up it as well, once she started letting her arrows fly. He knew his importance. The moment she started ambushing the enemy, they would be coming for her. Felloni's knife throwing abilities made him perfectly suited to guard her.

Calix and Uminos would head east to ambush the assassins from the raven furrow garden. Kasandra and Chan would head northeast, into the center of Sanctuary. They would weave their way between buildings, hiding in the shadows to attack any forces rushing toward Nadrian. Grax would be alone, heading north, to circle around the buildings and sneak upon any unsuspecting enemies. Although he was alone, he was taking the route with the fewest assassins, and was confident he could overrun them if he timed his attack right.

As she snuck ever closer to the great hall, Nadrian clung to the sides of buildings, cloaking herself in their protection. She dodged between buildings and other cover with Felloni close behind. They were not far from the great hall. With the swiftness of an eagle, she rushed toward her perch. She kept all her focus on reaching it. Felloni did not have this luxury.

Nadrian heard metal clash behind her, and found Felloni ambushed by two assassins. "Go!" he exclaimed, not loudly but nonetheless forcefully.

She drew a single shaft and fired it toward one assailant, barely missing him. She then turned and covered the last few steps to reach her destination. Jumping skyward, her hands grasped the edge of a board. After pulling herself up, Nadrian skillfully leapt to a higher grasp most never would have reached. She then ascended the side of the building as if climbing a mountain. On the final ascent, she spun as she jumped to land on the highest point of the hall. She kept herself close to the roofline, so that in the ever-fading torchlight in the east she remained completely hidden.

Felloni was no longer with her, but he had done his part. He had escorted her and saved her in the end. From this height, the only thing she needed to fear was other archers setting their sights on her. She had a feeling Felloni would not make it to the great hall.

Pushed back and retreating fast, Felloni was running out of options against his foes. They outnumbered him two to one, and a third assassin was closing ground quickly to assist them. Felloni blocked a spear thrust meant for his torso, and dodged a sword that followed it. His enemies pressed the attack, giving him no room to throw his knives. He could only defend as he was pursued on both sides. If he did not do something before the third assassin arrived, he would be doomed.

When the spear wielder pressed an advantage against Felloni, the follower of the light realized his enemy's spear was double-sided. Both ends were sharp points of unforgiving iron. That helped Felloni develop a plan. He waited until he could push back the sword threatening his left, then dropped his knives and grabbed hold of the spear just below the tip. He thrust the assassin's weapon back at him, planning to arm himself with the spear afterward.

His plan worked half of the way.

Felloni successfully used the assassin's spear against him, but his grip on his weapon remained firm. There was nothing Felloni could do to seize the spear from his enemy. Although he had bested his foe, he had nothing to defend himself against the fateful descent of the malicious sword. The sword-bearer sliced across Felloni's arm and the raven furrow took over from that point.

Felloni fell onto the soft Sanctuary earth next to the warrior he had defeated.

Nadrian, atop her archer's mount, was not oblivious to Felloni's defeat. As the finisher of her friend picked up the spear, Nadrian drew a silken arrow. She knelt amidst the shadows to find the perfect angle, and drew back her bow skillfully. It was crafted from the brightest and mightiest of the Haven Realm trees, and its aim would not fail her. Like a panther leaping from its hiding place, the lone arrow found its mark and Felloni was avenged.

She had no time to be proud. The third warrior reached his two fallen companions just as Nadrian pulled back a second arrow. He turned toward the great hall as a swift arrow sped toward him. With reflexes beyond those of a normal man, he shot out his hand and caught the arrow from the air. It was only a foot away from burying itself in the soldier's helmet.

Had this extraordinary feat been luck, or the training of many years, Nadrian was not sure. All she knew was that she had been discovered, and that this soldier was motioning to his allies of her location. There was no time for her to sit back and take few shots. She needed to empty her quiver before she was taken out. Hopefully, the others were in position to ambush the assassins, for they were coming for her.

Nadrian could no longer see the enemies she faced below, for the torchlight had faded. This did not deter her, however, for she had trained for moments like this. She watched the slight outlines of silhouettes in the darkness and relied upon her hearing. She listened for even the smallest of noises, but this was far harder than her training. These assassins had been trained well, for they were almost entirely silent. Almost.

Any slip of the foot or shuffling of a stone had an arrow soaring toward it. Though most of her shots hit the cold earth, some found their marks. Nadrian wondered how many arrows had simply missed, or how many had been adeptly avoided by her targets. All she could do was listen closer, rely on her training, and fire another arrow.

Not long after, two events occurred simultaneously. Archers set their sights on the great hall, firing their bolts and shafts with intent, and assassins were ambushed by the followers of the King. The initial damage caused was incredible. As Lavrin had guessed, the assassins planned on sneaking up on their foes, not the other way around. Ten assassins fell from the coordinated strikes. What the knights of the light had not planned was how fast the guardians of Sanctuary would regroup.

They took up defensive positions, rallied by each other's sides, and formed several tight clusters with weapons extended. They would not let themselves be tricked again.

This would have been the perfect opportunity for Nadrian to inflict more damage, but she was busy trying not to be hit by four assassin archers. As she rolled to her left, a shaft dug into the hall inches in front of her face. Its slender frame had been far too close to impact. Nadrian knew there was nowhere she could turn. She could not get down from the rooftop, and there was no cover to hide behind. She leaned back as sweat and fear beaded on her forehead. If she was going to go down, she would take them with her.

Nadrian knew from the flight of the arrows where at least two of the archers were. She fired as many volleys as she could. As many as she could muster, until she felt a sharp pain thrust into her side. It stung like a wildfire, but then her senses felt numb. She tried to resist, but was comforted only by two bodies hitting the ground from her shots. Her eyes collapsed from the heavy weight they bore. Nadrian fell into her coma, lucky that her body did not fall from the rafters.

The others retreated to the shadows, but were pursued by groups of enemies, groups much larger than their own. The warriors of both sides rushed about the paths of Sanctuary, trying to hide themselves to gain the upper hand. Though at first they snuck and hid, when the sides collided, there was no more secrecy - there was war.

Throughout Sanctuary, swords ricocheted as battles erupted. The skill of the assassins fought against the experience of the light. The foreigners had never faced such enemies as these guardians of the Titan's Heart, and the battle increased with every swing and block. The encounters were legendary, happening at mighty speeds and with unheard determination. No warrior was out of place; each had spent years mastering the art of their weapon, and did not fail to show their skill.

Chan and Kasandra fought against men much larger than them who were not only powerful, but agile. They struck at every weakness they could find. Uminos and Calix did not face better odds; their foes were many and tactful. Channeling all the true Seviathan within him, Uminos spared no mercy to his assailants. Calix and Chan had both learned from the highest masters in the way of the sword, but against so many enemies - foes who had been fighting against elite adversaries for decades - they had to rely on everything they knew or had ever known.

Suddenly, from chaos to silence, everything fell still. Little did he know, Grax was the only one to survive the intense battle. Hope was not lost, however, for very few of the enemy remained as well. As it was, there were four assassins remaining, and Grax was just about to defeat one of them. His hammer slammed into the bow of the guardian, shattering it into a thousand fragments. Grax did not stop his advance, for the assassin did not seem to mind losing his weapon. The guardian reverted to close-combat fighting, and forced him back, almost disarming him. Grax was not amused.

He let the assassin draw in close, blocked his sidekick and drew his hammer upward with all the strength he had. His enemy flipped over as he was thrown into the hard impact of a golden door. The door which entered the great hall soon gave way to Grax and his rage. Twice Grax had almost been defeated, and he would not let himself fall. Although he did not know how true it was, he felt as though everything rested on his shoulders. This mindset propelled him onward, onward toward the two warriors who were waiting for him in the great hall. They had heard their ally's struggle, and had come to face Grax themselves.

Grax recognized them as two of the Commander's personal protectors. They would be incredible in talent, as hard of foes as he had ever battled. They may be mighty, but so was he. Surely, he told himself, they have never faced someone like me before. Grax wasted no time in beginning the battle, for there was no reason to. They were ready for him; he was ready for them.

The first guard attacked with a dual-sided axe. Not far behind, the other carried a weapon Grax could only define as a crescent mace. It was long and straight, almost like a spear, its head was sharp and curved, pointed outward in both directions as if teeth. It was a menacing creation, but Grax decided it was not too different from his hammer. Both were long and could dish out punishment from both ends.

The assassins did not surround Grax, but nonetheless spread apart far enough to give them an advantage. He would have to thwart strikes from the front and the right to survive. It was a situation he had faced before, outnumbered and desperate. Grax had lived through numerous battles before, and was plagued by them in his nightmares. Though these enemies were different, he did not fear. He simply acted and reacted.

The axe swung for his leg, and he deflected it with an upward counter. The other assassin tried to pin Grax's weapon, but he responded with a three-step maneuver that left both enemies on the defensive. It was clockwork. He countered every attack thrown at him, calm and calculating. His strength was intimidating, even to assassins with supposedly no weaknesses. Everything seemed to be in Grax's favor, until his foes tried something he had never seen.

One of them threw his double-sided axe to his ally and charged Grax with a series of advanced punches and kicks. Blood trickled from Grax's damaged jaw. Grax eventually apprehended his unarmed adversary, only to find the crescent mace descending into his breastplate. It had been a distraction… and it had worked. This was it. This was his fall. He watched defeat swing downward with a grin of sharp teeth.

As the mace shot its sinister points into the forged steel of Grax's armor, it stopped. He could feel the tips of the weapon pressing against his chain mail underneath. The armor of the Haven Realm had saved him. No other craftsmanship could have withstood the blow. For the first time, Grax watched his opponent retreat, not out of discretion, but out of panic.

No time was wasted putting this man out of his misery. The broad stroke of Grax's hammer left the Sanctuary guard reeling on the great hall's floor. He lay underneath the chandeliers that no longer cast their light.

Grax tore the mace from his chest, and spat the salty blood from his mouth. His battle was far from over. There was one man he had not seen fall by a weapon of the light. The one man who now sat on Sanctuary's throne, though he was not a king. He was not a lord; he was a Commander.

CHAPTER 22

THE THRONE

It was a short walk to the throne room. Grax carried the weapon of another land in one hand, and the weapon of Sanctuary in the other. He stepped over fallen assassin warriors, the same warriors who had bested his friends. He knew now that he was the only one left, for as he ascended the steps to the throne room, he was greeted by the bodies of each of his friends.

They were still breathing, but they were clearly in a desperate state. It was as if they were held between life and death, and it was mortifying. Grax got the message loud and clear. If you enter this room, you will lay beside them. He did not care if he would be ambushed or not, but took the risk and knelt beside his wounded brothers and sisters, making sure they were alright.

When he lifted his eyes, the Commander stood in front of him at the top of the steps. He held a torch in one hand, vibrant and pulsing, and a sword in the other - a sword which should have needed two hands to carry. The Commander said nothing, but watched as Grax rose from beside his companions. They both left the steps and entered the throne room.

"I was hoping you would be the last to survive," the Commander said. "My scouts told me they had never seen you fight, but believed nonetheless that you were the strongest warrior. Evidently, they were not wrong. You intrigue me. Usually the greatest warrior has the hardest heart, but yours is wide open. Let's hope your kindness doesn't cloud your judgement now."

Grax clenched his teeth. "You have pushed my kindness too far. I'm guessing that's what you wanted. What other point would there be to lining my friends upon your footstool? You are a confident man, Commander, yet look at your army now. Your soldiers were not ready for us. Tell me, are you still confident?"

"No, but I am steadfast in my allegiance," the Commander answered. "The way I see it, my men just held their own against the greatest soldiers both Amcronos and the Haven Realm have to offer. Now my allegiance is to my fallen heroes of Sanctuary. I'm sure you don't see them the same way. I cannot wait for my legacy as the conqueror of the undefeatable. Did you know that's the rumor about your group? That you're undefeatable? How fun would it be to put that theory to rest once and for all?"

Grax beamed, not cockily, but knowingly. It was a smile that made the Commander wonder what he was missing. What did Grax know? "Do you want to know why we're undefeatable, Commander?"

The Commander raised an eyebrow. "Enlighten me."

"We're all flawed. We're all broken by scars of the pas. We're all human... well, you know what I mean. We recognize how amazing of a chance we have before us. This chance, this mission, has tested us before, but we've always found a way through it. We're fighters, down to the last drop of our blood. We each have unique skills, which are constantly pushed to their limits for the cause of the King. Our whole lives we've been pushed to the limits, and we've risen to the challenge. That's why we're undefeatable... we love a good challenge."

Symbolically, the Commander bowed to Grax, and he returned the gesture. They both took their stances, and held their arms firm. The Commander had since placed the torch on its stand beside the throne, and held his longsword before him. It was a weapon meant to be held with two hands. If he could hold the sword with one hand, how powerful would he be with the weapon in both?

In between flickers of fire, the battle erupted. Grax quickly found himself at a disadvantage. He had tried to overpower the Commander with two weapons to his one. It did not take the assassin's leader long to knock the mace from Grax hand. It collided with the ground in a clash.

Grax became far more centered against his foe with only his hammer. He broke the Commander's assault by launching several strikes toward his left side in a row. Most swords would have been shattered by the force of the mighty hammer. This longsword was of a rare kind - the kind that could brace against such a power. Grax pressed his foe into the throne, but he simply used it to support himself.

For a split second, Grax took his eyes off the fight, and onto the Titan's Heart... it was only a foot or two away. The Commander followed his eyes, and renewed his offensive with a fury. The blade seemed almost to crave the battle, like it could have continued fighting out of its master's hands. It seemed as though there were no fighters in the battle at all, only two weapons flying at speeds unfathomable, countering each other's attempts.

Grax would advance; his advance would be stopped. The Commander would seize an opportunity; it would amount to nothing. The fight circled the throne, the pinnacle of victory. It was a never-ending struggle, both sides becoming more and more weary. Grax felt as though his once strong arms would fail him if he did not do something soon. The Commander seemed completely unfazed on the outside, but his strength was also dimming.

Something had to be done. Grax knew that he had to be smarter, and swiftly an idea came to him. He would start to lose... or at least it would look that way. Grax broke from the hold his hammer was placed in and stumbled backward. He fell to one knee, and then braced himself on a column far from the throne. The Commander closed the ground in an instant. He did not want Grax to have one spare breath.

The fight turned bleak for the follower of the light, just as Grax had planned. It was almost impossible to counter all the Commander's attacks, so Grax had to fake very little. Just as hope seemed to flee from the throne room, it turned around to watch the last moment of the battle.

Timing his opening with excellence, Grax waited till the Commander's sword was about to be slammed down upon him. A death sentence. Almost. Grax launched himself upward, grabbed the Commander's hand with the sword and swung his hammer from behind the column and into the legs of his adversary. The knees of the legendary leader of Sanctuary buckled, filled with the poison he had created. Grax watched his foe fall, but then collapsed to his knees himself. A knife, the smallest of blades, was embedded in his side just under his armor.

The poison clouded everything. Grax roared in frustration; he was too far from the throne. He tried to drag himself in its direction, but the Commander's slender dagger impeded all movement. There was only one thing left for him to do. He barely had the strength left to draw his horn. With everything he had, with the daring that beckoned him to the challenge, Grax blew the horn. Its echoing call thundered through the cavern. Grax knew his work was done.

*****

She did not look left or right. She dared not veer off course. Her feet obeyed the steady words of Lavrin ringing in her ear. "Go straight for the Titan's Heart. Be ready for the call."

Kyra sidestepped the fallen assassin bodies and their ever-deadly poison weapons. Her feet almost tripped upon an outstretched arm reaching across the path. It was much farther to the throne room than she remembered, or maybe it was the darkness. Not even the fallen soldiers stopped her progress, until she saw them.

The ghostly pale bodies of her friends reminded her of the living shadows. Except this time, they did not seem to be in a nightmare. They seemed to be dead. There was no life in them. No movement. Only the slight whisper of their thin gasps for air relieved her. They seemed at peace... the peace that hangs as a balcony over the carmine and burgundy shades of death.

Kyra almost slapped herself. They would be fine... they had to be. She had almost lost sight of her mission, and this time Lavrin's words clung to her. She sprinted up the remaining steps and flung herself on the beautiful throne. Kyra wrenched the Titan's Heart from its clasp.

The cold tip of a heartless spear rested upon the back of her neck. Kyra spun around to see the Commander's doctor. He too had come to the horn's call. "You cannot hurt me," Kyra said. "I hold the Titan's Heart."

AUTHOR'S NOTE

The King served by the Forces of Light represents Jesus Christ. Just as they trusted in the goodness of the King, you can believe in the holiness of God. You do not need to say any special words, just believe in your heart Jesus Christ is the Son of God and know he died for your sins. You may say, "I don't have any sins, though." Or, "I don't need God." Have you ever cheated, even if only once? Have you ever disobeyed your parents? These are just two of several types of sins. These sins will cast you into the endless fires of Hell when you die.

Thankfully, Jesus Christ died on the cross to cover our transgressions. His blood can cover your sins and make you as white as snow. Please understand this does not mean your life will become perfect and there will be no more pain. It only gives you a hope of a brighter future that, just like Rowan and many others entered the Haven Realm, we will travel to Heaven after we die. It will be a place of unfathomable things, like roads of gold and gates of pearls. No pain will accompany us and sorrow will be but a thing of the past.

If you have already accepted the reality of God and have dedicated yourself to his will for you, I am thankful for this. I encourage you to read the Bible because it is a book like no other and can strengthen your faith tremendously.

Fight the good fight and stand against the forces of the devil. As Lavrin and his companions overcame their struggles, you can also defeat the sin in your life, and by doing so affect your church, community, and possibly the world! Never stop pursuing your dreams and make sure that whatever you do, you do it for God's glory. God bless. The great King of Light, may he live and reign forever, and may his followers prosper!

49482691R00275

Made in the USA
Lexington, KY
22 August 2019